Johauna stepped forward, preparing to brush aside the creature with her boot. "It's just a bat," she said in relief to Karleah, behind her. She extended her leg to kick the tiny, squawking animal out of harm's way.

"Wait! Jo!" Karleah croaked in sudden fear.

Something hard and heavy crashed against Jo's shoulder. The squire lost her balance. "What the—!" She fell to the cavern floor, only just glimpsing the massive object that struck her. Where the bat had once been, a seething lump of metamorphosing flesh now lay.

Convulsing. Transforming.

Books

The Penhaligon Trilogy
D. J. Heinrich

Book One
The Tainted Sword

Book Two
The Dragon's Tomb

Book Three
The Fall of Magic
October 1993

DUNGEONS & DRAGONS™
Books

THE DRAGON'S TOMB

D. J. Heinrich

THE DRAGON'S TOMB

Random House and its affiliate companies have worldwide distribution rights in the book trade for English language products of TSR, Inc.

Distributed to the book and hobby trade in the United Kingdom by TSR Ltd.

Distributed to the toy and hobby trade by regional distributors.

Cover art by John and Laura Lakey. Color map by Robin Raab.

DUNGEONS & DRAGONS, D&D, and the TSR logo are trademarks owned by TSR, Inc.

First Printing: April 1993
Printed in the United States of America
Library of Congress Catalog Card Number: 92-61085

9 8 7 6 5 4 3 2 1

ISBN: 1-56076-592-5

TSR, Inc.   TSR Ltd.
P.O. Box 756   120 Church End, Cherry Hinton
Lake Geneva, WI 53147   Cambridge CB1 3LB
United States of America   United Kingdom

For Lyle Graybow and Karl Kunze—
two fine men who died before their time.

They will be sorely missed.

Prologue

e came, just as I knew he would. Just as I knew he must. Humans are that way. Predictable. Idealistic. Bound by honor and vow and silly passion. Knights of the Three Suns, particularly, are that way. It makes them easy bait, as easy to kill as horses in a corral—and I've killed enough of those in my time to know.

But, truth be told, Fain Flinn was different. Flinn the Mighty, they called him, and for good reason. The first time I fought him, I discovered he couldn't be as easily slain as all the others. It was that damned great sword of his, that Wyrmblight. We could, neither of us, kill the other, and that sword mocked us all the while.

Yes, it was Flinn who shamed me—Verdilith the Great Green, scourge of Penhaligon—Flinn who shamed me into winning through subversion what I could not through battle. So I shed my lovely green scales and took human form. I insinuated myself into Baroness Penhaligon's good graces, even seduced Flinn's loving wife Yvaughan out from under him. . . . And, when all was in place, I turned a fellow knight against him, made him accuse the good

Flinn of dishonor.

I brought Flinn the Mighty to his knees.

It all worked too well. Flinn was stripped of title and honor, cast out of the fellowship of knights—out even of the Castle of the Three Suns. He became Flinn the Fallen, Flinn the Fool. And I became Yvaughan's loving husband. Thoughts of her still make my teeth itch. I'd even conceived a son by her, a glorious heir to my power.

But then that slip of a girl came along. She sought for Flinn the Mighty, and found him a hermit in a hovel. Until that time, I'd used abelaat stones to spy on him, to feed thoughts of despair and decay into his mind. I'd learned that prostrating and dominating my foe were far more enjoyable than killing him outright. But the girl, the clumsy bitch of a girl, got herself bit by an abelaat—one of Teryl Auroch's stray beasts from the infernal realms. The poison of the creature's fangs ran in her blood, blocking my eyes from Flinn, blocking my words from reaching his despoiled brain.

And she began to change him, as women always do to men. She reminded him of his honor, his glory, his nemesis, the Great Green! I should have known she would prove even more dangerous than he—unpredictable, naive, irrational in her love of Flinn the Fool. Before I could blink, Flinn had returned to flush me from the castle, to drive the mage Auroch away, to regain his honor and title. And he once again bore Wyrmblight!

The game was up. I was done with toying. I knew Flinn the Fool would make an idiotic attempt to hunt me down, to slay me. And, poetic soul that I am, I met him in the field where first we fought.

And I killed him.

I killed him despite the fact that my magic had failed

me, despite the fact that he used the girl's blink-dog's tail to strike at my flanks, despite the fact that he lanced my side and slashed my wings and ruined my arm. I killed him.

My poor arm. Of all my wounds, it pains me most. I change forms from dragon to mist to man to mouse, but always the pain follows me. I feel the urging of my flesh to split apart, to cease its struggle against death and be done. I feel the urging of my mind to dissipate on the wind, or spiral into some interior hell. I am morbidly wounded, insane with agony. Only hatred gives form to my mind. Hatred and the phrase that repeats with the pounding of my heart.

Flinn is dead.

I half expected to feel some sorrow at his parting, but I do not. He was dangerous, yes, but never a truly worthy adversary, never a creature worth engaging for the witty repartee. He was human, after all.

No. It was not Flinn who was my truest foe. It was Wyrmblight, a sword forged to slay me. Even now it resonates with that desire. I feel it in my wounds. I feel it in my aching mind, my still-beating heart. The bitch has it, I know—Jo is her name, like the name of a fisherman or a joiner. The blade is taller than she is, and yet she pretends she'll bring it against me. She and her comrades—that feeble crone mage and her brainless lackey, and the old mercenary Braddoc, one-time friend of the Fool. These dragon hunters offend me. The baroness sends greater forces against Greasetongue, the orc. In a single puff they would be gone.

Except for Wyrmblight.

Just as it shamed me the first time, it has shamed me again. Try as I might, I could not break that cursed, blessed steel, and my roiling plumes of green poison would not pass it. Worst of all, these wounds that Wyrmblight has cleaved will not heal.

So I wait in this lair of mine, wait for Jo and her pack of misfits to stumble in and kill me, as they must try to do. For they are human. If I cannot destroy them when they arrive, cannot snap the cursed Wyrmblight in two, I shall withdraw and again win by deceit what I cannot by war.

But I will kill them. They have angered me, and I will kill them. I will break the hated Wyrmblight just as I broke its bearer.

Chapter I

ritty ash from the still-smoldering funeral pyre whirled up in the midmorning breeze and stung Johauna Menhir's gray eyes. She blinked the tears back. Rubbing her swollen eyelids with the back of one grimy hand, Jo whispered, "No more." Her lips, dried out from more than four days' exposure to the late winter winds, split in a sudden grimace. "No more," she repeated hoarsely. "I'll cry no more for you, Fain Flinn." She shook her head sadly.

The wind shifted, and with it came a sudden hint of spring. The barren trees surrounding the tiny glade swayed gently, and for the first time Jo saw that the branches were about to burst with green. It was as if the world was oblivious to the death of Flinn, oblivious to the sacrifice he had made. It was as though the forest had already forgotten the titanic battle waged here between man and dragon. The hushed trickle of spring runoff filled Jo's reddened ears, and a crow circled lazily overhead.

Her hands gripped the great sword she held, a six-foot weapon fully an inch taller than she. "Wyrmblight," she murmured, as though to comfort herself with the name. The famed sword shone silver-white beneath the pale sky, untouched by the black taint that had covered it before. The four ancient sigils on one flat of the blade glinted brightly: Honor, Courage, Faith, and Glory. The four points of the Quadrivial. Flinn had attained the four points, but it had cost him his life. And now the sword was hers—her only physical reminder of the man who had sheltered her and taught her so much of life.

Jo's memories grew bitter, and the corners of her mouth tugged downward. A crack in her lips opened and bled a little. She stared at the fourth and brightest rune. "Glory," she spat. "If you hadn't sought glory, you wouldn't have fought Verdilith alone." No, that's not true, her mind whispered. Flinn went alone so we wouldn't be killed. He knew he was going to his doom; he wouldn't let us die, too. Her eyes wandered to the still-smoldering pyre.

"Oh, Flinn," Johauna whispered in a voice that broke, "why didn't you let me come with you? Why?" A thread of anger wound through the pain-filled words. "I was your squire! If I couldn't save you, I could have at least died with you!" One hand curled into an angry fist, and Jo stared unblinking at the pile of ashes. She ground her teeth, unable to voice the emotions welling inside her.

Wyrmblight glittered cold and lifeless in the young woman's hands. The warmth it had generated in its master's grip was absent for her, and she wondered if it always would be. For four days and nights Jo had stood vigil over Flinn's body; then she and the others had lit the pyre, and she guarded it during the day it took to burn. So cold and bitter had been the blade during winter's last throes that Jo had developed chilblains on her hands. But she hadn't noticed them then, and she ignored them now as she cradled the sword of elven silver and dwarven steel to her chest. "Oh, Flinn," Johauna whispered, "why did you have to die?"

Jo's gaze fell one last time to the ashes before her, the ghostly image of a man's body seeming to take shape amid the charred remains of oak and elm. Jo blinked once, and the form was gone. The embers had finally died out in this tiny glade in the Wulfholde Hills. All that remained of the finest knight the lands of Penhaligon had ever known was ash and distorted bone.

Flinn the Mighty was no more.

The squire's hand fell to her belt where a small, beaded leather bag hung—the one other possession of Flinn's. The pouch carried the abelaat crystals they had used for scrying. Three of the stones were orange in hue, created from the abelaat's own blood, but the other four were deeply red, formed from Jo's blood. A twinge of pain gripped Jo's shoulder as she remembered the eight-fanged creature biting into the joint, its poisonous saliva turning to stone in her wounds.

Jo touched the beaded bag. "Do I dare?" she whispered, unsure of her ability to control the crystals. When the stones were heated, they could be used to see or contact whomever the bearer wished. Some said they could even contact the dead.

The squire rubbed her tired eyes once again. "No, I can't," she murmured to the ashes. "Not now, anyway. I'd need Karleah's help." Jo looked behind her to the trail that led through the woods to her companions. The trampled snow had melted, leaving the brown richness of earth and a tinge of green. She blinked. Always before, spring had filled her with hope, but now she felt only empty.

They're waiting for me.

She blinked again and realized she didn't care. They're waiting for me, she repeated to herself, and I must go. Reluctantly, Johauna turned back to the remnant of the pyre. She held Wyrmblight before her, crosswise, and bowed low, her movements trembling and weary.

"Farewell, Fain Flinn, my lord—" Jo's voice faltered and could not continue, though her thoughts ended with "—my love." Jo closed her eyes wearily, then bit her cracked lips in sudden determination. "I will avenge your death, Flinn! Verdilith will die, and Wyrmblight will deliver the death blow," she said grimly. Jo clenched the sword again, this time drawing blood from her palms. She turned and hurried down the path, refusing to look back.

But she didn't need to look back to remember. The trail evoked the memory of the first time Jo had traversed it. Less than a week earlier she had stumbled through these woods, seeking Flinn and praying he was still alive after his attack on Verdilith, the green dragon. Jo had followed the path of blood, muddied snow, and broken branches all the way to the tiny glade she had just left—the glade where Flinn had died. Now the trail was brown and pungent with raw earth, and clumps of green lined its edges. It showed no evidence of Flinn's passing, as if it, too, had forgotten.

Suddenly Jo dropped Wyrmblight and fell to her knees. Cold mud clung to her legs, but she didn't care. Her arms crossed in a ragged embrace as she doubled over in pain. "Flinn! Flinn!" Johauna rasped, remembering how she had found his battered body, lying facedown in the trampled snow. She had turned him over, fearing the worst, but Flinn had been alive then, and for one precious moment Johauna had believed he would live.

But he didn't. He didn't live. Jo pressed her face between

her hands, determined not to give in to the despair and grief and anger that threatened to engulf her.

"How am I to live without you, Flinn?" Jo whispered, finally giving voice to the fear that had haunted her ever since Flinn had died in her arms. Who else will believe in me, teach me? Who else will have hopes and dreams for me, will have *pride* in me? Who else will *love* me? Jo wondered, her anger growing. Each day since Flinn's death, she had held her grief at bay. First she had stood vigil at the pyre, guarding his body for four days and nights from the wolves. Then she had waited the long hours it had taken for Flinn and the pyre to burn, not ceasing her vigil until the last ember died.

But now, there was nothing to stop her grief.

Jo doubled over and beat her clenched fists against the ground. Chunks of ice and rock bit into her skin, already fragile and damaged; chilblains opened and pus mingled with the blood of fresh cuts. "Why? Why? *Why?*" Bitter tears flowed from her unseeing eyes, and roaring filled her ears.

Jo paused and held out her hands before her, palms upward. Her hands were raw, the skin battered away. "Oh, Flinn," she murmured hoarsely, "let me join you." Jo looked past her hands to Wyrmblight, shining bright on the ground where she had dropped it. Catching a small, fearful breath, she placed her wrists to the sword's finely honed edge. The thin, razor-sharp edge of silvern steel stroked her skin.

A strange heat suddenly radiated from the sword.

Jo closed her eyes and slid her wrists against Wyrmblight's edge. She felt the fragile skin give way, and blood run in a sluggish stream from her veins, hot tears for the ground. Jo looked down at the stain of red on the white blade. A single tear escaped her eyes and splashed on the sword, hissing when it hit.

The young woman blinked, dizzy, vaguely wondering what she was doing. She raised her wrists from the edge of Wyrmblight and looked at the ragged wounds. Blood spilled forth and dripped onto the sword, splashing onto the sigils and hissing. One of the four sigils on the flat of the blade began to glow, and intense heat emanated from it. For a moment Jo was mesmerized by the pure white beauty of the glowing sigil; then she noticed that the blood on Wyrmblight had disappeared. Her eyes traveled from the sword to her bleeding hands and wrists. As she looked, a waving thread of white light stretched from the sigil. The light circled one wrist. Jo watched, speechless, as the white light took on the hue of blood and stitched itself about the gash. As it reached the opposite end of the laceration, the light gradually became pure white.

Jo blinked. "Flinn . . . ?" she whispered. The thread of light wove between her fingers, turned pink and paused, then encircled her other bleeding wrist. Jo held up her left hand and gasped. It was healed, completely healed. Only a tiny scar remained. She held up her other hand and it, too, was healed.

The waving thread of light retreated back to the third sigil. Jo reached out with her finger and tentatively touched it, marveling that she could despite its heat. "Faith," she murmured. She shut her eyes briefly, then stared above her at the surrounding trees. "Oh, Flinn!" she shouted. "You were the only one who ever had faith in me!"

The light from the sigil shot out and enveloped Jo. At first she was aware only of its warmth. Then, little by little, she felt the sorrow in her heart ease and become bearable.

The pain and grief still remained, but somehow she had gained the strength to bear them. Her mind was clearer, and the horror of the past week receded.

The words *have faith in yourself* rang inside Jo's mind. She thought it came from the light surrounding her. *Have faith, Johauna Menhir.* Slowly the light withdrew from Jo's body, leaving behind an unexpected calm, however small. Jo watched the light retreat inside Wyrmblight. Suddenly the warmth and glow were gone—Wyrmblight lay cold and lifeless once more in the trampled mud and snow. Jo stared in awe at the white blade, the words *have faith* ringing in her ears.

How long Jo knelt there in the melting snow and spring mud, she didn't know. She knew only that the sword had been a balm to her spirit, a balm that eased her sorrow. And now, in place of the pain, a new passion rose in Jo's weary mind: vengeance. At the pyre, she had vowed to avenge Flinn's death, and now she was suddenly determined to carry out that vow.

The dragon had brought him death, and the dragon would be destroyed by it. *Only then will Flinn's death and my life have meaning,* she suddenly realized.

Jo stood and picked up Wyrmblight. The woman frowned. She was a squire of Penhaligon, owing obedience to Baroness Penhaligon. But that obedience would likely interfere with Jo's desire to hunt Verdilith. Her thoughts turned grim. *Your loyalty lies with Flinn,* she mused, for it was he who helped you become a squire in the Order of the Three Suns. *Without him, you would never have reached the castle. Or if you had, they would have laughed you back to the rat-infested streets of Specularum.* Jo shuddered.

The squire touched the sigils one last time, then she

turned and continued down the path. Her steps grew increasingly sure. "Have faith, have faith," she chanted under her breath. She looked at the trees around her, noting how they burgeoned with buds, waiting to burst into green. But none of their vitality, their hope, seeped into Jo. She felt dead. Hurrying her step, she shoved her thoughts aside. "Have faith," she said a little unsteadily as she touched the silver bark of a birch.

Just ahead, at the end of the trail, the midday sun streamed into a glade larger than the one Jo had left. She hesitated before entering the glade, suddenly unsure of how to greet her comrades. You've been beastly to them, Jo told herself, callously berating them for "failing" Flinn, ignoring their grief. They'll understand, her logical half replied. They know I spoke out of anger and sorrow, not truth. Nodding once, Jo stepped into the glade and moved toward the encampment, keeping her eyes averted. If she didn't look out into the glade, perhaps the memory of her first sight of it wouldn't return. She quickened her pace, but the images were seared into her mind. She saw, once again, the terrible sight that had greeted her five days ago.

The crumpled, brutally savaged body of Flinn's griffon lay at this end. All about the creature, a score or more of staves, wands, and rods lay half-buried in snow. The once-pristine whiteness was marred by blood and churned mud from the battle Flinn had waged with Verdilith.

Jo bit the inside of her cheek. She had to face these memories and drive them from her mind or she would surely go mad. Jo stopped walking and forced herself to look at the glade. Her eyes grew wide.

Sometime during the last few days, the sun's rays had melted the snow. Gone was the white spattered with red. Dried tufts of grass and wildflowers lent a new, clean color to the glade. Jo blinked. Tans and yellows and browns and curtains of evergreen lay all about her as she knelt to take it all in. The trees had seemed so cold, so unfeeling the day they had witnessed Flinn's death. Now, spring was coursing through them, and the trees had sprouted buds.

Jo drew a ragged breath. If I can only endure, like the trees endure, she thought, I'll weather the winter of Flinn's death. Tears flowed freely from her eyes. "I understand." Jo slowly covered her face with her hands. The words *have faith* whispered once more through her mind.

A gentle touch on her shoulder made Jo look up. The concerned expression of Braddoc Briarblood's good eye met hers, though his milky eye wandered blindly away. Beneath the blind eye Braddoc's cheek twitched, puckering a deep hatchet scar that ran from his eyebrow to the cheekbone below, just short of the neatly plaited beard. Braddoc of the Cloven Eye had lost partial sight but not his life the day he had been attacked by an axe-wielding frost giant in the Altan Tepes Mountains. The dwarf's lips compressed a little, and Jo wondered if the usually laconic mercenary was about to say something.

Instead, Braddoc held out a gnarled hand to Jo. Three purple-and-white blossoms glistened there. They were snow crocuses, the earliest flowers to bloom in the spring.

"Braddoc . . ." Jo whispered. She reached out and took the fragile blossoms; she sniffed them delicately, then looked at her friend. "For Flinn?"

Braddoc shook his head. "No, they're for you, Johauna," he said sharply. "Flinn won't be needing these." The dwarf took Jo's arm and helped her rise. "Come, Karleah and Dayin are waiting. The time for mourning is past. It's time to go." Braddoc began walking toward the two canvas tents pitched at the other end of the glade. He stopped and eyed Jo quizzically when she didn't follow.

"I'm not sure the time to mourn ever ends, Braddoc," Jo said slowly. Her eyes slipped to the crocuses in her hand. "But you're right—it *is* time to go." She joined the dwarf, and together they crossed the ground leading to the camp.

Jo could see the smoke curl lazily away from the fire beneath the cook pot. Karleah Kunzay, an ancient, with-ered crone of a wizardess—and also a passable cook—was stirring something in the pot. Karleah ignored the approaching pair and busied herself about the fire. A sudden whiff of rabbit stew reached Jo's nose, and she sniffed appreciatively. Only then did she realized she was hungry.

The ten-year-old boy sitting at the camp saw Jo and Braddoc approach, and he stood in quiet anticipation. Dayin Kine had once been a shy wildboy hiding in Flinn's woods before Jo and Flinn offered him shelter. As Jo entered the camp, the boy brushed back his blond, shaggy hair and smiled tentatively. The smile was sweet in its innocence, and Jo couldn't help smiling back. Dayin's eyes were the color of the spring sky above, and they watched Jo intently.

The squire moved closer to the fire and saw that Kar-leah, too, was watching her with equal intensity. The creases around Karleah's black, beady eyes had furrowed more than their usual wont. Her lips were pursed, and the ancient lines crisscrossing her face had sunk deeper over the last week. Why, Karleah's worried! Jo thought in sud-den surprise. About me? A wave of guilt washed over Jo, and she felt her face flush. Her dismay deepened when Braddoc left her to join Karleah and Dayin on the other side of the fire. The three of them looked at Jo silently.

"I—" Jo began, then coughed. Get a hold of yourself,

she thought sternly. "The . . . pyre has finally burned out. Flinn is no more," Jo finished.

Braddoc and Karleah glanced at each other. The old wizardess looked down at Dayin, then put her bony arm around her apprentice's equally thin shoulder. Karleah nodded almost imperceptibly.

"Have you given any thought as to what to do next, Johauna?" Braddoc asked, his good eye looking up at Jo.

What to do next? thought Jo suddenly. Next? Why ask me? Jo turned away and placed Wyrmblight reverently on some nearby skins, buying a moment to think. Can it be, she thought, that they expect *me* to make the decision? She turned back to the others, and all three were looking steadily at her.

"I . . . hadn't given it much thought," Jo said truthfully, "but I know that the first thing I intend to do is find Verdilith." Seeing their dubious faces, Jo added grimly, "The dragon must die. I won't rest until Verdilith is dead." Her gray eyes flashed.

"While you stood vigil over Flinn's body," Braddoc said after a discreet pause, "I followed the path Verdilith made through the woods. It wasn't hard. He never once took to the sky—I think Flinn must have damaged his wings." The dwarf grinned savagely.

Karleah began dishing up plates of steaming stew and bread and handing them to Dayin to pass out. Jo accepted one gratefully and took a place by the fire. She touched the sword lying behind her, and the words *have faith* seemed to echo through her.

As Braddoc opened his mouth to speak again, Karleah thrust a bowl into his hands and grunted, "Eat." Snapping his mouth shut, he, too, sat by the fire. Dayin joined the dwarf and began eating his stew, using his bread as a ladle.

The fastidious dwarf shot him a censoring glance, then dug in with his spoon. A tiny drop of broth spattered Braddoc's yellow jerkin and leather breeches. He frowned and wiped the spot away immediately. Jo smiled. He's a strange fellow, she thought. So brusque and yet so persnickety about his appearance. Though his clothes were travel-stained, they were free of crusted mud, unlike Jo's and her other companions'. The dwarf spent far more time at the stream washing his things than the rest did.

"What happened to the trail once the dragon cleared the woods?" Jo prompted the dwarf.

Karleah harrumphed at Braddoc as she sat down, and Jo turned to the older woman. The wizardess bit into a steaming piece of meat and, seemingly oblivious to the heat, said to Jo, "He lost it. Wouldn't think a creature so close to the ground *could* lose a trail—a dragon trail at that—but the dwarf did."

"I did not lose the trail!" Braddoc barked.

"You sure enough did!" the old woman retorted.

Jo held up her hand for silence, about to speak, but the words died on her lips. The gesture she had just made was one of Flinn's, and she was shaken. She didn't know whether to be surprised that she used the gesture or heartened that she was following in his footsteps. Jo managed to say, "That's—that's enough bickering, please. Just tell me what happened after you broke through the woods, Braddoc."

Braddoc shot Karleah an I-told-you-so look with his good eye, then turned back to Jo. "The trail continued once I was through the woods and into the Wulfholdes," the dwarf said sharply. He paused, then shook his head. "Flinn severely injured Verdilith, by the looks of the blood trail the dragon left. In fact, I'd wager it was a close fight.

My guess is Flinn very nearly—"

Jo winced and put her hand to her eyes. Braddoc halted his words, and Jo silently thanked him. By the Immortals, she thought, Flinn *would* have lived if I had been there, regardless of Karleah's prophecy.

"Johauna . . ." Braddoc said tentatively, his voice quieter than Jo had ever heard. "I'm sorry I said that. I thought you'd be comforted to know that Verdilith paid dearly for—"

Jo winced again. "Thank you, Braddoc. I know," she said heavily. "I just wish I'd been at Flinn's side, like a good squire—"

"Don't think that, girl," Karleah cut in with her high-pitched voice. "Fain Flinn rode to his doom that day, and he knew it. He knew, too, that any who went with him would meet their doom as well. Flinn did a brave deed that day—don't belittle it by thinking you could've saved him."

Jo looked at her plate of food and then at Karleah. "You believe your prophecy, Karleah; I'll believe my instincts. I could have saved him." Jo frowned bitterly.

Karleah snorted, and her dark eyes glittered at Jo. "Harrumph! My prophecies have never failed me, girl. Had you been in the glade with Flinn, you both would have died."

And how much better that would have been than this! Jo's heart cried. She gripped her bread tighter and stared at the crone. "Believe what you like, Karleah," Jo said coldly, "and leave me to do the same."

"I'm glad you didn't die, Jo," Dayin said softly, his eyes shining at Jo. The young woman stared at the boy, unable to decide if she felt grateful or annoyed at his feelings for her. Dayin's eyes averted from Jo's before she could decide.

The boy's shoulders hunched slightly, and Jo turned back to Braddoc.

"So you were able to follow Verdilith's trail into the Wulfholdes?" Jo asked briskly, determined to change the conversation. She bit into a piece of bread.

Braddoc nodded, swallowing some food. He said, "Yes, I followed the trail—it was clear and obvious. Then I rounded a hill and—"

"—and the trail disappeared! The dwarf lost the trail!" Karleah cackled. She slapped a bony knee beneath the shapeless gray shift she wore.

A wicked grin slowly crossed Braddoc's face as he fixed his good eye on Karleah. "That's where you're wrong, old hag," he said gleefully.

"Eh?" Karleah's tiny black eyes widened suddenly, and her mouth hung open. "That's not what you said before," she noted worriedly.

Braddoc nodded slowly, still grinning. He waggled a finger at Karleah. "I didn't tell *you*, old woman, because I wanted to tell Johauna first," Braddoc said and then turned to Jo. The smile left the dwarf's face. "I may have lost the trail, but I haven't lost the dragon."

"What do you mean, Braddoc?" Jo asked. She placed her cleaned plate by the fire, then licked her lips and frowned. An odd aftertaste lingered in her mouth. I hope the rabbit wasn't spoilt, she thought, then thought better of it. Karleah never brought home carrion when she hunted in wolf form.

Braddoc held out his hands toward Jo. They shook slightly. "Johauna! Listen to me!" he said excitedly. "I lost the trail *because the trail ended!* The trail ended at the hill!"

"The hill? What hill, Braddoc?" Jo asked, just a shade testily. She blinked rapidly, trying to stifle the sudden urge to close her eyes. The lack of sleep is catching up with me, she thought, but I won't sleep now. I don't dare. "The Wulfholdes are all hills!" Jo yawned abruptly.

Braddoc glanced quickly at Karleah and then turned back to Jo. "Does one particular hill—a slightly rounded hill, with a stunted pine nearby—interest you?" Braddoc asked quietly. Beside him, Karleah drew her breath in sharply. Dayin looked up from his food, then leaned closer.

Jo blinked, only then aware that she had stopped breathing. Then, with a long intake of air, she asked, "You found the hill? You found Verdilith's lair? You found the dragon?"

"You're sure it's the same hill we saw in the crystal?" Karleah asked sharply.

Jo interrupted, "Is it *the* hill, Braddoc? Did you find the dragon?" She yawned again. A great desire for sleep washed over her, but Jo shook herself mentally. I know you're tired, she thought, but there are more important things than sleep. You must listen to Braddoc.

The dwarf stared at Jo, his good eye not blinking. Jo struggled to focus her eyes on him. Nodding, Braddoc said, "Yes, it's the right hill. But I spent the better part of three days searching and I couldn't find an entrance any-where—nothing!"

Jo's vision swam. She stood shakily, oblivious of the concern on her three comrades' faces. "W-we have to find an entrance somehow. We must. Surely we can reach this hill before sundown—"

Karleah broke in. "Not today, Jo." The old woman stood, too, and put her hand on Johauna's arm.

Jo's russet eyebrows rose in perplexity as she struggled to understand the wizardess. Then anger knitted her brow.

"Why n-not today, Karleah?" she stuttered, angry at her sleepiness. "You're not in charge—"

"No, I'm not," Karleah said agreeably. The crone lifted one thin hand and touched Jo's cheek. She nodded at the younger woman. "No, Jo, you're in charge. But you're exhausted and need to rest. I think the powder I put in your stew is beginning to work. . . ."

Johauna's eyes rolled backward as she fell into Braddoc's waiting arms. Karleah drugged me? Jo thought in disbelief. She could hear her friends' concerned voices, but the voices seemed to come from far away. A roaring filled her ears, and a strange lethargy seeped into her body. She struggled against it, suddenly afraid of what her dreams would bring. No! she cried, unaware that she made no sound. No! I mustn't sleep! I mustn't sleep!

But the sleeping powder and her own exhaustion were too much for Jo. Fatigue descended, surrounding her and dragging her into dreaming. Jo's last conscious thought was one of mingled dread and longing: she knew that in her dreams, Flinn would live again. She knew, too, that when she awoke, he would not.

But, for now, she dreamed of Flinn.

ia ia ia ia ia

Flinn lay in a world of cold and ceaseless flames. He was naked. He was dead. And the body that he occupied was somehow like his own, and somehow different. It floated numbly about his consciousness, as though his limbs were made of water and sponge. And the world of flames around him seemed to purify his watery form.

The knight clenched his fists, noting the strength in his hands. His arms felt stronger than they had in a very long time, perhaps stronger than they had ever been. He glanced at his body, his chest, his thighs; everything was smooth and strong, as though he were a statue freshly chiseled by a master sculptor.

All his scars of battle were gone.

With some effort he stood, noting only then the shadowy trees that towered in a ring about him. The ground beneath his feet crackled and broke, the only sound in this strange place of flickering light. He saw that he stood upon a burned-out pyre of wood and realized this was probably the same wood used to burn his mortal body. He was not surprised to discover that his soul had form, a perfect form of which his body was only a crude simulacrum. And then, with inhuman calm, he knew where he was.

The Realm of the Dead.

Whatever he was doing here, and wherever he was to go would certainly be revealed in time.

As he peered more intently into the flames, Flinn saw one other figure in the clearing. Johauna Menhir. She knelt, frail and fearful, upon the ground, Wyrmblight clutched loosely to her side. She was more beautiful and more graceful than Flinn had noticed with mortal eyes. The knight stood for what he thought must have been a long time, staring at the form of the woman he loved. She was more perfect here than in his memory, and his passions raced the longer he stared. He knew that these were the first feelings he had had since death. He stepped off his grave to embrace her.

Johauna's image was instantly dispelled as the fires about him spread in a roaring rush that engulfed the whole world. Johauna was gone, the trees, the sky . . . only the ceaseless flames remained. For a moment Flinn felt rage and pain, but he quickly cooled his feelings. The land of the dead had its own laws. Though he did not feel them yet in his thoughts, his heart knew they would be revealed.

In Johauna's place, a perfectly spherical boulder as high as Flinn's waist appeared, a primitive spear thrust clean through its width. It was a perfect stone, and a perfect spear, and the knight recognized the symbol of his most favored Immortal patron.

Diulanna, Patroness of Will, beckoned from the flames in the distance. Flinn, naked, strong, pure in spirit and body, walked toward her.

❧ ❧ ❧ ❧ ❧

Karleah came out of the tent and nodded coolly at Braddoc. The dwarf ducked through the flap and looked at Jo's sleeping form. Braddoc had carried Jo into one of the tents and laid her on the sleeping furs, then Karleah had undressed Jo and made sure she was sleeping peacefully. The dwarf, however, mistrusted Karleah's magical powders and ministrations and was determined to check on Jo himself. Braddoc knelt now by Jo's bedroll and pushed a straggling lock of hair from her eyes. He smiled. For some reason, it pleased him that her hair color so closely matched his. Johauna's was just a shade darker than his red mane.

The dwarf tucked a wolf skin a little closer around Jo's shoulders. His expression grew grim when he heard the girl moan a little. He slid Wyrmblight within her reach and set her hand lightly on the hilt. Braddoc fancied the girl's face smoothed a little. In her condition, he thought, she won't be able to lift the blade, let alone injure herself with it. With a final nod, he turned and left the tent.

Karleah and Dayin looked at him expectantly. "Is she

settled?" the old woman asked, her voice neutral.

Braddoc nodded, then joined the others at the fire. Dayin sat at Karleah's feet. He was sorting a number of dried twigs, some of which still held leaves and berries. Part of his lessons with the witch, Braddoc assumed. "Yes, she's settled," Braddoc said flatly. He shook his head. "Poisoning her like that wasn't such a good idea. I think she's having nightmares."

The old woman frowned, then shrugged. "Of course she's having nightmares; the powder only guarantees sleep, not sweet dreams. But Jo needs to rest. I don't think she's slept any since Flinn's death."

"Will she be any better in the morning, Karleah?" Dayin asked softly. His young face puckered with worry.

Karleah touched the boy's shaggy hair briefly. "I think so, dear," she said in a gentle voice Braddoc had never heard from her. The old hag has a heart after all, he thought. Karleah continued, "Jo placed too many of her hopes and dreams on Fain Flinn. She would have discovered that in time—if only she'd had time. But we'll help her learn how to find new dreams for herself."

"How long will she sleep, do you think?" Braddoc asked. He pulled out a whetstone and began sharpening his battle-axe. The edge was already keen, but sharpening the blade again gave the dwarf something to do.

Karleah squinted up at the midafternoon sun. "All day today and through the night, I suspect—perhaps longer," she answered.

Braddoc's only response was to grunt. He flicked his thumb across the battle-axe and smiled, well pleased with his work. He almost wished something other than wolves would dare return to these woods. But the terrible battle that had been fought between dragon and man had

frightened away all creatures, and it would be some time
before they would return.

Karleah pointed at a wrapped bundle near one of the
tents and said to Dayin, "Let's try again, boy."

Silently Dayin retrieved the bundle and unwrapped it at
Karleah's feet. Inside were nearly a dozen wands. All were
handsomely crafted, adorned with glittering gems and
made of rare, precious metals. All were magical, inscribed
with both ancient and recent runes of powers.

And not a one worked.

Verdilith had brought the wands with him in preparation for meeting Flinn, Karleah surmised, but for some
reason all the magic had been leached from them. Braddoc
frowned. The only logical explanation was that Verdilith
hadn't known the wands were drained when he brought
them to the glade. The other obvious answer, that there
was something about the glade that negated magicks, had
been ruled out by Karleah two days ago. She had tried to
use her own spells and magical items to reenchant the
wands, but they would not hold the magic.

Dayin picked out a slender wand of silver embellished
with mottled turquoise. "Try this one, Karleah," he suggested. "Let's see if we can enchant this one."

Braddoc glanced over with little interest. The work-
manship on this particular wand had not captured his
fancy, for the silver was crudely cast. "She tried that one
the day before yesterday, Dayin," Braddoc said gruffly. "If
you're intent on being a wizard like Karleah, you'll have to
learn to be more observant of the little details." He was
being pedantic, he knew, but Braddoc was hoping to goad
the boy. Dayin's passivity rankled the dwarf. He blamed
Karleah for the child's behavior—behavior Braddoc
thought was far too calm.

Dayin turned to the dwarf. "If you remember Karleah trying to use it, what did she do?" Dayin asked, a little testily. The boy's tanned nose wrinkled. Good, thought Braddoc. Get mad; don't be so sweet!

"Why, that I don't recall," Braddoc said smoothly, "but I do remember the outcome: nothing!" He laughed abruptly, pleased with his little joke.

Karleah smirked at Braddoc. "Harrumph!" she muttered caustically. She turned to Dayin and said, "Pay no attention to him, boy. Dwarves don't know magic . . . or humor. Now, let's try this wand of yours once more."

The old wizardess held the wand before her and began murmuring an incantation. His attention pulled from the battle-axe, Braddoc watched a scene he had witnessed many times the past few days. Beside Karleah, Dayin began a counterchant. His voice blended with Karleah's, and the sound swelled and filled the air of the glade. The wizardess's bony fingers hovered above the wand and traced invisible runes in the air. Dayin pulled powders and other items from the little pouches Karleah had given him and dusted the wand—all to no avail.

"I don't understand," the crone muttered, her dark eyes snapping. "I just don't understand. We've established that all the wands in this glade are no longer magical, but that doesn't explain why I can't enchant them!" Karleah scratched her chin. "I've enchanted empty wands before— even some of my own, now that I think about it." The old woman's bushy, peppered brows knitted.

"Is there something wrong with the wands themselves, Karleah?" Dayin asked, staring at the silver item the wizardess had dropped.

Karleah shook her head. "No, they're fine, for the most part. Oh, a few were trampled in the fight, of course, but most of the wands are perfectly formed—they should serve as fine new vessels for magic. All I need to do is enchant them!"

Braddoc raised one brow and cut in, "Maybe you're not a good enough mage, old hag."

Karleah turned on the dwarf and hissed, "Not good enough!" The woman's voice rose to a shriek. "*Not good enough?* Why, I'll show you 'not good enough'! " Karleah pushed back one sleeve of her nondescript gray robe, and Braddoc dove for his shield. The dwarf managed to raise it only an instant before a flash of blue light struck the shield and exploded into tiny sparks.

After the last fizzle sounded, Braddoc peered over the shield toward Karleah and Dayin. The crone's expression was mixed, telling him nothing, and the boy was frowning in disapproval as usual. Braddoc turned the shield over and waved away the last of the smoke. He saw with a measure of satisfaction that Karleah had missed the center of the shield. "We'll count that as one for me, old crone," he jeered.

Her ancient features flexing, Karleah waved vaguely toward the shield, and a blue light from her fingertip shone over a blackened scorch mark, "Mark's closer to the center than to the edge. My point."

"It's a tie!" Braddoc protested, pointing out that the latest scorch mark rested squarely on the circular line that divided the iron hub from the wooden rim. Three fainter black marks touched the inner circle of metal, while only two marked the outer wood.

"It's a tie?" Karleah replied, incredulous. "Ties go to me, eh?"

Braddoc shook his head. "I think not, hag. Ties belong to the dodger. That makes it three to three." The dwarf shook his head again and laughed. "I just pray one of these days you don't *really* miss, Karleah!"

The wizardess sniffed haughtily and then said, "The day I miss, Braddoc, is the day you forget to dodge!" Her black eyes twinkled at the dwarf suddenly, taking away some of the sting.

Dayin broke in, his voice sharp with concern. "I don't think you two should play this game," he said urgently. His summer-sky blue eyes flickered between the dwarf and Karleah. "Someone's going to get hurt."

"No one's going to get hurt," Braddoc rejoined, annoyed at the boy. "Karleah and I both know what we're doing. Besides, it's useful practice for me to stay in shape as a fighter. Though, truth to tell—" Braddoc's good eye winked at Karleah "—the first time the hag took a potshot at me I was a little surprised!"

Dayin glanced at the wand he was holding, his brow wrinkling with anger. Come on, boy! Braddoc thought. Let it out! Show us your anger; show us you're alive! When Dayin did nothing more than purse his lips, Braddoc frowned. Same reaction as always, Braddoc thought. The boy had plenty to be angry about: his father had maliciously abandoned his young son, he'd had to survive for two years in the wilderness, and only a few weeks ago he discovered his father was the evil mage Teryl Auroch. Even one of these events would send Braddoc on a tirade, he knew, but Dayin always contained his anger.

The boy was faultlessly useful in camp and always pleasant and conciliatory. Braddoc suspected that Dayin blamed himself for his father's leaving and thus tried to remain as unobtrusive as possible. Perhaps Dayin would not risk losing his temper for fear the others would also abandon him. Whatever the cause, the boy's manner grated on Braddoc's nerves, and the dwarf deliberately tried to provoke the boy on more than one occasion. So far, nothing had cracked the child's resolve.

Dayin held up the wand. "Karleah, you said the wands were drained of magic. I'd say it's more than drained. They've been altered so that they can no longer hold magic, as if every spark of enchantment had been removed," Dayin conjectured. His young blond brows knitted in imitation of Karleah's bushy gray-black ones. Braddoc stifled a laugh.

Karleah nodded sagely. "I'm afraid that's the conclusion I've come to, too, Dayin." She shrugged. "Whatever did it must be powerful indeed. I've never run across a spell that could do that!"

"What do you propose to do with them?" Braddoc asked, eyeing one particular wand that had caught his attention with its chased gold filigree set with emeralds that shone in the sunlight.

Again the old woman shrugged. "They're useless to me. We can bring them back to the Castle of the Three Suns, but the mages there are mere bunglers next to me."

Braddoc raised a brow at Karleah's statement but wisely chose to say nothing. He never timed his taunts of the wizardess too closely; he was well aware her magic missiles were of a low-key variety, and he didn't want to push her to anything more powerful.

Karleah continued, "We'll find out what's what at the dragon's lair. I'm sure of it." She turned to Braddoc. "If you've really found the hill we saw in the crystal, dwarf, then I can find us a way in, even if you couldn't."

Braddoc drew the whetstone across the edge of his battle-axe one last time before he looked at Karleah. "I found it, all right, but like I said—" the dwarf shook his head "—there's no entrance to the lair. None whatsoever."

The crone's faced crinkled into myriad wrinkles as she suddenly grimaced. "Leave that to me." Her black eyes glittered in the setting sun.

Chapter II

ohauna awoke late the next morning, feeling sluggish. A strange, twittering sound had awakened her, surrounding her and lifting her from her dreams. She pushed the sound away, unwilling to discern its source. Flinn is dead, she thought, and I'm alive. I'm alive to avenge his death, and avenge it I will. Her teeth clenched, then her hand wandered across the furs until she felt the cold, comforting steel of Wyrmblight. She could hear someone moving about outside the tent, and she knew it was time to join her comrades.

Jo sat up in the furs and looked around the dark canvas tent she had shared with Karleah during their journey through the Wulfholdes. From one tent pole, the old wizardess had hung several knapsacks and bags, brimming with smaller bags, vials, and boxes. Jo swore Karleah must have brought every herb, dried relic, and powdered substance she possessed. It had taken Jo a while to get used to the pungent aroma. Sometimes the odors invaded her sleep and gave her strange dreams, though last night's dreams were surely caused by the drug Karleah had given her in the stew.

Rubbing her eyes, Jo threw back the furs and dressed herself, the cold air speeding her movements. She tugged on her boots. They were finely crafted of heavy burgundy leather, and they were a source of pride to the poor orphan girl from Specularum. Jo stroked the silver buckles as she tightened the clasps running up the sides. She remembered being given the boots, along with her other clothing, at the Castle of the Three Suns. A faint smile flickered across Jo's face. The young woman had teasingly displayed her new boots to Flinn in their rooms at the castle, and she remembered now the warm, admiring glance he'd given her.

"Stop it, Jo," the young woman whispered aloud. Don't torture yourself. Flinn's dead, and your memories of him must be, too—at least for a while. You can't survive if every little thing reminds you of him. Jo fastened the clasps of the other boot hurriedly, struggling to keep her thoughts from Flinn. She stood quickly, picked up Wyrm-blight, and left the tent.

Jo blinked in the sudden light. The sun was nearly straight overhead in a cloudless sky. The sheen of green from a swaying branch caught her attention. Why, she thought, it wasn't just a dream! Spring is really here! The twittering she had heard earlier was the chirp of birds— thousands of birds. Jo saw blackbirds lining the tree branches above her, their trilling voices filling the air in a celebration of spring. The squire impulsively waved her arms above her head and shouted. The birds, silenced for a moment, abruptly took to the air. Their wing beats were nearly as loud as their singing had been. Almost as one, the entire flock swirled up from the branches and shot into the sky overhead. They descended almost immediately to other trees, farther off. A moment later, the woods again rang with the sounds of ten thousand bird voices.

Jo felt her lethargy leave her. The birds were an omen of healing, of repairing the damage that had been done. Jo stepped toward Karleah, who was sitting near the small campfire.

"Mornin'," Karleah said tersely. "Or should I say good day?" The old woman's brows lifted in mock disapproval. She turned back to the shirt she was mending.

"Blame it on your potion, Karleah," Jo rejoined. She sat beside the wizardess and pulled off a chunk of the bread warming by the fire. Jo ate greedily, suddenly aware of how hungry she was.

The old woman grunted. She licked the thread attached to her needle and made a stitch or two before she asked, "You feeling better?" Karleah's tiny, dark eyes were keen.

Jo met the woman's gaze without flinching. "Yes," she said slowly, "I'm 'better.' Healed, no—better, yes."

"Take your time, girl," Karleah said. The old woman reached out and awkwardly patted Jo's hand. "You're young, you'll heal. I know that's hard to swallow, but it's the truth."

Jo turned her eyes to the loaf of bread as she pulled off a second piece. She felt the muscles of her face constrict and harden. Yes, I'll heal, she thought. I'll heal the day I've made Verdilith pay for taking Flinn's life. Aye, and Sir Brisbois and Teryl Auroch, too. They all had a hand in Flinn's death. *Sir* Brisbois. Jo grimaced as she recalled the man who had brought about Flinn's fall from grace, from the knighthood. That smug bastard will pay, just as dearly as the wyrm! Jo vowed.

The young squire added a stick to the fire, though it didn't need it. She looked back at Karleah, suddenly aware the old woman had been watching her closely. Jo said calmly, "Where's Braddoc and Dayin?"

"Went to tend the animals," Karleah said. She tied a knot, then bit the thread off. She held up a rough shirt. "I declare, that boy is hard on clothes." The old woman grabbed her staff and used it to stand. "They'll be back soon. Finish that bite of food, will you? We've eaten already. Dayin found some tubers this morning in the softening ground." Karleah grunted in pain suddenly. "I'm glad it's finally spring. Winter's hard on old bones. . . ."

Jo's thoughts turned inward, and the sound of Karleah's voice receded and joined that of the blackbirds'. The squire sat cross-legged before the fire and balanced Wyrmblight across her knees. Gently, reverently, she touched the silver blade, her fingertips barely grazing the four raised sigils. Eyeing a speck of dirt, Jo fished through her clothing to find a rag to wipe away the offending spot. The only thing suitable was a small cloth from her belt. Jo stroked the midnight-blue swath with reverence. It was a remnant of Flinn's first tunic as a knight in the Order of the Three Suns. Flinn had torn up the tunic to bandage her wounds, but Jo pieced the strips together and restitched the three golden suns across the field of blue, the emblem of Penhaligon.

The young woman returned the cloth favor to her belt, tucking it in securely. She brushed away the dirt on the sword with her hands. Wyrmblight, Wyrmblight, she silently besought the sword. I will avenge Flinn's death, but how? How? *Have faith.* The words echoed inside her soul. *Have faith.* Jo sighed and looked up.

Braddoc and Dayin were returning with the mounts. Jo's horse Carsig, Braddoc's long-legged ponies, and the horse Karleah rode were tied to a lead rein. The animals

were tackled, ready to journey. Following without a lead
came Fernlover, Flinn's pack mule. Fernlover was braying,
and the sound was heartbreaking. Poor thing, Jo thought
suddenly. You miss Flinn, too. You know we're getting
ready to leave, and he still hasn't come back.

The dwarf handed Dayin the rein, and Dayin tied the
mounts to a nearby tree. They began nibbling at the new
growth surrounding the campsite. Braddoc strode closer to
Jo, who stood and faced him squarely.

"Is it time, Johauna?" Braddoc asked, his one good eye
focused on Jo.

She nodded. "Yes," she said steadily. Jo looked from
Braddoc to Karleah and then to Dayin. She nodded again.
"Yes, it's time. We break camp and ride. We've a dragon to
kill!" Her gray eyes glittered in the spring sunlight.

     🐾 🐾 🐾 🐾 🐾

Johauna held on to Carsig's rein and knelt beside the
dwarf. When speaking with Braddoc Jo often preferred to
be on his level. She looked the direction the dwarf
pointed. The rugged Wulfholdes surrounded them like
great black walls, threatening to close in. The last time Jo
had traversed these hills, the ground had been white with
treacherous ice and snow. Now touches of green crept
through the gray here and there, masking the shale and
flint that made up the backbone of the land.

"There," Braddoc pointed. "That's where the trail
ended. The blood disappeared. Either Verdilith took to
the air there, or else he changed into something so small I
couldn't follow his tracks."

Jo stared up at the large hill directly ahead of them. Carsig snorted and shook his head, and she shushed the

gelding. The hill was smoother, more rounded than most in the Wulfholdes, and there was a scraggly pine nearby. "You're right," she said slowly. "That is the hill we saw in the crystal the time we asked to see the dragon's lair. But, Braddoc, I barely recognize it; I don't think I would have if you hadn't forewarned me."

The dwarf nodded. "I know. What with spring here, I hardly recognize it either. I might not have if I hadn't seen the hill almost a week ago, when it was still under winter snows."

Jo looked at her friend and smiled. "Thank you for following the trail so promptly and not waiting for me," she said quietly. "I wanted to come with you . . ."

Braddoc's good eye flickered to the silver clasp he had given Jo for her hair the day they had met, then returned to Jo's face. "You kept the vigil, Johauna," he said huskily. "You did Flinn proud."

The squire shook her head and turned back to the hill. "You're sure there's no entrance?"

Braddoc said adamantly, "As sure as I'm a fourth cousin twice removed from the King of Dwarves, I am." Jo smiled at the warrior's manner. He only invoked his remote tie to royalty when he was at his most resolute. "I tell you, Johauna, I searched every square foot of that hill and every hill for a mile around." He shrugged. "I had nothing better to do, so I searched. There's no passage large enough for a human or dwarf—let alone a dragon—to get through."

"Then the dragon must shapechange each time to get into the lair, is that what you're saying?" Jo asked suddenly. "That makes sense. We know Verdilith can change shape; we saw him change at the great hall in the castle. And Flinn told me once that Verdilith could change without even using magic—'the damned Anointing of Immortal Alphaks,' Flinn called it." Verdilith's ability to change form had cost Flinn his honor, and his wife. "Are there smaller passages?" Jo asked.

Braddoc nodded. "Aye—more than just a few, too. I caught sign of a weasel's entrance over to the east near the base of the hill." Braddoc pointed at a small rock pile. "If the weasel's hole winds all the way to the center of the lair, Verdilith could get in through there."

Jo frowned. "To get through a weasel's tunnel, the dragon would have to be pretty small. He'd have to try to get in while the weasel was away or else risk fighting while he was in his injured state, wouldn't he?" Jo shook her head. "No, from your description, Verdilith was far too hurt to risk fighting a weasel underground. He must have used a different passage to get inside."

The dwarf bared his teeth in a vicious smile. "Yes—and I think I know which passage it is! Or, rather, which passages *they* are." Braddoc pointed to the rocky summit of the hill. "The crown is littered with tiny crevices, crevices so tiny only a bat or a mouse could crawl through them."

"How do you know they go all the way through?" Jo asked.

"Two days ago I saw half a dozen bats exit the hill—and they came *through* the crown. That's how I found the crevices. That has to be the way Verdilith got in; it has to!" Braddoc said earnestly.

Jo stood and turned to Karleah and Dayin as the two of them dismounted. Jo watched in concern as the old wizardess nearly fell when her feet touched the loose shale covering the ground. Dayin hurried to Karleah's side and handed the crone her staff. Slowly the pair made their way toward Jo and Braddoc.

"Karleah? Are you all right?" Jo asked tentatively as she saw how heavily the old woman leaned on the boy.

The wizardess shot the young squire a thunderous look. "Don't 'Karleah' me, girl," Karleah said testily. "A little saddle stiffness never killed anyone. If you're thinking to send me home, you've another think coming." She gestured at the hill with her staff. "Besides, how're you going to get in there without me?"

Jo shrugged. "Short of our digging frozen earth, Karleah, you're it. Braddoc swears the only two entrances are the weasel's lair over there or the crown of the hill." Jo pointed to the two areas. "What do you think? Can you get us inside? Could you teleport us inside, all at once? My blink-dog's tail could have carried me alone in there, if it hadn't gotten lost."

"Alone to fight a dragon," Karleah echoed irritably. "Think, girl!"

Jo's eyes narrowed for a moment, and she touched the hilt of Wyrmblight. I wouldn't be alone, she thought. She half expected to hear the sword repeat the words *have faith* to her, but the blade was silent.

The old woman cocked one eyebrow. "I've an idea," Karleah drawled slowly, "but it's going to take a bit of doing." She shook her head. "I don't like the idea of transporting us to a place I've never been—"

"But we've seen the inside of the lair, Karleah," Dayin interrupted, "through the crystals. Isn't that as good a vision as having been there?"

Jo looked hopefully at Karleah, who scratched her chin and was silent. Jo prompted, "I'm sure whatever you have in mind will get us inside, Karleah, but teleporting *would* be the quickest. We've already lost so many days that I hate the idea of waiting any longer. He's had nearly a week to heal—"

"Yes, yes!" Karleah interrupted, waving her hands impatiently. Sighing, she said slowly, "It's possible the dragon gave us a false vision when we saw his lair through the crystals. Have you thought about that?"

"Yes, it's possible," Jo said equally slowly, "but I think it's unlikely." Jo stretched to her fullest height and towered over the tiny crone, a technique she had seen Flinn use on the guards when he had entered the Castle of the Three Suns. She doubted Karleah would succumb to intimidation, but Jo had to try. She would tear the ground asunder with her bare hands if it was the only way to enter the lair and avenge Flinn's death. "If you can get Braddoc and me in immediately via some kind of spell, Karleah, I think you should do it," Jo said coolly.

The old woman frowned but stood her ground. She looked up at Jo for a long moment before finally saying, "Very well, I'll teleport you, but I'm coming with you. You may need me."

"And me!" Dayin called out.

Jo put a free hand on Dayin's shoulder. She said sincerely, "Dayin, I know how much you want to come with us, but there's an equally important task outside the lair: tending the animals. If we don't come out of there alive, it'd be cruel to leave Carsig and the others tied to a tree to starve themselves to death. Besides, between orcs and abelaats, you'll have your hands full keeping the mounts safe and hidden until we come back. Will you do it?" Jo didn't add that she couldn't afford the distraction of guarding Dayin while she was battling Verdilith.

"But—" Dayin began.

"A good soldier follows orders to the letter, Dayin," Braddoc said gruffly. "The best help he can give is to do what he's asked. Take the animals to that hill over there and keep watch at a distance. If something strange happens, retreat farther south, then wait for us."

Jo nodded, then added grimly, "And if we don't return in, say, two days, head back to the castle. The castellan will take care of you. Of that I'm sure."

The boy nodded, placated. "I liked Sir Graybow. He was nice." Jo smiled. The aging castellan had been Flinn's mentor—and his good friend. Without Sir Graybow, Flinn would never have had the chance to present his case and demand justice from his false accusers.

Dayin gathered the mounts' reins, then turned and left the trio still standing at the base of the hill. Jo looked from Karleah to Braddoc and said, "This is it." She twisted Wyrmblight in her hands. "You know I don't expect either of you to come with me," she said seriously.

Braddoc and Karleah snorted in glottal chorus. Had Jo's heart been any less heavy, she would have laughed.

"This isn't even worth discussing, Johauna," Braddoc said disdainfully. "Of course we're coming with you. That's final. Now, get on with your spell, witch."

Karleah rummaged through her pockets and pulled out two amulets. She handed one to Jo and the other to Braddoc. The squire shifted the charm back and forth, catching the faint runes in the sunlight. Its rough links of tarnished gold held an oval of beaten silver. She looked at Braddoc, who raised his brow, and they both turned to the wizardess.

"They're pendants," Karleah noted unnecessarily. "They'll protect you—or at least they should. I've never used them—never had need to 'til now. I traded for them more'n a year ago, so I hope they're all right."

Jo bit her lower lip. "What do you think we'll find

inside the dragon's lair, Karleah?" She put her amulet on.

The old woman shrugged. "Verdilith's an old wyrm; he knows how to protect himself. Chances are, the lair's booby-trapped left and right. You can be sure those entrances Braddoc found are."

"Will your teleport spell get us in past the traps?" Jo asked.

Again the older woman shrugged. "Past the ones the dragon has at the entrances, yes. Past anything inside, well . . . I can't say for sure. 'Course, Verdilith may have this whole area charmed against that kind of entry. My spell might not even work."

Braddoc pulled the amulet over his head and gripped his battle-axe. "I trust my reflexes and my weapon, old hag, but I'll wear your charm anyway." He grimaced uncomfortably at the magic medallion around his neck.

"Harrumph," Karleah snorted. "You'd better. The amulet should help, especially if we find ourselves in the *middle* of one of Verdilith's surprises."

Jo stroked the hammered silver. "Are you going to be all right, Karleah? Do you have a charm of your own?"

"Don't worry about me, girl," the wizardess retorted. She held up her ornately twisted oak staff and fingered a few carved runes on it. "My staff is all the protection I need." She planted the staff's tip in the rocky soil in front of her. "Now, reach out and put one hand above mine."

Jo and Braddoc did as they were bid, each putting out a left hand to grasp the smooth wood of the staff. Jo gripped Wyrmblight with her right hand, the sword held canelike, with its tip resting on the soil. The great sword's six feet of steel made it too heavy to be wielded with but one hand. Jo bridled at the indignity of setting the sword's tip on the ground, but she wanted to be ready for whatever she would face. Karleah closed her eyes and began to murmur softly, words spilling from the old wizardess's lips.

As the incantation wore on, the squire looked down at the dwarf and said calmly, "If the Immortals favor us with luck, Braddoc, Verdilith will still be nursing his wounds, unprepared to meet Wyrmblight again."

"That's hoping for a lot of luck, Johauna," Braddoc answered smoothly. His brown eye glinted at Jo. "Let's hope we are so lucky."

Jo ground her teeth and nodded. "For Flinn!" she shouted just as Karleah finished her spell.

The strange feeling of being yanked from the physical world seized Jo. Next came the disjunct sensation of existing momentarily in a separate state, and Jo knew she was traveling through the solid rock of the mountain. Her blink-dog's tail had allowed her to blink from one place to another, but never had she traveled more than twenty yards or so, and never felt the medium around her. Now, she had the odd sensation of wading through earth and rock, and the impression that whole minutes passed by. The feelings lasted longer than her longest blink ever had, and she had time enough to worry that the spell had failed. Then hard earth, smooth and cold, formed beneath her feet.

Jo released Karleah's staff and dropped to a crouch immediately, Wyrmblight swinging into position before her. The squire blinked her eyes, trying to focus them in the sudden blackness of the dragon's lair. The inside of the cavern was dark save for the twinkling of tiny lights far above Jo's head. For a moment she wondered if Karleah's spell had transported them to somewhere beneath a night sky. Then, in the gloom surrounding her, she made out a stalagmite projecting up from a sandy floor.

Behind Johauna a sudden hiss broke the silence, and the squire whirled about. Light flared from the top of Karleah's staff; Jo held back her sword. Easy, girl, Jo admonished herself. No need to take off Karleah's head. Jo glanced at Braddoc and nodded to the far side of the wizardess. The dwarf moved to flank Karleah, and Jo did the same. Whatever the cost, she and Braddoc would protect the old woman.

The light from Karleah's staff extended in all directions, and Jo could see to the farthest corners of the immense cavern, though the edges were but dim outlines. Before Jo and her companions lay an enormous chamber, its length too vast to properly judge. About one-third that distance separated the ceiling from the floor. The tiny spots of light Jo had mistaken for stars still twinkled overhead; in fact, they seemed to shine more brightly now that Karleah's spell had lit the cavern. They seemed to be little crystals, and Jo wondered briefly if they were anything like the abelaat stones.

No Verdilith in sight. Before Jo knew whether she was frustrated or relieved, her attention was drawn to the huge mounds of glittering coins and gems lying not more than a minute's walk away.

Jo stared at the flowing mound of treasure, a mound so vast she could not see it all without turning her head. The mountain of riches sparkled with gems and pieces of jewelry, casually lying beside golden goblets, platinum plates, and copper kettles. Coronets and diadems winked at Jo, and for a moment the orphan from Specularum couldn't believe her eyes. Such utter opulence couldn't really exist. Johauna heard Braddoc gasp in disbelief as he, too, gazed in wonder at the mound. For a long moment, the squire was lost in the gleaming magnificence of the wealth. Then the memory of Flinn returned, and she threw off her avarice.

Jo shot out a warning hand when Braddoc took a step forward. She stared intently into the eyes of her two companions and shook her head in warning. Braddoc frowned, then nodded. Jo gestured for the three of them to start circling around the cavern before checking out the treasure hoard. The squire glanced briefly at Karleah's light, and for a moment she resented it. With that second sun blazing in the cavern, even the blind bats would know of their presence. Now that they knew, though, it made no sense to put out the light. The idea of stumbling through the dark and into Verdilith's maw certainly didn't appeal to Johauna Menhir.

The three stepped forward, weaving their way through the stalagmites and piles of rocky rubble that littered the floor of the cavern. Jo's senses strained to detect any sign of life—movement, blood, noxious breath, the shudder of giant footsteps. . . . But she sensed only the sand crunching beneath her boots and the vision of gold swaying before her. She tore her gaze away deliberately and stared at the cavern surrounding them.

She continued walking along the edge of the cavern, taking care to stay within the more protecting confines of the wall. The treasure pile was so vast and high that the green dragon could easily be lying in wait behind it. Perhaps he lay in the open area beyond the treasure—the area that was so clearly the wyrm's lair.

Where is Verdilith? Jo thought angrily, then tried to calm herself. You're using anger to cover fear, girl, she told herself sternly. Could Flinn have injured the wyrm so badly that we'll find a dead dragon? she wondered. Having heard many tales of the recuperative spells dragons use, that seemed highly unlikely. No, Verdilith has to be some-where just up ahead, Jo thought. She lifted the heavy sword slightly higher.

As she moved along the wall of the main chamber, the stalagmites became taller and more tightly clustered. Several of the larger ones obscured the squire's view, and Jo grew worried. The stone pillars also cast looming shadows in the light of Karleah's staff. Jo's tension grew, and her hands gripped Wyrmblight tightly. The perfect place for an ambush, she thought. Her ears strained for some sound and her eyes sought to pierce the occasional patch of gloom.

Then Karleah's light faintly gleamed off a shadowy, scaly mound ahead. More gold? Jo wondered suddenly, her heart beating fast. Or the dragon's chest scales?

A minute flapping movement on the ground a few feet away distracted Jo. She halted abruptly. Karleah and Brad-doc stopped behind her. "Did you see it?" Jo whispered tersely, breaking the silence. Her voice sounded harsh and inordinately loud in the cavern.

Karleah shook her head, and Braddoc peered forward.

Still staring at the spot where she was sure she had seen movement, Jo inclined her head slightly toward the dwarf. "Something moved! It's just ahead—up by that next pile of rocks!" she said.

Braddoc and Karleah both stared at the patch of lighted sand cradled by two stalagmites and smaller rocks. Strained moments passed, and Braddoc said, "I don't see—"

Then, suddenly, the three of them saw the little flutter of movement that had caught Johauna's eye. There, on the sandy floor of the dragon's cavern, crouched a bat. A ray of light shifted and hit the creature, and Jo saw the tiny thing clearly. It flapped its wings helplessly, then opened its mouth and squealed.

Chapter III

ohauna stepped forward, preparing to brush aside the creature with her boot. "It's just a bat," she said in relief to Karleah, behind her. She extended her leg to kick the tiny, squawking animal out of harm's way.

"Wait! Jo!" Karleah croaked in sudden fear.

Something hard and heavy crashed against Jo's shoulder. The squire lost her balance. "What the—!" She fell to the cavern floor, only just glimpsing the massive object that struck her. Where the bat had once been, a seething lump of metamorphosing flesh now lay.

Convulsing. Transforming.

A *dragon-size* lump of flesh.

Jo rolled to her feet, a snarl on her lips and Wyrmblight in her hands. The blade shone faintly, and its hilt was warm to the touch.

"Stand back!" shouted Karleah, waving her staff at Jo and Braddoc. The old wizardess struck the ground with the staff. It stayed upright by her side, its ball of light illuminating the cavern still. Karleah pulled back her sleeves and immediately began murmuring an incantation, her gnarled hands blurring with speed.

Ignoring Karleah's instructions, Johauna swung Wyrmblight above her head and leaped forward, shouting, "*Fliiiinn!*"

As Jo hurtled toward the transmuting lump of matter, it exploded in size and shape, taking Verdilith's form. The squire hurled Wyrmblight down onto the beast in a massive, two-handed arc that carried every ounce of strength and willpower she possessed.

A sudden, blinding flash of blue light came from Jo's left and struck Wyrmblight before her blow could reach the dragon's flesh. The blue streaks of Karleah's spell flared brilliantly, magic clashing with elven silver and dwarven steel. A tremendous shudder of energy traveled up the blade and into Jo's arms, almost wrenching the sword from her hands. The full force of the blow struck her body, and Jo was thrown backward across the cavern.

The squire's flight ended almost forty feet later when she struck a stalagmite. The stone projection caught Jo in the back, and breath exploded from her body. She tumbled to the stony ground. Her spine felt snapped in two and tears of pain stung her eyes. Jo struggled for air, but her lungs would not respond. Sharp, stabbing pains pierced her chest.

Am I dying? she wondered frantically. Why can't I catch my breath? I've got to kill Verdilith. I can't die until he is dead! The squire's fingers tightened on Wyrmblight, still clutched reflexively in her hand. Please, let me live, she pleaded to the sword. Let me outlive the dragon, if only by moments! She struggled to control the fear that washed over her.

The Great Green, Verdilith, separated Jo from Karleah

and Braddoc. Around him lay stalagmites, crushed to rubble beneath his newly formed claws of ivory. His emerald-green hide was laced with myriad cuts, and fresh blood seeped from unhealed wounds. A gaping gash nearly a foot deep and more than three feet long bled profusely along the dragon's right side. It was a serious wound, though perhaps not mortal, and it looked fresh. Jo had expected Verdilith to be healed by now, healed with the extraordinary spells he knew.

In the instant that all these thoughts flooded through Jo's spinning mind, the great green dragon reared back in fury, extending and fluttered his giant, batlike wings. Wind whistled through numerous holes in the wings' fragile membranes. A few of the holes were so large that Jo knew the dragon couldn't fly.

Attack! Jo cried silently to her friends. Just beyond the beast, she could see Braddoc and Karleah; they stood like statues, poised as they had been when Jo had made her lunge. Apparently Verdilith's magic is far more powerful than Karleah's, Jo thought with a moan of pain.

Struggling desperately to move, the squire braced Wyrmblight against the ground and tried to pull herself upward. She rose to one knee before agonizing pain twisted through her back, forcing her back to the stony cavern floor. With an extreme effort, she held her head up and looked toward the dragon and her comrades. Why are they just standing there? she thought anxiously. Why don't they *do* something?

The dragon turned his enormous head toward Jo, and the curved amber horns on his brow glinted coldly in the light of Karleah's staff. Through her haze of pain Jo wondered if Verdilith had somehow read her thoughts. She saw the golden, malevolent eyes staring at her, perhaps gauging her ability to harm him. Then, with slow and deliberate malice, he stepped toward Jo and extended his trembling right claw. She gasped, struggling back from the razor-tipped talon. Eyeing her evilly, Verdilith lowered the massive claw, setting the ivory tip of one nail on the flat of Wyrmblight.

"No!" Jo shrieked, trying desperately to yank the sword away. It wouldn't budge; the sigil for Glory was snagged on the dragon's claw. Wyrmblight's hilt felt suddenly red-hot in Johauna's grasp. With one quick flick of his talon, Verdilith wrenched the sword from Jo's hand and sent it skidding across the stone floor toward him. The hilt struck sparks in the darksome lair as it passed.

"Wyrmblight," the dragon whispered in greedy awe, pinning the sword beneath his claw. Careful not to let the blade touch his flesh, he prodded it toward a cluster of stalagmites. There, with the caution of a jeweler, he slid the sword between a tight pair of rock columns. Then, setting his claw on the hilt, he began to bend the blade sideways. "Good-bye, Wyrmblight," the dragon mumbled venomously.

"No!" Jo cried out again, struggling to get up. Her body cried out in pain but, gritting her teeth, she slowly rose to one knee.

With a ghoulish smile on his spearlike teeth, Verdilith snapped the blade harshly to one side. Instead of breaking, however, Wyrmblight cut hissing through the rock columns and dropped loose. One of the stone pillars, sliced in half, broke free from the cave roof and fell like a massive tree into the lair. The resulting *boom* shook the stony ground beneath Jo, and made her ears ring.

"You can't destroy it, Verdilith," Jo shouted in agonized triumph. "Not you! Wyrmblight was forged to kill you, and it'll stay whole until its purpose is fulfilled."

Verdilith turned his enormous head toward her and regarded her with all the disdain he would have for an injured fly. The vast lids over his slitted eyes drew into a dubious and irritable line.

"Quiet, bitch," he murmured, green gas spilling gently from his nostrils and rolling over her.

Choking, Johauna croaked out, "Karleah! Do something!" She clamped her eyes closed against the stinging gas and rasped, "Braddoc, attack! Fight, damn you! Fight!" Every battered muscle in her back screamed with the drawn breaths.

Unconcerned, Verdilith snagged the sword once again. He shifted his weight to his back haunches and assumed a sitting position. Only then did Jo see his wounded left arm. A jagged laceration, nearly three feet long, puckered rawly across the inner flat of the claw and up Verdilith's forearm. Exposed white tendons, likely snapped by Wyrmblight, extruded from the claw and arm; the limb was withered and virtually useless. Somehow Jo knew the wound would never heal, though the skin surrounding it might finally pucker and close over. She grinned with evil satisfaction. "Good for you, Flinn," Jo whispered huskily, taking shallow breaths. "You've maimed the bastard for life!" She gained her feet and staggered toward Karleah and Braddoc.

The dragon studied the sword, cautiously lifting it in his claws. Setting her teeth in determination, Jo inched closer to her friends. Verdilith's eye turned distractedly toward her, and he let out a roar that reverberated through the cavern. A cloud of noxious green mist erupted from his maw, covering Jo and the statuelike forms of Karleah and Braddoc.

Jo held her breath and dropped again to her knees. Watching her, Verdilith grinned. Slowly he snaked his long, sinuous neck toward her. The beast's ivory fangs glinted, and his gums glowed with green bile. A long, snakelike tongue flickered out, licking away the viscid fluid. The stench that rolled from his mouth nearly made Jo retch. The dragon lowered his head, a head the size of a small cottage, to Jo's level. His golden-orange eyes gleamed moistly, and little puffs of poisonous mist plumed from his nostrils.

It was the first time Jo had ever really seen the dragon, and even the pain in her back and lungs retreated in the face of her sudden terror. Nothing could have prepared her for this sight. Nothing could have prepared her for facing Verdilith.

"Ssssoooooooo," Verdilith hissed in a long drawl, "you are the foolish successor to foolish Flinn?" An amber eye flickered to the sword, dangling in Verdilith's good claw. Even beyond her grasp, the sword seemed to whisper *have faith* to Jo. Heeding the words, she tapped the anger inside her—her only hope to fight off the terror of his presence. This fiend *killed* Flinn! she shouted to herself. You must avenge that death, broken bones be damned!

The dragon's tongue tested the air, and droplets of green spittle splashed at Jo's feet. "Your magicks and your sword are too feeble to defeat me," Verdilith continued. The words sounded clipped and strangely alien to Jo, as if they were coming from a great distance instead of the few steps that separated Jo and her foe. "Your precious Flinn proved that. Your attacks now prove that. Your comrades are dead, and so are you." The dragon opened his jaws, revealing rows of deadly, spearlike teeth.

He dropped Wyrmblight before her.

"Go, ahead," he seethed. "Take the sword. Kill me if you can."

Jo grappled the blade, struggling to clutch its hilt with her weary hands. Finally securing her hold, she raised the sword and thrust it toward the dragon's head.

With something akin to a purr, Verdilith lowered his face toward the sword and rubbed it lovingly along his jaw. The keen, hot edge of steel lightly sliced into the tender facial skin of the dragon, hissing as blood poured slowly onto it. A spark of pain appeared for a moment in Verdilith's massive eyes, but quickly transformed into a dull glow of pleasure. Jo wrenched fiercely at the blade, trying to redirect it toward the dragon's throat. Wyrmblight swung about, leveling toward the creature's throat, but Verdilith caught it lightly between his massive teeth.

Without releasing his bite, the dragon murmured, "A mere shaving implement, this." He stared mirthlessly at Johauna, his golden eyes narrowing. Despite the dragon's words, despite his apparent lack of concern about the blade, Jo saw a moment of fear in those great, slitted eyes. He blinked it away, and the wound on his face gently dripped blood onto the stone beside her. "Why need I destroy a shaving implement?" Verdilith continued, his voice strangely tense. "Especially, when I can destroy its bearer?"

"To arms, children of stone! To arms!" came the ragged shout of Braddoc Briarblood from some distance behind the dragon. As Verdilith whirled his huge head toward the call, a thud of metal sounded.

Verdilith shrieked.

In the same moment, a roaring funnel of wind suddenly formed in the cavern. It grew rapidly, swirling to one side of the cave, some distance away. Johauna wondered if

Karleah would be able to control the air elemental in time to actually threaten Verdilith.

Whether or not she could, Jo's time was at hand.

Scrambling unsteadily to her feet, she charged the beast's exposed breast. Her gray eyes flashed with anger and dread anticipation as she pulled Wyrmblight back for the killing blow. "For Flinn!" Jo lunged unevenly with the blade, letting her stumbling body impart its force to the attack. Still, it was a weak thrust at best, and misdirected, but the sword shone suddenly bright in its path. It glanced off the scales of the creature's breast and dug into the dragon's crippled left claw. White mist from the blade clung to the raw wound and turned red.

The dragon screamed again. He reared, his massive wings flapping wildly to help him keep his balance. Jo dropped to the ground, shielding herself from the buffeting wind. Karleah's wind funnel swept closer, nullifying the winds from Verdilith's wings.

Braddoc, axe glinting in hand, landed a solid blow on the wyrm's wounded side. Verdilith seemed oblivious, gnawing his wounded arm in blind rage. Retreating from the creature's thrashing tail, Karleah stepped amongst a forest of rock columns. From there she directed the wind tunnel toward the dragon. In moments, it engulfed him, pummeling him with coins and gems and dust.

With supple, wicked grace, Verdilith swung his head back toward Jo and hissed, his voice rumbling deep and low through the long, twisted neck. "You've earned my hatred, squire! You and that accursed blade are no more!"

Jo blinked the dust from her eyes and tried to see beyond Karleah's tornado. One moment, he was a dim outline in the swirling storm, the next, he was gone altogether. Then, as quickly as it had come, the tornado vanished. A harsh

hail of coins and gems followed for some moments afterward, leaving only a drifting cloud of sand, glittering in
Karleah's magical light.

There was no sign of the dragon.

Stunned, Karleah and Braddoc stared back at Jo from
across the empty hall.

The squire slumped to the ground, the strength gone
from her body. She clutched Wyrmblight in her arms.
Braddoc and Karleah raced toward her, the dwarf reaching
her first. He knelt by Jo's side and smoothed tousled hair
and grit from her face.

"Johauna!" Braddoc said urgently. "You're hurt!"

Karleah knelt beside the dwarf and said testily, "Well, of
course she's hurt! She took the full effects of my most
powerful missile spell—a spell, I might add, that *would*
likely have killed Verdilith in his condition." The old
woman tapped the silver-and-gold medallion on Jo's chest.
"It's nice to know this thing works, dear. You'd have been
dead otherwise."

Jo smiled feebly, but was too weak to respond further. I
may not have died then, she thought, but I'm about to die
soon. She looked at Karleah's suddenly frowning face.

"When Wyrmblight intercepted my magic, the spell
somehow rebounded on the dwarf and me," Karleah
explained. She began gently prodding Jo's body, and every
now and then Jo gasped in pain. "We couldn't move; we
were paralyzed," Karleah continued. "We saw and heard
everything, fortunately. Only after we were gassed by that
behemoth were we freed." Karleah jerked her thumb
toward Braddoc, who held up his amulet, and said, "There
again we were lucky."

"How are you, Johauna?" the dwarf asked. "Where
does it hurt?"

"My back . . . and lungs," Jo whispered, the stabbing pains in her lungs forcing her to take shallow breaths. "Never . . . mind me. What . . . about . . . Verdilith?"

Karleah glanced at Braddoc, who returned the old woman's look. Then Karleah looked away, and Braddoc turned to Jo. "I'm afraid he got away, Johauna," the dwarf said slowly. "He turned to mist and . . . disappeared."

Jo closed her eyes. I'm going to die, Wyrmblight, she thought to the sword. I'm going to die, and I haven't avenged Flinn's death, and I won't live to see Verdilith's death. She pulled the blade closer to her, her fingers unconsciously seeking the four sigils. Perhaps I can fall asleep and then die without so much pain, she thought as a heavy darkness descended on her.

Jo felt consciousness begin to slip away. The pain retreated, taking with it Jo's hopes and needs, dreams and desires. She fought against the gentle insistence surrounding her. *Give up the sword*, whispered her mind. *Give up avenging Flinn's death. Your time has come to depart from this world.* Jo fought against the words. "No!" she shouted. In the indistinct blackness that closed around her, she ran, her soul suddenly given form. She waved her arms wildly, trying to ward off the insistent thoughts of defeat hammering at her.

"Flinn! Flinn!" she called frantically. "Wyrmblight, where are you? Where is Flinn?"

Then, somehow, he was walking toward her in a vision, a glowing figure surrounded by the blackness of death. He was whole and hale again, and seemed younger than Jo had ever seen him. A smile lingered on his lips beneath his dark moustache, and there was only a little iron streaking the black hair. The scars across his face were barely visible. Flinn held his hands out to her, palms upward. Jo looked up from them, across his broad chest now clothed in his midnight-blue tunic from the Order of the Three Suns, and on to his dark eyes. They were shining down at her, and Jo felt her heart break. He had never seemed more beautiful or more majestic.

"I can't come to you yet, Flinn," Jo sobbed. "I promised you! I have to avenge your death. Please help me return."

Flinn still smiled at her with love and understanding.

Jo almost reached out for him, but she stopped herself in time. "Where . . . are you?" Jo asked instead, gesturing around at the darkness.

Flinn laughed low, a chuckle that held none of its old cynical bitterness. "Ah, Jo!" he murmured. "Return to your body. Have faith—we will meet again someday."

The image of Flinn disappeared in the blackness that surrounded Jo, but the words *have faith* echoed through her soul. She felt like crying, whether from great joy or deep sorrow, she didn't know.

From a tremendous distance, Jo heard Karleah murmur, "Look at that, Braddoc! That—that glowing mist is covering Jo's body!"

"Aye, and it's coming from the sword!" Braddoc responded.

"What do you make of it?" Karleah inquired.

Jo's eyelids fluttered, and she heard Karleah and Braddoc both gasp.

"Johauna! You're alive!" the dwarf cried.

"You've a penchant for stating the obvious, dwarf!" Karleah vented. Jo felt hands gently touching her. Then she heard the old woman hiss in sudden realization. "Of course! The sword healed her!"

Jo's eyes opened fully, and she focused on her two comrades kneeling beside her. The squire smiled slowly. "Now who's stating the obvious?" She held out her hands. "Help me up."

The two helped Jo rise to her feet. She felt a little shaky. That's to be expected, she thought wryly. After all, you've just come back from the dead. Jo stretched, the muscles in her back moving without pain. She tentatively took a deep breath; the stabbing ache wasn't there. She smiled at the two concerned expressions staring up at her.

"I'm fine. Really," she said.

Karleah blinked rapidly. "Forgive my staring, Jo," she said, "but it's been a while since I've seen a dead person."

Braddoc snorted. He handed Jo her sword and hefted his own battle-axe. "She's not dead anymore, so don't go treating her like she's *un*dead, will you?" The dwarf looked up at Jo with his good eye and jerked his thumb behind him. "The dragon's gone. We won't get our vengeance today. But let's at least load up on some treasure and return to the castle. Maybe if the baroness is in a generous mood, she'll let us keep a piece or two for ourselves."

Jo shook her head. "I'll help you bring some treasure back to camp, but I'm coming back here with supplies. Verdilith's injured; he'll return to his lair sometime soon."

Braddoc shrugged. "We've got maybe a week's worth of rations left, if we stretch it. But you're right. It makes sense to harry the dragon now before he heals and regains all his powers."

As the three of them started across the cavern floor, Karleah stopped to get her staff. She frowned at the ball of light, but Jo didn't bother to ask why.

"I don't think Verdilith's healed any since Flinn attacked him," Johauna said seriously. "Aren't dragons supposed to have lots of healing spells?"

"So the sages say," Karleah answered absently. She was

looking around nervously. "And I can't divine why the dragon wouldn't fight us with spells, particularly since he was too injured to really engage in physical battle."

"We can puzzle that out later," Braddoc interrupted as they reached the edge of the golden hoard. The magical light flickered across the vast mounds, which spread out as far as the light would reach.

Hadn't the light extended farther before? Jo wondered. She dismissed the thought, thinking that perhaps the area of illumination diminished naturally as the spell wore on. "Karleah," Jo murmured as she and Braddoc moved toward the piles of gold, "you keep watch. We'll get a few things and be right back."

"Make it fast, Jo," the old wizardess called. "I want to get out of here soon. . . ."

Braddoc wandered to the right, and Jo circled to the left. She began wading through the gold and silver coins littering the floor, enjoying the shift and clink of coins slipping by her boots. She paused every now and then to reach out to touch some gem or gold-chased bauble. Her eyes flitted from necklaces and brooches to rings and bracelets to encrusted footstools and ornamented portrait frames. Jo's brain reeled. How could there be so much wealth in the world? she wondered. How could there be so many exquisite, *exquisite* things? Johauna picked up a fire opal the size of her fist and an aquamarine diadem and tucked them in her belt. For the most part, however, the poor orphan girl from Specularum was too overwhelmed to greedily gather treasure. Johauna continued to walk on, her eyes touching on pieces of metalwork that would have paid a king's ransom in the present age.

Some unknown time later, Braddoc came up behind Jo and touched her arm. The squire jumped. "I've been calling you for the last minute, Johauna," the dwarf said. "Don't let the dragon's treasure root in your brain. It'll take over your thoughts, mesmerize you, consume you—you'll stop eating or sleeping or thinking of anything but the treasure."

"Really?" Jo said thickly. She reached out a finger and stroked a cupboard made of gold, inlaid with jade.

Braddoc jerked her arm. "Come along! It's a good thing I'm here—the treasure's gotten to you already."

Jo scowled, trying to think. It was true she hadn't thought of anything but the riches she'd seen, but she couldn't have spent more than a few minutes . . .

"We've been picking through the hoard for more than an hour now," Braddoc said testily, as though sensing her thoughts. He shifted his bulging knapsack on his shoulder. "Karleah's been nagging us to leave for that whole time."

"How . . . how does the treasure get to me like that?" Jo asked. Her thoughts were beginning to clear.

The dwarf shook his head. "It just does. The dragon sleeps on the treasure, you know. I think his essence permeates the gold and traps the unwary. Even I'm not immune to it. Karleah had to tap me with that staff of hers before I was able to shake it off."

The two rounded a mound of treasure and found Karleah anxiously pacing. She whirled toward them in a pique of nerves and held out her hands.

"There you are, you old stump!" she snapped, waggling her withered finger at Braddoc. "I sent you after Jo a quarter hour ago! There's no time to lose! We must leave immediately!" the old wizardess urged. "Come!" She gestured for them to move closer.

Jo saw that the light atop Karleah's staff had faded, giving off the dull illumination of an oil lantern. Jo's thoughts cleared completely, and she tightened her hold on Wyrm-blight. "What's wrong, Karleah?" Jo asked.

The old woman shook her wrinkled head rapidly. "No time to explain!" she cried. She held out her staff before her. "Quickly! Put your hands above mine as you did before! We must leave now!"

Jo and Braddoc hurried to do as the wizardess bid. Karleah began murmuring her incantation, an undercurrent of fear lending urgency to the words. Jo closed her eyes and braced herself for the unnerving shift through space and matter.

The old mage had frenetically muttered many phrases before Jo felt the magic began to weakly wrap about her. But, even then, the sensation was all wrong. The magic felt unsure, its grip on the three tenuous and fragile at best. The spell that had brought them into the lair had been like hurtling over water aboard the steady deck of a ship. *This* spell, though, was like falling—falling and rising and falling. Images of rock and sand intermixed with images of sky and ground, as though they were shifting back and forth above and below ground . . . as though they were slipping down through the world into the nether realms, then back up again.

And it seemed an eternity.

Jo thought she heard Karleah murmur, "Something's . . . no, it's not right—something's wrong—" Jo tried to open her eyes but couldn't. Keep a grip on the staff! she told herself. If you let go, you might end up inside rock!

Moments stretched to minutes and then on into endless days before the uneasy travel passed and Jo felt herself returning to her solid form. She opened her eyes and blinked dazedly at Karleah and Braddoc. The dwarf returned her gaze with the same measure of disorientation.

The wizardess let go of her staff and collapsed to the ground.

"Karleah!" The shout came from Dayin, who stood nearby. Karleah had teleported them to the hill where they'd asked Dayin to stay with the animals. We're safe, Jo sighed as the realization of where they were set in. She turned to Dayin, who was helping Karleah sit up.

"What's the matter, Karleah?" Johauna asked. She gestured back toward the hill covering the dragon's lair. "Why was that such a rough transport? Are you still able to send me back to the lair to kill the beast?"

The old woman's tiny eyes were wide with terror. "Something's wrong! There'll be no going back to the lair. We've got to get back to the castle, Jo . . . immediately."

Jo bit her bottom lip and narrowed her eyes. "But I've sworn vengeance for Flinn's death. That dragon is never going to get any weaker than he is now! I've got to kill—"

"And I tell you all my magic has been drained from me!" Karleah interjected. Her black eyes flashed. "Don't you see? We almost didn't *make* it that time! I *can't* send you back to the lair because . . . my magic's gone!"

&a &a &a &a &a

Verdilith watched the creatures vanish. They flickered in and out for many moments, and he wondered if the old woman's spell would fail. When at last it seemed unlikely that they would return, he seeped out of the crevice in the ceiling he'd hidden in. His misty form floated gently to his bed of gold, the mist settling through the mound.

The dragon rued the theft of some of his hoarded treasure, all save one piece. He'd known every item the squire and the dwarf picked up, and he'd been tempted to attack again. But he had held his rage in check and watched and plotted. He was too weak now to attack them all, especially now that his magic had been drained away. But he would not always be weak. That would change. That would change.

Verdilith's misty form sank into the cracks between his coins and jewels and other items. He sank down to the very depths of his treasure. Ah! It is good to touch the first gathered, he thought as he reached the very roots of his hoard. And it is good to be rid of that box!

An evil chuckle emanated from the mound of gold and spread out through the cavern. The dwarf had found the box and couldn't resist it: preternaturally featureless, marvelously simple, finely crafted, solid and guileless, like the brain of the dwarf himself. The iron box had called to the iron in the dwarf's soul. When he had picked up the accursed box, a shadowy smile formed along the cave's misty ceiling. Verdilith considered the other items the grubby creature had pilfered to be almost fair payment, a kind of service fee for taking Teryl Auroch's horrible box from his lair.

The dragon assembled his thoughts, a difficult task in this form, particularly situated as he was within the treasure. Teryl Auroch gave me the box, knowing what it would do, knowing it would drain me. Now the mage himself will know the pain he has caused. Verdilith frowned mentally, then added, I serve him no longer. By the time he comes looking for his precious box, it will be lost, I will be whole, and Wyrmblight and its bearer will be broken.

The dragon turned his thoughts to the squire and her comrades. Invaders. Ignorant and weak. Women, two of them were, he reminded himself. He had thought Flinn's death would be vengeance enough for him. But it isn't Flinn. The sword's the thing. It's what cut me. It's what hungers like a tongue of steel for the taste of my blood.

He shifted, coins and gems sifting down, disquieted, around him. I had held that sword in my claw, he thought, incredulous. I had wrenched it against the stones. Why could I not break it? Why did I let the bitch escape with it? She will die for this. But not merely die. She will suffer and die. It is a matter of poetics.

And the sword . . . I must destroy it. But how? Upon this question, he thought for a long while.

Perhaps days.

At last he thought, I must see Teryl Auroch about this sword. He will have something to destroy it. The mist that formed the dragon's body threatened to seep away into the ground beneath his treasure. With a struggle, Verdilith pulled the mist closer together. He would have to change now; he was too weak to hold this form together much longer. Ordinarily, changing back into his natural form would be a simple and sensible matter; ordinarily he could heal his wounds in dragon form. But these were desperate days.

The dragon gnashed teeth of mist, disturbing a single coin as he did so. That accursed box! he thought. It stole his healing spells, rendered his magic items worthless, seemed to drain his very soul. Only his natural ability to shapechange remained—his gift from the Immortal Alphaks.

Verdilith shuddered. He had to pull his form together and change now . . . or dissipate and die. But he feared the change. His wounds were worse in dragon form—tearing wider, filling with gems and filth. For that matter, the transmogrifications were growing longer, more difficult, as he weakened. But death would be worse.

The dragon pulled the mist up and out of the treasure hoard until he was floating above the golden mounds. With a supreme effort, he focused on the transformation. The mist gave way to something more corporeal; it solidified, shaped itself, and hardened. Scales formed, hair grew, and blood pumped through his veins. Talons and fangs lengthened and sharpened. The dragon opened his golden eyes, and his body dropped a little to the treasure hoard below.

His left front claw buckled under pressure, and Verdilith fell immediately, writhing in pain. He screamed. The dragon clutched the claw to his copper breast. Searing pain shot through the wyrm's arm, and then he succumbed to merciful blackness.

Verdilith fell into a dark sleep, his slumber broken by fitful dreams. His left arm throbbed, and he tried to stretch his claw. The arm moved a little, and the pain subsided momentarily, but then it came back fiercer than before. The green wyrm gave a little whicker of distress. He sank deeper into tortured dreams—dreams fueled by his foreclaw, dreams centering on the flashing great sword and the darkness of death that surrounded it.

A strange, high-pitched whimper of fear escaped the dragon's curled lips, along with a drop of greenish-yellow spittle. The odor of poisonous bile wafted into Verdilith's nostrils and the dragon quieted, comforted by the familiar stench. His dream deepened, and somewhere inside him the pain was joined by hatred for the sword.

Chapter IV

A man on a chestnut horse approached Johauna and her companions as they turned their mounts onto the castle road. Parts of the knight's armor shone in the late afternoon sun, and the rest was covered by a midnight-blue tunic embroidered with three golden suns. Behind him rode two guards, each carrying their spears upright in formal greeting. Jo had wondered if the baroness would send a guard to formally meet Flinn and his comrades upon their "victorious" return to the castle.

Jo clenched her jaw. Only there's no Flinn to return triumphant, she thought. The baroness is greeting a party who has lost its hero—a party who hasn't even avenged that hero's death. Jo's mind slipped back a few days to a conversation she'd held with Karleah and Braddoc. They'd been sitting around the campfire the night after they'd attacked Verdilith. Karleah was adamant about leaving in the morning and heading back to the Castle of the Three Suns.

"Look, I understand that you think you've lost your magic, but—" Jo began again.

"There's no 'think' to it, Jo!" Karleah interjected. Her

voice cracked with strain and anger and, Jo thought, fear. "Something inside that lair has stolen most of my spells! I'm afraid to use any more for fear they'll disappear, too!"

Jo tried to calm the distraught woman, who had begun to pace again. "I understand that, Karleah," the squire said, "but I want to stay here and at least watch the lair! You and Braddoc and Dayin can head back to the castle. Then send me a mage who *can* help me get back inside."

"Bah!" Karleah snorted. "One of those pansy (meaning no disrespect to the flower) mages *might* be able to get you in, but not out!"

Jo stood up and held her hands toward Karleah. This argument had gone on long enough. "What do you *expect* me to do, Karleah? Will you tell me that much, huh?" Jo's voice rose. She took a step forward and slashed the air with one hand. "At Flinn's pyre, I swore I would avenge his death!" Her eyes flashed at the older woman. Karleah had the grace to look momentarily chagrined, but Jo wasn't mollified. "I *must* stay here—"

From his position by the fire, Braddoc spoke up for the first time that night. All the time Jo and Karleah had argued, he'd been idly rummaging through his backpack, looking at his treasures from the dragon's lair. Dayin had stayed by the dwarf's side, obviously seeking Braddoc's stoic protection against the volatile argument between the squire and the wizardess.

"No, Johauna," Braddoc interrupted, "that's not what you *must* do—that's what you *want* to do." The dwarf picked up a stick and stoked the embers. He eyed Jo with his good orb, the firelight glinting off the blind one.

Jo rounded on Braddoc. "Oh, yes? Is that what you think? Come on, Braddoc! You know what Flinn meant to me!"

"Yes. I do," the dwarf said imperturbably. He tossed aside his stick. "I also know you swore an oath to Baroness Arteris Penhaligon. When a knight dies, the squire must immediately report to the castle for reassignment . . . or dismissal. Which oath is more important to you, Johauna, the oath of vengeance or of honor?" Braddoc stood and drew himself to his full height. "I could tell you which was more important to Flinn, but I think we all know. If you aren't going to be a squire any longer, Johauna, then I'm leaving in the morning."

"Leaving!" The word exploded from Jo's lips. She put her hands on her hips and stood before the dwarf.

Braddoc nodded. "You heard me." He shook his handsome russet head, the newly plaited beard gleaming with a golden braid he'd found inside the lair. "Remember: I'm a mercenary at heart. I was one before you ever met me." He gestured at the rest of the booty he'd stolen from Verdilith. "I've got a few baubles I can sell to keep me in comfort the rest of my life, plus an interesting box to spend my time puzzling over."

"But—!" Jo exclaimed, cutting short her words. She changed her tactic. "What about Flinn? I thought he was your *friend.*"

Braddoc didn't bat an eye. "*Was* is right. What about Flinn? He's dead. I can't help him any more. He wouldn't expect me to, either."

Jo leaned backward, her eyes caught by Braddoc's expression. "And what of me? Am I not your friend?" she asked quietly after a long moment.

The dwarf pursed his lips before saying slowly, "Yes, you are my friend, Johauna Menhir. But you have a choice to make here, and that is, which of the two oaths you have sworn will you honor first? If you choose your desire to avenge Flinn's death, I can't help you now. If you return to the castle, I *can* help you. I'd like to take over where Flinn left off on your training."

The last sentence held such a ring of concern and sincerity that Jo had to swallow a sudden lump in her throat. She glanced away at Karleah and Dayin, both of whom were silently watching her, then she turned back to the dwarf. "Can't—" Jo began, then coughed "—can't you go to the castle with Karleah and Dayin and send back help? I can guard the lair. . . ."

Braddoc crossed his arms. "You're forgetting one thing, Johauna," he said quietly. "*You* are the squire, not me. Flinn's dead and Verdilith is still alive. It's *your* job to report that back at the castle." Braddoc turned and began walking away toward his tent. "I won't do your job," he tossed over his shoulder.

Jo watched the dwarf retreat into the darkness. She rubbed her hands together wearily. Just as she saw Braddoc pull back his tent flap, she called out, "All right! All right! I'll . . . go to the castle." She added when she saw Braddoc turn back toward her, "I will do my duty as a squire in the order, but I *will* request assignment to avenge Flinn's death."

"And we'll go with you," Braddoc replied. Karleah and Dayin nodded assent.

Jo rubbed her eyes and pushed aside the memory of that conversation. Tensions had run high between her and her comrades, but they'd lessened the last few days on the road. Now the party had almost reached the Castle of the Three Suns. The knight and his guards were approaching her, and soon she'd have to make some sort of formal report to the baroness. Jo bit her lip but didn't slow her horse, Carsig.

Show no hurry, she thought. Show no grief. Flinn died in glory; to show your pain is to mock his death. Jo's face set in rigid lines, and her teeth clenched together involuntarily. Every step she took back to the castle meant she was that much farther from avenging Flinn's death, and that rankled inside her. But, she thought, I have a duty to perform.

Just as they reached the halfway point of the long, narrow road that wound up to the castle, the knight and his guards met up with Jo's party. Jo pulled Carsig to a stop. Behind her, Karleah, Dayin, and Braddoc halted their mounts as well. Jo heard the dwarf grumble as Fernlover, the pack mule, tried his best to continue on. A tiny smile tugged at Jo's lips. The mule had had enough of wilderness travel and longed for the comfort of a stable. Jo recalled the softness of the bed she had stayed in here at the castle, and she suddenly wanted only to retire to a clean, warm room. She quashed the desire immediately and turned her attention to the knight, a man she didn't know.

"Greetings, Sir Knight," Jo said courteously. "I'm Squire Menhir, and these are my companions."

"Well met, squire," the knight rejoined, looking over the group. If he was perturbed at the absence of Flinn, the knight's face did not betray him. "I'm Sir Sieguld, and I'm here to escort you to the baroness." Sir Sieguld turned his horse around. Jo and the others fell in step behind him, and the guards brought up the rear.

Jo approached the Castle of the Three Suns and wondered if it had changed in the short time she'd been away; so much of her life had. But the familiar white towers were still there, marking the four points of a diamond, one being the main approach to which they were headed.

Three other towers marked the center of the outer walls, which presented a formidable barricade to the world. These seven outer structures stood four stories high.

Jo passed under the main approach and saw again the single tower that rose twice as high as the others from the center of the castle. This structure was the keep, or donjon, as Flinn had called it. Sir Sieguld continued to ride through the slate-lined courtyard leading toward the inner portion of the castle. Peasants hawking their wares gave way before the knight and his guests. Jo was reminded vividly of her first trip to the castle at Flinn's side, but she ignored the pain that threatened to rise.

Some of the peasants stopped and stared at the procession; a few began nudging their fellows. Others pointed fingers, and a low murmur rose in the gathering crowd. Jo silently willed the knight to move faster. Please, she thought, please don't let them recognize me!

Just then, a peasant with a booming voice called out, "'Oy! Ain't that the squire of the Mighty Flinn?" Others took up the cry, and Jo found her horse surrounded, cut off from Sir Sieguld and Karleah behind her. Grimy hands grabbed at Carsig's reins to draw her attention. Jo glanced in desperation at the peasant who had given voice to the people's thoughts. The tall, burly man swung down from his wagon and worked his way through the throng. Carsig started to fidget at the nearness of the people closing in on him, and the gelding reared halfheartedly.

The peasant caught Carsig's rein in a black-gloved hand and quieted the horse. His black hair was unkempt but clean, and his face and bare arm were covered with more black hair. Jo looked down at him in anger but was distracted by his flashing golden eyes. She wondered briefly if she had ever seen a man with such unusual eyes before.

The peasant's voice boomed throughout the courtyard, so that every man and woman could hear. "'Oy, miss! Ye *are* Flinn's squire! Where be the Mighty Flinn?" he asked in mock concern. He held up his gloved hand and turned to the crowd. "Or has Flinn the Mighty fallen *again*?" Some of the crowd bristled at the insult, but a few of them joined the booming peasant's laughter.

Jo jerked Carsig's rein from the man's hand. He tried to regain control of the gelding, but Jo kept the horse prancing. "I'll thank you to leave me and the name of Fain Flinn alone!" she said loudly. The peasant laughed brutally and caught the beleaguered horse. Jo was about to force Carsig to rear, knocking the man away with his hooves, but a commotion just ahead stopped her.

Someone was coming from the donjon. The crowd, protesting mildly at first, soon parted quickly and quietly for the man and his horse. Sir Sieguld stepped his mount aside, too, and at last Jo caught sight of the fully armored knight. With a stern and disciplined silence, the knight pulled his horse to a stop immediately before Jo.

Her attention drawn from the malcontent peasant, Jo held up her hand in greeting, and the knight did the same with his gloved hand. Then Jo caught the flash of a gold pendant hanging about the man's throat. It carried the stamp of a gyrfalcon, a large white raptor that hunted the rocky reaches of the surrounding Wulfholdes. Only then did Jo recognize Sir Lile Graybow, castellan of the Penhaligons. Reaching up, he took off his helmet.

The aging castellan nodded to Jo, unaware that his thinning gray hair had been ruffled by the helmet. His watery blue eyes looked over Jo's comrades, lingered on the supplies tied to Fernlover's back, then circled back to Jo. "Squire Menhir!" the castellan barked gruffly, loud enough so that all the courtyard could hear. "Your report!"

Jo sat straighter on Carsig. Once, and once only, she thought. "Sir Graybow," Jo began formally. Then, to her horror, she felt her eyes fill with tears and spill over. No! Not now! she thought wildly. Not in front of the castellan!

Unexpectedly, Sir Graybow urged his horse forward a step. He took off his metal-and-leather glove and put his gnarled hand over Jo's. She looked into the castellan's eyes and saw only kindness there. She smiled bleakly, wiped her tears away with the back of her hand, and nodded at the castellan, who withdrew his hand. Jo looked away once, took a deep breath, and turned back to Sir Graybow. Her composure had returned, and she nodded again gratefully.

"What happened, Squire Menhir?" Sir Graybow asked more quietly. The crowd of peasants literally leaned closer to hear.

"We . . . we attempted to track the dragon, and at first we failed," Jo said coolly. "One night, Sir Flinn left our camp. He found Verdilith in the same glade where they had fought their first battle, and—" Jo stopped, unable to go on. Something felt lodged in her throat. Silently she implored the castellan.

Sir Graybow said only, "Continue, squire."

Jo drew her breath. She would get no quarter from him. She suddenly realized she respected him for that. Jo nodded and said as calmly as she could, "We . . . found . . . Sir Flinn the next day, barely alive. He . . . died shortly after that, and we paid our last respects according to the old tradition—by burning his body." Jo's voice sank to a whisper. The nearest peasants murmured in awe and quickly relayed the information to those behind them.

"And Verdilith?" the castellan asked, equally calmly,

though Jo had seen a flicker of emotion cross his face at her tale of Flinn's end.

Jo shook her head. "The dragon survived Sir Flinn's attack, Sir Graybow. We . . . tracked the wyrm to his lair, and we confronted him inside, but . . . the dragon escaped. My companions and I are out of provisions and in need of rest." Jo hesitated. "They thought it best to return."

The castellan's face grew stern, and he admonished Jo, "Never be too proud to come back to the castle to report a setback; time for completing a mission will come if you are patient enough. Remember that if you wish to remain a squire in the Order of the Three Suns, Johauna Menhir."

Jo heard only the terrible *if*. Her face blanched, and she reached out to touch the castellan. "Sir Graybow," she murmured, disregarding the peasants who leaned still closer, "what do you mean 'if'? Am I not still a squire—?"

Once more the castellan closed his hand over Jo's, and she saw again the spark of kindness in his pale eyes. "Don't worry, my dear. That's something to be discussed later. First things first. We'll get you settled, and then the baroness will want you to report at council. Follow me." The castellan turned his horse around, signaled for Sir Sieguld to follow after Jo and her companions, then moved his mare into a trot back to the donjon. The peasants parted the way immediately.

As Jo fell into place behind Sir Graybow, a new fear entered her heart, one she'd avoided considering before. Can they really take away my status as squire? she thought miserably. With Flinn dead, I have no knight, that's true. I guess I just assumed I'd be assigned as squire to another knight. That thought seemed suddenly repugnant to Jo. The idea of working closely with someone other than Flinn didn't sit well with her.

Carsig carried Jo smoothly under the gate separating the outer portion of the castle from the inner. She passed low buildings lining the perimeter of the inner wall, then the guards' dormitories, craftsmen's dwellings and shops, stables, and the like. She and the castellan rode on through the gigantic, rose-granite courtyard. It was even larger than the last one and it led the way to the castle proper— the donjon. Sir Graybow slowed his mare to a walk, and Jo did the same with her gelding.

Hawkers and merchants milled about, vying for cus-tomers. Starving peasants begged for food. A shepherdess herded a small flock of sheep across the castellan's path, and Graybow pulled up short, waiting for the last pregnant ewe to pass by. A man proudly displayed the paces of a pair of matched draft horses to a ring of interested buyers. A number of knights and their squires engaged in practice swordplay. They stopped immediately upon seeing the castellan. Several pointed and saluted, then they began gathering their things and hurrying to the large central tower.

The donjon was eight stories high, its windows placed at equidistant intervals. Its walls of white limestone shone as if newly scrubbed. Jo looked south of the donjon at the far tower; it had been Flinn's home many years before and had been the home of his former wife before her recent death. Then, every window of the tower had been fitted with bars of black iron, and behind those bars had flitted birds of all colors and sizes. Jo noted that the bars were being removed; a man perched precariously atop a tall lad-der as he removed yet another. So the tower's been reclaimed from the birds, Jo thought. Yvaughan's passion must not have appealed to Baroness Penhaligon. Or per-haps the baroness wanted no reminders of her mad cousin,

Jo thought, recalling some bits of gossip she had heard the last time she had been at the castle.

Sir Graybow led the way past the donjon and on toward one of the castle's numerous stables. A stable girl ran up and took Carsig. Sir Graybow dismounted and gestured for Jo and the others to do the same. Jo, Dayin, and Braddoc all dismounted with alacrity, but Karleah hesitated.

"A . . . little help, if you please," Karleah whispered gruffly. "I'm feeling . . . a bit fatigued." Her face was ashen, and the veins of her neck stood out, pulsing wildly.

Jo was shaken by the wizardess's weakness, and she saw the same emotion cross Dayin's face as they helped Karleah off her horse. The old mage nearly fell when her shoes touched the stable floor. "Sir Graybow," Jo began, but the castellan had already gestured toward the guards.

"You'll have the same chambers as before, Squire Menhir," Sir Graybow said. "My men will take Mistress Kunzay to her room and call the healers at once."

"I need rest—not healers," the old woman interrupted irascibly. "I don't want any clerics prodding my bones and murmuring incantations and forcing me to drink funny-colored potions made of newt brains and what-have-you."

"Let them help, Karleah, please," Dayin said in his most pleading voice. "Please," he said again. Karleah nodded, relenting. A smile touched Jo's lips; no one could refuse Dayin when he asked for something.

The guards nodded toward the castellan and then left, one carrying the old wizardess. Dayin looked at Jo for permission to follow, and she gestured for him to do so. He flashed a quick, sweet smile at her and then ran after the guards. Braddoc stepped next to Jo's side, carrying his bulging knapsack. The stable girl came back for Jo's horse, and then Jo turned to the castellan.

"Sir Graybow," Jo began tentatively. She flexed her grip on Wyrmblight and then began again, more boldly, "Sir Graybow, if the council is still meeting, I'd prefer to make my formal report now and . . ." Jo hesitated, feeling her request was silly.

"And?" the castellan prompted. He added, "To gain what you want in life, you must learn to ask for it, squire."

Jo took heart at the gentle reminder to stick up for herself. ". . . and—and to find out what's to become of me now that—" Jo hesitated once more "—now that I have no knight to sponsor me."

Sir Graybow nodded. "Perhaps it is best to make your report now, Squire Menhir. The council is still gathered. I had thought to let you rest overnight and give your report in the morning, but perhaps you have the right of it. Come with me." The castellan turned and began striding across the courtyard.

Jo glanced quickly at Braddoc, who nodded his intentions to follow her. Jo caught up to the castellan and matched her steps to his. Sir Graybow frowned and said beneath his breath, "Four paces behind and to the left, squire. I'm a knight, remember. And for goodness's sake, straighten your tunic."

Johauna winced at the irritation she heard in his voice and felt frightened all of a sudden. I've forgotten what little etiquette Flinn taught me! she thought to herself as she quickly shifted her golden tunic into place. Jo took her position behind the castellan and marched onward.

They entered one of the many side doors to the main castle, and Jo was freshly impressed with the Castle of the Three Suns. She'd forgotten how lovely the place was, with its soaring stone pillars, patterned granite floors, and magnificent tapestries. Light shone everywhere from all the magical lanterns.

In silence the castellan led the squire and the dwarf through numerous hallways, up several flights of stairs, and finally to a pair of ornately carved, closed doors. Jo remembered those tall, distinctive doors, for they were the doors that led to the "small" meeting room to which Flinn, Jo, and the council members had retired to discuss Sir Brisbois's punishment after Verdilith had fled the great hall. Behind those doors, too, had been the scene of Baroness Penhaligon's formal declaration of Flinn's reinstatement as a knight in the Order of the Three Suns and Jo's own instatement as a squire.

"This is your last chance, Squire Menhir," Sir Graybow stated, one hand on the gilt, curved doorknob. He eyed Jo quizzically, but with compassion.

Jo shook her head. She returned the castellan's look, then said slowly, "I must make a report, Sir Graybow; I realize that. I would prefer to—to discuss Flinn's death tonight, so that I may seek Verdilith and win vengeance that much quicker."

The old warrior arched one gray eyebrow, and Jo was poignantly reminded of Flinn. Had he picked up the habit from his castellan? "As you wish, Squire Menhir," Sir Graybow said formally, then opened the door.

The castellan, Jo, and Braddoc stepped into the meeting room. As one, the council members stopped speaking and turned to stare at the intruders. Jo held her breath. The sun had begun to set on the surrounding Wulfholdes, and now sunlight streamed through the four arching windows of leaded glass. Strands of golden light fluctuated in the room, covering everything with a gilt patina.

Enchanted, Jo stepped forward. This was the room that had witnessed Flinn's greatest triumph—her greatest triumph, too. Once again, she saw the intricately carved stone ceiling thirty feet above, the pale murals almost obliterated with age, the huge tapestries depicting numerous battles in Penhaligon's history. . . . But, most of all, she stared at the magnificent windows lining one wall, opening out to the setting sun. One by one, the brass lanterns throughout the room were magically lighting in response to the growing darkness.

Fourteen knights and nobles were seated around an elaborately carved, U-shaped table. Sir Graybow moved to stand before the person seated at the center of the table. She was dressed in blue and silver, and, as she stood, a silver coronet shone in her chestnut hair. Baroness Arteris Penhaligon inclined her head toward the castellan and said regally, "Sir Graybow, I see you have returned." The other council members fixed their gaze on Jo and Braddoc.

Sir Graybow bowed and said with respect, "Yes, Your Ladyship. I also bring with me Squire Menhir and Braddoc Briarblood. The squire, you may recall—"

"I am aware of who Squire Menhir is," Baroness Penhaligon interrupted. "Pray, take your seat, Sir Graybow." She gestured to the empty chair at her left, then continued, "Am I to understand, Squire Menhir, that you are here to make your report?" Jo felt the woman's agate-brown eyes bore into her.

Sir Graybow gave Jo a little push before walking toward his seat at the table. Jo hesitated a moment longer, then strode farther into the room. She stood before the U-shaped table, directly across from Baroness Penhaligon. The castellan gave her a little nod of approval. Braddoc sauntered over to a chair standing against a wall, carried it to a spot behind Jo's back, and sat down. Jo was momentarily irritated by the dwarf's cavalier attitude, for etiquette demanded that he not seat himself until instructed to do so, but she quelled the thought. She had more important things to attend to.

Baroness Penhaligon nodded coolly to Jo and then sat down. Jo bowed slightly in return and said, as formally as she could, "Baroness Penhaligon, members of the council, I come bearing tidings of Sir Fain Flinn."

The council members other than the baroness and Sir Graybow murmured to each other, and Jo waited for them to be silent. An older woman spoke up—Madam Francys Astwood—a friend of Lord Maldrake's. She had been covertly hostile to Flinn, and even unrepentant when she learned that Maldrake was Verdilith in human form. "Are we to take it that some tragedy has befallen the good knight?" Madam Astwood asked in mock worry.

Jo gritted her teeth. Remember the lessons in diplomacy Flinn taught you! she scolded herself. Jo forced herself to nod cordially in the woman's direction. "Yes, a great tragedy for Penhaligon," she said. "We have lost the greatest knight the Order of the Three Suns has ever known." Jo stopped, suddenly aware that absolute silence had befallen the room. "Er, at least in my humble opinion, madam," she said, hoping to cover her diplomatic gaffe.

Madam Astwood smiled icily. "There are, of course, those who believe as you do, miss—er, Squire Menhir," the lady said smoothly. "Others, of course, believe differently." The woman raised her pale eyebrows, flecked with gray. Jo felt suddenly insulted. She bristled.

Baroness Penhaligon interrupted before Jo could make her retort. "Pray continue with your report, Squire Menhir. Sir Flinn is a beloved member of our order—" the baroness glared in Madam Astwood's direction "—despite his unwarranted fall from grace. We would know what has become of him."

Jo related her tale, picking up when she, Flinn, and their
companions had left the Castle of the Three Suns only a
few weeks earlier. Jo told the council of their search for
signs of Verdilith's passing in the Wulfholde Hills northeast
of the castle, and how fruitless that search had been. She
told the council, too, of Flinn's departure in the middle of
the night to confront Verdilith single-handedly. He did
this, Jo told them, so that Karleah Kunzay's prophecy of
doom would not come to pass for any but himself.

Standing in that room, bathed by the light of the magical
lanterns, Jo's eyes misted over with tears as she told them of
the final day of Flinn's life. Her storytelling instincts took
over, and Jo's imagination colored her recounting.

"And Fain Flinn struck one last, final blow with his
mighty blade, Wyrmblight," Jo said softly, her words echoing off the walls in the silent hall. "Not even Verdilith, the
great green, could recover from that blow. He turned tail
and fled, but so grievous were his injuries—so badly had
Flinn harmed the malevolent wyrm—that Verdilith could
not fly. Instead, the dragon crashed through the barren
winter undergrowth. He left a trail of blood and broken
branches that the greenest hunter could follow.

"But it was not such a hunter who followed that trail—
it was Fain Flinn, Flinn the Mighty. Grievous, too, were
his wounds, but he did not hesitate in his duty. He was a
knight in the Order of the Three Suns; he had sworn to
kill the dragon who menaced Penhaligon," Jo swallowed
abruptly, disregarding the tear that escaped her eye.

"And so Flinn the Mighty took up Wyrmblight and
stumbled after the dragon, determined to slay the wyrm.
But at the body of his faithful griffon, Ariac, Flinn fell to
one knee. He said good-bye to the crippled bird-lion, and

perhaps he thanked him, too, for trying to save his life. We will never know.

"Flinn followed the dragon's path of blood, his own adding to the trail. He fell, but would not relent," Jo paused and slowly looked at each council member one by one. All were engrossed and saddened at the tale. Even Madam Astwood look chagrined. "He would not relent," Jo repeated, "but instead dragged himself through the trampled snow and mud. He would not fail, he told himself, he would not fail."

Jo's throat constricted, and she looked down at the sword she held in her hands. She looked back at the council and fixed her gaze on the castellan, warming at the empathy she sensed in him. "We found him late that day," she said simply, "and he was still alive, though a lesser man would have surely died." Jo's hands clenched on Wyrmblight. "He seemed to have clung to life until we could reach him, for shortly after I arrived, he died—" Jo choked on the words before she could embarrass either Flinn or herself by saying "in my arms."

The council members remained silent while Jo collected herself. Then Madam Astwood spoke up, her tone laced with irony. "How touching," she said cattily. "It's a shame the man did not defeat the dragon, for he would surely have attained the fourth point of the Quadrivial then. That was always Flinn's goal. What a pity he didn't succeed. But, then, so few knights do really attain all points of the Quadrivial. Such knights are really quite rare." The woman's statement set Jo's teeth on edge, and something close to hatred rose in her breast. She struggled to find a fitting retort.

A hand upon her arm made Jo stop and look down. Braddoc stood beside her, his one good eye fixed on her.

He pursed his lips, and Jo nodded to him. Braddoc took Wyrmblight from Jo's hands and stalked over to Baroness Penhaligon. Sir Graybow, on her left, remained calm, but the knight on her right rose and drew his sword. Braddoc paused momentarily, grunted in the man's direction, then dropped the sword on the table in front of Arteris. Jo came to stand by the dwarf.

"There," Braddoc said and pointed at the blade. "There's all the proof you need that Fain Flinn attained the Quadrivial." The council members gathered near and peered at the silver-white sword.

Bit by bit, the four sigils on the flat of the blade began to glow. The runes depicting Honor, Courage, Faith, and Glory released a warm, white light. Then the four spots of light merged and grew brighter still, forcing Jo and the others to squint to see them.

Glory was attained, whispered the blade to Jo. By the stunned look on Sir Graybow's face, and others' too, Jo realized the sword had spoken to everyone. *The Quadrivial was attained*, Wyrmblight whispered.

Suddenly the glow from the sigils diminished one by one, until only Glory was left alight. Then it, too, faded into the sword. Wyrmblight lay on the table, once more simply a sword of renown.

ía ía ía ía ía

"But, Karleah, I don't understand!" Dayin protested. The old wizardess was heedless, pacing their chambers, pulling open drawers and rifling through them. Dayin raised his voice. "We just got here! Why do we have to leave?"

"I told you, child," Karleah snapped, "it's just getting worse and worse. My powers have diminished even faster since we arrived. I need my safe valley, my books and things if I'm ever going to find out why. I've been jittery ever since we left the dragon's lair, and I just don't feel safe here in the castle. Ah ha!" Karleah pulled out a piece of paper, then a quill and a pot of ink from a drawer. She hurried to the table and sat down, spreading the paper before her.

"What are you doing, Karleah?" Dayin asked nervously. He had little tolerance for this agitation from Karleah. It was the same odd mood that had possessed his father those many years ago—had possessed him in those weeks before he'd abandoned Dayin to the harsh wilderness. Now Karleah, whom he loved and trusted more than anyone, was acting the same.

"I'm writing Jo a note," Karleah began, dipping the quill into the ink. She was poised as if to write, but paused and looked at Dayin. "Does she know how to read, do you suppose? Well, no matter—someone will read it to her, if necessary." The ancient crone scribbled away in a sprawling hand, dipping frequently into the black ink. Dayin huddled near, peering over Karleah's thin shoulder.

Johauna—

I must return to my valley immediately, and I am taking Dayin with me. Do not worry—we are both well. We will work on the boy's training as a mage, and perhaps I can discover a thing or two on my own.

You see, more than merely my teleportation spell failed us at the dragon's lair. My light spell did, too, and my wind funnel. Further, my staff's magic has begun to fade. I know these are not mere coincidence, and I intend to discover what—or who—is draining my magic.

We'll be in touch. Do not worry.

Yours, Karleah Kunzay

"What do you mean, 'don't worry'? What's there to worry about, Karleah? Karleah?" Dayin tugged on the wizardess's arm. His blue eyes were wide with fright. "Are we ever going to see Jo and Braddoc again?"

The old woman turned to the boy and looked at him with something akin to exasperation. Then she smiled reluctantly and drew Dayin into her arms. The boy closed his eyes in relief. All will be well soon, he thought. Karleah will take care of me.

"Always, child," the old woman murmured. Dayin smiled. Karleah had read his mind! It pleased him when she did so, for he knew she did so only with those whom she trusted. Karleah gave him one last squeeze, then said briskly, "Come. It's time we were off."

"Are you sure you're well enough?" Dayin asked anxiously.

The old woman blinked her dark eyes rapidly. "I feel fine enough, aside from my magic," she said, then shrugged her shoulders. "I want to leave now."

"What will we do about food and supplies?" Dayin sensibly asked.

"We'll take one tent and some of the gear; I imagine the equipment's still in the stables, along with the horse that Graybow lent me, and Braddoc's pony for you," Karleah answered, gathering up the few personal belongings they'd brought with them to the chambers. "We'll stop at the kitchen on the way out. I'll get some foodstuffs—have no fear."

"Why should I fear, Karleah?" the boy asked innocently.

Karleah pulled up short and looked at Dayin. She ruffled his shaggy blond hair and said softly, "Because something happened in the dragon's lair, Dayin. Something happened to my powers. It's more than the loss of a few simple spells; it's a loss of much of my inner magic." Karleah cocked her head to one side and added, "I've even lost the magic that lets me change into a wolf."

Dayin shook his head, his eyes widening in fear. He had seen Karleah once or twice in her wolf form, and he had envied her. She'd promised to teach him how to change into an animal when the time came. Could she still teach him now? he wondered.

"I've lost the first magic I ever knew, Dayin," Karleah said, her raspy voice quiet and her eyes wandering about the room. "Either something has stolen my powers, or I'm turning senile. Either way, I don't want to be rendered helpless and stuck here in this stone block. I want to return to my valley. There, I'll know what's what."

ia ia ia ia ia

Johauna's eyes stretched wide, and her face blanched. "I will not give up Wyrmblight, Baroness Penhaligon! I cannot," she said staunchly. Jo heard the hollow ring of fear inside her words. Her hands gripped Wyrmblight all the harder.

Arteris sighed, then fixed Jo with her stony brown gaze. "Young lady—"

"I'm a squire, Your Ladyship," Jo broke in quickly, "until you decree otherwise." She bit her lip, appalled at her brazen interjection. Apologize! she told herself. Apologize immediately and maybe she'll forgive yet another faux pas. No! her other half spoke up stubbornly. No! I will not be bullied this way! She can't take Wyrmblight away from me! I'll give up being a squire before I let her take Flinn's sword from me!

Arteris smiled coldly, her lips forming more of a

grimace than a true smile. Beside her, Sir Graybow abruptly rubbed his cheeks, hiding his mouth and keeping his eyes on the table. Jo felt sudden remorse; the castellan had tried to warn her, but to no avail.

"I'll ignore this *one* intrusion, Squire Menhir," Baroness Penhaligon said graciously enough, though Jo couldn't help hearing the undercurrent of threat running through it, "but *only* because of the bond I know squires feel for their masters. That bond is now broken—" but not forgotten, Johauna thought mulishly "—and you have no use for the sword. Wyrmblight is a treasure that should be displayed for all to see—"

Jo couldn't contain herself. "But—!"

Sir Graybow coughed loudly, effectively cutting off Jo's torrent of words. The glance he cast her was murderous, and that alone quelled the squire. He pulled out his handkerchief and blew his nose noisily, then turned to the baroness with elaborate courtesy. "My sincere apologies, Your Ladyship," he said loudly. "Pray forgive me." Arteris inclined her head.

The castellan shot one more black look at Jo before gesturing toward the sword. "It's a most intriguing prospect before the council, Your Ladyship," Sir Graybow continued smoothly, "the question of what to do with Wyrmblight, the most renowned sword in all of Penhaligon." Jo opened her mouth to speak, and the castellan said quickly, "And what are all our options, do you suppose?"

"I believe," the baroness said without hesitation, "that we have but two options: to put Wyrmblight on display or to leave it in the hands of Sir Flinn's squire." Arteris paused, her agate eyes glittering coldly at Jo. "*If* Sir Flinn's protege can contain her passions, she may tell us why she feels she ought to bear the sword."

Jo made a move to speak, then stopped and glanced at Sir Graybow. She wondered if she had misread Arteris's invitation. But the castellan nodded, a slight smile of encouragement on his lips. Jo turned back to the baroness. "Your L–Ladyship," she stammered, then gripped Wyrmblight tighter. *Have faith,* the blade whispered. "Your Ladyship," Jo began again, her voice growing stronger and more sure, "I feel I should bear the sword for one specific reason, if no other." She paused for effect and swept her eyes over the council members. "Sir Flinn would wish me to wield it. Of that, I am certain." One or two of the council members murmured to each other, then silence fell once more in the room.

Lady Arteris rubbed her fingers together. "Clearly, you cannot bear the sword unless you remain a squire for Penhaligon. However, the knight who chose to sponsor you has, most regrettably, died, Squire Menhir," the baroness said with unusual gentleness. "This puts you in an awkward position. We currently have no knights who are without squires. We could give one knight two squires to train, but in the past we have found that detrimental to the squires' learning." Arteris paused to let that information sink in.

"I am without a squire," Sir Graybow said distinctly. All eyes turned to him.

"By tradition the castellan is usually without a squire, Sir Graybow," Arteris said after a momentary silence. "A castellan has too many duties to properly attend to the training of a squire."

"Save when he is training his replacement," Graybow rejoined.

"But you took on Sir Flinn as your squire, presumably with the intent that he should one day replace you,"

Arteris said equably. "Sir Flinn has since died."

"And has left behind the woman he chose worthy to be *his* squire," Sir Graybow said neutrally. He turned his head toward Jo, and she swore the old man winked at her.

"I . . . see, Sir Graybow," Arteris was at a loss for words. She looked at Jo, then turned back to the castellan. "It must be pointed out that you were considerably younger when you took Sir Flinn as your squire so many years ago. How do you propose to provide training for Squire Menhir?"

"I shall, of course, provide instruction in the virtues of knighthood, in etiquette, in reading and writing, geometry, tactics, and the like. As to the combat training, I intend on enlisting the aid of Braddoc Briarblood," Sir Graybow gestured toward the dwarf. Jo turned to her friend. Although Braddoc's face remained passive, Jo had caught the fleeting look of surprise in his one good eye. "If that is agreeable with friend dwarf, of course." The castellan inclined his head toward Braddoc.

The dwarf cleared his throat, took a step forward, and bowed low toward Sir Graybow, and then the baroness. "I should be honored to assist in any way I can, Sir Graybow. I would consider it a privilege to so repay old debts to my lost comrade." Jo had to repress a smile at the sound of such formal speech from her friend.

Lady Arteris was not so easily swayed. "I know nothing of you, Master Briarblood, save that you have the acquaintance of Sir Flinn and Squire Menhir," she said coolly.

Madam Astwood nodded to the baroness and said, "With your permission, Your Ladyship?" At Arteris's nod, she continued, "I have heard of this dwarf. He has led the life of a mercenary for many years, his sword for hire."

The baroness arched one eyebrow at the dwarf. "Is this

so, Master Briarblood?" she asked coldly.

Braddoc glanced at Jo and then bowed again to the baroness. "Yes, what Madam Astwood says is true—to the extent that she thinks it is true."

The baroness frowned, and several members of the council murmured in confusion. "You speak in riddles, sir?" Arteris asked severely. "Pray explain yourself."

"It is true that I have led the life of a mercenary, Your Ladyship," Braddoc said simply, "but I am no mercenary. I am the nephew of Everast XV, king of Rockhome, my ancestral lands. He bade me learn of your ways, and it was he who suggested I roam your lands as a mercenary that I might judge your mettle."

Several members of the council rose to their feet in alarm. Even Sir Graybow stood, though his face was filled with consternation rather than fear. The baroness held up her hands and motioned for silence. When she received it, she said, "This is most extraordinary, sir. And what, may we ask, is the purpose of such subterfuge?"

"To discover if the Estates of Penhaligon are a land that the Dwarves of Rockhome could do business with," Braddoc said readily. He bowed at the baroness, his movements the graceful and elegant maneuver of a courtier. "And I am pleased to say that, on behalf of King Everast XV, we dwarves would like to open up mutual trade agreements." Braddoc smiled at the baroness, then at Jo.

The squire had always wondered where Braddoc had gotten his finicky manners—they had seemed out of place in a true mercenary. Jo smiled back at her friend. Now she knew.

The baroness's expression turned civil, and her brows arched faintly. "I . . . see no objection then," she said slowly, looking over her council members. When none was forthcoming from them, she turned back to Braddoc and smiled. "I shall look forward to arranging trade discussions with you and your uncle, Master Briarblood."

Braddoc bowed low, his beard sweeping the floor, and returned silently to his chair. Jo looked expectantly at the baroness, and she gestured at the castellan.

Sir Graybow turned to Jo and said, "Squire Menhir, you are, of course, at liberty here. You may choose to leave the Order of the Three Suns now, if you like."

Jo's hands tightened on Wyrmblight, and the thought of Verdilith rose in her mind. Her lips grew grim. She faced Arteris squarely. "What of the status of Wyrmblight—" Jo paused slightly, then added "—Your Ladyship?"

Baroness Penhaligon sighed heavily, then said, "We will honor Sir Flinn's wish that you receive Wyrmblight, though we have none but your own word that that was his wish. Wyrmblight is yours to keep, Squire Menhir, but only if you remain a squire of this castle."

Jo nodded at the castellan, then turned to the baroness and said, "Your Ladyship, I would be proud and pleased to remain a squire in the Order of the Three Suns under the care and training of Sir Graybow."

Jo bowed low, holding Wyrmblight to her side. The silver-white blade felt warm to the touch.

Chapter V

ohauna Menhir swung Wyrmblight around her shoulders in a wide, arcing stroke. The edge of the blade was met by Braddoc's wooden practice shield, and Wyrmblight clove into the oak. The leather sheath around the blade gave way; Wyrmblight's edge was so keen that it cut through one blade guard after another. Jo wrenched the blade loose and stepped back a pace, holding Wyrmblight before her. She tore away the leather streamers, keeping her eyes fixed on the dwarf. Braddoc shifted his battle-axe and raised his shield a bit higher. The dwarf slowly began circling the young squire.

Jo smiled impishly at her friend. During this last month at the castle, she'd come to enjoy these practice sessions. Braddoc's constant camaraderie had kept the pain of Karleah's and Dayin's departure to a minimum. Indeed, between Braddoc's sparring and the castellan's lessons, Jo had had little time to think of anything else. And a recent note from the old wizardess had assured Jo that all was well.

The young squire and Braddoc were in one of the castle's many smaller courtyards. Three other sparring

partners practiced their maneuvers, two of the squires
using swords, and one young half-elf wielding a polearm.
At the far wall, an archery range had been set up. Two
squires were there, shooting arrow after arrow. Before Jo
and Braddoc had fallen to, Jo had watched the archers.
One was quite good; the other was far less skilled than Jo,
despite her inexperience. Flinn had started teaching her
archery only the past winter. She was hoping to practice a
bit today after her bout with Braddoc.

A sudden gust of spring wind blew a trailing lock of
hair into Jo's mouth, and she spat it out immediately. The
momentary distraction allowed Braddoc an advantage,
however, and the dwarf leaped forward. His battle-axe—
the edges dulled by a boiled leather sheath—sliced through
the air in a stroke parallel to the granite courtyard. Jo,
unable to bring the unwieldy Wyrmblight up fast enough
to block the blow, leaped backward. The axe whistled by,
just touching the leather practice jerkin Jo wore.

Braddoc grunted. "It's a good thing they make fighters
put guards on their weapons."

Jo responded by swinging Wyrmblight in an upstroke.
The blade sank into Braddoc's shield again. "Yes," Jo said
as she worked the blade free. "I wish I could get a guard to
stay on Wyrmblight. I could hurt you, Braddoc."

The dwarf chortled as he and Jo stepped apart and
began circling again. "Don't worry about it, Johauna. If
you can nick me with Wyrmblight, then I deserve it!
Yow!" Braddoc jumped in pain as Wyrmblight just glanced
across his shoulder. The dwarf touched the wound and
then pulled his hand away. It was red. Braddoc grimaced
and said wryly, "Or maybe not!"

Jo lowered Wyrmblight and stepped forward in concern. "Did I hurt you, Braddoc?"

The next thing Jo knew, the pommel of Braddoc's battle-axe was in her stomach. She doubled over, but didn't fall to the ground. "Why, you—" she said through teeth clenched in pain and anger.

Braddoc raised one mocking finger. "Uh, uh, uh!" he admonished. "Flinn taught you the rudiments of fighting—fighting honorably, that is. I intend to teach you how to *really* fight!" Braddoc grinned suddenly. "I may be the nephew of King Everast, but even I know how to fight dirty. You, Johauna Menhir, are bound to meet people who don't fight fair—and I want you to be prepared!"

Jo's eyes narrowed as she slowly closed the gap between her and Braddoc. "If that's the case, my *friend*," Jo said smoothly, "then try this!" Jo swung Wyrmblight over her head and leaped forward, bringing the shining great sword down in a crashing blow. The metal tip rang off the granite stones, not the wooden shield Jo had expected. To her side laughed the dwarf, suddenly, maddeningly, nimble.

"You'll have to do better than that, Jo," Braddoc said mockingly. "That little love bite earlier was a lucky stroke—took no skill at all."

Angered, Jo swung the heavy sword in a horizontal arc, twisting it so the flat of the blade would hit Braddoc in the small of the back. She hoped to knock the wind—and the pride—out of the little man. She didn't want to hurt him. Not much. But Jo's stroke went awry. Braddoc simply crouched, and there was no way Jo could halt the sword's stroke. The weight of the swinging blade dragged her off balance, making her twirl around without control.

Thump! The flat of Braddoc's battle-axe smashed into Jo's unprotected thigh. Already off balance, she spun from the impact and sprawled heavily to the granite stones. Wyrmblight fell beside her, the harsh clang of metal ringing throughout the small courtyard. Two of the sparring couples and both archers turned to stare at her. Jo felt her face flush crimson, and her panting turned even more ragged. She'd met a few of her colleagues, but she had never been the center of their attention before.

She didn't like it.

Jo shook her head, refusing to let her embarrassment ruin today's sparring lesson. She looked up at the dwarf, who stood calmly before her. Braddoc wasn't even winded! Jo held out her hands, palms upward. "Braddoc," she asked, "what am I doing wrong? I was so much better and quicker against Flinn! At least I *think* I was!"

Braddoc rubbed a balled fist against his milky eye for a moment, then sat beside Jo. He stared at Jo with his good eye and released a long, grim, I-didn't-want-to-be-the-one-to-break-this-to-you sigh.

"What? What is it?" she asked, her voice rising in pitch. She returned the dwarf's gaze.

Braddoc's look grew thoughtful. Carefully he tucked a few stray strands of Jo's reddish hair, so much like his own, back into her leather practice helmet. Then he said slowly but clearly, "Wyrmblight's too big for you, Johauna."

Jo jumped to her feet. "Too big? Too big?" she shrieked. Once again a practicing pair stopped to look at her. Jo lowered her voice. "What do you mean, Braddoc?" she insisted. Her eyes were narrow with annoyance.

The dwarf shrugged but refused to stand. Jo knelt on one knee beside him and peered intently into his face.

"What do I mean? Just what I said, Johauna," Braddoc said simply. "Wyrmblight's too big for you. The sword's too long and too heavy. You haven't got the—"

"It's a man's sword, that's what you're saying, isn't it?" Jo said bitterly. She couldn't deny the truth, however. Sparring with Braddoc the last few weeks had shown her just how poorly she wielded Wyrmblight. Her arm, shoulder, and back muscles ached every day after only a few swings. Her strength seemed to be growing, however, and that had given her hope.

Unexpectedly, Braddoc put his hand on Jo's knee. "Look. If it makes you feel any better, I couldn't wield Wyrmblight either," he said. He gave the girl's knee a squeeze and then drew his hand away.

Jo frowned and said nothing for several moments. Finally she asked quietly, "Are you saying I should give up Wyrmblight? Perhaps give the sword to Baroness Penhaligon, like she wanted me to?"

Braddoc shook his head adamantly. "No, I'm not saying that at all," he said, his good eye fixed on her. "Flinn would want *you* to have Wyrmblight—that much nobody will argue about."

"Nobody?" Jo asked suddenly. "What about Madam Astwood? What about Arteris? Maybe Flinn would want Wyrmblight put on display for all the people to see. Surely he'd prefer that to having me smash it against the ground all day." Tiny lines of worry crossed her face.

The dwarf smiled at the squire and patted her hand. "Yes, Flinn would have been pleased about having it on display—" Braddoc paused for effect "—but he would still prefer *you* to have it. You reminded him of all that was good and right and noble, Johauna. You alone are worthy of his blade."

Jo hung her head, refusing to meet Braddoc's eye. "I—I don't know about that," she whispered, "but that's not the point here." Jo looked at Braddoc. "The point is, Wyrmblight *is* too big for me—"

"That doesn't mean you can't learn how to use a *form* of

Wyrmblight," Braddoc interjected.

Jo sat down, tucking one leg under her chin. One of the other sparring couples—a sword-wielding human and a half-elf with a polearm—danced nearby, casually avoiding the sitting pair. Jo looked up at them for a moment, then stared at Braddoc. "What do you mean, a *form* of Wyrmblight?" she asked.

The dwarf shrugged. He gave Jo an appraising stare, from the top of her practice helmet down her lanky form to her burgundy boots. "You've a tall enough build. With some work, you could learn to use Wyrmblight as the blade is now." He held up a cautionary finger as Jo's face brightened. "Mind you, that would require a lot of work—far more training than I'll ever be able to give you."

"Then what do you suggest?" Jo asked, crestfallen.

Braddoc turned away and rubbed his hands, intent on peeling back the loose skin of a callus. "You, er, could consider having Wyrmblight reforged into a smaller—"

"Reforged!" Jo shrieked a second time. This time she ignored the stares her shout garnered. She grabbed Braddoc's arm and shook him. "Reforge *Wyrmblight*? Are you crazy?" she shouted.

The dwarf stared at her, his face suddenly, utterly serious. Jo was taken aback by his expression, and her hold on his arm lightened. "No, I'm completely sane, Johauna Menhir," Braddoc said slowly. "If you search your memory of the calling you had at the spring, I think you'll agree that that's the only true answer."

"The spring . . ." Jo murmured, her mind reliving the day she had met Braddoc. She remembered the evening she'd spent in the dwarf's sweat lodge, remembered the wondrously chill water, the swirling vapors, the vision. In it, Jo stood before a forge, waiting for a smith to pull something from the fire. Her stance was strangely expectant, and Jo wondered now if what she so eagerly awaited *was* the reforging of Wyrmblight, as Braddoc suggested. In the vision, Braddoc stood beside her, and Flinn was nowhere in sight. Jo narrowed her eyes and looked now at Braddoc.

"I can't believe that's what the vision means," she said simply, then shook her head. "I can't. Reforging Wyrmblight would be sacrilege. I will not dishonor Flinn's memory so." Or his spirit, Jo added to herself. She shook her head again. "I will not do it."

Braddoc returned her gaze, then shrugged. "What will you do with Wyrmblight?" he asked steadily.

"Learn how to use it, of course," Jo answered. She rose to her feet and pointed at their belongings on a nearby bench. "In the meantime, I have the sword Flinn gave me in Bywater, and I have his bow. Practicing with both will hold me in good stead until I develop the strength and skill to properly wield Wyrmblight." Johauna extended her hand to the dwarf and helped him rise.

Braddoc grunted, then said, "You are persistent, I'll grant you that."

Jo grinned, her first genuine smile since Flinn's death. "I am *nothing* if not persistent!" When Braddoc broke into a laugh, Jo did, too, though hers was hesitant and short-lived. A bell sounded nearby, and she frowned and picked up Wyrmblight. "It's time for my etiquette lesson," Jo said, her voice edged with irritation. She handed Braddoc his shield as he picked up the battle-axe lying at his feet.

"Just be thankful Sir Graybow got you out of taking those classes with Madam Astwood," Braddoc replied sternly. "From what I've gathered, Johauna Menhir, you've been given a lot of leeway in your training here at the castle. Don't be so quick to mope—someone'll interpret it as ingratitude." Braddoc began unlacing the axe's protective guard.

"Oh, I *am* grateful, Braddoc," Jo said earnestly as they began crossing the courtyard. The other squires were doing the same; Jo noted thankfully that none seemed to be listening to their conversation. "It's just that I'm not understanding all the little intricacies! And, Braddoc, there are so *many*!" Jo sighed heavily. She stopped at a bench where she had left her belongings, picked them up, and continued onward.

"Give it time," Braddoc soothed. "You'll learn. From what I've seen of Sir Graybow in the council meetings, he's a master of etiquette. You couldn't learn from any better."

"I know, I know!" Jo despaired. "It's just that I don't understand *why* there should be a difference between addressing an empress and a queen! But I've got to learn, Braddoc, I've just got to! I want so much to be a knight like Flinn—and he was so good at etiquette, too, even after all those years away from court." Jo's voice rose in vexation. Her long legs had lapsed into a brisk pace, and she had to slow down when she realized Braddoc was trotting to keep up.

"Ask Sir Graybow," Braddoc answered lightly. "He'll be able to explain it to you in a way you can understand."

Jo stopped suddenly and looked down at her friend. Her eyes narrowed and she bit her lip. "It's just that—it's just that I feel so . . . so at a disadvantage around the other squires, Braddoc."

The dwarf's eyebrow rose. "Why?" he asked in astonishment.

Jo shrugged and looked away. "I figured it out the other day, Braddoc. Do you know, I'm the only orphan here? I'm the only one without any formal schooling, without any family lineage. Why, I don't even remember my parents' names!"

Braddoc sighed heavily and looked down at his polished boots. He rubbed the tip of one with the other, then looked back at Jo and shook his head. "I don't know what to tell you, Johauna," he said slowly, "except that I'm proud of you. You're here on your own merit—that and a little luck and persistence."

The dwarf pointed at the other squires gathering by the courtyard's entrance. "Coming from royalty myself, I understand what it's like to have lineage and money, like those folks have. But lineage and money don't make me respect them. *You* I do respect—and so did Flinn and so does Sir Graybow. Just keep that in mind the next time these kinds of thoughts get you down." He tapped Jo's arm with his battle-axe. "Now, let's get you inside for that etiquette lesson."

"You're right, my friend," Jo responded positively, her eyes shining down at the dwarf. They continued to walk toward the archway. In some ways I have it much easier than the other squires, Jo thought suddenly, and I shouldn't complain. I'd hate to learn etiquette from Madam Astwood; she and I would have come to blows in the first lesson. Besides, none of the other squires has the opportunity to study with Sir Graybow, and he's the most respected knight here in the castle. Jo smiled shyly at the thought of her new mentor, then noticed that the eyes of one of the other squires followed her: Colyn Madcomb, the young man who couldn't fire a bow. He was holding one of the doors to the western tower open for Jo and Braddoc, and his smile at Jo was merry and interested. Jo turned her head aside and swiftly entered the tower. She didn't wait for Braddoc.

"Wait up, Johauna!" Braddoc scrambled after her, his short legs trying to keep pace with Jo's long ones.

Jo told herself to relax and slowed her pace. They entered one of many side stairwells in the western tower and slowly began to climb. A few weeks back, a large delegation from King Everast XV and a contingency from Duke Stefan Karameikos had forced Jo and Braddoc out of their guest chambers in the central tower. Sir Graybow had kindly invited both Jo and Braddoc to share his spacious quarters rather than bunk down in the soldiers' building, and the squire and the dwarf had readily accepted.

Although the political envoys had left the castle, Sir Graybow extended his invitation, stating that he enjoyed their company. The castellan had a floor of his very own in the western tower: a bedroom for each person plus a spare for guests and a wide open area connecting all the rooms. There was even a kitchen, and Sir Graybow had his own cook and scullery maid. Jo had never lived in such luxury before, and she still wasn't accustomed to the idea of having someone do the drudge work for her. She frequently dismissed the cook and the drudge, particularly when Sir Graybow was away.

"Too bad Dayin and that witch left us. The old crone would have loved climbing all these steps as much as I do," Braddoc said, slightly out of breath as they entered the fourth level of steps. The stairs were designed for human legs, and Braddoc detested climbing them. They wound their way up the middle of each tower and were tightly formed. He had to constantly lean into the next turn even as he was taking the next step.

Jo smiled down at her friend. "You know, Braddoc," she said mischievously, "that's only the third or fourth time you've mentioned that this week. I think you miss Karleah as much as I do."

"Humph!" the dwarf snorted, but said no more.

Jo and Braddoc reached the castellan's floor and entered through the only door. A sparsely furnished living area surrounded the circular stairwell. Only two rugs dotted the floor; woven of red and black, they helped counter the room's austerity. The furniture was utilitarian, though comfortably upholstered. A few fine tapestries graced the rough white walls. Jo never tired of gazing at them and asking the castellan for the stories woven there. The bedrooms and kitchen branched off the living area. Candles in sconces lit the chambers at night, their delicate golden glow further endearing the chambers to Jo; she found the magical lantern light in the rest of the castle too harsh for her eyes.

Jo hung her short sword and the bow on the pegs in the wall next to the stairwell, but kept Wyrmblight beside her as she always did. Sir Graybow's fine silver long sword hung in its black-and-gold sheath in its usual spot, and she knew the castellan was already here.

The door to Sir Graybow's room opened, and the aging castellan entered the living area. The man's face, grim and shadowed, broke into a grimace at the sight of Jo and Braddoc. "I'm glad you're both here. I have some news for you."

Jo and Braddoc drew closer, the squire holding on to her sword. The dwarf set his gear on the green marble floor near his bedroom door. "What is it, Sir Graybow?" Jo asked. Braddoc merely grunted.

The castellan kept his eyes on Jo. "It's about the dragon—Verdilith," he said heavily.

Jo's heart sank. *He's dead!* she thought. *And I—I mean* Wyrmblight—*didn't strike the killing blow!*

"What happened?" Braddoc asked. "Did your knights find the lair with the directions I gave them?"

"Directions?" Jo turned on Braddoc. "You gave directions to Verdilith's lair? Why?" She turned back to the castellan. "Tell me what's going on here! Is Verdilith dead? Did you send out a party after the dragon without telling *me?*" Her fingers clenched on Wyrmblight. "I've sworn an oath to avenge Flinn's death, and—"

"And you're not skilled enough to complete that oath without the loss of someone's life—" Sir Graybow interjected "—most likely yours." He took a step closer to Jo, who fought the urge to back away. "Jo, I asked Braddoc for directions to the dragon's lair. He gave them to me, and I swore him to secrecy."

"Why?" Jo whispered, though she knew the answer.

"Because you would have gone after them," the castellan said coolly, "and you simply aren't *ready.*" He sighed. "I sent five knights and two mages to corner and slay the dragon. That's my job. I couldn't let Verdilith heal and plot while we waited for you to be ready for your vengeance."

"Flinn—" Jo began.

"Fain Flinn would have been the first to have agreed with me," Sir Graybow reminded her. "And you know that." The castellan gestured with his hands. "Jo, others here—*knights,* not squires, mind you—are as eager to slay the wyrm as you. With eager hands and a wounded dragon, I had to proceed."

Jo glanced at Braddoc, who pursed his lips and shrugged. The squire turned back to the older knight. "What—what happened with the party you sent?" she asked at last, try-ing to instill her voice with a knightly reserve.

"The knights found the lair, and the mages got them inside," Sir Graybow replied. He turned away and began pacing. "Verdilith was there, all right. He slew one knight and then escaped—" Sir Graybow paused to draw a tight breath "—apparently with the aid of a wizard."

Jo and Braddoc looked at each other, then said simulta-neously, "Teryl Auroch!"

"Exactly," the castellan replied. "My people recognized him immediately." The knight resumed pacing. "They were obviously in the process of relocating Verdilith, for virtually all of the treasure had been removed. I doubt the wyrm will ever return to that cavern."

Jo felt a surge of wicked joy fill her and was only slightly chagrined by it. Yes, she thought, yes! I can still be the one to avenge Flinn's death! Jo turned away from the oth-ers, embarrassed that she hadn't shown—couldn't show—the proper sorrow for the knight who had been slain, or suitable consternation over the dragon's escape.

Braddoc spoke to the castellan. "If it's all right with you, Sir Graybow, I'll be leaving shortly."

The castellan nodded as Jo turned nervously back to the dwarf. "You're leaving?" she asked Braddoc. "You're not leaving . . . because of me, are you?" Sir Graybow dis-creetly withdrew to the trestle table at the side of the liv-ing area and began arranging the books there.

The dwarf brought his hands together. He said to Jo, "I'm leaving for a few days—nothing special. No, I'm not leaving because of you, or because of what you've just found out, or because you're happy that Verdilith's still out there for you to hunt down." He paused, shaking his head in slow warning. "I'm going to check on my home, gather a few things, and then return." He smiled when he saw Jo's blushing, crestfallen face. "Don't worry, Johauna. I'll be back in time for the initiation ceremony. Have no fear."

Jo took a step toward the dwarf. "Why don't I come with you, Braddoc?" she asked and then gestured at the castellan. "I'm sure Sir Graybow wouldn't—"

"I'm afraid you're wrong there, Jo," Sir Graybow interrupted. Jo turned to the castellan, who pulled out a chair for her and motioned her toward it. The squire hesitated, then quietly took the proffered seat. "Thank you," Sir Graybow said quietly, touching the table before her. "You have much left to learn during this last week before your initiation. There is no time to spare."

Jo watched Braddoc retire to his room and heard him begin to pack a few belongings. She looked up at the kindly face of her mentor, and her brows knitted in perplexity. "But . . . Braddoc didn't mention this trip to me until now," she began.

"At my request," responded Sir Graybow. He took a step toward the other end of the table. During their lessons he preferred to stand, and Jo had grown accustomed to the arrangement. "We didn't want to distract you from your lessons, either with the sword or the quill."

"But he's my friend—" Jo said, then gave voice to what really troubled her. "He's my friend, and I'll miss him—"

The castellan nodded, his pale eyes filled with understanding. "I know, Jo, I know. You miss Karleah and Dayin, and now Braddoc's leaving you, too. But he'll be gone for only a little while." The old knight hesitated, then Jo saw his eyes crinkle into what sometimes passed for a smile. He said firmly, "I'm your friend, too, Johauna. Don't forget that." He gestured toward the papers covering the table. "Come. It's time to begin your lesson."

Jo leaned Wyrmblight against the nearby wall and pulled her chair closer to the table. Sir Graybow had never questioned her desire to have the sword constantly near her. If he had, Jo's only response would have been that she found the presence of the blade comforting. She lightly touched the four sigils, wishing Flinn would talk to her again through the blade. No matter how hard she pleaded with the Immortals and the sword itself, Jo had never again seen Flinn as she had in her wounded delirium.

Have faith, the blade whispered back.

Jo's fingers lingered on the third sigil, and for the first time she wondered why the sword never admonished her about the other points of the Quadrivial. Then the thought came to her: *Without faith you cannot attain the others.* Sir Graybow cleared his throat, and Jo turned to him, startled. The words had been so faint that she wondered if it had been her own mind or the sword speaking.

The squire looked at the castellan and said lightly, "I'm ready, Sir Graybow. What intricacy of courtly manner am I to learn today?" She smiled at the castellan to soften the teasing in her words. Her respect for the aging knight had grown with each new thing he taught her, and she wanted to convince him she was a fast and serious learner. Sir Graybow frowned as if lost in thought, then opened his mouth to speak.

Braddoc came out of his room then, a knapsack and a bedroll over his shoulder, as well as an iron box about a foot square. Jo recognized the unusual box Braddoc had taken from the dragon's lair, and she asked, "Have you had any luck yet getting that catch to open?"

The dwarf looked up distractedly, apparently surprised that anyone else had noticed his growing obsession with opening the box. His eye lingered for long moments on Jo before he shook his head and said, "No, none. I mentioned it to a mage named Keller, and he's offered to have a look at it for me while I'm gone. Damnedest construction I've ever seen." Braddoc shook his head again and glanced over his shoulder at the peculiar box. "Marvelous though, simply marvelous." His eye, seemingly a bit watery now, turned toward the castellan and his student. "Well, I'll take my leave now, Sir Graybow," the dwarf said formally. He gave a slight bow to the castellan, then turned to Jo. "Take care, Johauna. I'll be back soon."

Impulsively, Jo stood and hugged her friend, who was too weighted down with gear to return the gesture. Tears stung her eyes, but she blinked them away immediately. Braddoc would never appreciate my crying, she thought. She returned to her seat at the table and looked at the dwarf. "Please hurry, Braddoc," she said simply.

A strange look came over Braddoc's face, but Jo couldn't fathom it. "You say the strangest things sometimes, Johauna Menhir," Braddoc said. He shook his head, gathered the rest of his things, and quit the room without a backward glance.

Jo turned back to the castellan. She looked expectantly at him and asked, "You were about to say something, Sir Graybow?"

The older man looked quizzically at Jo, then suddenly shook his head. "No, nothing—just an old memory," he said lightly. He picked up one of the books on the table and began leafing through it. "Let's begin the lesson today with the ceremony of the joust. . . ."

Curiosity got the better of Jo, and she asked hesitantly, "What . . . memory was that, Sir Graybow?" She had never asked the castellan a personal question before, and she wondered now if he would take affront at her prying.

The book snapped closed, and Sir Graybow abruptly looked at Jo. His watery blue eyes did not blink, and his face remained carefully blank. Jo could only stare back at her mentor and think how stupid she had been to commit such a foolish mistake. The castellan looked away as he rested the book on the trestle table.

"I . . . was thinking how much you reminded me of . . . my oldest niece," Sir Graybow said, his voice distant and quiet. He turned his back to Jo and gazed out the window.

"Your . . . niece?" Jo asked neutrally. "I didn't know you had a niece."

The castellan slid the book back and forth across the table's cherry surface. His brows drew together, and he said in an even more remote voice, "I had two, actually."

A tiny silence followed, broken only when Jo finally asked softly, "Had—?"

The castellan nodded, his brows still knitted and his attention still on the book beneath his hand. "Yes, had," he said in a flat voice, made emotional by its directness. "They . . . died . . . many years ago."

Conventional manners dictated Jo murmur some platitude, but she found herself gripped by the desire to know more about Sir Graybow's sorrow. The words, "How . . . did they die?" slipped out before she could catch them.

The castellan continued to methodically rub the book across the table, though Jo saw now that he was beginning to fray the book's edges against the corner of the table. She didn't dare point that out to him. His knuckles on the book were turning white beneath the aged skin.

"Elowyn was . . . fourteen and Fritha . . . twelve," Sir Graybow said. His gruff voice was so gravelly that Jo barely understood him. His unblinking eyes remained locked on the book he held. Jo leaned closer to hear his words, for the man's voice had become a whisper. "Their parents died of plague. Somehow they were spared and came to live with me. I was their only kin.

"It was early winter, and the old baron was holding a great hunt," Sir Graybow continued slowly. Jo assumed he meant Baron Arturus Penhaligon, Arteris's father and the man to whom Flinn had been so devoted. She strained to hear Sir Graybow's next words. "The girls were marvelous archers, both of them, and they pleaded with me to let them join the hunt.

"I couldn't say no to them, and the baron couldn't either." For the first time the castellan lifted his hand from the book and looked about the room. Jo had the impression he was looking back into a distant time, when the castle had a very different lord. "They joined us on the hunt, and we spotted a giant boar almost immediately. It fled south of here, into the Moor, where apparently it made its lair."

Jo drew her breath. She'd heard tales of how dangerous wild boars were, particularly if injured or cornered.

The castellan continued, "They were young, and they'd never been on a hunt before. They spotted the boar and immediately raced after it. We lost sight of them. Then the boar circled back and caught me and the rest of the party. Elowyn's and Fritha's arrows had bloodied it, but not seriously injured it. It was mad, furious for blood, and it turned on us. Three of my men died before we downed the beast." Sir Graybow stopped speaking. Jo saw his extra chin quiver as he swallowed several times.

When a respectful silence had passed and the castellan still didn't say anything, Jo said tentatively, as gently as she could, "What . . . happened to . . . Elowyn and Fritha?"

The castellan took a deep breath, and his eyes closed

and sank into the folds of his face. He touched his forehead and then nervously brushed back his thinning hair. His hand shook.

"We followed their trail as best we could, though it grew dark fast that time of year," he said huskily. "To make matters worse, the girls were hopelessly lost. They headed deeper into the swamp. Soon we were lost, too; no one knows the Moor well. But at least we had camped in the wilderness before and knew what to do. Then the rain began to fall.

"Some called it quits for the night and set up camp, but a few stout fellows stayed with me—Flinn was one such. One by one, though, they had to turn back; the last one made Flinn return with him, telling him the baron needed him. I couldn't fault them for leaving. Elowyn and Fritha were my nieces, not theirs."

Jo wasn't surprised to hear Flinn's part in the tale, and she knew he would have been torn by Graybow's obvious need. Jo pictured Flinn standing before the castellan, winter rain freezing them. He would want to believe there was still hope for the two young girls lost in the great marsh in winter, but would know there couldn't be. And he would also know that his allegiance lay first with the baron. In the end, he had no choice.

"I drove my horse onward. My lantern blew out a dozen times before my tinder grew too wet to light it. I didn't need it anyway—the wind blew so much debris and rain that I couldn't see even with light. But I'd hoped it would attract the girls, and I missed it for that reason." Graybow's voice had become a hushed, ghostly whisper, and his breath curled in gray wisps from his lips.

"I stayed to the high ground, praying my nieces would do the same. But the weather grew colder and nastier, the wind more chill and biting. The rain turned to sleet, then to snow. I pushed my horse to cross channels of water, forcing him to carry me on to the next patch of icy ground." The castellan's voice had grown gruff, and Jo could almost hear the frigid waters sluicing past the stallion's legs.

"I kept going. When my horse finally collapsed, I left him wallowing in a frozen morass of swampland. I stumbled, dazed, away, not even thinking to end his misery." The castellan stopped and swallowed, then continued, "I began to walk through that swamp. The water came up to my waist in most parts, and over my head in others. The winds howled, and the snow whirled about me so fiercely I knew I was only walking in circles; I had no sense of direction.

"How I kept going, I don't know. I only knew I couldn't stop until I found my girls. I called. I walked and I called all through that night and on into the next morning. I called my nieces' names until my throat was raw and my spittle red." The castellan picked up the book and stroked the frayed edges. It was a long minute before he continued.

"I stumbled across their bodies late the next morning by accident. They were in the water, frozen; the water was no more than two feet deep. Ice covered the surface of their little pond—and their little faces."

The castellan dropped the book abruptly. He looked at Jo, his eyes suddenly naked with emotion. "There'll be no etiquette lesson today," he said gruffly. With long, swift strides he made for the stairwell and hurried out the door.

Chapter VI

ir Lile Graybow smiled his approval as Jo crossed the floor between them. She grinned back, then looked down at herself. She had polished her dark maroon boots until they shone, the silver clasps glistening against the heavy leather. Her new breeches, provided by the baroness for tonight's ceremony, were midnight blue and made of a light, summery cloth.

Jo picked at the nape and said, "These aren't likely to last long," she said, somewhat scornfully.

The castellan laughed, and Jo shyly smiled at him. "Jo," the man said, "these are pants to wear only on special occasions—perhaps even only this once."

Jo frowned. "To wear only once?" she asked, perplexed. "Isn't that awfully extravagant? Can the baroness afford breeches for everyone for every occasion?" she asked anxiously.

The castellan rubbed his heavy jowls. "What is the matter with you, my dear?" he asked kindly, though he tried to mask that by making his voice even more gruff. His pale blue eyes almost disappeared in the folds of his face.

Then realization touched his face. "Ah," he said quietly. "Were you very poor?"

Jo blinked once or twice rapidly. Sir Graybow had a most disconcerting habit of asking astute questions. She walked toward one of the tower's windows. She could see servants scurrying about below in preparation for the night's festivities. She turned to face the castellan. "Yes," she said simply, "I was very poor."

"Tell me about your parents," Sir Graybow suggested. He sat down on one of the nearby settees. Jo leaned against the rough stuccoed wall and looked at the castellan, while Sir Graybow continued. "Flinn told me about them—how they never showed up at the port in Specularum as planned," Graybow said gently. "What a terrible loss for a little girl."

As always, Sir Graybow's sensitivity undid her. Jo had never known anyone who was so habitually kind. Even Flinn had never been actually *kind* to her. Jo looked down at her hands, resting on her lap. Beneath her hands shone the golden yellow tunic of a squire. Midnight-blue threads created a swirling floral embroidery around the center of the tunic, and an intricate lacework about the tunic's edges. Jo was proud to wear that tunic tonight, to be recognized before all the people of Penhaligon as worthy to wear it. She picked off a stray thread and then looked at Sir Graybow, who was sitting nearby and waiting patiently. Jo shrugged.

"Did you know I have a brother?" Jo asked quietly. "At least I think I have a brother. I remember my mother holding a crying baby and hugging him so fiercely he cried all the harder."

"When was this?" Graybow asked gently. His face softened with concern.

"It was the day they put me on the ship," Jo said slowly, her eyes glazing over. "Mother kissed me good-bye, and all the while the baby screamed. She kept fussing with him, and so I turned to my father." Jo's thoughts retreated back in time, and she saw her six-year-old self once more on a wharf.

"Why do I have to go ahead of you and Mama, Papa?" Jo asked her father.

A man with flaming red hair, a full moustache, and merry eyes knelt beside her. He wore a leather apron over his grimy clothes, and his bare arms smelled of burned hair and molten metal. Her father worked at a foundry, and Jo had grown accustomed to the way he smelled. In fact, she little recognized him the day after his monthly ritual bath. He put his hands on her shoulders and kissed her cheek, then sat back on his heels. It was the first time she had ever seen her father's eyes dim, and Jo saw tears welling up there.

"That's a long story, Jo dear," he said, "and you're too young to really worry about that. We'll . . . we'll be with you soon. I promise. I do." Jo felt the same awful way she did when her mother sent her out at night searching for her father. Jo would find the man in some filthy gutter, a bottle nearby and his pockets empty.

"Papa," Jo said as she touched her father's tousled hair, "are we out of money again? How can we afford to send me on ahead?"

Her father glanced at the ground and murmured, "Ships don't cost money, dear. People ride them for free." Jo bit her lower lip. Papa's lying again, she thought.

Her father tucked her flyaway hair back into Jo's two braids and then said with a smile, "You have your blink-dog's tail, don't you now?" Jo solemnly nodded and patted the bulging pouch at her waist where she kept her most treasured possession.

"Good," her father said. "Use it when you need to escape bullies or what have you, but don't let anyone see you use it. Those same bullies will try to take it away from you."

Jo nodded again. "When are you and Mama joining me, Papa?" she asked. A little tear trickled down her cheek.

"Oh, soon, Jo dear, soon! I promise! I really do!" her father said and pulled her into his arms. "Now, I want you to be a good girl and mind the steward. He knows where to take you when you get to the city. All right, Jo dear?" Her father took her chin in his thumb and finger and gave it a little shake. Jo smiled bleakly.

The ship's steward called, "Last board! Last board! Boaaard up!"

Jo's father gave her one last swift hug, then stood and turned to his wife. He took the squalling baby from her. Jo hugged her mother fiercely, treasuring the touch and warmth of her broad, clean arms, which always smelled of bread. Jo's mother said nothing, though tears trickled down her freckled cheeks and wet a few stray strands of her chestnut hair. Her mother gave her one last kiss, then took the baby from her husband's arms. She looked down at her daughter.

"Mama?" Jo asked, not understanding why her mother wouldn't say anything.

Her mother busied herself with the baby. "Not now, Johauna," she said. "Baby's crying."

"Can I hold him good-bye?" Jo asked.

The mother clung to her infant and savagely shook her head. "No, Johauna! It's time for you to go." She pointed toward the ship. "Now, go on! Go on!" Jo backed away, not understanding why her mother suddenly seemed so hurtful.

Behind them two sailors began pulling the boarding plank, and Jo's father carried Jo toward the ship. One sailor groused at the delay, but the other extended his hand toward Jo and helped her board. He even wiped away a tear before putting her on deck.

"Good-bye, Jo dear!" her father shouted and waved. Beside him, her mother waved, too, though the gesture was reluctant. She turned away soon. Jo heard the baby squalling his good-bye to a sister he probably would never know he had.

The plank clattered as it landed on the ship's deck, and then, slowly, the ship began pulling away from the dock. Jo stood by the railing, clutching the salt-hardened wood with her small hands, until her father and mother disappeared.

Jo's thoughts returned to the present, and she looked at the castellan. "I was only six," she whispered. "The steward sent me to this place with hundreds of other children, but there wasn't room for me. They turned me away. At first I thought it was a home for children until their parents came for them. But it wasn't an orphanage. It was a sweat shop. People had sold them so many children that they were turning the extras away."

Jo scratched her forehead. "My parents, of course, never came for me. Every day I went to the docks, and they never came for me. All I had left to remind me of them was my blink-dog's tail. How my father got the tail, I'll never know. Now . . . now I don't even have that. Flinn used my blink-dog's tail in his fight with Verdilith, but I couldn't find it after the battle." She paused and added, "I like to think the tail helped him live long enough for me to see him before he died."

"Jo dear . . ." began the castellan.

Jo looked at the aging knight and then slowly smiled. "My father called me that," she said haltingly, "and I never remembered that until now. Perhaps there are some good memories to my past after all." She smiled, though her lips trembled a little.

"You're a very special young woman, Johauna Menhir," Sir Graybow said earnestly after a pause. "It's time a few people recognized that, and tonight at the ceremony they will." The castellan paused again, then picked up a nearby goblet and fidgeted with it. Jo knew the man well enough by now to understand he was nervous. She waited patiently.

"I . . . I've been thinking, Jo," the castellan began, "about our position here at the castle."

Jo felt immediate alarm. Have I done something wrong? she thought. Am I breaking some rule of etiquette? "Is . . . something the matter?" she asked cautiously.

Sir Graybow set down the cup. "Only something that I feel can be easily remedied, if you agree."

"Agree?" Jo asked. "To what?"

"I'd like to make you my heir, Johauna," the castellan said clearly, his eyes on Jo's face.

Jo expelled her breath, only just realizing that she'd been holding it. "I . . . see," she said, then nodded slowly. "Elowyn and Fritha were your only kin?" she asked as kindly as she could.

The wrinkles around the castellan's eyes deepened. He said quietly enough, "Yes, they were. As I said, you remind me of Elowyn. I have no heir, and you have no kin of your own that you know of. We are knight and squire and—I think—friends, too." The castellan's smile was sad though not bitter.

Jo nodded slowly, her eyes unable to leave Sir Graybow's face. "Yes," she said softly, "yes. If you want me as your heir, I would gladly accept."

The castellan gave her a brief hug and then backed away, saying, "Good. That's settled. I'll make the announcement at tonight's ceremony." He smiled again at Jo, and this time, his expression held no sadness. "I'm very proud of you, Jo, and I'm more pleased than I can say that you're willing to adopt me."

Jo colored a little at the praise. After living for six years with an alcoholic father and thirteen years on the streets of Specularum, Jo had little practice in accepting praise. Unable to say anything, she looked about the room. "I hope Braddoc arrives in time to see the squires and knights initiated," she said, deliberately changing the subject.

Sir Graybow laughed, a chuckle much like a bark. "What you mean to say, young lady, is that you hope the good dwarf sees *you* initiated in the order!" The older knight smiled at Jo's sudden discomfiture. He smiled at her a moment longer, then added, "I'm sorry Karleah and Dayin won't be here tonight."

Jo looked down at her hands. She'd received a message from Karleah yesterday to that effect. "Yes, well," Jo said slowly, "Karleah's very close to discovering why she's lost her powers. And I understand her concern. . . ." Of course, I thought I was a concern of hers, too, Jo thought, then tried to push her disappointment aside.

Somewhere in the tower a bell sounded, ringing the three-bell stroke for assembly. The people will be starting to gather in the great hall for tonight's ceremony, Jo thought. Her cheeks flushed, and she turned her bright eyes to the castellan.

Sir Graybow stood and said, "Hold on a moment, Jo. I have something for you." He entered the kitchen.

Jo stood and picked up Wyrmblight. The sigils seemed to glow in the evening light, though Jo fancied it could be simply a reflection from the candle sconces that Jo had lighted at sunset. She held the blade before her and whispered, "Oh, Flinn. Why aren't you here with me? What is my moment of triumph without you?" Her eyes smarted.

Wyrmblight warmed to the touch, and Jo felt a measure of comfort. *Have faith* whispered through her mind.

The castellan returned, bearing a burgundy-colored sword sheath in finely tooled leather. He held it out to Jo, who set Wyrmblight aside.

"What's this?" she asked as she eyed the peculiar arrangement of belts.

"It's a harness rig for a great sword," Sir Graybow responded. "Here, let me." He picked up one part of the harness, which Jo saw served as a belt. It was wider than her palm and studded with grommets. The castellan fastened it at her waist, making sure it rested snugly against her. A second similar construction looped over her shoulder and under the opposite arm. From both dangled leather straps and silver snaps and buckles. Sir Graybow took Wyrmblight and silently began fastening the blade in place.

Jo looked over her shoulder closely. Wyrmblight was too long to actually sheathe, for no one could quickly withdraw a great sword from a case. But the leather straps of this harness were so designed, Jo saw, that a single pull would undo them. *It obviously takes much longer to buckle the sword into the harness,* Jo thought as the castellan finally finished.

"There," Sir Graybow said. "A proper harness for a proper sword—" he smiled at Jo, the many wrinkles around his eyes crinkling "—for a proper squire."

Jo practiced bending and kneeling, checking the balance of the hanging sword. The harness held Wyrmblight securely in place, the tip of the sword about a foot off the floor. She wouldn't be able to sit with the sword strapped in place, but she doubted she'd have much opportunity of that until after the ceremony. She touched the rich burgundy leather and the silver appointments reverently.

"Thank you, Sir Graybow," she said simply. "The harness is beautiful." She looked fondly at the man standing before her. "It will be a relief to have Wyrmblight with me, properly sheathed, tonight. It's irksome not having my hands free."

The castellan nodded, a pleased expression on his face. He put his hand on Jo's arm and turned toward the stairwell. "Come, Jo," Sir Graybow said gravely. "It's time for your initiation as a squire in the Order of the Three Suns." He smiled at the young woman.

Jo's answering smile was solemn, for her thoughts had turned inward. If Flinn cannot be with me now in my shining moment, she thought, at least his sword and his mentor can. And when the time comes, when I *am* ready to take on Verdilith, I *will* find that wyrm and slay him. I *will* avenge Flinn's death. Jo nodded to herself, seeing only then the concerned expression in the castellan's eyes.

☙ ☙ ☙ ☙ ☙

Braddoc Briarblood eyed the man in front of him, then kicked his calf with the sharp tip of his boiled-leather boot. The man yowled and turned around, searching for the perpetrator. You're looking a little too high, mister, Braddoc thought maliciously as he stepped around the man. He wiggled his way between two more humans and breathed a sigh of relief as he reached the upper balustrade's railing. The balcony overlooked the interior of the castle's great hall.

At last! Braddoc thought. I didn't think I'd ever make it in time. He put his battle-axe and knapsack between his feet. The dwarf leaned over the stone balcony and peered into the crowd of people below. The great hall of the Castle of the Three Suns was filled with people, though not as packed as the hall had been during the open council last winter when Braddoc, Jo, Karleah, and Dayin had seen Flinn confront his accusers.

The dwarf's trip had proven uneventful. His home was still secure, though a pair of raccoons had moved inside the house. After leaving his home, Braddoc had circled back past the dragon's lair and found no sign of Verdilith there, though of course he hadn't been able to get inside the lair. Still, the castellan's report seemed true. Verdilith was gone.

The last task Braddoc had set himself was the most difficult, for he had visited the site of Flinn's funeral pyre. There the dwarf had scattered the few remaining ashes and said his own good-byes to Flinn. Then he had begun a methodical, diligent search for the one gift he wanted most to give Johauna: her blink-dog's tail. Braddoc checked his pocket for the bristly fur and again thanked the Immortals that he'd been successful.

All in all, the trip had been most productive and uneventful—until he'd stabled his pony at the castle not half an hour ago. As he had turned from his mount, a large, black crow had fluttered in the stable entrance and dropped a parchment in his hands. The crow had squawked and flapped away before Braddoc could even

feel surprised. Remembering the peculiar bird, the dwarf
pulled the parchment out again and smoothed it against
the stone railing in front of him.

Braddoc—

*Dayin and I cannot attend the initiation ceremony; I am close
to discovering what has stolen my magic and hope to recover my
spells before I return to the castle. The timing is crucial. Even so,
I wish I could attend the ceremony, if not for Johauna's vanity, for
her safety. I've sent Harrier, my messenger, to deliver a warning to
you: Be ever vigilant at the initiation ceremony. I have dreamed
of Jo coming to harm that night, and hope this missive reaches
you in time to avert it or somehow ease it.*

Tell Jo we will see her soon.

                                        Karleah Kunzay

"Old witch," Braddoc muttered into his beard. "What's
'harm' supposed to look like? I wish you'd been a little
more specific."

Braddoc folded the note and stuffed it in his belt. Squinting, he looked out into the great hall, searching for anything or anyone that seemed remotely unusual. His eyes ran
along the clean architectural lines of the ribbed vault above,
searching for a dark spot or irregular shape that might be
hiding a lurking assassin. He saw no such sign, only soot
trails from a time when the castle had used torches. Braddoc harrumphed. Four immense chandeliers hung from the
vault, attached to it with ornate, wrought-iron housings.
Each chandelier carried a dozen sconces, all elaborately
chased with touches of gold and silver. Magical light
poured forth from the tops and bottoms of the sconces,
casting gaunt shadows over the vault. The dwarf smiled
grimly. Those massive chandeliers could easily conceal

some crossbow-toting villain. Though he strained his eyes
to make out such a form, he could see none. The fixtures
swayed slowly, silently in gentle eddies of air from the vault.

"Have to keep my eye on those."

Next, his attention turned to the seven other balconies
overlooking the great hall below, three on his side of the
hall, and four on the other. They were crowded with
eager peasants and merchants—the riffraff like himself.
Given the density of the throng, an attack could easily
come from any one of the balconies.

"'Scuse, please," grunted a burly blacksmith, shoving
Braddoc into the stone rail and crushing him against it as
he pushed by. As soon as the man's large stomach stopped
pressing against him, the dwarf whirled angrily about,
hand on the dagger in his belt. The blacksmith was gone.
Bristling, Braddoc stared into the churning crowd around
him to catch a glimpse of his assailant, but the man had
disappeared as though he had never been.

"Bloated idiot," Braddoc mumbled, drawing a handkerchief from his pocket and rubbing at a line of black grease
on his shoulder. "Filthy, bloated idiot." He pulled the ker-
chief away, staring irritably at the two spots that now
marred it. One spot was black and grimy like grease. The
other was red as blood. "Bad omen," Braddoc noted, the
breath in his bruised lungs catching short. Trying to shake
off the chill that washed over him, he turned his attention
to the great hall below.

The floor was a vast mosaic of interlocking tiles that
formed some grand design Braddoc couldn't make out.
The surface of the pattern was obscured by the people, sitting in thick rows on the floor. The lines of them extended
from one wall to the other, like a furrowed garden of villagers. Young pages ushered more peasants into the already

packed hall, gesturing for them to tighten the existing
rows. The pages, little more than children themselves, also
tirelessly cleared the red-velvet aisle in the center of the
hall.

"Could be any one of 'em," Braddoc muttered, eyeing
the crowd. His hand slipped a second time to his pocket,
checking for the blink-dog's tail. His fingers wrapped
around the beaded handle, and he peered once again at
the swaying chandeliers, the burgeoning balconies, the
crowded floor below. . . . "I just hope this thing works."

Noise swelled at the front of the hall. Suddenly a dozen
or more people, including Baroness Penhaligon and Sir
Graybow, filed into a cordoned area where the council
table sat. Long and rectangular—imposing even at this distance—the table rested on a low dais and was attended on
the far side by high-backed chairs. Only pages, squires,
knights, and nobility were allowed beyond the ropes that
marked the cordoned area.

"Let's hope this starts it," Braddoc said to himself. He
was tired of waiting, especially since he had hurried
straight to the hall, with trail dust still clinging to him.

Baroness Penhaligon waited for the castellan to pull out
her seat, then sat down. The council members stood by
their respective chairs and waited. The crowd, none too
quiet a moment before, grew noisier still. A man behind
Braddoc pressed forward, practically leaning over the dwarf.
Braddoc jerked his elbow back and connected with the
man's thigh. The human said, "Ooof!" but backed away
peaceably. Oh, to be back in Rockhome! Braddoc sighed,
feeling nostalgic for the short folk of his dwarven homeland.

Arteris raised her hand. A dozen trumpeters, six to
either side of the dais, stepped forward and blared out the
call for silence.

It's begun, thought Braddoc. His eyes left the stage and combed the audience.

🜚 🜚 🜚 🜚 🜚

Jo pressed against the delicate iron grillwork that screened the small anteroom from the great hall. She couldn't see beyond the backs of the first row of people. Braddoc could be anywhere out there! she thought. She could only hope she would catch sight of him as she walked up the aisle.

The squire wrapped her fingers around the metal grillwork. Her hands were perspiring from the heat of the small, crowded room, and she hoped to cool them. She glanced nervously to each side of her. Eleven other men and women were gathered with her, each wearing the same golden tunic Jo did. Most of them were young like her, though one man sported a grizzled beard. Jo wondered what had prompted him to become a squire in midlife.

In a separate cluster stood seasoned squires who were about to be promoted to knighthood: two men and three women, one obviously elven. Jo hadn't had the nerve to approach the elf maiden, even for a simple greeting, for she admired the elven race above all others. Tonight's ceremony was too distracting and emotionally taxing to let her overcome her shyness and approach the golden-haired, violet-eyed beauty.

Jo furtively watched the soon-to-be knights, who were talking quietly among themselves. Some were trying to feign nonchalance, but Jo sensed their excitement nevertheless. They're about to become *knights* in the Order of the Three Suns! Jo thought, then caught one of the women trying to surreptitiously rub a tarnished spot from her armor. Jo smiled. Unlike the squires, who had already been given their golden tunics, the knights would receive their midnight-blue tunics from Baroness Penhaligon herself. The tarnish will never show then, Jo thought charitably.

Trumpets sounded then, and Jo turned back around and pressed against the grillwork. Beside her, a young man did the same, and Jo glanced at him. She blushed and averted her eyes immediately when she saw that he was looking at her. "Hello," said Colyn Madcomb, the squire who had opened the door for Jo in the practice courtyard a week ago.

Jo blushed, unable to say anything to the young man with the merry eyes. She couldn't help noticing that his eyes were an interesting combination of green and brown, and that they were framed by black, curly lashes.

The trumpeters finished their introductory theme, a fanfare that had been used since the beginning of Penhaligon's days as a court. The people responded by slowly quieting. Baroness Penhaligon regally stood and began to speak, her voice echoing through the great hall. Jo strained to see past the people still moving about in the hall, but she lost sight of the dais. She would have to be patient: she and the other initiates weren't allowed into the great hall until a page opened the door and escorted them to the council area.

"Gentle folk, commoners and royals alike," rang Arteris's voice, "welcome, one and all." Arteris paused while the audience erupted in the traditional cheer of greeting.

"In the tradition of our forebears," the baroness continued, "tonight we celebrate the initiation of those who have been found worthy to join the Order of the Three Suns. . . ."

Jo rubbed her sweaty hands on the legs of her trousers, then fidgeted with the collar of her tunic. Her thoughts drifted away, and she remembered Flinn telling her he believed she would one day become a knight in the order. His words and manner had been filled with such earnestness, such faith, that Jo had believed him with all her heart. It had been the first time since her parents had sent her away and betrayed her that she had believed anyone so fully.

Oh, Flinn! Jo's heart cried. I have such doubts! How I wish you were here! Once again, the words *have faith* entered Jo's mind. She smiled sadly and put her hand on Wyrmblight. "I'll try," she whispered, "but it's so hard without you."

Then suddenly the door opened and a young woman poked her head inside. "It's time for the squires," the page said. "The castellan will announce your name shortly— begin walking down the aisle at the pace he taught you." The page smiled sweetly and held open the door.

Jo's heart thudded, and she barely heard Sir Graybow announce to the audience in the great hall, "We have found twelve persons worthy to become squires in the Order of the Three Suns." Listen, girl! Jo admonished herself. It'll never do to miss your name!

Sir Graybow called out, "Colyn Madcomb, from Greenheight in the County of Vyalia, now squire to Madam Francys Astwood. We bid you welcome to Pennaligon." The young man with the merry eyes flushed and stepped out onto the velvet-strewn aisle. Jo clenched her hands.

Moments passed slowly, agonizingly, while Squire Madcomb walked the long hall to the dais. The audience responded with a round of cheers and clapping when the young man reached the council members. Jo felt faint.

Then the words Jo longed to hear rang out. "Johauna Menhir, from Specularum in the Estate of Marilenev. We bid you welcome to Penhaligon," came Sir Graybow's strong, gruff voice. For a moment Jo couldn't move. Then she caught sight of the page hurrying toward her, and the motion spurred Jo forward. She stepped onto the velvet walkway.

As she walked the long aisle, Jo was too overwhelmed to even think of looking for Braddoc. To each side of the aisle, people sat in neat rows on the floor and peered expectantly up at her. She swallowed convulsively; Sir Graybow was speaking.

"—formerly to the Mighty Flinn, the order's most renowned knight, who recently died in battle against the vile wyrm Verdilith. Johauna Menhir has accepted the position as squire to the Castellan of Penhaligon," Sir Graybow was saying. Jo flushed at the proud tone in his voice. Her eyes were bright as she continued down the walkway. To each side of the aisle, people twisted and shifted to get a look at the young woman. Jo was almost halfway to the dais.

Sir Graybow continued, "Squire Menhir has also graciously agreed to become my ward—"

His words were cut off by a sudden screeching noise, as of metal twisting and groaning under pressure. Jo stopped and looked around, trying to locate the sound. The protesting metal screeched louder, a piercing wail echoing off the stone walls of the hall. Some in the audience rose to their feet in confusion; they began to murmur, their cries mixing with the grating noise. The screech came again, though this time more muted. Jo looked up.

There, four stories above her head, a huge, wrought-

iron chandelier pitched precariously back and forth. Its
magic sconces cast swirling, ghostly shadows across the
ribbed vault, and a green-gray mist seemed to hover about
the chandelier's iron mounting. Jo gasped, raising her arm
up over her head, squinting at the brilliant, hypnotic
lights. Suddenly, the chandelier began to flicker, as did all
the other magical lanterns inside the great hall. Women
and children screamed and cried out in panic, and the
sounds masked the screeching of rending metal above Jo.
In the next instant, the floor filled with running people,
shouting, fleeing from the hovering doom.

It seemed like Verdilith's first attack on the great hall.

The lights flickered into blackness. Abruptly, someone
slammed into Jo and flung her forward through the racing
dark. As she hurtled heavily to the ground, panic swept
over her, then crunching pain. Jo struggled to break loose
of her assailant, tugging helplessly at the sheathed and
tangled great sword harnessed to her.

With a rumble more felt than heard in the chaotic din
and darkness, the chandelier's mounting tore free of the
stone ceiling. A horrible and sudden silence in the crowd
answered the rumble, and in that shocked hush, the gentle
clink of iron chains filled the hall. Jo stiffened in fear,
knowing the chandelier was directly overhead. Whoever
had knocked her aside clutched her collar in tight fists and
dragged her, rasping, across the mosaic floor.

Jo's feet tangled with her assailant's, and the two of them
fell heavily to the stone floor. With a deafening thunder,
the iron chandelier crashed to the floor, its massive metal
frame less than a sword's length from Jo. The lights flickered once, and Jo saw the grimly terrified look of Braddoc
Briarblood holding her.

Then all was blackness.

The crowd panicked, running toward the entry doors, trampling any who had remained sitting or had fallen to the ground. Children cried. Jo heard prayers being spoken and curses as well.

Sir Graybow's voice rang out stentorianly, "Stay calm! Stay calm and sit down! The lights have failed—that's all. We are *not* under attack. Please remain calm; we will have light soon." Several knights entered the hall carrying lanterns, which they began passing out to the other knights, squires, and pages.

"Braddoc! Braddoc!" Jo said shakily, sitting up next to the dwarf. "Are you all right?" she asked, her breath coming in labored wheezes.

"I was about to ask the same of you," the dwarf noted huskily.

"You made it to the ceremony," Jo mumbled, and the moment the words had left her lips she realized how stupid they sounded.

"You have a gift for understatement, Johauna," Braddoc said, rising to his feet and coughing.

"Yes," Jo said absently as she tried to dust the powdered stone from her clothing. Lantern light flickered by the pair now and then casting strange and eerie shadows onto the hall's walls. The audience was still confused, and pages and squires hurried about trying to calm frightened men and women and comfort crying children. Groping in the darkness, Jo's shaking hand found Braddoc's shoulder and she blurted, "How . . . how did you know? About the chandelier, I mean. How did you get here in time to save me?"

"A little gift of mine, you might say." Braddoc held out his hand. The light was so dim that it took Jo a moment to make out the curved form of the blink-dog's tail. "Or a little gift of yours, more truthfully."

Jo took the bristly tail and ran her fingers over the beaded handle. "How—? Where—?" she began, unable to continue.

The dwarf shrugged. "I . . . stopped to pay my respects to Flinn. I thought I'd look around while I was there and see if I could find it. Dwarves can be notoriously tenacious when we want to be, you know." He took the tail and flipped it over, then handed it back. "I'd thought some animal would have eaten it by now, but there must be enough magic left in it to make it distasteful."

Jo looked at her friend. "How did you figure out how to use it? I taught Flinn the particular bark command to trigger the teleportation, but . . ."

Braddoc rubbed his elbow and said, "Oh, I heard you use it once or twice." The dwarf smiled ruefully and shook his head. Then he sobered. He fixed Jo with his good eye. "I almost didn't make it, Johauna. I couldn't get the right tone. If I hadn't—" The lines around his eye creased in worry.

Jo touched his hand and bit her lip.

A page ran up to Jo and Braddoc and asked, "Squire Menhir, you're wanted up front by the castellan. Immediately. Do you need any help?"

"No, thank you," Jo said automatically. She stood and Braddoc did the same. Together they began pressing forward through the crowd. The audience was beginning to settle now that more light had entered the hall. Most were sitting on the floor, huddling in small groups. The flush of fear had given way to curiosity, and the screams and moans had given way to muttered speculation.

Trumpeters blared the peal for silence once more. Jo and Braddoc hurried forward. Baroness Penhaligon stepped to the end of the dais and raised her hand.

"People of Penhaligon," Arteris said loudly, "I pray you calm yourselves. Our mages inform me that the chandelier's mountings were slowly corroding in the ceiling. As it began to work its way loose, it broke the incantations that lit this hall."

Jo and Braddoc reached the dais, and Sir Graybow gestured for them to join him. They did so with alacrity.

"The ceremony will commence immediately, for we are all too proud of the friends and family we admit this night into the Order of the Three Suns to cease the ceremony here," Arteris continued. "Heaven help us if the pride of Penhaligon should be brought to its knees by faulty lamps. We'll celebrate as we did in days of old!" The baroness's uncharacteristically impassioned speech brought a ragged cheer from the crowd.

"The good castellan will check on getting us additional light, and so I am turning his part of the ceremony over to Madam Astwood. She will announce the remaining squires and introduce you to the new knights in our order." The crowd, pleased that the ceremonies wouldn't be canceled, answered with a heavy round of applause. Smiling tightly, Arteris finished, "I pray you enjoy yourselves, good people of Penhaligon. And I enjoin you to remain after the ceremony to partake of the fine wine and food the pages will dispense. I must take leave of you for a few minutes, but I shall return shortly. Madam Astwood, pray continue with the initiation." Arteris bowed slightly and turned toward the knight, who strode forward as Arteris retreated.

Madam Astwood called out, "Thank you, Your Ladyship! We look forward to your return." The woman gestured toward the people, "And now, people of Penhaligon, let us bid welcome to young Squire Aldney Blackbuck late of the Rugalov village—"

Sir Graybow nodded, then began moving rapidly away. Jo and Braddoc fell into step behind him, and they met up with the baroness as she neared a small door at the side of the dais. Arteris strode through the door and rapidly down a short, dark hall that led to a stairwell. Jo was not surprised to see that torches lined the walls of the passageways and stretched away into the distance. So, the lanterns failed elsewhere, too, she thought, as she followed the castellan up the stairs. Behind her, Braddoc was grumbling beneath his breath.

As Jo hurried to match the baroness's pace, she struggled to keep a smile of excitement from her lips. She was part of a special detail, the baroness's own personal entourage. Jo wanted desperately to ask where they were going, but, seeing the determined step of the baroness, she reined in her tongue. They turned down a familiar hall. There, the baroness threw open the doors to the small council room and greeted the three men and one woman who arrived from the opposite hall. Once everyone had entered the chamber, the baroness peremptorily shut the doors—just short of slamming them—and whirled on those gathered.

"What is happening here?" Arteris demanded, glaring. "Why did the magic fail? Are we under siege?" Her agate-brown eyes flashed at the four mages, who glanced nervously at each other. Arteris strode forward and took her accustomed seat at the center of the U-shaped table. The mages moved to the side of the table and sat down slowly. Watching Graybow, Jo set her teeth and tried to look as calm and stern as he. Sir Graybow, glancing sidelong at Jo, positioned himself before Arteris, between the mages and his baroness.

"Well?" Arteris demanded. "All the lights in the castle falter and fade on a single day? In a single hour? How can this be?" The baroness focused her wrathful eyes on the oldest wizard. "Aranth? What is the meaning of this?"

The man named Aranth stood. He flicked a nervous look at his comrades before facing the baroness. Jo felt sudden distrust form in her heart. What is he hiding? What is he afraid of? she wondered.

"Your Ladyship—" the mage said formally.

"Dispense with the formalities, Aranth," Arteris snapped once more. She crossed her arms, apparently unconcerned about wrinkling her lovely blue-and-silver gown.

"We—we believe Teryl Auroch may have somehow infiltrated the castle," Aranth began.

The baroness's eyes narrowed. "What proof have you of this suspicion?"

Aranth smiled wanly, clutching the collar of his robes for an uncomfortable moment. "No direct proof, My Lady. But we've noticed a general, magical malaise over the castle—some kind of subtle but powerful spell that's affecting all the magic here. Its been weakening the light spells, the magic items, even new incantations."

"Why wasn't I told of this 'malaise' earlier?" Arteris demanded, her sharply trimmed nails beginning to rap impatiently on the table. "This *is* a matter of castle security—a grave weakening in our magical defenses."

"I apologize personally for that, Your Ladyship," Aranth replied, punctuating the statement with a shallow bow. "The effects of the spell have been slow, but cumulative. Though we now believe the spell has been in effect for some weeks, its influence on our magic only became obvious this morning, and has since then grown acute."

"What—if I may be so bold—" interjected Graybow,

thoughtfully stroking his chin, "does this 'malaise' have to do with Teryl Auroch?"

"He is the only mage we know of with enough power to cast such a spell," replied Lady Irys, the female mage, as she rose to her feet. She was a slight, middle-aged woman of plain appearance. "We've discovered Auroch is a much more powerful wizard than we had been led to believe. And, he's the only one with a clear motive to cast such a spell."

"And that motive is . . . revenge?" Arteris inquired.

"No," Aranth said simply, then thought to quickly add, "Your Ladyship. I fear it runs deeper than that. Teryl Auroch originally insinuated himself into this court—into your trust—for some evil purpose. We believe his purpose was left unaccomplished when he was driven out by Flinn. We believe the spell he has cast must be calculated to bring about his unfulfilled plans."

"Dominion over Penhaligon," Graybow whispered in awe to himself, though the words cut through the silent room.

"What?" Arteris snapped, rising to her feet.

Graybow, shaken from his musing, blinked twice and said, "It only makes sense. Auroch is a ruthless, power-hungry mage. If he cannot rule Penhaligon from within, he will do so from without."

"This is all guess and conjecture," Arteris noted, striking her palms firmly on the tabletop.

"Not all," Jo responded quietly, her voice quavering. Graybow glanced toward her quizzically. His gaze was sharpened with irritation that she had not observed proper etiquette in addressing the baroness. Jo, unaware of her mentor's attention, took a weak step backward, bracing herself with a trembling hand against the table.

"Squire Menhir?" Graybow blurted in quiet alarm, reaching out a hand to steady her. "What is it?"

Jo, catching her breath, shook her head gently and murmured, "The mages are right. Auroch *is* behind it."

Graybow's hand was firm on her arm. "How do you know?"

Jo looked up into her mentor's face, anger and fear naked in her eyes. "I saw Verdilith here."

"What?" chorused Arteris and Graybow.

"The day we returned from the dragon's lair, after battling Verdilith . . ." Jo explained, ". . . a black-haired man accosted us; he ridiculed Flinn." Her voice began to break, but Jo clenched her jaw and gathered her resolve. "He had golden eyes and wore a long leather glove over his left hand and arm. Verdilith has golden eyes, and his left arm was maimed by Flinn."

"That proves nothing," Arteris noted coldly.

"Excuse, please, My Lady," Braddoc interjected, stepping forward, "but someone matching that description ran into me in the great hall. He left a streak of blood on my tunic, blood that must be from his left arm. And, just before the chandelier fell, I saw a greenish mist whirling about the ceiling mount. I think the man and the mist were both Verdilith, transformed."

"I . . . see," Arteris said, throwing Jo a sideways glance. "Verdilith and Auroch seem to be back to their old tricks." She paused, her eyes patiently measuring each person in the room. "Now we have a vague idea what is happening, but I've not heard a single suggestion as to how to stop these schemers. What do you intend to do about this rogue mage?" Arteris asked icily, not batting an eye. "And what do you intend to do about restoring magic to the Castle of the Three Suns?" Jo felt a twinge of reluctant admiration at the baroness's ruthless tone.

Aranth fidgeted with his fingers. "We will, of course, restore the magic as soon as possible, Your Ladyship. I caution you that this may take—"

"Do not caution me, Aranth!" the baroness said coldly. Her agate eyes flashed at the wizard. "You are my head mage, and I am sorely disappointed in you. You will have the magical wards and defenses restored by tomorrow. Magically locked doors and gates, magic cords . . . everything. Do I make myself understood?"

Aranth bowed and said, "Understood, Your Ladyship." He leaned back, his eyes averted, but his lips curled in resentment.

"And the lights must be restored by the next day—all of them restored," Arteris continued. "Understood?"

The three mages reluctantly nodded. Aranth said, "To do so, we will need to discover a way to break the enchantment. That may take time."

The baroness's eyes were like spheres of ice. "The less time, the better for you." Her chill gaze warmed slightly, and she added, "The better for all of us. In the meantime, Sir Graybow, I want you to step up security. Double the guards throughout the castle, and treble them before magically warded portals. I don't care if you must draw from the ranks of the squires and knights to do so. Security in the castle is the utmost concern."

"Yes, My Lady," Graybow responded, with a gracious bow.

"And I want Auroch found," Arteris finished. "Found and slain, and his head paraded on a pike."

"We will use every means at our disposal to magically detect the whereabouts of the rogue mage, Your Ladyship," Aranth said quickly. "We will undo the damage he has wrought."

Arteris pursed her lips at the mage but said nothing. Jo could clearly see the baroness's thought: Fools. I'm surrounded by ineffectual fools. Jo smothered an irreverent smile, then felt the smile fade as Arteris turned to Sir Graybow. "My mages, Sir Graybow, plan to search for Auroch with their rapidly failing magicks. I pray my castellan can devise a more reliable plan. What do *you* plan to do, castellan?"

A gentle smile tugged at the corners of Graybow's mouth, as though he had been waiting to be asked that question. "My scouts have discovered someone who—I am convinced—will know the whereabouts of Teryl Auroch," Sir Graybow said slowly. Jo felt her heart begin to pound uncomfortably. A rushing noise filled her ears. "I intend to send Squire Menhir and Master Briarblood after the man."

Sir Graybow paused, the grim, determined smile deepening across his lips. "The man is Sir Brisbois."

Chapter VII

ave you lost your senses?" Arteris raved at Sir Graybow. She looked away, her lips pressing into a thin line. Regaining her composure, Arteris leaned toward the castellan and splayed her hands across the wide expanse of table before her. "Tell me, Sir Graybow," the baroness asked sarcastically, "by what logic do you send an untrained squire after a former knight who is, by all accounts, a man of dishonor and treachery?" Arteris arched her eyebrow.

Johauna hurriedly took the last step separating her from Sir Graybow. She raised her hand and was about to speak, but the castellan caught her wrist and flashed his eyes at her. Jo pursed her lips and kept silent. The castellan gave her hand a brief squeeze as he released it, then turned to Baroness Penhaligon.

"My 'logic,' Your Ladyship," Sir Graybow responded drily, "is this: Brisbois, for all his dishonor and treachery, is a coward—no match in battle for my squire and her associate. Furthermore, Brisbois is merely a tag for the whereabouts and weaknesses of Teryl Auroch and Verdilith, the true villains. While Squire Menhir and Braddoc are pursuing Brisbois, I need every other experienced knight and squire to guard the castle against further attack from the mage and the dragon. You yourself said that the castle's security was paramount."

"I did, indeed," Arteris said, lifting her hands from the table and standing erect. She drew a breath in preparation to speak, but Graybow was already talking.

"And, most importantly, I am your castellan and have been for many years now. *I* have every faith that my squire and her companion are best suited for this task. If *you* have faith in me as your castellan, you should have faith in my choice of assignment." Lile Graybow lifted his bushy eyebrows slightly and stared at Arteris.

The baroness blinked stoically. Her expression remained inscrutable for a long moment. Finally, she coughed once, delicately, and said, "You are correct in your assumption that I have every faith in *you,* Sir Graybow." She fixed her penetrating gaze on the castellan. "As such, I will extend that faith to your squire. But know you this, Sir Graybow—" Arteris pointed at the castellan "—I do not want to discover that this choice of yours has been dictated by either infatuation or senility. Do I make myself clear?"

Sir Graybow bowed low. "Yes, Your Ladyship, you do. And no, you will not." Jo caught the briefest trace of a smile lingering around the castellan's lips.

"In that case, Sir Graybow," Arteris said wryly, "I suggest you adjourn to brief Squire Menhir and Master Braddoc. I wish to talk with these—" there was the briefest pause "—mages. Please attend me later tonight." The baroness nodded dismissal to Jo, Braddoc, and the castellan, then turned to the mages. Jo saw Aranth actually squirm before she turned to follow Sir Graybow out the room.

The castellan maintained a quick pace through the halls and stairwells that led to their chambers, despite the lack of adequate light. "This will take some getting used to," he murmured when he discovered that one hall was virtually unlit. He stopped, put his hand on Jo's arm, and squeezed it. Graybow said gruffly, "We've a lot to discuss tonight, Jo. I suppose I should have asked first if you wanted to go—"

Jo shook her head vehemently, unable to see much of Sir Graybow's expression in the dark. She gripped the man's hand. "No, sir," she said strongly, "I *do* want this opportunity—I do! If you won't let me hunt Verdilith yet, I can avenge Flinn's honor if not his death—"

Sir Graybow raised a gnarled forefinger in warning. "No, there will be no talk of that," he said sternly. "I am sending you after Brisbois to bring him in, not to seek vengeance." Sir Graybow's voice had a hard edge to it that Jo had never heard him use with her. "Understood?"

Conflicting emotions warred within Johauna, and for a moment she couldn't respond. Then she quelled all her thoughts and said lightly, "Of course, Sir Graybow. You can count on me."

Something in her tone made Sir Graybow pause to look at the young woman, but the darkness hid her expression. "Jo . . . ?" he began, his voice like a low growl.

Jo closed her eyes and felt her skin flush. "Yes, sir?" she forced herself to say with just the right degree of concern.

The castellan peered at her once more, then, seemingly satisfied, he turned down the hall. Jo and Braddoc fell in step beside him.

ÎÎ ÎÎ ÎÎ ÎÎ ÎÎ

Early dawn found Jo and Braddoc mounted on horse and pony and traveling south on the smooth, hard-packed Duke's Road. Only a few ruts, puddles, and frost boils hampered the steady, ground-eating canter they set for the animals. The road was the finest thoroughfare around and was used by almost anyone traveling across Penhaligon. Originating in Specularum, to the south, the Duke's Road worked its way north through Kelvin, on through the southern Wulfholdes to Penhaligon, then through the Wulfholdes again as it wound its way north to the Altan Tepes Mountains.

The River Hillfollow bordered the western edge of the Duke's Road. Its bank had come alive with a flush of vivid green as the trees burst into leaf. The Wulfholdes surrounding Jo and Braddoc seemed pale by contrast, though a few tenacious shrubs and grasses dotted the shale slopes. Jo glanced at the river, her eyes drawn by the glint of sparkling waters. She remembered they'd have to cross that river to get to the tiny village of Rifllian, which was just on the other side of Castle Kelvin to the south. Brisbois was supposed to be hiding in the village. She turned to Braddoc.

"There's a ford at Kelvin, isn't there?" Jo asked.

Braddoc nodded, his long-legged pony cantering to keep up with Carsig's stride. "Aye, there is," the dwarf replied. "We'll cross the river there, and then the Duke's Road branches westward. We take that into Rifllian."

And that's where we'll find that—that traitor, *Sir* Brisbois! Jo thought savagely. It rankled Jo that Brisbois's title was still intact—at Flinn's gracious request, the title had never been officially stripped from the man. The "knight" was a menace. Surely discrediting Flinn with lies and betraying Flinn as bondsman were only two of Brisbois's heinous crimes, Jo told herself. Her fist clenched on

Wyrmblight's pommel, then forcibly relaxed. Calm down, girl, she told herself as she tried to find something else to concentrate on. *Duty, not vengeance.* She'd repeated the phrase in her head many times already, but still the words rang hollow. Once, she even found herself hoping Brisbois would provoke an attack so they could kill him on the spot.

Shaking her head to clear it of the destructive thought, Jo glanced at Braddoc. "Didn't you meet Flinn in Rifllian? What's the village like?" she asked.

Braddoc's beard, braided into a single plait, bounced up at his pony's canter. He tucked it back into his wide, silver- and sapphire-studded belt. "Rifllian?" he repeated, then snorted. "It's not much of a place, that's for sure. My comrades and I—"

"What *were* you exactly, Braddoc? You weren't really mercenaries—you said so yourself to the baroness," Jo cut in quickly. "What did you do?"

Unexpectedly, Braddoc laughed. "There's a lot you don't know about me, Johauna Menhir!"

"Then tell me," Jo entreated lightly. "We've—what? one? two? days on the road before we reach the village? I'd like to know more about you and how you met Flinn."

The dwarf looked at Jo oddly for a moment. A sudden break in his pony's rhythm drew his attention away from Jo. The animal pulled up sharply and halted. "Likely a stone," Braddoc murmured as he dismounted and looked at the pony's legs. Jo pulled Carsig to a halt and watched Braddoc.

The pony was favoring her left forehoof. Braddoc leaned against her while facing the animal's rear. Onyx obediently shifted her weight, and Braddoc slid his hand down her leg and picked up the hoof. He cupped her hoof with one hand and pulled out his knife. Gently he scraped away loose gravel and packed mud with a blunt hook on the knife's pommel. "Here it is," he said as he probed deeper. Using the hook, he carefully dislodged and removed a sharp, jagged piece of granite. The dwarf eyed the rock with disfavor, then threw it away. He set the pony's hoof back down and remounted.

"The sole looks bruised," Braddoc said to Jo. "Let's slow to a walk and let Onyx recover." He added after a moment, "That'll give me time to answer your questions in a more sensible fashion, rather than bounce along and lose half my words." The dwarf fell silent.

Jo nudged Carsig into a walk. "Think she'll pull up lame?" the young squire asked momentarily. She knew she might have to prime the pump to get the reticent dwarf talking about his past. A little banal chitchat could do the trick.

Braddoc shook his head. "I don't think it's that bad a bruise, and she's moving pretty good now." The dwarf opened his mouth, then closed it suddenly. He glanced at Jo and stroked his beard.

Jo bided her time, taking in the countryside, which was far different from the streets of Specularum, where she had spent her early years. The Wulfholdes gave way to gentler hills and meadowlands. The Hillfollow still curved to the west, and the road matched the river curve for curve.

Overhead, birds flocked here and there, some still heading north to summer ranges. A flock of snowy geese flew high above the ground in a deep V; their cries echoed faintly in Jo's ears. Then Jo heard the eerie, lonely cry of a solitary loon as it winged its way toward the river's waters. She smiled in wonder. How different these birds are from Specularum's raucous gulls! she thought. During her years in the port city, Jo saw only gulls and pigeons. The wealth of birds in this untamed land startled and pleased her.

The terrain leveled into gentle rolls before Jo finally turned to Braddoc. "Well?" she asked tersely. The dwarf had never taken this long to answer her questions before.

"Well what?" the dwarf asked mildly. His good eye caught Jo's.

Jo sighed elaborately. "You were going to tell me about your life as a supposed mercenary and about how you met Flinn," she added in a rush. She saw Braddoc tug on his beard—a sure sign of nervousness—and she smiled reassuringly at him. "You're my friend, Braddoc—" Jo grew suddenly serious and sincere "—probably my best friend in the world, what with Flinn gone. I'd be honored if you'd tell me more about yourself."

Braddoc looked at Jo thoughtfully, trying to match his pony's stride with her horse's. He turned away and said slowly, "I told the truth to the baroness when I said I'm not a mercenary, though I'd pretended to be one. And I told Arteris at least a partial truth when I said my people were interested in opening trade relations with Penhaligon." Braddoc paused, as if pondering what or how much he should say.

"Go on," Jo urged.

Braddoc looked away from Jo and patted Onyx's shaggy neck. Both the horse and pony were still shedding their thick winter coats. Jo groomed Carsig twice daily in an effort to remove the gelding's thick hair.

"I . . . I'd prefer if you didn't ask me any more of my past, Johauna," the dwarf said so quietly Jo had to lean toward him to hear. "I've said more than I should, and anything more might compromise your position at the castle."

Jo blinked, feeling a mixture of surprise, disappoint-ment, and a little resentment. I thought we were friends, she said to herself, then quelled the thought. We *are* friends, Jo reminded herself. If Braddoc has something in his past he'd rather not share, so be it. Jo nodded slowly and said, "I'll respect your wishes for now, Braddoc, but you've done the one impermissible thing around me: piqued my curiosity." Jo smiled roguishly. "I'm giving you fair warning. I intend to know all about this by the return trip to the castle."

Braddoc snorted but didn't deign to comment.

"Tell me about your meeting with Flinn then," Jo sug-gested. The dwarf was with his band of supposed merce-naries then; surely he'll let slip some clue about his past, Jo told herself. And, besides, I'll get to hear more about Flinn.

"I'm sure you've heard Flinn's side of the tale," Braddoc began, then suddenly smiled. "I remember the first time I saw Flinn." The dwarf laughed aloud.

"Yes? Was it funny?" Jo asked quickly, excitement creeping over her, though her heart shrank with grief and pain at the thought of Flinn. Jo had learned all the tales of Flinn the Mighty and had become a fair storyteller as a result. But she knew next to nothing about Flinn's life after his fall. Braddoc hadn't met Flinn until then, and she was determined to draw as much of the dwarf's informa-tion as she could.

Braddoc laughed again and nodded his head. "Oh, yes!" he chortled. "My men and I were at an inn in Rifllian—the Flickertail, if I remember correctly—having an ale, minding our own business. In walked this tall, angry man. Flinn was just spoiling for a fight that night."

"Did you know it was him?" Jo asked, picturing the

scene. She could see Fain Flinn's tall, muscular form burst through the tavern door, a door that held the weathered image of some unrecognizable bird. Flinn would be grimacing, his eyes glowing like smoldering embers. He would snarl some greeting to the innkeeper as he looked around. Braddoc and his men would be in one corner of the tavern, peacefully minding their own business.

"Oh, we knew it was Flinn, all right," Braddoc answered. "Everyone knew Flinn the Mighty—newly Flinn the Fallen—by sight back then. People couldn't help but stop and stare at Flinn. Like I said, he was spoiling for a fight that night, but all he really wanted was a plate of stew and an ale."

"What happened when Flinn looked around the tavern?" Jo asked.

"The innkeeper asked him what he'd have, but Flinn only asked for water," Braddoc answered. "I knew he must be flat broke then, for it only cost half a copper for a loaf of bread; Flinn obviously didn't even have that."

"Then what happened?" Jo asked. She was a little surprised by the dwarf's suddenly loquacious manner, but she figured Braddoc hoped to distract her from asking any more questions about his own past.

The dwarf laughed. "I said something sarcastic like, 'That's a fitting drink for a man'—implying, of course, that Flinn wasn't much of a man if he could only drink water." Braddoc chuckled again. He directed Onyx around a large frost boil in the road and continued, "That was all it took. Flinn snapped. He leaped at me, my men leaped between, and they beat each other up. Flinn put up a good fight, but in the end it was *him* lying on the floor looking up at *us*."

"Go on," urged Jo.

"I looked down at Flinn, this man I'd heard so much
about in the last few weeks. I looked at him, and I
thought: This man hasn't got a dishonorable bone in his
body. And I held out my hand to him," Braddoc paused.
"He didn't take it immediately, but I think that's because
his bruises were puffing up and obscuring his vision."

"He finally took your hand?" Jo asked.

"Aye, he did," Braddoc nodded. "I helped him up,
dusted him off, and apologized for my lot. Then I invited
him to have a bit of food with me. We sat down then and
there and ate. We were friends from that moment on until
the day he died."

Jo said nothing, and the silence that fell was marred
only by the trilling of birds and rhythmic clopping of
hooves.

Braddoc mused quietly for a few moments, then said,
"Before his disgrace, people followed him around, pester-
ing him to take up their causes. But he understood that.
He knew he was their hero, and he knew they looked up
to him." The dwarf shrugged, then shifted in his saddle.
"At the same time he was an intensely private man. Sometimes the two sides of his life were difficult to reconcile."

"Surely the people stopped dogging him after his fall?"
Jo asked. She was getting to know a side of Flinn she
hadn't considered before.

"Well, in one way, yes, and in one way no," Braddoc
answered readily. "Trouble is, the hero worship was
replaced with a malice and cruelty."

"Is that why Flinn was so angry the night you met?" Jo
asked in sudden inspiration.

Braddoc nodded. "I'm sure of it. This was several
months after his dismissal from the order, understand.
He'd been drifting, trying to find work, I'm sure. His

reception in Rifllian was probably typical: callow and brutish." Braddoc shifted in the saddle, his short legs obviously wearying of the ride.

The late afternoon sun was beginning to set. They topped the crest of a hill, and Jo spied a cluster of towers rising above the tree line a few little valleys away. They were nearing Castle Kelvin. She and Braddoc would stop there for the night, then make for Rifllian and Brisbois tomorrow morning. She pointed toward the towers and asked, "How long to Kelvin, you think?"

"Two hours, maybe a little more," Braddoc replied. He frowned at the clouds looming from the south. "We might get some rain before then, though. Onyx seems better; let's pick up the pace." The dwarf urged his pony into a canter, and Jo gave Carsig the rein. The big gelding nickered and easily matched the pony's stride.

The pair traveled in silence for the next hour. The road was smooth, and the animals' pace was swift, but the clouds proved faster still. It wasn't long before the once-clear sky turned dark and overcast. Distant rumbles of thunder grew progressively louder and more sustained, and the clouds boiled black with rain. Jo and Braddoc kept to the winding Duke's Road, catching glimpses of Castle Kelvin through the trees every now and then and hoping to reach it before the clouds let loose.

In time, they rounded another curve of the road. Braddoc pointed at a walled gate not five minutes' ride away. "Ah, there's Castle Kelvin now," the dwarf said eagerly. "They've got a fair-sized merchants' quarters here on the north side. We should be able to find a decent room for the night and a place to stable the animals. Then we'll get an early start in the morning for Rifllian."

"I hope Brisbois hasn't left by the time we get there," Jo

said with an edge of anxiety in her voice.

"Doesn't matter," Braddoc replied gruffly, guiding his pony around a large rock in the road. "In the inn room tonight, we'll use one of the abelaat stones to pinpoint him. Doesn't matter where he goes, as long as we've got stones to spy on him."

"No," Jo said quietly. She kept her eyes focused on a spot between Carsig's ears.

"We can—" Braddoc continued, then abruptly stopped. "What did you say? Did you say no?"

"Yes, I did," Jo said quietly, still staring at Carsig's ears despite Braddoc's intent stare. "I said no. I will not use the crystals to find Brisbois."

"But why?" the dwarf's voice cracked an octave. "It makes perfect sense! We locate Brisbois through the crystal and then corner him. We'll know exactly where to find him, and we can make sure he doesn't escape!"

"I know," Jo said even more quietly. She shook her head, her red braid flapping forward. "But I won't do it."

"Why?" Braddoc demanded.

Jo glanced into the dwarf's good eye, then back to the road. "Because Karleah says she may be able to contact Flinn through the abelaat crystals . . . because I've only got a few crystals left." Jo's voice rose, and her hands drew Carsig's rein so tight the gelding was forced to carry his head too high. "Because I want to use every one of those crystals to talk to Flinn—" Jo choked on her words and clenched her teeth. The warm taste of blood reached her tongue, and she realized she'd bitten the insides of her cheeks. She loosened her grip on Carsig and bowed her head.

She could feel the dwarf's gaze upon her, and she knew Braddoc wanted her to look up at him. Jo ground her teeth. I can't! I can't! she thought. As much as I want revenge on those who betrayed and murdered Flinn, I want even more to talk to Flinn's spirit. Jo knew, without question, that Braddoc's plan for the crystals was much more sound than her own. Karleah Kunzay had told Jo there would be no guarantees, that the crystals would likely burst if she tried contacting the dead.

"Jo . . ." Braddoc began, then stopped. He said slowly, "I see we both have things we'd rather not talk about. Let's leave it at that."

Long moments passed, and Jo was roused from her misery by a sudden clap of thunder. She looked up. Dark storm clouds filled the sky, wind tossed the trees about them, and fat raindrops began to fall. Jo and Braddoc approached the gate to Castle Kelvin, and Jo felt relieved that they wouldn't sleep outdoors tonight. I hope we find a stable and an inn soon, she thought. She glanced again at the sky as a white-hot jag of lightning reached down from the cloud and clawed through the forest, filling the air with roaring thunder.

Jo looked over at Braddoc and smiled tentatively. The dwarf looked the other way. "Well," Jo said in an attempt at levity, "looks like we timed our arrival just right." She held up her hands as the rain started coming down harder.

The dwarf snorted and refused to look at Jo. "Look for an inn. I'm hungry, and I want a bath."

🐚 🐚 🐚 🐚 🐚

The man leaned back in the rough wooden chair and took a draw of the bitter, pungent ale in his mug. He rested one long, lanky leg on the corner of the equally rustic table before him, then crossed his other leg over the first. He surveyed the tips of his badly worn leather boots, the maroon so faded as to be a nondescript brown. The once-silver buckles were tarnished irreparably. He took another draw of ale, then looked about the tavern.

It was the foulest establishment he'd ever been in, barring none. The room was tiny; it housed only four tables, assorted chairs, and a short counter. A film of smoke hung in the air, making the tavern seem even more cramped and closed in. But the rain had started coming down hard, and he didn't have a place to stay tonight. The Elder Tavern seemed as likely a place as any to wait out the storm.

Besides, he might be able to shake the youth who'd been following him the better part of the day. He took another swallow of the bitter ale and grimaced.

The only other customers in the place were two old men. They were rolling and smoking some filthy weed as they played a game of stones. The stench of the smoke was overwhelming. Every now and then, one of the geezers would go into a hacking cough and spit phlegm onto the floor. Although a layer of sawdust covered the hard-packed dirt, the sawdust hadn't been changed since the day it had been laid out. Someone had added extra layers of sawdust and rushes throughout the years, and the floor had developed a strange, rolling appearance. One of the ancient men coughed again, this time spitting up blood as well as mucus. From some dark corner a scraggly dog came out of the shadows, wandered over to the bloody pile, and began snuffling.

The only woman in the place looked the man's way and caught his eye. He gave her a bold appraisal. Once truly a serving "girl," the woman was now a little mature for his tastes. She was also a trifle overblown, like a rose that had passed its perfection. He met the woman's eyes, and she smiled coyly. A little dimple played in her plump cheek, and she swayed back and forth ever so slightly.

It's been a while, he thought. Too long, in fact. He downed the rest of his ale and held up his mug, an inviting leer creeping to his lips. The woman smiled back readily. She slowly wiped her hands across her stained apron, pressing her short, fat fingers into the cloth to outline her bodily curves. She winked and smiled once more, then turned around seductively and picked up a small ale cask from behind the bar.

Come on, come on! the man thought. I don't want to be at the courting stage all night. Suddenly his attention was captured by the sound of the door scraping open and rain splashing on the threshold. Through the obscuring haze of smoke, he saw someone enter and close the door. The two old men never looked up from their game. The serving woman frowned, then put down the cask she'd picked up and began searching for the cleanest tankard.

He watched the figure enter the tiny tavern room, hesitate, then walk toward him. His eyes widened. It was the youth who'd been following him. Casually he moved his hand to the knife at his belt.

The thin, dirty urchin held out a slip of paper and said, "Here, this is for you. I was told to deliver it by a quarter of ten bells." When the man made no move to take the note, the boy placed it on the table. He turned around and, shying away from the serving woman, left the tavern.

The man stared at the stained slip of paper, lying crumpled on the coarse table before him. Should I? he wondered. How brave am I?

The woman retrieved the cask and walked over to the man, her hips swaying languorously. He glared at her, and she stopped walking. Her beaming face fell into lines of discontent and disillusion. The man's lip curled into a sneer. *Another five years for you, woman, and that expression you wear will be habitual*, he thought. *Maybe three.*

He turned his attention back to the paper, wondering if it could be magically trapped. It was so blotched and sodden, so crumpled by the waif's grip, that he thought it unlikely. Gingerly, he reached out and picked up the paper. It was folded into fourths. The man bent back the first fold and braced himself. He half expected some sort of explosion, but nothing of the sort happened. He stared at the paper and wondered if the next fold was trapped. If he hadn't been so damned curious, he might have never known.

With a cautious breath, he gently bent back the second fold. He winced as he did so and closed his eyes. Still no explosion, no trap of any kind. Using the surface of the table, he blindly smoothed the rough paper flat. Drawing another deep breath, he opened his eyes.

It was a simple note, and not the scroll-casted spell he had feared.

Come to the alley behind the rendering hall, just after ten bells. There, I will meet you.

The note was signed with a sigil reminiscent of a wild bull's horns. The man snarled. Then somewhere, faintly, he heard the first chime marking ten bells.

🐂 🐂 🐂 🐂 🐂

Waves of searing heat passed through him, purging every tissue of his unearthly body. Still his feet bore him across that place of flame, still he kept his mirrorlike eyes on the Immortal that guided him. And in place of the constant, dull thudding of his mortal heart, he felt the insistent words resound and repeat in his breast: *have faith, have faith, have faith.* . . .

With solid, reverent steps, Flinn followed on the heels of his patron, Diulanna. In life she had been his inspiration, and he had followed her immortal path. Now, in death, she led his soul across the tumbled, stony ground of this netherworld, led him through the cleansing fire. He had seen visions of others along the way, other Immortals he knew were the friends of his patron—Thor, the Thunderer, and Odin, known as the All Father. They had saluted Flinn on the path and he had saluted them back, remembering how he had called for their blessings on the battlefield. Now he knew his call had been answered.

It would not be long before he reached his final destination. It would not be long before he would again feel the earth of the mortal plane beneath his feet.

Chapter VIII

"I tell you, we're lost," grumbled Braddoc as he and Jo turned down yet another alley in the town surrounding Castle Kelvin. "And I don't know why we had to hostel the animals at the stable instead of the inn. We wouldn't have gotten lost like this if we had—" Braddoc pulled his cape's hood a little farther down his face "—and we wouldn't have gotten so soaked!"

"We aren't lost," Jo countered as she skirted a puddle and then stepped quickly through a veil of dripping water to get under an overhang. The streets of Kelvin were poorly lit in this part of town, and the late night and the rain added to the gloom. Jo suppressed a shudder. They had found a reputable hostel for Carsig and Onyx on the far side of Kelvin and then taken this shortcut back to their inn. The buildings surrounding her and Braddoc had deteriorated from pleasant, well-kept establishments to progressively harsher and seedier hovels. Gone were brightly painted signs proclaiming a business's name. Many of these buildings looked abandoned, and only one in every four or so boasted a number or name.

The smoke-darkened windows of the district glowed with only faint glimmers of candlelight, if any light at all. Jo felt fear grow inside her as the number of windows with candles decreased until the streets were utterly dark. She stretched her long legs a little more, hoping to find their way back faster. She tried to keep under roof overhangs as best she could. Braddoc followed close behind her, and she felt a measure of comfort at the dwarf's presence and low, continuous grumbles. Suddenly she stopped and gave him a brief hug, to his consternation. "I know how cities are laid out," Jo said reassuringly. "We're going to get back to the inn quicker this way. Trust me."

Tower chimes rang ten bells, their peals sounding tinny and hollow in this forsaken side of town. Jo wished they were back in the snug little inn Sir Graybow had recommended to them. She wanted to be clean and dry and sipping honey wine before a roaring fire.

Just beyond the glow of the next street lamp, Jo saw someone moving—the first living soul they'd seen for a long while. The man's shoulders were hunched over, and he was hurrying. Jo wondered if Kelvin had a curfew and whether they enforced it. She grimaced. Specularum had a curfew for the part of the city Jo had lived in. Of course, Jo thought wryly, no one willingly entered the slums to make certain it was kept.

"The inn's stable wasn't all that bad, Johauna," the dwarf said suddenly, perhaps to break the gloomy silence that had fallen on the pair.

Jo was grateful for the chance to talk. Kelvin was beginning to spook her. "Wasn't that bad?" she exclaimed nervously. "Why, did you see what was in that one nag's stall? Did you?"

As they crossed a street, the dwarf's good eye whirled

white in the light of a shuttered street lamp. "No . . ." he murmured.

Jo nodded vigorously. "It's a good thing you didn't, Braddoc. You would have been appalled. There was barely a fistful of corn mixed in with rice—*rice*, mind you! That's no way to feed a fine challenger like that. The rice'll expand and give him colic if his owner runs him hard tomorrow."

"You called the stallion a nag a moment ago," Braddoc said. An undercurrent of humor laced his words, and Jo spotted a gentle smile on his lips.

"Well, the horse *will* be a nag after a night in that stable," Jo retorted. "Either the rice or the sea hay the innkeeper put down for bedding—" Jo sniffed and then almost gagged. They were nearing a rendering hall. The smell of processed fat, entrails, and rotting animal parts rose in the wet air. Jo hurried her pace still more.

"Even so, you might have let us stable the animals there—we could have taken care of them ourselves, you know," Braddoc rumbled. The dwarf stepped into a deceptively small puddle and sank suddenly up to his knee. He jumped out quickly and cursed under his breath. He shook his wet leg and swore once more.

"What? And have that place charge us three times as much as an honest hostel would?" Jo demanded. She touched the knot of coins in her belt pouch, which she had securely fastened and concealed in the small of her back. She had caught many a cutpurses' act in Specularum. The young woman shook her head vehemently. "I'm not going to spend Sir Graybow's money by throwing it out the window at an inn like that—"

Sudden shouts, accompanied by the clang of steel on steel, interrupted Jo. She and the dwarf stopped abruptly, their hands leaping to their weapons; Jo was thankful she and Braddoc had stopped short of the lamplight. The sounds came from some distance away, though how far was difficult to say with the muffling rain. The shouts seemed to be coming from a dark alley. Jo wrinkled her nose. Next to the rendering hall, of course, she thought. She looked at Braddoc, who fixed his good eye on her and shrugged.

Sure, Braddoc, leave the decision up to me! she thought with a touch of dismay. Jo loosened one of the two tabs holding Wyrmblight into place. Her bow was back at the inn, but she also had her knife if the fight were in quarters too tight for Wyrmblight. The Immortals know I haven't mastered use of the great sword yet, Jo thought wryly, but maybe the thugs'll be scared by it and back off.

It was then that Jo knew what she was going to do. Her first impulse had been to run, to leave the hapless person to his or her problems. But that was a reflex she'd learned from the streets of Specularum. She was a squire now in the Order of the Three Suns. No, Jo thought firmly as she unleashed Wyrmblight. Briefly her finger stroked the blade's sigils, and she thought: The path to righteousness, to the Quadrivial, lies down that alley. She touched Braddoc's shoulder and pointed for him to take the left. Jo slid toward the right, keeping her back to the wall of the rendering hall.

Little light filtered through the rainy gloom into the alley. Fortunately, the way was clear of debris. Jo sidled down the alley, her fingers touching the coarse saw-cut boards of the building behind her for reassurance. She could just make out Braddoc's form less than five steps away. His battle-axe glinted once or twice. A faint light spilled into the alley from around the back corner of the

rendering hall, and Jo and Braddoc stopped just short of
the light.

From around the corner came shouts, curses, and cries
of pain mingled with the sounds of clashing weapons and
armor. Jo paused, trying not to breathe the foul air. She
wiped a few dripping strands of hair from her face and
wished the rain would stop. Jo was close enough to make
out words, and she heard one man yell, "Scurvy dog—!"
before the sickening thud of a club against flesh cut the
words short. His curse ended in a cry of distress. Jo waved
her hand at Braddoc, and then she and the dwarf stepped
around the corner and into the light.

The tableau that met Jo's eyes was one she had seen
many times in Specularum. Three men surrounded a
fourth. They were one of two things. Thieves? she
thought quickly. No, not in this part of town—nothing to
steal. Thugs then—thugs sent to do some sort of "persua-
sion."

The man in the center had fallen to his knees and was
doubled over in pain. His sword lay in the slick mud, rain
splattering down upon it and burying it. He reached out
to grab it. One of the other men—a big, burly brute of a
man, naked from the waist up—hit the injured man's hand
with a cudgel; Jo thought the beast was half ogre. The
wounded man screamed, and the two other men surrounding him raised their weapons. One carried a heavy,
ironbound staff, while the other had a sword.

Jo and Braddoc charged forward. Jo drew Wyrmblight
in a flashing arc over her head and shouted shrilly toward
the half-ogre, "Come on, you mole-brained monster!"
Braddoc meanwhile positioned himself between the
injured man and the two human thugs. One of them
pushed the other and yelled, "Run!" He leaped away, but

tripped on the injured man's sword and sprawled to the muddy ground.

The other ruffian jumped toward his comrade, warding Braddoc away with his brandished sword. The dwarf's teeth gleamed fiercely as he stepped nearer to the sword's tip. Scrambling to get up, the fallen thug ran headlong from the scene as his comrade swung his sword to engage the dwarf. Braddoc attacked, smashing the sword back with a solid swing of his axe and following through with a jab to the belly. The man stumbled backward a pace before returning the blow, his teeth gritted in a grim smile. Braddoc narrowly deflected the sword with the head of his axe and fell back to regroup, his hands stinging. He was just deciding to swing low for the bandit's vulnerable legs when he ran briefly against the half-ogre's tree-trunk calf.

Looking up, Braddoc saw with a startled gasp that Jo was swinging Wyrmblight in a horizontal arc toward the half-ogre's exposed belly. But the beast man was more nimble than he looked. In one quick motion, the half-ogre backed up and kicked the dwarf away from his foot as though he were kicking a small dog. As Braddoc crashed into a pile of crates on the opposite side of the alley, the tip of Wyrmblight cut shallowly into the half-ogre's fleshy stomach. Ignoring the gash, the nearly naked monster stepped toward Jo. He was close to eight feet tall and covered with coarse, wiry hair. Golden hoops dangled from his nose and ears. He snarled, and short tusks gleamed in the lamplight.

The half-ogre swung the cudgel and almost caught Jo across the jaw. She ducked just in time, nearly falling on the slick mud of the alley. The rain seemed to be tapering off, and she hoped that would prove a blessing. The brute is fast, she thought as she spun away from a second blow. So much for tales of slow, stupid ogres!

Catching a foothold on the slick cobbles, Jo swung Wyrmblight in a high, overhand arc. Again, the ogre stepped back to avoid the blow, but Jo had anticipated that. The razor-sharp tip of the sword dug easily into the top of the bulging belly and exited underneath. Blood spurted from the wound and hit Jo. A sudden wave of sick excitement swept over her, and she wanted to strike the ogre again. She felt momentarily repulsed at her own blood-lust, then pushed the thought aside. She swung Wyrmblight horizontally, aiming to split the brute's belly with one blow.

The half-ogre's cudgel landed squarely against her stomach, and a wheezing groan escaped Jo's lips. The stroke had sneaked past her guard and underneath her own stroke. Jo stumbled backward, feeling a pain in her side as she tried desperately to draw a breath. The rasping inhalation told her that her ribs were only bruised, not broken. Gamely, she held Wyrmblight before her, one hand on the pommel, the other clutching the blade in the center. Her eyes blinked rapidly, trying to see in the falling rain.

The brute stepped toward Jo and raised his cudgel. Jo gasped another breath and clutched the sword hilt with both hands, preparing for the blow. The cudgel came crashing down, catching the razor edge of Wyrmblight. The force reverberated through the sword, into Jo's hands, and on through her arms. In pain, Jo crumpled to her knees. If she'd had breath to spare, she would have screamed.

The half-ogre brought the cudgel up over his head, preparing the same blow to smash his adversary into the paving stones. He raised his hairy arms high overhead, and his bulging, bleeding belly shook. I can't survive another blow like the last one, Jo thought in desperation.

She drew Wyrmblight's pommel downward and flipped the tip up. The half-ogre's arms began to descend, the cudgel following. Jo grabbed Wyrmblight by the middle of the blade and thrust upward awkwardly. The blade's tip caught the half-ogre's belly and punctured through the exposed flesh. Jo stood and used the force of her body to thrust upward, twisting Wyrmblight as she rose. "For Flinn!" she muttered through bared teeth.

With a growling shriek, the half-ogre dropped his club, which glanced off Jo's shoulder. He staggered backward. Jo held on to Wyrmblight and watched in sudden, vicious satisfaction as the half-ogre's entrails stuck to the sword. The massive creature rolled unevenly to the ground and was still.

As she tugged Wyrmblight free from the viscera, Jo saw Braddoc Briarblood charge the remaining thug, the corner section of a crate still clinging raggedly to the dwarf's shoulder. Braddoc's battle-axe flashed, cleaving squarely into his adversary's elbow. Jo watched in morbid fascination as the forearm dangled from a bit of sinew before dropping with a thud to the muddy ground. The man blinked once, stupidly, then collapsed. Braddoc stepped forward and touched the thug's neck. Satisfied that he sensed no pulse, the dwarf turned to Jo.

"Are you all right?" Braddoc asked matter-of-factly.

Jo coughed a little and drew her breath. "Yes," she said, though her breath was labored. She leaned against Wyrmblight and stood a little straighter. Her breathing grew easier, and she looked past the half-ogre.

The thug who had been fighting Braddoc lay facedown in a puddle of bloody water, his sword beneath him. Jo

blinked, aware that the rain had finally stopped. At least
we won't have that to contend with on our way back to
the inn, she thought tiredly. She turned her attention to
the injured man she and Braddoc had rescued.

The man groaned and touched his bruised face. Jo put
her hand on Braddoc's shoulder for support, and the pair
approached cautiously. The man struggled to his feet,
holding his bleeding head. "Thank you," he said in a voice
hoarse with pain. "I don't know what I'd've done . . ."

As the man's face turned to the light, Jo's eyes went
wide. It's him! she thought wildly. He's shaved the moustache and goatee, but it's him! What's he doing in Kelvin?
He's supposed to be in Rifllian! Jo knew the answer even
as she finished the thought: The tiny village hadn't offered
enough interest to a lecherous miscreant like him. The
pain in her side throbbed, a roar filled her ears and
drowned out the rest of Brisbois's words, and Jo clenched
her teeth.

She stepped defiantly toward him and spat, "You!" Her
eyes flashed in rage. She let the man stare at her, let recognition dawn slowly in his hazel eyes, before her hand flew
out, slapping him brutally across the face.

🐺 🐺 🐺 🐺 🐺

The old she-wolf moved through the thick evergreens,
soft now with spring growth. The branches were gentle
on her scarred black hide, which was thin with the loss of
her winter pelt. She bent her head to the ground, every
now and then snuffling the wet needles. She whined, then
continued her search.

Karleah Kunzay pricked her ears at a minute noise, a
noise she would never have heard in human form. A

rabbit, her wolf senses informed her. She lifted her head and scented the air, casting about for the rabbit's location. A moment later she pinpointed its whereabouts; she focused her golden eyes on the underbrush before her.

Ah, there it is! Her wolf lips curled, rippling over canines still white and sharp. She lunged, and the chase was on. The cottontail, fat with spring food, dodged beneath a branch and scampered for denser cover. The wolf leaped the branch with no space to spare, conserving precious energy, and dived after the rabbit.

The cottontail veered to the left, and the old wolf smiled. A young one, she thought, and none too smart. A wilier rabbit would have headed right, toward the thorn bushes. This one had chosen the bottom lands near the stream. The wolf whined and panted as she raced after the rabbit. She'd catch it near the stream, for the undergrowth there was sparse and would offer little cover.

The rabbit broke through to open ground and squealed in fright. In a single bound the wolf caught up to her prey. She extended her jaws, her lips drawn back in a snarl. The young cottontail paused, trembling, for a moment, then kicked out with its strong back legs. The blow met the wolf squarely in the face, and Karleah rolled off balance into the soft spring earth.

She gained her feet and lunged toward the rabbit. Instantly the cottontail fled toward the stream, and the wolf snarled. Another mistake! thought Karleah. The young rabbit should have retreated to the dense brush. The old wolf leaped after the rabbit. The cottontail zigged and zagged, squealing in fear, but to no avail. The she-wolf's jaws snapped down on the soft flesh.

"Ouch! Karleah, that hurts!" The words came out in a funny, strangled hybrid of rabbit and Common. The wolf relaxed her powerful jaws and dropped the transforming Dayin Kine to the ground. His long ears shrank, his body grew, and his soft fur disappeared and was replaced by naked skin. Brown rabbit eyes gave way to the summer-sky blue irises of a young and innocent boy. He blinked and looked up at the wolf standing above him; the wolf panted heavily, her saliva dripping onto the boy's skin. He wiped it off hastily and made a face. "I hate it when you do that!" he complained.

The wolf sat down. Karleah looked at Dayin through her golden eyes, and her wolfish appetite whispered what a morsel the eleven-year-old boy would make. But she calmly ignored the lupine cravings.

"What'd you think, Karleah?" Dayin asked brightly. "Did I do good? It took you longer this time to catch me."

Karleah whined and prepared to speak. She had spent years learning how to contort her lips, tongue, and vocal cords in order to speak Common while in wolf form. She said slowly, painfully, "Better, yes, boy, but . . . still bad." The wolf whined again and licked her lips, striving for control. "Could have . . . killed you."

Dayin sat up and threw his arms around the old she-wolf. "Oh, Karleah!" he cried. "You'd never hurt me!" He ruffled the wolf's black fur and added, "Besides, I've got one of my spells back, and I would have used it on you. See?" The boy threw his hands up in the air, and a brace of white doves suddenly appeared above his head. They fluttered away to a nearby branch and peered down at the boy and wolf. He added happily, "And I get birds now, and not feathers. I never knew how to do my spells right until you showed me."

The wolf growled low, then let out a series of barks.

Dayin watched Karleah closely, trying to fathom the wolf language. He said, "I think I understand, Karleah. You want to know about my spell returning, right?"

"And . . . when," the wolf choked out the words in Common. Her tongue stuck, and it was a moment before Karleah could straighten it.

The boy lightly stroked Karleah's fur and then said, "It was either yesterday or the day before when I tried the spell again. You know how you asked me to try my failed spells several times a day?"

The old wolf nodded, and Karleah's mind drifted for a moment. It had been terrifying to discover at the dragon's lair that much of her spell-casting ability had been drawn away, and even more frightening that it hadn't returned by the time they'd reached the castle. The discovery of Dayin's inability to cast the only two spells he knew—producing doves or roses from thin air—had somewhat mollified Karleah. She'd begun to fear she'd grown too old for spell-casting.

In the sanctity of her valley, Karleah's ability to change into a wolf was the first power to return, as though its magic was somehow more deeply rooted in her being than the memorized spells she had lost. The return of that one ability almost made up for the loss of most of her other magical powers. Unable to teach Dayin anything other than the rudiments of magic, she concentrated on teaching him how to change into an animal, a power that could only be learned for a single animal. The wolf shook her head. Why the boy had chosen a rabbit to be the only animal he could transform into, she didn't know. Her wolf half reminded her that Dayin's choice had its advantages, and Karleah recalled the taste of rabbit hair. She whined a little.

"Well, I tried and tried and tried," Dayin answered. "And one day it just worked." The boy's face went blank with concentration, and then he threw up his hands a second time, this time clapping them. A shower of rose petals of all colors rained down on the boy and the wolf.

"'mpressive," the wolf said low.

Dayin shook his head. "I never get this spell right. I did this for Jo back in Flinn's cabin. Wanted whole flowers but all I got then was petals, too." He distractedly rubbed his arm.

The wolf, attracted by the boy's movement, instinctively sniffed at the inside of Dayin's elbow. Her lips curled back, and her cold nose nudged the boy, searching for his other elbow. Dayin, brow furrowing, let her sniff his other arm. Through her golden eyes Karleah saw for the first time the tiny, circular scars marking the boy's skin, scars several years old. Her sensitive wolf's nose quivered at the strange, lingering odor of the inner elbow's skin. The she-wolf growled and backed away, the hairs on her shoulders standing on end.

"Karleah?" Dayin cried. "What's wrong?"

"Dress," the wolf said. "Return . . . home, now." The black she-wolf turned and slipped away into the long-needled pines surrounding her. There was not even a whisper of noise to mark her passing.

The wolf loped through the trees populating Karleah's valley. She wandered her territorial range, stopping now and then to leave her scent. She had to work off a little of the terrible excitement that had gripped her at the sight of the boy's scars. An answer to what had stolen her magic was beginning to fall into place, to congeal in her mind, but she was still missing some vital clue to complete the explanation. The she-wolf whined in impatience as she continued her roaming. The answer was there, if she could only find it! Finally, footsore and weary—forgetful of the hunger that had gripped her—she headed back into the valley that sheltered her home.

Her wolf paws rustled through the evergreen vail vine, a creeping plant that provided Karleah's valley with its first line of defense. Would-be trespassers were caught by the tenacious vines, which telepathically transmitted images of the captives' lives to Karleah. Flinn, Jo, Braddoc, and Dayin had all entered her valley last winter. Even in winter the vines had yielded complete information of everyone— except Jo, whose blood had been tainted by that of the abelaat. The wolf growled low, sensing a piece of her puzzle before her.

The old wolf stopped, scratched her ear, and yawned. Think! The answer's here, she admonished herself. Jo had been bitten by an abelaat, a beast from another world. Karleah mused. There was a certain advantage to living through such an attack: the poison in the creature's saliva rendered the person immune to most forms of scrying or other magical detection. The vail vines hadn't registered Jo's presence because, to them, she wasn't even there.

Knowing she was on the verge of discovering the final clue, Karleah moved on, her paws rustling through the vines. She stopped suddenly. Her wolf brows wrinkled in a semblance of a human frown. The vines, she thought, why, the vines told me nothing of Dayin, either!

The wolf leaped forward, intent on reaching home. She entered the thick grove of pines that surrounded her cabin. The web of magic she had long ago spun in these woods still remained strong, enfolding her house in other-worldly shrouds of darkness and silence. As she plunged into the magically warded woods, the spells took effect;

Karleah was suddenly lost in a world without sight or sound. As often as she had passed through this enchanted grove, Karleah was still troubled and dizzied by the black silence. She sympathized with first-time visitors to her home. Only through long practice could she now cut straight through the grove to her cottage without getting trapped by the magicks; those who stumbled into the woods uninvited wandered about in endless, panicked circles, unable to find a way out. Some few, truly despicable folk, had actually starved in that small woodland.

The old she-wolf emerged from the inky region of the pines into a bright, sunlit glade. There her home stood, a cottage built of stone with a thatched roof and two tiny windows. The door was open and waiting in welcome.

Karleah willed herself to shapechange. Her arms and legs grew longer, the wolf hair dropping to the forest floor and disappearing with a slight snap. Her tail disappeared. Her muzzle shortened while simultaneously her head grew rounder and took on a human cast. She took a step forward on what had been her forepaws, and almost fell over. Karleah looked down at her human hands and frowned. "I hate when that happens," she grumbled.

Beside the door, she had left her shapeless gray shift, which was ornamented with basswood twigs. She pulled it over her ancient, shriveled body, then picked up the staff she'd left behind as well. She never worried about the possibility of it coming to harm in her valley. There were wards aplenty to keep out those who might lust after such a staff of power. "Not that anyone'd want you now," Karleah grumbled aloud to the staff, "since you seem virtually useless." She ran her fingers across the smooth wood, noticing that only a few faint runes remained on the aged surface of the staff.

Dayin came and stood in the doorway. He looked at the wizardess, expecting her to repeat the comment she'd made almost every day since returning to the valley. She didn't disappoint him.

"Look at this!" she croaked, holding out the beautifully carved oak staff. It was appointed with plain bronze bands, which bound its ends. Dayin moved closer, hoping to see that some of the thin runes had reappeared in the staff's wood, but fearing that more had disappeared. Karleah had quite a number of spells stored thus in the staff—or she had before escaping Verdilith's lair.

"Look at this!" she said again, waving the staff. "It barely radiates any magic! It's still drained! If you've gotten your spells back, you'd think my staff would've, too!" The old woman complained bitterly.

"How about your personal spells?" Dayin asked. He took Karleah's arm and helped her enter the small cabin.

The old woman leaned her staff against the rough-hewn table that stood to the left of the door and snatched up a charm that lay on a bench beside it. Plodding distractedly forward, she sat down in her rocker, the only comfortable piece of furniture in the cramped confines, and set her feet on another bench. The fire had fallen to embers in the fireplace, but the room was plenty warm. The old wizardess's eyes traced longingly over the pots, jars, and pouches that cluttered the mantle, and the sheaves of herbs dried hanging from the rafters overhead.

"No, not a one of my spells has come back," she said sadly, rubbing the charm between aged fingers. "I suppose I'm more an herbalist than a mage anymore."

"But I was drained, too," Dayin offered, "and now I'm back to fine." He handed the old wizardess a cup of tea and then sat down at her feet.

"Yes, and I think I know why, too," Karleah rejoined. "Dayin, roll up your sleeve and hold out your arm. I want to look at those scars again." The boy silently complied, and Karleah stroked his tender skin with her gnarled, bony fingers. She grunted. "These scars are old. Do you remember how you got them?"

Dayin shook his head. "No, I didn't even know I had them." He touched his skin and peered at the pale spots. "But what've these to do with your spells?" he asked curiously.

Karleah leaned back and looked at the boy. Once you would have asked that with fear and impatience, she thought. It's good to see that you are becoming more courageous, more self-assured. She leaned forward and ruffled his hair.

"Tell me about your father, Dayin," Karleah countered. "Tell me all that you remember about his making the abelaat crystals. You thought he died in an explosion, didn't you?"

"Yeah—at least he disappeared then," Dayin said with a shrug. The boy's eyes were distant and blank, as though he were once again viewing the events of the time, but from a safe distance. "There was an explosion, yes, and it ruined our tower. Then my fath—the man disappeared. I searched and waited, but he never showed up." Again the shrug. "Of course I thought he was dead . . . and to me he is. When he changed his name to Teryl Auroch, when he became an evil wizard, my father died." Dayin's blue eyes gazed squarely at Karleah, and she saw deep hurt lingering behind the blankness there.

Karleah pulled the boy into her thin arms. She gave him a swift hug, then pushed him away. "There's work to be done, boy," she said huskily, "and no time for that." She leaned back in the rocker. "Now. Tell me about the crystals."

The boy frowned. "That was such a long time ago, Karleah. I've told you all I remember," he said. "Can't you use that vail-vine charm on me to find out? You know, the one you told me about that makes people tell the truth?" He looked at the wizardess.

Karleah rested her elbows on her knees and put her chin on her cupped palms. She'd made a vail-vine charm hundreds of years ago, back in the days when she constructed magical things. Maybe it was still around. Without a word, Karleah stood and began rifling through the shelves and cabinets that lined the walls of her cabin.

She remembered the amulet because she'd crafted it with such care. She'd arranged three vail-vine leaves, cast them in copper, and then enshrined the leaves inside the pale heart of the original vail-vine mother plant. Over the years, she'd brushed the charm with a mixture concocted of concentrated vail-vine fluid, other powerful truth serums, and substances she'd long since forgotten. The mother vail vine eventually encased the amulet with woody plant growth, and Karleah had all but forgotten about it. Then, one day, she'd come across a strange, tuberous growth on the vine. She removed it, and inside found the charm, now the essence of a vail vine's power. But the amulet was attained at a cost; the mother vine died.

Karleah snapped her fingers and reached for a round wooden hatbox stored on top of her hutch. She pulled the box down, then hesitated. With trembling fingers she lightly stroked the still-elegant moire satin that lined the outside of the box. The color had faded from a rich plum to a nondescript gray. Karleah muttered to herself, "Stop acting like a doe-eyed fawn. That was years ago. Memories of him can't hurt you."

"Who, Karleah?" Dayin asked. He came and stood beside the wizardess as she set the box on the table.

Karleah ignored the boy. She took off the box's cover. Inside was a tissue-thin, patterned cloth. The wizardess pulled back the material to reveal a round hat of white velvet. Above its tiny brim was wrapped a feather of exquisite azure beauty. A multifaceted diamond graced one side.

Dayin caught his breath in awe. "Is it . . . magical?" he asked breathlessly.

Karleah snorted. "Not hardly," she answered crisply, "and that's what makes it all the more special." She reverently set the hat aside, then reached into the box and pulled out the remaining item. It was the vail-vine amulet. Karleah eyed its tarnished leaves, its once shiny copper now covered with a dull green patina. The gold chain it hung from had fared better, for it still shone. She smiled and said, "Well, the green's more appropriate for a vine amulet anyway."

Dayin squinted in concentration. "What does it do? And what do I do?"

"Nothing," the old woman said. She placed the chain over the boy's head and then looked into Dayin's eyes. "You have a choice, child," she said slowly. She pointed to the first leaf. "If I stroke this first leaf, you and I together will see what I wish to know. At least I hope so. My charm may not be strong enough."

Karleah pointed to the middle leaf. "If I touch this leaf, I will discover what I wish to know without your reliving the incident. And the third leaf will reveal information to me of someone nearby—without their knowing." Karleah paused and looked at the amulet. "At least I think that's how it went; I'm not sure any more." She shrugged and said, "Quite a clever piece of work, if I do say so myself. Which will it be, boy? Do you want to remember what I wish to discover, or would you prefer to be untouched by all this?"

The boy's eyes grew wide with fear and confusion. "If . . . if I don't have to know what's going on, I'd like that, please," he said, his voice quavering. Then his lips puckered. He said quietly, "I know that's not very brave of me—"

Karleah nodded and cut Dayin off, saying, "All right, child, I understand. Perhaps that'd be for the best. I have my doubts if the charm has any power anyway. Even if it did, it might not even work—I've never used it before. Just stand there, and the charm'll do the rest." Karleah began to slowly stroke the central verdigris leaf. She looked into Dayin's eyes and let her mind open up. Channeling her thoughts through the amulet, she gently eased Dayin's mind open as well.

The old woman had a sneaking suspicion about what had caused Dayin's scars, and she wasn't surprised when her charm met resistance in the boy's blood. Karleah's wrinkles deepened, and the lines about her mouth puckered into a grimace. Her suspicions were growing stronger, but she wanted proof—absolute proof. She reached farther into Dayin's psyche, using the amulet to probe more specifically and perhaps bypass the toxin in the boy's blood that clouded her scrying.

Karleah stared deeply into Dayin's blue eyes, unaware that her own black ones almost sank into the folds of her face. The memory she wanted lay there, just beyond her reach. She struggled to grasp it, her mind carefully pushing past the veils of thought. Her eyes locked mercilessly with his, and her finger continued to stroke the center leaf of the charm. With a controlled sigh, she began also to stroke the first leaf. She needed the boy's help.

Pain exploded inside Karleah's mind. Pain from a giant, eight-fanged maw biting into a child's tender arm. Pain from the searing track of poisonous spittle, coursing through a small body. Karleah stepped backward, unable to bear the agony of the piercing fangs any longer. She dropped heavily into her chair and looked up at the boy.

Dayin's face was devoid of color, as if his very blood had been drained away. His eyes stared blankly like huge saucers, wide and brimming with pain. Karleah inwardly rebuked herself for forcing the experience on the boy. She opened her mouth to say something, but Dayin spoke up.

His voice was barely a whisper. "My—my father . . ." Dayin stuttered, "he brought in that creature and let it . . . let it feed off me, didn't he?" Dayin's eyes blinked blearily, and he rubbed his arms. "And he—he made crystals with my blood. Crystals for him to see through. And—and he kept healing me, so that he could make more crystals. He—he healed me with herbs . . . the same herbs he gave to Flinn to heal Jo. I never knew how I knew. . . ." The boy began to shake.

Karleah took Dayin in her arms. There was nothing she could say, nothing she could feel but horror and compassion.

Chapter IX

"I tell you, I'm innocent!" Brisbois yelled. He wiped the blood from his lip with the back of his hand and glared at Johauna Menhir, standing before him. The man swayed and almost slipped on the wet ground, and Jo tensed. Fall! she thought viciously. Fall so I can kick you! Brisbois held his left arm awkwardly to his side and said hoarsely, "I had nothing to do with—"

"Liar!" Jo shouted and slapped his battered face again. This time he did fall to the slick ground. She lifted her foot to crush his hand.

"Ease off, Johauna," the dwarf said, pulling her aside. "The man's hurt."

Jo rounded on Braddoc. She grabbed the dwarf's shoulder and shook him as hard as her bruised ribs would allow. "How can you say that, Braddoc? This man agreed to be Flinn's bondsman, then attacked us! He—"

Braddoc gripped Jo's arm. His fingers tightened so hard that Jo cried out in pain. "*He* didn't attack us—Auroch did!" Braddoc said intently.

Jo wrenched her arm free, her eyes blazing at the dwarf.

An ugly sneer distorted her lips. "He stood by while we all battled Auroch's tornado of fire! What more do you want?" her voice rose shrilly. Jo started to tremble, but clenched her teeth and forced the impulse down.

Braddoc put his hands on her arms and forced her to look at him. He murmured, "Johauna . . . killing Brisbois isn't going to bring back Flinn."

Jo choked back a sob. Her eyes blinked rapidly. I will not cry! I . . . will . . . *not!* she thought harshly. Image after image of Flinn flooded her mind. She saw again the icy street of Bywater on the day she'd heard the children taunting Flinn, "Flinn the Fallen! Flinn the Fool!" She saw the lines of pain in his darkened face as he haltingly told her of his fall from grace. She saw the glory that shone brightly in his eyes when he was reunited with Wyrm-blight. She saw his crimson, crumpled form, couched in a well of bloody snow.

Stepping backward, Jo held up her hand and shook her head. She looked from Braddoc to Brisbois, lying on the ground, and she fought down the urge to kick the man. Her heart filled with hate. "I say we kill him," she hissed. "I'll tell Sir Graybow we couldn't find him—"

"I tell you, I'm innocent!" Brisbois interrupted hoarsely, a touch of fear behind the bravado. One side of his face was swollen almost beyond recognition. He shifted, struggling to rise from the mire, then winced as his left arm dangled awkwardly. "I didn't attack Auroch in the castle because I knew it wouldn't do any good! I—"

"Quiet, cur!" Jo fell to her knees beside Brisbois and held up her hand menacingly. She ignored the stabbing ache in her side. Her ribs would heal; her heart would not.

"Let him speak, Johauna!" Braddoc barked suddenly. Jo

turned to him and opened her mouth to put the dwarf in his place, but Braddoc said tightly, "Think a moment what you're doing here, Johauna. Think! Sir Graybow trusted you to carry out a mission of retrieval, not vengeance. If you kill him now—whether he deserves it or not—you'll be betraying your oath to the baroness . . . and to Graybow!"

Johauna stood slowly and ruthlessly quelled the remorse his words inspired. She poked Braddoc's chest and said angrily, "*You* think for a moment who falsely accused Flinn, who goaded those knights to drag him down and beat him. *Think?*"

Braddoc seized Jo's hand and gripped it against his chest. In the faint lamplight that illuminated the back of the rendering hall, he stared at Jo. His white eye gleamed, and for one awful moment Jo wondered what he *could* see with it. "Listen to me!" the dwarf said urgently. "Verdilith was behind all that—"

Jo rebuked, "Brisbois denies being charmed by the dragon! He says—"

"If Verdilith could charm Flinn's own wife into defaming Flinn, he could certainly charm Brisbois into doing the same," Braddoc said as he released Jo's hand. The squire took a step back.

"Yeah?" she said, angrily rubbing her hand. "So what's your point?" Little flecks of spittle accompanied her last word.

Braddoc rubbed his beard. "My point—" he began.

Jo shook her head and made a chopping motion with her hand. "He *betrayed* Flinn!" she interrupted the dwarf. "He gave his word as bondsman to Flinn that he would act in his behalf for one year!" Jo stalked over to Brisbois, still lying on the ground. In one swift gesture, she grabbed his

clothing and yanked him to his feet. Her hands clutched
his collar, and her gray eyes flashed at him. "And the first
chance you had, you escaped with your friend Teryl
Auroch! No serving as bondsman for you!" She released
him roughly, backed a step away, and spat at the knight's
feet, hoping to trigger a fight.

Through puffy eyes Brisbois glared back at the young
woman, ignoring the spittle. "That's where you're wrong."
He ground the words out reluctantly, cradling his injured
arm to his side.

Jo stared at the man, her eyes incapable of blinking. "If
you hadn't left him," she breathed, "it might have been
you who'd died instead of Flinn!" She sneered. "Because
you're in cahoots with—"

"I'm not in league with Auroch! I never have been. I
hate the man," Brisbois snarled, "and I can prove it!" His
eyes remained on Jo's face as he carefully pulled out a
piece of coarse paper. He handed it to her.

Johauna stared at the paper, at the bloody fingerprints
Brisbois left on it. She opened it up and read aloud to
Braddoc, "'Come to the alley behind the rendering hall,
just after ten bells. There, I will meet you.' And then
there's the sigil of a bull's horn." Jo's eyes glittered at Brisbois. She lifted one eyebrow and said smoothly, "The sign
of Auroch, no doubt."

"Yes," Brisbois spat out. "He spirited me away against
my will when . . . when he left your chambers at the
castle. . . . I escaped him, but he's been hounding me ever
since. I thought . . . I thought I could perhaps bargain
with him in the alley . . . make him leave me alone. But
he . . . he sent those thugs to kill me." The man's voice
came in ragged gasps.

Jo held up the note. "Oh? So you think the fact that

you'd bargain with Auroch should make us trust you?" she asked angrily. She threw the note down into the muddy water at her feet and stepped on it, twisting the paper into the ground with her heel.

Braddoc took a step toward Brisbois, who was on the verge of collapse. The disgraced knight weakly waved Braddoc away. "Let me finish," Brisbois said, his words not much more than a whisper. "Jo. You're smarter than this. You just want a scapegoat for your anger."

Jo winced at the man's familiarity and clenched her hand. "Watch your tongue, Brisbois," she snapped.

"Auroch's been hunting me," Brisbois continued with some exertion. "I know too much about him—I compromise his safety. He'd've found me sooner, too, if I'd not bought this amulet from a backstreet mage I know . . ." He pointed to a simple pendant hanging from his grimy neck. "And I've kept moving, too, to . . . to throw him off track. Still, his goons found me fast enough. They . . . they sent me that note, and I . . . I thought I could maybe cut a deal. . . . I couldn't run forever." The man paused and then said, "Cut a deal, or kill him."

"Only Auroch had the same plan," Braddoc noted stiffly.

Brisbois nodded his swollen head. Brisbois looked at Jo and began to tremble. He took a breath of air through lips so swollen they could hardly open.

Johauna looked from Brisbois to Braddoc and back to the knight. Her mouth curled into a sneer, and she said, "You bastard liar." She spat in Brisbois's face.

"That's enough!" Braddoc roared. He grabbed Jo's arm and dragged her a few steps away. The dwarf stared at her, twitches of anger working across his features. "Johauna, I'm ashamed of you! *Ashamed,* do you hear?" As if to reinforce his words, he took his hand off the young woman's arm.

Enraged, Jo tore into the dwarf. "He's lying, you fool! He'd say anything to avoid going back to the castle! He'd kill Auroch to save his hide, and he'd kill us, too."

Braddoc waved his hand. "The man would have died here if we hadn't happened—"

"He faked it! He's faked it all!" Jo shouted. "Somehow he knew we were here! He hired those thugs—"

"Excuse me," Brisbois said in a whisper that cut through the humid air. He tried unsuccessfully to raise his hand. "I don't mean to interrupt . . . your decision of my fate," he said, his eyes whirling in his head, "but I think I . . ." Brisbois's expression went blank, a mocking smile seeming to curl about his battered lips, and he crumpled to the wet ground.

"I *knew* this would happen! I just *knew* this would happen!" Braddoc fumed. He handed Jo his battle-axe and knelt by the injured man. Jo refused to move; she watched in stony silence as Braddoc checked Brisbois. "His arm's broken—thankfully not his sword arm—and he's got a lot of bad bruises. His face looks awful." Braddoc stood and began gathering the man's lanky body over his shoulder.

Jo licked her lips, and her eyes narrowed. The wind shifted a little, and the stench of the rendering hall hit her full in the face. "Throw him into the dead animal pen," she said brutally. "Tomorrow he'll be a candle—not a traitor." Her lips pulled downward.

"Wish I had a *real* squire to give me a hand," Braddoc barked unexpectedly. "I'm bringing this man back to the inn. He may or may not be innocent, but he *is* injured. You can either stay here and pout or join us." The dwarf grunted as he shifted Brisbois's body on his shoulder.

Braddoc started walking away, back through the alley they had entered.

Unmoving, Jo watched Braddoc sway as he disappeared past the lamplight's range. Her glimpse of Brisbois saw his broken arm swing loose from the dwarf's hold. The arm jerked and dangled, moving unnaturally. The squire smiled coldly, and her eyes didn't blink. For a long time she continued to stare after the pair, her expression frozen, until she could no longer hear Braddoc's shuffling gait.

The squire turned away, then suddenly raised her fists to the sky. She threw her head back and cried in rage, "*Fliiinnnn!*"

The rain began again to fall.

ᵮᵃ ᵮᵃ ᵮᵃ ᵮᵃ ᵮᵃ

Karleah entwined her fingers together and then stretched out her arms, cracking her knuckles and her elbow joints simultaneously. Granting the boy a sidelong glance, she began to rummage through a basket of dried herbs on the table before her. As her fingers slipped among the dried stalks and tightly woven bags, the old woman peered up at the boy through her bushy brows. It was on the tip of her tongue to say, "You've grown," but Dayin's expression was too sad and confused for such an innocuous observation.

"What are you looking for, Karleah?" Dayin asked quietly. His sky-blue eyes were shadowed with pain, but he hadn't cried. There was an edge to his gaze that had been lacking this morning. Karleah wondered if the boy would ever cry again.

"Let me present a puzzle to you, boy." Her long fingers delicately pulled the orcbane from the feverfew. "Let's see if you get the same answer I did. Sit down."

"What's this puzzle about, Karleah?" Dayin asked, a tinge of interest coloring his voice. His eyes shone a little brighter.

Karleah frowned as she stared at the boy. "Why do you suppose the dragon brought useless wands of power with him to his fight with Flinn?" she asked. "Verdilith knew he and Flinn would fight; he knew Flinn would finally join him in the glade where they had first fought many years ago. So why did the dragon bring useless gadgets along? And why did he refrain from casting his own spells? Tell me, Dayin."

The boy stared at Karleah and then blinked twice. He shook his head and said, "They must've been drained, just like your spells were drained." Dayin paused, waiting for Karleah to say something. She remained silent, and he continued, "So whatever drained the spells must be in the glade where they fought, or in the dragon's lair itself."

"Almost right," Karleah replied, amused at the boy's sincerity but gratified to see that he was working out the puzzle on his own. "Where were my spells drained, in the glade or in the lair?"

"The lair," Dayin blurted, sudden recognition breaking over him, "so whatever was draining magic must have been in the lair, right?" The boy stopped, his blue eyes clouding a little.

Karleah nodded and said, "Yes, Dayin?" Let the boy work it through, she told herself.

"But that's not quite right, either," Dayin said suddenly. He propped his chin with his hand. "Because I wasn't ever *in* the lair, and I lost my spells, too. And you lost more spells after we left the lair; your staff kept being drained, even after we got to the castle."

Karleah played with a forget-me-not twig, then looked at the boy. "And . . . ?" she queried.

Dayin's brows knit again. "And . . ." he said slowly, then his brows rose, "and so that means somehow I've been near whatever drained you and the wands of magic. It must have been something that attached itself to you in the cave. . . . Something like dust, or water, or spores . . ."

". . . or treasure," Karleah nudged impatiently.

Stunned, the boy stared at the wizardess. "Do you think all that stuff works like a magic magnet, Karleah? Sucking out enchantments from everything the treasure comes near?"

Marshaling her patience, Karleah responded gently, "You saw all the things Jo and Braddoc brought from the lair. Tell me about them."

Dayin's eyes wandered to the ceiling. "Jo had a really pretty opal, I remember, and a crown with some blue gems on it. She had lots of coins, a weird dagger, some pearly things . . ."

"And Braddoc?" Karleah coaxed.

"Braddoc had, let me see, a jeweled dagger that you could hide stuff inside the hilt. And he had a giant goose egg encrusted with gold and gems." Dayin pointed suddenly at Karleah. "Oh! And a box! That funny box that wouldn't open!"

Karleah smiled, touched her nose with one finger, then reached out and touched Dayin's. "You've got it, Dayin! Dragons hoard treasures of great value. All the objects you mentioned would fetch a fortune in the marketplace—all except that plain iron box. It had to have some reason for being there, some great value to the dragon, and I think drawing magic must be what it is."

"Are you sure, Karleah?" Dayin said, suddenly discouraged. "It was awfully plain—just iron and all that."

"Ah, but you saw what happened when Braddoc tried to open that 'simple' box," Karleah rejoined. "There's much more to that box than meets the eye, my boy."

"But the box didn't even seem magical . . ."

"Of course not," Karleah replied, a bit more harshly than she intended. "It's antimagical. It somehow acts as a magnet for magic and draws it out of anything that is near it." She smiled at Dayin, well pleased at his deductive powers. "So, the riddle is solved." Dayin responded to her keen-edged smile with a look of concern. "Don't worry about it; I'll have Braddoc drop it in the bottom of a deep gorge in the Wulfholdes. That should . . ." Karleah's words trailed off as the boy's expression of concern deepened into one of horror. "Dayin?" Karleah asked worriedly.

Dayin shook his head. "K-Karleah!" he whispered. "Didn't Braddoc say in his message—? Didn't he give the box to a mage at the castle, since he couldn't open it? Didn't he?"

Karleah stared at Dayin. She scratched her lower lip with her strong white teeth. Finally she said, "Well, I'll be damned." The crone shook her head, then grabbed her staff and used it to stand. "Saddle up, boy. We've a trip to make."

ⁱⁿ ⁱⁿ ⁱⁿ ⁱⁿ ⁱⁿ

"Stand away from the window."

The noise came from somewhere behind him. Verdilith couldn't make out who might be speaking, nor did he try. The words were simply part of the dull roar of pain that sometimes hummed and most often screamed through his fragmented mind. Pain. It was both curse and blessing to him. It wouldn't leave him, not even long enough to let him sleep. But, by its very intensity, it defined the core of his being—it kept his mind from dissipating on the wind. He cradled his maimed arm, watching with mild delight as his body restlessly changed from the form of Lord Maldrake to that of the blacksmith . . . of Brisbois . . . of the pitch squire . . . of Teryl Auroch. He had neither the will nor the attention to keep any form for long. Besides, surely his transformations unnerved the speaker behind him.

"I said stand away from the window! You'll be seen."

Verdilith didn't know who spoke, and he didn't care. He only knew that it wasn't Wyrmblight.

Wyrmblight.

If there was a name for his pain, it was *Wyrmblight*. It grated on him that the sword still remained, out there in the hands of a fool, out there, ready to strike from the darkness. The sword haunted him. The thought of the four runes, glowing and bright, burned like brands into his spasming mind.

Through human ears—Maldrake's ears, to be precise—the dragon heard the noise again. "Maldrake! For the last time, *get away from that window!* I don't want anyone to see you."

Verdilith turned his head toward the sound. It was the paltry human speaking, the mage who called himself Maloch Kine . . . and Teryl Auroch. Ah, yes, his "rescuer" from the Knights of Penhaligon, the dragon's friend and master. But Verdilith knew Auroch's true motives—it was Auroch who had given him the box that ate magic, Auroch who had drained his power, Auroch who had made him vulnerable to the sword. Soon, Verdilith would have his revenge. But first, he would accompany the mage, play his games long and well. Only then would he gain a magical means to break the damned-blessed blade.

Verdilith withdrew from the window into the inn room
He walked with shuddering steps toward the mage, pas
the bed where he had spent the last week in sleepless fits
past the mage's tables crowded with magic paraphernalia
Jars and vials and tubes bubbled with Auroch's foul con
coctions, the smell of which was sweet to Verdilith. Surely
with the aid of these accoutrements, Auroch could devise
some magical means of destroying the hated sword
Indeed, Verdilith wondered if the man already had th
means. But Auroch would surely force the dragon throug!
a maze of lies before providing any solution. Such was th
way with Auroch: everything he spoke was a lie, especiall
his offers of healing.

"Maldrake? Won't you sit down?"

Concentrating to retain the form of Maldrake, Verdilit!
forced his spinning mind to focus on that little room, o
the little man that still called to him. As his vision cleared
Verdilith let his human face twist into a small, almos
polite, smile. He approached the withered old mage and
felt the wound across his arm burn like acid. But h
allowed no sign of agony to show on his face, his gree!
eyes gleaming wide and eager. He took the proffere
chair, greedily scanning the bubbling beakers.

"My men should have finished with Brisbois."

Verdilith glared at the mage through slitted eyes. For
moment, Auroch stepped back, away from the intens
gaze. The dragon let a small plume of poisonous ga
escape from Maldrake's nose.

"Why didn't you simply kill Brisbois yourself?" h
hissed. Remembering the reason for tolerating Auroch
the dragon added politely, "Such a thing would be simpl
for you."

Auroch at first made no reply, turning as a beaker cradled above a small burner begin to boil. He removed the glass container with his bare hand and placed it inside a small wooden black box. As the mage placed another beaker atop the flame, he said, "Brisbois is a mere mouse in the house. I'm far more interested in the master."

Verdilith let Maldrake's head nod slightly, again scanning the room. He was familiar with magic and its creation, but did not recognize any of the mage's devices. The items Auroch toyed with seemed not of this world, as alien as the box that ate magic. "Ah, and I assume that the master you refer to is me."

"Of course you assume so," Auroch replied with a hint of annoyance in his voice.

Verdilith shifted uneasily in his chair, but the wound on his side rubbed against the leather. It was as though Wyrmblight itself were jabbing him, reminding him of his torment. "Surely we agree, human, that you desire to keep me within your grasp."

"So that I may heal your wounds, Maldrake, so that I may heal your wounds," Auroch appeased smoothly. "These things you see about you—"

"Are part of your self-promoting machinations," Verdilith interjected mildly. "As, you think, am I. And now you wish to blackmail me into carrying out your schemes."

The magician lightly dropped the tools he was using onto a table, frowning in irritation. He ran fingers through his thick hair and sat down heavily in a chair behind the table. After a moment, he sighed and raised his eyes.

"What is it you want?" he asked leadenly.

Verdilith would not allow himself to be fooled by the human's theatrics. The man was too powerful, too otherworldly to be so affected by the dragon's moods. Clearly,

Verdilith was pivotal to Auroch's plans to destroy all things magic. But Verdilith didn't care if Auroch would engulf the world in flames, as long as Wyrmblight, the sword blessed to destroy him, were first shattered.

"You know what I want, Auroch. And to get it, you know I will do what you want," he softly replied, letting another trail of poison seep from his lungs through the body of Maldrake. He was lying. He cared nothing for the mage's desires.

"You distrust me," Auroch noted calmly.

"Return my magic, and I will return my trust," Verdilith replied.

Auroch nodded, as if to himself, and stood. He turned to a large cabinet directly behind him. "Restoring your magic is a feat I cannot perform. But to prove my good intentions to you, I shall give you what you desire *before* you ever act on my behalf." He made a gesture with his left hand, and there was a loud click from the cabinet's door, which swung partially open. Verdilith tried to peer inside, but his wounded side forced the air from his body. A small trail of venom dropped from Maldrake's lips and fell on the floor. The rug burned.

The sorcerer closed the door with another gesture and placed a long, reddish gemstone on the table. The stone, about the length of Auroch's shaking hand, rattled heavily on the wooden tabletop, and its edges flashed a sinister light in the mage's eyes.

"I have no use for riches," Verdilith muttered, eyeing the shimmering gem. "Your 'rescue' deprived me of a hoard worth more than a million such stones."

"Doesn't the shape look familiar?" Auroch teased, running a finger along the edge of the stone. "The shape and the color?"

"An abelaat stone?" Verdilith asked in a growling voice. "What good is that for destroying Wyrmblight?"

"Not an abelaat stone," Auroch corrected, smiling evilly, "but an artifact fashioned to *look* like an abelaat stone."

"What good is that?" Verdilith repeated, purposely spewing noxious breath into Auroch's face.

"This stone will give you a window on the progeny of Flinn—on Squire Menhir, the bearer of Wyrmblight. You will know everywhere she goes, every word she speaks. You will learn every secret of the blade she bears, of its magnificent strengths, of its one, great weakness."

Verdilith eyed the softly glowing gem. "What weakness? I clutched that sword between my own fingers and wrenched it against stone, but it would not break."

"Every weapon has its weakness," Auroch replied, "just as every man does. You found Flinn's weakness in his glory and relentless pride . . . and his wife, Yvaughan."

"Yes," Verdilith mused, gently stroking his maimed arm. "But I could speak directly to the mind of Flinn, plant the seeds of destruction in him."

"You can speak to the squire through this stone, too," Auroch said, lifting the gem from the table and setting it gently in Verdilith's hand. "You can take the form of Fain Flinn and appear to her in the stone."

The gem felt hot in the dragon's human hand. He peered into its bloody depths, a line of bilious drool sagging across his lip.

"You can poison her heart, like you poisoned the heart of Flinn," Auroch continued, breathless. "You can twist her so she will happily give you the sword—even help you destroy it."

Yes, Verdilith thought, gazing into the crystal. Yes, this

gemstone could deliver the sword of Flinn and the squire of Flinn into my hands. In the glinting light of the stone's facets Verdilith's mania to smash the blade calmed and deepened, and he began to desire a more satisfying, more poetic vengeance. Certainly, Wyrmblight would be shattered and the squire destroyed, but only after Verdilith had insinuated himself into the heart of the girl.

Johauna was her name.

He would steal Johauna away from Flinn as he had stolen Yvaughan. With a clicking, whirring sound, the wheels within wheels had begun to spin in Verdilith's dragon brain.

"How can I track the squire with this?" Verdilith asked, allowing his rumbling dragon voice to issue from the mouth of Maldrake. "How can I see her? Speak to her?"

"Simply give her the stone," Auroch said. "Tell her she can use it to see Flinn. Tell her she must keep it secret, or the stone will shatter. Then, to see or speak through the stone, you need merely peer into a mirror and wish it so."

Verdilith raised his eyes from the gem, now clutched tightly in his palm. "Why would you give this to me?"

Auroch walked back to the table and leaned comfortably on it. He fixed his deep blue eyes on to the dragon's green ones and said, "It serves my purposes, as do all things. In exchange for this priceless gift, I ask only a simple service from you. There is a boy named Dayin traveling along with the bearer of the sword. I want the boy returned to me."

"Why don't you retrieve him yourself?" Verdilith asked through Maldrake's lips. He continued to stare at the gemstone.

Auroch's eyes flashed angrily. "Do as I say, dragon, and I may let you work with me again." His wizened features softened, and he said, "As a token of my friendship, I will tell you a secret. The wounds you suffer so mightily are incurable while Wyrmblight is whole. But, when you break the blade, your wounds will finally heal." The mage leaned forward slightly, staring deeper into the great serpent's eyes. "But, if you don't bring me the boy, I shall make certain you are torn limb from limb, and nothing will heal you again."

Without another word, the human returned to his bubbling flasks. This final mention of the accursed blade sent Verdilith into another paroxysm of pain, and he choked off his rising whimper. The pain was so great he almost believed what the magician had said. But the dragon knew that nothing could ever heal his wounds. Whether Wyrmblight remained whole or not, he would bear these wounds to his grave, of that Verdilith was sure.

But that didn't matter to the dragon as he rose from his seat, the acid from his human mouth having destroyed the chair and some of the floor. He slowly walked toward the table and lifted his arm to pocket the gem. The pain flared again and for once Verdilith found he could ignore some small part of it. The stone felt delicate in his hand. Fragile. But from this fragile gem, he knew he might finally have the vengeance he sought.

Or his own death.

It truly did not matter. Once the blade and the bitch were destroyed, he would betray Auroch for spite and let himself be torn limb from limb.

❧ ❧ ❧ ❧ ❧

Jo's weary step grew a little faster as she recognized the Hap'n Inn, where she and Braddoc were supposed to stay for the night. Not that there's much night left, she thought, remembering the hour or so she had stood outside the rendering hall, trying to reconcile her rage at Brisbois and her grief for Flinn. She stopped to shift Braddoc's battle-axe, which fit poorly in Wyrmblight's harness. She had carried Wyrmblight in her hands all the way from the rendering hall; it had given her a sense of security she'd sorely needed as she walked through the gloom alone.

Almost by instinct, her fingers sought the four raised sigils. *You have lost faith tonight*—the sword again—*but it can be reclaimed. Have faith, Johauna Menhir. Have faith!* The words rang in Jo's mind, but not in her heart. Duty alone had prompted her to return to Braddoc to help him bring Brisbois back to the Castle of the Three Suns. That and the fact that she couldn't fail Sir Graybow. Jo's benefactor had expressed his good opinion of her directly to the baroness.

Jo reached the alley leading to the exterior stairs. She took a step into it, then stopped. The alley was dark, far darker even than the one near the rendering hall had been. Shouldn't there be a light near the stairs? she thought. Hadn't there been one lit when they set out for the hostler's? Perhaps the rain or the wind had extinguished it, she thought. The squire glanced toward the front of the inn. A shuttered lantern rested by the door, casting a star-like pattern of minute lights from holes punched in its sides. Pretty but not very illuminating. Still, it was brighter than the gloomy alley. Jo held Wyrmblight a little higher. *I can go through the front, I suppose, and risk stepping on the people sleeping in the common room.* She took a step in that direction.

Something shifted in the darkness near the stair. Jo dropped to an immediate crouch, Wyrmblight gleaming before her. The gloom was too great for her to make out anything more than a general impression. Some creature, hunched and draped in rags, lurched toward her.

"Who goes there?" Jo called out firmly, only a trace of fear in her voice.

The figure halted for a moment, sniffing oddly in the darkness, then continued toward her. Jo retreated a step, trying to sidle toward the inn's front door. The creature paused, its darksome eyes piteously studying Jo from beneath a tattered hood.

"Please," came a thick, rasping voice. "I mean you no harm. I only wish to know if . . . you are Squire Menhir? The one who was bitten by the watcher in the woods?"

". . . watcher?" Jo asked tentatively. Her eyes adjusted minutely, and she could make out the creature's crooked shoulders.

"An old term," the voice responded. Jo couldn't tell if it was male or female, only that it sounded old and infirm. "Some call them abeylaut, or abelaat. Are you she?" The figure took one tentative step, and this time Jo did not back away. She kept Wyrmblight at the ready, however.

"And if I were?" she countered.

"I have . . . something for her, if you are she," the voice grated. The figure knelt, removed something from its cloak, and placed it on the stony ground. It then stood and backed away. "It is for you," it said, pivoting on a heavy, thudding boot and starting away down the alley.

Jo called after the mysterious creature. "Wait! What is it?"

The cloaked figure stopped, and Jo thought it turned around. It said, "It is a crystal, a crystal of the first abeylaut. Through it you may join with Fain Flinn. But beware: if you speak of it to anyone or anything, the stone will shatter into a thousand pieces, which will lodge in your flesh and work their way into your heart." The figure began walking away again.

Jo bit her lip, unable to believe the infirm being, but unwilling not to. "How do I know this isn't a hoax?" she called loudly.

The figure did not stop. "Try it," she heard faintly, "and discover the truth."

The next moment, only shadows remained in the darksome alley. Trembling, Johauna knelt on the ground and looked at the gem, taking care not to touch it. It glowed faintly, unlike any abelaat stone she had ever seen, and it was larger, too. Whether or not it was an abelaat stone, it was a thing of power. *But why give it to me? Why?*

Cautiously Jo picked the stone up. It took up most of the palm of her hand and felt warm to the touch. She ran her fingers across the four sigils of her sword and murmured, "Wyrmblight, is this stone an abelaat crystal?" She waited for some sort of response, but the blade remained cool to the touch, and none of the sigils glowed. She tried other questions, all pertaining to the stone or the cloaked figure, and at first received the same silence after each question.

But then, a voice spoke. *Keep the stone, Jo. It bears my heart. It bears my love.* The words hadn't come from Wyrmblight, but they had come all the same. Perhaps it was her own weary mind that had spoken. Perhaps it was the stone itself. But an insistent, irrational hope told her it was the voice of Flinn.

Blinking, Jo realized suddenly that dawn was lightening the sky. The alley, which a moment before had been impenetrably dark, now glowed with morning light. A lump in her throat, Jo lifted the stone and gazed, mesmerized, into it.

"Flinn," she whispered, hoarsely. "You *are* in this gem, aren't you?"

Her words were answered only by silence.

Glancing from side to side, hoping no one had seen the precious stone she bore, Jo tucked the crystal inside her belt pouch. She'd worry about it tomorrow, after she'd had some sleep. Maybe she'd talk to Braddoc about it, she thought for a moment, but a suddenly spasm of fear clenched her heart. Braddoc would insist on giving the treasure to the baroness, who would imprison it—the heart of Flinn—in a glass case for all the world to see. No, Jo thought. I will keep it a secret, my silent, constant communion with Flinn. Nodding, she headed down the alley, up the stairs, and into the hallway running the length of the inn.

At the seventh door on her left, Jo stopped and listened through the plain pine door. She heard someone stirring. Good, she thought, Braddoc's up and I won't disturb him. Jo opened the door to the room she had planned to share with Braddoc. The castellan had given her money enough for two rooms, but Johauna was frugal to a fault after living so many years on the street.

Jo entered the small room just as Braddoc sat down on the only chair, situated by one of the two narrow beds. A curtainless window behind the dwarf let in a little light, supplemented by a candle on a table between the beds. From the look of the melted wax and the stubble remains of the candle, Jo knew the dwarf had been up the better part of the night. Braddoc looked at Jo and grunted a greeting, then turned to Brisbois.

The squire's eyes shifted toward the man on the bed. Brisbois's injuries had been dressed, Jo saw. His broken arm was in splints and a sling, and white strips of bandage nearly covered one side of Brisbois's face. He was murmuring in his sleep, and his free hand jerked spasmodically. Jo set the battle-axe in the corner with Braddoc's other things. She undid the harness and stretched her back, then rested the sword next to the bed along the far wall.

Jo sat down on the edge of Brisbois's bed, but was careful not to touch the man. For some moments, she watched him sleep, then turned to Braddoc. The dwarf's good eye was on her.

Jo gave Braddoc a little smile. "I hope you didn't have too hard a time bringing him back here by yourself."

Braddoc snorted. He shook his head. "I've had the healer in. Brisbois'll live, if that's all right with you." The dwarf stared at Jo.

The young woman's eyes widened for a moment, and she turned away from Braddoc's gaze. "That's good," she said quietly. "I'm sorry about how I acted. I want to do what Sir Graybow asked of us." She turned back to the dwarf. "At least, that's what I want to do now. Earlier tonight was a different matter."

Braddoc looked at her and said slowly, "I don't understand you, Johauna. I don't." He turned to the injured man, then reached out and tucked the blanket a little closer around Brisbois's neck. Beside Braddoc, the candle on the table sputtered and went out. The room was bathed in the half light of the rising sun, and, moment by moment, the light grew in the tiny room. Jo felt it touch her face, and she closed her eyes against its caress.

The squire stood and then lay down on the other bed. She groaned as stiff muscles tried to loosen up. Gesturing at Brisbois, she said. "Is he able to ride in an hour?" she asked.

Braddoc stared at Jo and then said slowly, "Yes . . . but I think—"

"That's all I want to know," Jo said coldly. "That's all I need to know."

Chapter X

ot even the dreary, cloud-covered sky could dampen the mood of Squire Menhir as she approached the Castle of the Three Suns. Keeping her victorious smile tightly concealed, Johauna rode behind the young knight who had met them on the approach. She watched the gentle bobbing of the blue plume on his helmet as the knight's stallion trotted toward the gate. Noting his arched back and broad shoulders, Johauna tried to sit as straight on Carsig as he sat on his horse.

"You're as bad as Flinn," Braddoc hissed tersely over her shoulder.

Jo glanced back at the dwarven warrior, riding stern and disgruntled astride his pony. "As *good* as Flinn, you mean," she snapped with an indignant smile. As she did so, she caught a glimpse of the pathetic prisoner in the queue behind Braddoc. The man, slumped, shackled atop one of the pack mules. *Sir* Brisbois. He still holds his title, but not for long, Jo told herself. Vengeance tasted sweet. The very day after Sir Graybow had sent her out to retrieve Brisbois, she returned, her mission complete, her quarry broken and humbled—ready to talk. She would do the same to Verdilith, and Teryl Auroch. The spirit of Flinn would have its vengeance.

The knight at the head of the procession saluted the gate guards and continued on into the main entrance. Jo reined Carsig in for a moment, noting only then that she had been following the knight too closely. It was the excitement of the capture, she railed herself, urging Carsig forward.

As the party passed through the gates, entering the slate-paved marketplace, the bustling crowds drew back to make room for them.

"Look! It's Brisbois, the traitor!" a gray-haired beggar man said.

The cry drew the attention of a fabric merchant nearby, who strayed, incredulous, from his cart. "Never thought I'd see him rounded up!"

"The proud boy's been humbled!" called a wiry cobbler from a small shop along the wall.

A cluster of peasant washerwomen drifted steadily toward the procession, whistling and whooping as they came.

The knight at the head of the parade tightened his hold on the reins of his steed, who was stamping nervously as the crowd converged.

"Look who done it, too!" the cobbler shouted, rushing forward now. "It's Flinn's girl!"

Jo reddened visibly at the remark, uncertain whether to be flattered or angered. But one of the washerwomen answered for her by slapping the cobbler in the face with a wet rag. "She's not Flinn's girl! She's her *own* girl!"

"She's Squire Menhir," Braddoc supplied with a reluctant cough. Jo flashed him a glance, but the dwarf merely nodded her direction.

The procession had slowed, almost halting in the face of the growing mob. A brace of children, running from a crowded corner of the market, came stomping up, their young voices raised in shouts.

"Brisbois the Bungler! Brisbois the Boor!"

Jo laughed aloud and wondered if the children knew how similar their taunts were to those used against Flinn. Over the cries of the children she could hear a flurry of other voices: "Where did you find him?" "How'd he get wounded?" "Who's the dwarf?" "Tell us what happened." "Did he put up a fight?"

The knot of folk around her tightened, pressing against her legs and her mount. Noting Carsig's uneasiness, Jo signaled to the knight ahead of her. He pivoted his steed about with some difficulty in the crowd and shouted, "Back. Let us through to the donjon!"

"Tell us the story!" a few voices demanded of Jo, ignoring the knight's order. Their calls touched off other shouts from the crowd, which drowned out the knight's next commands.

Jo bit her lip, watching the young, red-faced knight try hopelessly to move the crowd. When she saw he was getting nowhere, Jo turned sheepishly toward Braddoc. The dwarf merely shrugged and mouthed the words, "You're the storyteller."

Jo nodded grimly and scanned the sea of faces. Their voices raised a din that must have reached to the donjon itself. They wanted her to tell them what had happened; they wanted her to tell the story of Brisbois's capture. But she'd never told a story to so many people before—for that matter, she'd never told a story that wasn't about Flinn. Her tongue felt like a ball of lead in her mouth, and the events seemed to jumble in her head.

Carsig nickered and took a gentle sidestep, and Jo saw that Braddoc's pony had nudged the horse. The dwarf's face was impassive, but he nodded minutely in Jo's direction. "Go on," he mouthed.

Jo nodded back, a nervous smile on her lips. She swallowed hard and lifted her hands in a gesture to quiet the crowd. "It's really not much of a story," she shouted out as the clamor died down.

"Tell it anyway!" the cobbler cried.

Jo bit her lip; she didn't know how to begin the telling. "I—ah . . ." she started, then flushed: she'd forgotten to adopt her storytelling tone. Lowering her voice and taking a deep breath, she said, "Some days ago, the honorable Sir Lile Graybow, castellan of this mighty fortress, learned the whereabouts of the ignoble rapscallion, the defamed *Sir Brisbois.*" Jo paused, her heart in her throat. The crowd seemed to have appreciated the phrase *ignoble rapscallion,* responding with a smattering of boos and hisses. And her emphasis on the knight's undeserved title garnered even more jeers.

It was a good crowd.

Warming to the task, Jo continued. "Sir Brisbois, I tell you—this worm of a knight, this knight of the wyrm Verdilith—" more hisses "—was the man who falsely accused Flinn the Mighty. Sir Brisbois was the man who willingly brought the glory of Flinn and of Flinn's sword Wyrmblight to an end. And though Flinn forgave the rapacious monster—though he spared the man's life and made him bondsman—Sir Brisbois repaid this kindness with desertion and treachery."

In the chorus of disapproval that followed, the townsfolk around Brisbois's mule began prodding the pathetic figure with their fingers. The knight didn't respond, except with an angry, bloodshot glare.

"So the noble Sir Graybow decided that Brisbois must be captured and tried. Being the one-time mentor of Flinn the Mighty, Sir Graybow dispatched Flinn's former squire and his long-time friend to hunt down the vile man, to bring him back to the castle so that all the folk of Penhaligon might have vengeance for their fallen hero."

"We were supposed to retrieve him for questioning," Braddoc corrected loudly, breaking into Jo's account. "That's the story. Now, in the name of the baroness, let us through."

"Quiet," called someone from the crowd. "Let the squire finish!"

Jo, glaring hotly at her companion, shouted out, "We journeyed across the rugged Southern Wulfholdes unto Castle Kelvin, a pig sty of a place beside the gleaming towers of Penhaligon." The crowd responded with cheers and whistles. "There, we found the man fully entrenched in his element—floundering about in the mud of a gutter, beside a vat of rotting animal parts, and surrounded by a trio of grimy thugs."

"Did the thugs give you trouble, squire?" called out the cobbler excitedly.

"Not with that sword of hers," the washerwoman interjected, playfully flipping her rag in the cobbler's face.

"In fact, the thugs were no problem at all," Jo answered, almost laughing. "They were doing our work for us. They'd been beating up the infamous *Sir* Brisbois for some moments before we arrived."

The crowd let out a whoop of surprise, and some of the listeners began to clap.

"You didn't get to lay a hand on him?"

"Of course I did," Jo responded with mock indignation. She raised her hands before her and made a separate sweeping motion with each. "I slapped him first with the right, and then with the left!"

Amid the gales of laughter, a blacksmith bellowed out, "What then?"

"Then my level-headed companion—" Jo shot Braddoc a surly glare "—advised me against any further retribution against the filthy cur." She consciously deepened her voice again and said, "Though Squire Menhir's fists had not yet wrought their full vengeance upon the evil knight, though she was driven in that moment to unmake Sir Brisbois with the very blade he had darkened by his evil—" Jo dramatically seized the hilt of Wyrmblight and pulled it with a crackling pop from the shoulder harness. She held it up, cold and brilliant in the silver sky "—Wyrmblight, sword of Flinn the Mighty, nemesis of Verdilith the Great Green—though the very Immortals seemed to be crying out to the squire to wipe this wretched filth from the face of the world, the dwarf stayed her hand. Yes, he stayed her hand, though every impulse told her to slay him!"

A rumbling commotion had begun behind Jo, and as she looked over to see its cause, the crowd shifted, and a stream of villagers pressed toward her. Shouts broke out in the crowd, redoubling into a roaring tumult. Jo's eyes went wide as she saw that Brisbois was held in the hands of the throng. They had dragged him from the mule, kicking and bellowing—dragged him through the churning crowd. Only as they reached the side of Jo's horse could she discern what they were shouting.

"Kill him now!" they cried. "Kill him now!"

Wyrmblight, still raised in the raking wind, seemed to tremble with anticipation in Jo's hands as the people lifted

Brisbois up toward her. The gem in her belt-pouch was hot, as though aflame, and a small voice in the back of her skull seemed to say *Kill the traitor, Jo. Kill him as you have wanted to these many months.* It was not the sword speaking, she knew, but the vengeance sounded sweet indeed.

"Kill him now! Kill him now."

Jo's grip on the sword faltered, and the blade fell toward the shackled form. A hand, strong as iron, clamped onto her fist and raised the sword before it struck home. Wide-eyed, Jo blanched as she saw Sir Graybow's granite features next to hers. He sat on horseback beside her, having pushed his way to her through the mob. His very presence quieted the crowd.

"That, my dear," he said, his voice devoid of warmth, "is enough of that."

*** *** *** *** ***

Johauna, Braddoc, and Graybow hurried down the long halls of the Castle of the Three Suns, escorting Brisbois among them. The two guards who had met the trio at the gate followed them, making sure Brisbois would have no opportunity to escape. Graybow had not said another word to Jo from the time they had cleared the mob, and Jo felt chagrined by his silence. She wasn't going to kill Brisbois, she told herself, it was just a story that had gotten out of hand. Jo winced as a slight misstep jarred her bruised rib, despite the tight wrap Braddoc had applied to it. And her injuries were nothing next to Brisbois's. The day in the saddle had obviously aggravated the knight's wounds. His face was a mixture of purple bruises and pale fatigue, and he clenched his teeth against the pain. Brisbois glanced back balefully at Jo, then fixed his eyes once more on the hallway.

As they rapidly made their way through the corridors, Jo saw that many of the magical lanterns still hadn't been repaired. She wondered how Arteris was handling the delinquent mages. The scattered torchlight lent an eerie look to some of the longer halls and in some areas the smoke collected and stung Jo's eyes and nose. This was not the same glowing castle she and Flinn had entered some months before.

Two guards stood outside the meeting room entrance. One turned and threw open the doors as Jo and Braddoc approached. The guard announced in a clear, strong voice, "Your Ladyship, Castellan Graybow escorts Squire Menhir, Master Briarblood, and Sir Brisbois to your council chambers." The guard bowed and stepped aside.

Graybow, Jo, Braddoc, Brisbois, and the two guards behind them entered the room. The entire council was assembled, and the visitors' entrance had apparently interrupted some meeting. Jo noticed that three of the castle's four magicians were also in the room, sitting before the council members as if to give a report.

The chamber's heavy doors closed with a bang. Jo and Braddoc stepped forward, Brisbois reluctantly doing the same. The two guards took up positions behind the knight.

The mages and all fifteen members of the council turned to face Jo. Baroness Penhaligon rose and demanded, "Your report, Squire Menhir!"

"Master Briarblood and I intended to journey to the village of Rifllian, where we had been told Master Brisbois was hiding," Jo began stiffly, trying to be succinct. Still embarrassed that her overblown account had gone awry, Jo wanted to avoid a rambling report. "We stopped in Kelvin at the end of a day's ride. While there, we came across Master Brisbois being beaten by three thugs—"

"You and Master Briarblood are not responsible for the knight's condition?" Sir Graybow broke in.

"No, sir," Jo said quickly. She saw the castellan's little nod of relief.

"Continue, Squire Menhir," Arteris said. She took her seat at the table.

"We rescued Master Brisbois from the thugs; we killed two, but the third escaped." Jo turned to look at Brisbois, but the knight refused to meet her gaze. "Sir Brisbois claims to have been made a pawn, kidnapped by Teryl Auroch. He was given a note, which I am afraid I no longer have in my possession. Master Briarblood will confirm that the note bore the sigil of Auroch."

"Is this true, Master Briarblood?" Sir Graybow inquired.

The dwarf nodded. "Sir Brisbois says it was the mage's sigil—a curved line, like the horns of a bull."

"That is the sigil," the castellan replied. "We will accept this by the honor of your people." A nodded again, a slight smile on his lips.

Jo continued: "The note told Master Brisbois to meet the mage at a certain time and place—"

"A time and place in which you discovered I was being beaten to death," Brisbois interrupted harshly.

Arteris pounded her fist against the table. "Quiet, *Master* Brisbois! You will have your say. This is a court of honor—despite those who still pretend to possess it." Arteris pointedly eyed the stained midnight-blue tunic Brisbois still wore. "Continue, Squire Menhir," the baroness said.

"It is true that we found Master Brisbois at the time and place indicated on the note," Jo said. "And it is true that we saw no sign of Auroch. Master Brisbois says he has no love for Teryl Auroch—"

"We will let the man speak for himself, Squire Menhir," Arteris interrupted testily. "Continue with what you know to be true."

Johauna nodded. "We returned to our inn, tended to Master Brisbois's wounds, and rode out this morning."

Sir Graybow glanced at Brisbois and said, "Did Master Brisbois give you any indication that he did not want to return to the Castle of the Three Suns? Did he try to escape last night or today?"

Jo did not want to answer the question: she knew it would lend credence to Brisbois's claim of his hatred of Auroch. She wanted Brisbois punished at any cost, but knew that she must answer truthfully.

"No, Sir Graybow, Master Brisbois did not resist us in any way." Jo hesitated. She was about to add, "But he was in no condition to do so," but Sir Graybow held up his hand for silence.

"Thank you, Squire Menhir," the castellan said. He gave Jo a warning glance, and suddenly Jo was glad she hadn't made the petty qualifier to her statement.

Sir Graybow nodded to one of the guards, who left for a moment to bring in three extra chairs. "Please take a seat, Squire Menhir and Master Briarblood," the castellan said gruffly. "I'm sure sitting is the last thing you want to do after a day in the saddle, but perhaps you can rest a bit while we finish today's proceedings."

Jo sat gratefully, taking care to position Wyrmblight between two of the chairs. Beside her, Braddoc sat, too. He gave a tiny sigh of relief that only Jo heard. She smiled inwardly.

Silence fell in the room as everyone waited for Arteris

to speak. She folded her hands on the table before her and fixed Brisbois with her agate-brown eyes. They were hard and stony and inflexible, without an ounce of mercy in them. Sir Graybow had told Jo that the baroness was growing more and more like old Baron Arturus every day, and her present mood seemed to support the claim.

"Do you know why we sent Squire Menhir and Master Briarblood after you, Master Brisbois?" Arteris asked calmly.

Brisbois was caught off guard. "Ex-excuse me, Your Ladyship?" he asked.

"Do you know why you were brought here?"

Brisbois's puffy face took on an impassive cast. "No, Your Ladyship, I do not." Brisbois obviously could not meet the woman's stony gaze.

"Then let me inform you," Arteris said graciously. "You are here because it is believed by our court mages that Teryl Auroch has destroyed the magic in the Castle of the Three Suns."

"Destroyed—?" Brisbois blurted. He turned his attention to the council and looked at each person in turn. "You must believe me! I know nothing of Auroch's plans—"

"Then why did you leave with the mage after he attacked Sir Flinn and his party here in the castle?" Graybow interjected suddenly.

Brisbois shook his head angrily. "I didn't leave with Auroch willingly! He abducted me as he disappeared."

"Are we to presume you have quit his company?" Arteris asked and added quickly, "and, if so, how did you escape from so powerful a mage?"

Brisbois's face displayed emotions ranging from anger to shame; he looked aside at the floor. After a few moments, he turned to Arteris and addressed her squarely, "Auroch spirited us away to Specularum, Your Ladyship. We appeared on a crowded dock, and I took advantage of the confusion to slip away. The attack had drained Auroch, and he was not capable of retrieving me."

Baroness Penhaligon considered the knight's words, her face devoid of emotion or thought. "And what have you done in the weeks since this abduction, Master Brisbois?" Arteris asked impassively.

Brisbois took a deep breath, as if he were about to reveal some grave personal secret. Jo found herself entranced, despite her anger.

"At first, I sought to escape Auroch's influence. He is obviously more powerful than I, and I feared for my life," Brisbois replied leadenly. "But I slowly realized that if the man were as powerful as I thought, I could not hope for any real escape. My only option was to kill him before he killed me. I have been running from him only to gain opportunity to decide how I might kill him."

"Where is Auroch now? Rifllian? Kelvin?" Sir Graybow asked.

Brisbois rubbed his brow, then said, "He stayed for a while in Specularum, and I tried to figure out how to trap him there. But he tracked me down, so I escaped the city and traveled north on the Duke's Road. I stopped in Kelvin, hoping to buy some time there." Brisbois paused.

"You were never in Rifllian?" Graybow asked.

"No, sir, I was not," Brisbois said readily. Jo stared at the knight intently.

"My sources—" began the castellan.

"Were misinformed, Sir Graybow," Brisbois said steadily. "I *arranged* for them to be misinformed."

"What!" demanded Graybow and Arteris simultaneously.

The other council members murmured to each other, and even the three mages shot questioning looks at Brisbois. The castellan stood and shouted, "Explain yourself, Master Brisbois!"

The knight shrugged. "I led your informants to believe I was in Riflian in the hopes of throwing Auroch off the track as well," he said clearly. "I also hoped you might send someone after me, someone who might encounter and dispatch Auroch in Riflian."

Arteris exclaimed, "Surely you must know that you are an outlaw to the order? Surely you must know that breaking your bond with Sir Flinn was the final stroke in your dismissal. This new transgression—willful misdirection of the order for your own purposes—may well have won you your death."

Brisbois inclined his head in the baroness's direction. "Yes, Your Ladyship, I do know all that," he said. "But I also know that I could not take on Auroch by myself. I hoped for an envoy from the castle to back me up. If I could prove my good intent by battling side by side with the order against Auroch, perhaps you would have allowed me to return to the Order of the Three Suns." Brisbois looked at the council members. Jo's eyes darted daggers, but he avoided looking at her.

The room was brutally silent. Eventually, Sir Graybow stood. "You hoped for many, many things, Master Brisbois," the castellan said slowly, "and I am appalled at your lack of humility!" Sir Graybow turned away from the table and stalked over to one of the windows. He shook his head. The sun was setting, but the magical lanterns had not begun to glow. One of the guards began lighting lanterns.

Arteris rose and said slowly, "Are we to infer, Master Brisbois, that you wish the court to show you leniency once more?" Her voice was laced with astonishment.

Brisbois's cheek rippled. He nodded and said, "Yes, Your Ladyship, I do."

"This is . . . most unprecedented, Master Brisbois," Arteris said coldly. "Pray, tell us how you possibly esteem yourself worthy of this grace beyond grace!" The baroness took her seat.

Brisbois gestured in Jo's direction. "I came willingly with Squire Menhir and Master Briarblood. I in no way harmed Sir Flinn—"

Johauna jumped up. "Yes, but you didn't help him, either! You let Auroch attack—"

The castellan swung around from his position at the window. "You are out of order, Squire Menhir!" Sir Graybow shouted thickly. He pointed at Jo. "Sit down at once, or remove yourself!"

Stunned, Jo sat down in her chair. She looked at Sir Graybow, and the blood drained from her face. Jo turned to Braddoc for sympathy, but the dwarf only gave her a warning shake of his head.

The castellan returned to the table and bowed formally to the baroness. "My apologies, Your Ladyship, for the actions of my squire," Sir Graybow said gruffly. "I assure you, Squire Menhir's outburst was the last you will ever hear from her."

The baroness stared at Sir Graybow and said icily, "And I assure *you*, Sir Graybow, that that *is* the last such outburst I shall allow." Arteris turned to Jo and stared pointedly at the young woman. Jo swallowed hard.

Sir Graybow looked at the council members, then addressed the baroness, "Your Ladyship, determination of Master Brisbois's fate is something we may postpone. The death of our castle's magic is not." The castellan bowed slightly and took his chair.

Arteris looked at Brisbois, who was swaying noticeably now. She pursed her lips, then gestured for a guard to give the man a chair. When Brisbois sat down, Arteris said "Your involvement with both Verdilith and Teryl Auroch your conspiracy against Sir Flinn and the principles of the Order of the Three Suns—these transgressions alone give us reason to suspect you in the plot that has destroyed our magic."

"I know nothing of this!" protested Brisbois. The council looked at him, as the words rang hollowly through the room. Brisbois said nothing more, and Arteris continued.

"Only a few of our mages have any spells or powers left to them, and virtually none of our enchanted items work." The baroness paused and steepled her fingers. "Master Brisbois, to put it plainly, we suspect you of conspiring with Teryl Auroch in the destruction of our magic. How say you?"

Brisbois blanched. "I am innocent, Your Ladyship." His voice rang with sincerity, though Jo was hard pressed to believe him. You're guilty of other things anyway, and they will be exposed, she thought.

"You still haven't addressed the castellan's question. Do you know where Auroch has been the last several weeks and do you know where he is now?" Arteris asked coolly.

"As I said, Auroch was in Specularum and then traveled north along the Duke's Road. He was in Kelvin as recently as yesternight—" Brisbois said slowly.

"Excuse me," Sir Graybow cut in. "Did you actually see Auroch in Kelvin, Master Brisbois? Might he have sent you the note from elsewhere?"

Brisbois blinked. One eye had completely closed over and his bruises had darkened to deep purple. "You are correct, Sir Graybow," he said after a moment. "I did not actually see Auroch in Kelvin. I only assumed he passed through Kelvin because of the note and because he had been traveling north." He turned to the baroness. "To my knowledge, Auroch has not been in Penhaligon at all since he attacked Sir Flinn." Brisbois shook his head. "That is not to say that he didn't have the time or the magical means to travel to the castle."

"Do you know where the mage is *now*, Master Brisbois?" the baroness repeated testily.

"No, Your Ladyship, I do not," Brisbois replied slowly. "I last saw him on the Duke's Road just south of Kelvin. I assumed he entered the town there." Brisbois sighed and then said, "What makes you think Auroch is responsible for the failure of your magic? Isn't it possible that Verdilith has done this to you?"

"It is one and the same," Sir Graybow said. "Haven't you heard? After Sir Flinn died in single-handed combat with the dragon, a detachment from the castle engaged Verdilith in his lair. The dragon escaped with the aid of Auroch."

Brisbois nodded impatiently. "Yes, I have heard the tale! Every inn is abuzz with the story of Flinn's life. Why, some of the minstrels claim Flinn the Mighty is not dead, but being transformed into an Immortal."

Jo caught her breath; her hand rose, but Braddoc grabbed it and shook his head at her. Jo held her peace and listened avidly to the knight.

". . . an unlikely event," Brisbois was saying, "considering the difficulties involved."

"Though if any man in known history could have become an Immortal," Sir Graybow interrupted, "it would have been Sir Flinn." The castellan's expression was grim.

"Er, yes, Sir Graybow," Brisbois said hastily. "My point is that the minstrels will tell any tale, and so I hadn't believed their reports of Auroch and Verdilith together again, especially since the mage seemed so preoccupied with killing me."

One of the doors to the council room opened to admit a guard. He coughed politely, but, before he could speak, an old woman pushed forcibly past him. Following her was a young boy. Karleah and Dayin! Johauna thought. She almost rose but remembered her place just in time.

The guard would not be outdone, however. He stepped before the intruders and announced to the baroness, "Your Ladyship, the wizardess Karleah Kunzay and her apprentice request—"

"I didn't 'request' anything. I demanded," Karleah interrupted the guard and stepped around him. Arteris made a dismissing gesture, and the guard returned through the door to his post outside. Karleah stepped forward, Dayin by her side. He cast Jo and Braddoc a quick smile.

"To what do we owe the meaning of this intrusion, crone?" Arteris asked. Her voice was colder than it had ever been to either Brisbois or Jo. "I should have you thrown out, but I am assuming this is important." Arteris arched her brows haughtily.

"Where is the box?" Karleah demanded. The wizardess's lanky gray hair seemed to stand on end.

"What box?" Arteris asked angrily.

Braddoc jumped to his feet and stood beside Karleah. "Your Ladyship," he said, his eyes suddenly wide with alarm. "I know the box of which Karleah speaks: the iron box I took from Verdilith's lair!" Jo stood and joined her friends. She noticed Sir Graybow's eyes and pursed her lips. Her friends were more important than protocol.

"It's the key to this magical conundrum," the old crone supplied.

Arteris turned on the mages, who had been silent all along. "Master Keller," she said to the youngest, "did you not tell me that this . . . box was simply a puzzle box, an item *definitely* not magical?"

The mage stood and stared from Karleah to Arteris. He stammered, "Y-yes, Your Ladyship, I did."

"You fool!" Karleah shrieked. She threw up her bony hands and advanced on the mage. "Don't you *know?* The *box* is what's drained away all your castle's magic, and much of mine!"

The young man's face blanched. "I—I didn't know," he stuttered.

"That box must be hidden far, far away," Karleah said in a voice deadly serious. "That box must be dropped in the deepest gorge, the farthest sea, whatever! It must be removed from all sources of magic *immediately!*" She gave the mage a push with her oaken staff. "Go, get the box. Give it to Braddoc, that unmagical dwarf who brought it here in the first place. He should take it away."

The young man was shaking so badly he almost fell over on top of Karleah. "I—I—I can't, old crone," he said fearfully. "I can't get the box!"

"What!" Karleah shrieked. Never before had Jo seen the old wizardess more upset. Why, it's almost as if Karleah's terrified, Jo thought suddenly. Can the box really be that powerful? "What have you done with it, fool?" Karleah roared. She raised her staff.

The oldest mage, Aranth, stepped forward and pulled young Keller away. He, too, was shaking, but he said with some semblance of calm, "The puzzle box was a disruption to my mages—they were fiddling about, trying to

open it when they should have been working on restoring
the castle's magic. I sent it away so we could get back to
work."

"Sent it where?" Karleah asked, breathlessly.

"To a cousin of mine," Aranth said. "He loves such
puzzles, as do all those wizards up there in Armstead."

Karleah's face turned white, and Jo swore some of the
woman's hair did, too. "You . . . you sent the box to . .
to Armstead?" Karleah whispered. "You sent the box to
the most . . . magic-filled place in the country . . . ?"

Karleah's eyes rolled back in her head, and she crumpled.

"Karleah!" Dayin shouted as he knelt next to the wizardess's fallen form. Jo knelt, too, and lifted Karleah's head
onto her lap. Jo looked up at Sir Graybow, but the castellan was speaking in Arteris's ear.

"Karleah! Karleah!" Jo whispered as she stroked the old
woman's lined face, marveling at the deep seams.

The baroness's voice rang out authoritatively, "Council
members, please leave. This is a matter I would discuss
with the mages. Guards, take Master Brisbois to the
dungeons. Sir Graybow, attend the wizardess and her
companions."

Madam Astwood eyed the baroness sulkily. "Your Ladyship, it is inappropriate to make decisions concerning the
Estate of Penhaligon without our counsel and knowledge."

Arteris fixed her icy gaze on the mistress of etiquette.
"In times of dire threat, security must come before free-
dom of knowledge," the baroness said. She continued in a
voice loud enough to carry to all the council members,
some of whom were already at the door. "And should
word of this leak out to anyone—*anyone,* mind you—I
shall personally see that each and every one of you is

emoved from the council." The council members cast quick glances at each other, then slowly filed out of the room.

The two guards had Brisbois by his arms when the knight called out, "Baroness! Please, I would remain!"

Arteris hesitated, then looked at the castellan. Sir Graybow rubbed his chin, then shook his head. "No," the castellan said, "I cannot permit it. The security of the castle is my affair. If either Auroch or Verdilith is the cause of our troubles, Brisbois might reveal our plans." Sir Graybow gestured for the guards to take Brisbois away. The man left without another word.

Jo and Dayin watched with trepidation as Karleah slowly recovered from her swoon. Out of the corner of her eye, Jo noticed that the majority of the council members had filed out of the room at a gesture from Sir Graybow.

"What . . . what happened?" Karleah muttered.

Jo and Dayin helped her rise. They settled her on a chair. The baroness and Sir Graybow stood nearby, expressions of concern filling their faces. The three mages tried to look equally interested in the old woman's welfare, but were obviously anxious about their own. Karleah looked back and forth between Sir Graybow and Arteris. "Sending that thing to Armstead, indeed!" she spat. "Whose pea-brained idea was that?"

The castellan looked to the three huddled magicians, then turned to Arteris and whispered, "I know you wanted to discuss the matter with your magely advisors, My Lady, but I think we should dismiss them as well. Each is as suspect in this plot as Master Brisbois."

The baroness gave each of the sorcerers a penetrating gaze, and Jo suspected that this gaze had been used to

elicit the truth from lesser men many times before. After
moment, Arteris pursed her lips and nodded to herself
She turned to Karleah and said, "I cannot suspect every
one, Sir Graybow. I think these mages are more bungler
than traitors. Let them stay."

The insult notwithstanding, the mages seemed to ease
bit.

"As you wish," Sir Graybow said, then turned to th
mages. "When did you send the box?"

Aranth answered, "It left with four guards almost
week ago. They should be in Armstead any day now. Ar
you saying that this—thing, will destroy the magic there a
well?"

Karleah pursed her lips and sucked in her cheeks. He
face was suddenly gaunt and strained with fatigue. "Yes."
She bowed her head and nodded gravely. "But I don'
think the box simply drains magical energy: otherwise
why would Verdilith have kept it in his lair? The drago
obviously had the box for a reason—and he must have le
us steal it for a reason, too. It must have another purpose."

"Perhaps it needs to gather a certain amount of powe
before it can fulfill its true purpose," Aranth suggested ten
tatively. "If the box arrives in Armstead, it may gathe
enough magical energy to . . . to destroy all of Pen
haligon."

"If Verdilith and Auroch created it," Karleah finished, "
would agree."

The baroness made a slight noise, and Sir Graybow pu
his hand on the woman's shoulder. Arteris leaned towar
the castellan minutely, the first time Jo had ever seen th
woman display any weakness. "What can be done?"
Arteris asked quietly.

"Surely we can prevent this catastrophe," Sir Graybo

said to Karleah. "Treacherous sorcery has never yet defeated the Quadrivial." His gruff voice rang in the room, and Jo felt suddenly heartened.

Karleah shrugged. "We can intercept the box, I suppose," she said slowly. "Perhaps your guards are slow, or have met with disaster."

Sir Graybow nodded, then helped the baroness to her chair and sat next to her. Jo and the others sat down as well.

"This is what we will do," the castellan began, his deep voice reassuring and authoritative. "Squire Menhir," he said formally, "by virtue of your prompt return of Master Brisbois, your proven rapport with Karleah, who knows most about the box, and the fact that I am surer of your motives than of any other knights and squires at this point, I send you after this box. You must stop its arrival at Armstead any way you can."

The baroness looked askance at her castellan and said, "I'm sorry, Sir Graybow, but I believe that one of the more experienced knights should be given this task."

"Normally, that would be true, My Lady, but there is one overriding reason for my choice. Squire Menhir has something no other knight possesses."

"And that is?"

"Wyrmblight. If the dragon Verdilith is involved in these events, the sword forged to slay him must go along."

"But she is only a squire."

"I will send her in the company of Master Briarblood, a fighter equal to even our most experienced knights." Sir Graybow looked at the dwarf, who nodded his head slightly. "And Karleah Kunzay will go as well, a mage who exceeds our mages in experience and intuition—as shown by her discovery of the box's power.

"In their initial assault on Verdilith's lair, Squire Menhir and her companions proved themselves more effective than the full regiment of knights and mages we sent afterward. And, given the problem of security, I would prefer to send a small, potent strike force rather than a marching army."

"Do you agree to go, Karleah Kunzay?" Arteris asked.

The old wizardess rubbed her chin for a moment. Then, looking at Jo, she said, "Aye, I'll go, but on one condition: that only one more person accompanies us, and I choose whom." Karleah turned to Sir Graybow and Arteris, who traded stunned looks.

Graybow peered at Karleah. "And who would that be?"

Karleah grunted. "Master Brisbois."

Jo stood and cried, "What? Are you crazy, Karleah? That man's in league with Auroch—"

Karleah snapped, "Hush up, young lady. I've got more intuition in my little toenail than you have in your whole carrot-topped head! Brisbois is innocent. He's also the only one who knows anything about Auroch's whereabouts and plans. He completes the strike force. We've got our sword-bearer . . ." She looked at Jo, Wyrmblight resting against the chair beside her. The crone's gaze then shifted to Braddoc. "We've got our warrior, our spell-flinger (and assistant)," she continued, patting Dayin's shoulder. "Now we need an information man, and Brisbois is it."

"With Brisbois in our camp, Auroch has a *certain* chance of finding out what we're up to!" Jo shouted. The castellan grabbed her arm and flashed her a warning look. Jo reluctantly took her seat. She crossed her arms.

Arteris spoke up. "It would seem that the disposition of Master Brisbois must be addressed now, rather than later as we had hoped." She paused and looked at Jo. "The council had not quite come to a decision, and now other factors have arisen that would further color their judgments."

The baroness steepled her fingers again and set her gaze on Jo, who felt suddenly uncomfortable.

"Squire Menhir, as heir to Sir Flinn's blade, what would you have us do with Master Brisbois? Would you grant him mercy . . . or death."

Jo stared at the baroness, her mouth suddenly dry. Her arms felt like lead, and she let them come uncrossed. "*My* decision, Your Ladyship?" she asked, breathless.

The baroness nodded. "Yes, squire. The decision is yours. Master Brisbois has clearly betrayed his duty, not once but twice. The first time, Sir Flinn asked that the man be spared, asked that Master Brisbois act as his bondsman for one year, in hopes that he could be reformed. Sir Flinn's mercy, of course, went astray."

"I know all this," whispered Jo.

Arteris nodded. "And now, Master Brisbois has betrayed his duty a second time, not honoring his sworn word as bondsman," the baroness said. She shook her head sadly. "We have not determined if Brisbois joined Auroch willingly or was indeed abducted by the mage. But, either way, he rendered to Sir Flinn none of his service as bondsman. And, in a feeble attempt to return himself to our good graces, Master Brisbois willfully misled the knighthood," Arteris paused, letting the point sink in. "By all rights," Arteris continued slowly, "the man deserves no further mercies. He is clearly without honor. He is possibly in league with Auroch and Verdilith. And he may do us great harm. His execution would be warranted, and I will sanction it with only a word from you to do so."

Sir Graybow covered Jo's hands with his own and said,

"The choice is yours, Squire Menhir. You are Sir Flinn's former squire. Not only are his memory and his sword entrusted to you, but his commitments are yours as well." He paused and then said, "As we all saw in the market-place, the people of Penhaligon cheer your mission of vengeance, whether I do or not. So, I leave the choice to you: mercy or death."

"Mercy or death?" Jo muttered in bewilderment. Those two words hammered at her soul. She wanted her revenge, now even more than in the marketplace. During the council meeting, Brisbois had smoothly laid out excuse after excuse, lie after lie, and Jo had grown only more angry. He was *not* innocent. Brisbois had defamed Flinn. Brisbois had burned Flinn's home and befriended Flinn's killer. He had vowed his service as bondsman and then fled when Auroch had attacked. A score of true offenses rose to the surface of Jo's mind, accompanied by a hundred imagined ones. And her anger deepened. The stone in her belt pouch seemed to throb in sympathy with her hatred, and a voice in her head whispered, *Give him death, Johauna; for the sake of Flinn's soul, give him death.*

But Flinn had let the man live. The irony of the situation suddenly struck Jo: Brisbois had dishonored Flinn by saying he had denied mercy to a foe on the battlefield. The charge was not only false, but absurd. Flinn demonstrated his mercy by granting a second chance to the very man who had falsely accused him. It was Flinn's mercy that had saved Brisbois, had let him keep his title, had let him live.

Jo felt the anger in her begin to crack. For so long this grim vow of vengeance had eclipsed her mind, eclipsed her being. And, in its deep shadow, Jo's soul had withered. Her single-minded quest to hunt down and kill the slayers of Flinn seemed suddenly hollow, destroying rather than building her soul.

It was making her more like Brisbois, less like Flinn.

No, Jo told herself. True knights exhibit not only Honor, Courage, Faith, and Glory. True knights also exhibit Mercy.

"If I am the heir to Sir Flinn's estate as well as his commitments," Jo said clearly, "then I can only do as he would have done: I grant mercy to Sir Brisbois." Jo's eyes glittered suddenly. "But Master Brisbois must fulfill his sworn word as bondsman."

Conflicting emotions flitted across the castellan's face, and Jo wondered just what the man was thinking. Finally, he turned to Arteris and said, "If you so approve, Your Ladyship."

The baroness gave a slight nod.

Karleah caught Jo's eyes and said, "Looks like we'd better get that man out of the dungeons, then. We've a box to find."

Jo nodded slowly, her heart pounding in her chest. A niggling voice in her mind told her she had made the wrong choice, and for the wrong reasons.

Chapter XI

I wish I could go with you, Jo," Sir Graybow said as he gave Jo a leg up into her horse's saddle. He looked up at the squire and then clasped her wrist in farewell. Jo smiled sincerely, peering into the man's eyes.

"I wish you could, too," Jo whispered.

Sir Graybow smiled wryly. "Duty calls." The skin around his light blue eyes wrinkled a little.

The young woman nodded. "Duty is important. And I know that your first loyalty must be to the castle." Jo shook her head, her gray eyes intent. "You have given me things that no one else could. For that, you have *my* loyalty, and I will try my best not to fail you."

"That's all I can ask, Johauna," Sir Graybow said, looking down the road. "You *do* know which way to go now, don't you?" he asked teasingly.

"Oh, aye!" Jo responded with a laugh. "You only kept us up the better part of the night memorizing your maps!" The castellan's questioning gaze didn't soften. Shaking her head, Jo recited, "Head due northwest through the

Wulfholdes and enter the Altan Tepes Mountains. From there head north by northwest until we reach the end of the Altan Tepes and the Black Peaks take over. Follow the trail to Armstead." She looked down at the castellan. "How'd I do?"

Sir Graybow nodded. "Fine, Jo, fine." The man frowned. "It's been years since I've seen the Black Peaks, and a more treacherous mountain range I've never found. There aren't any villages along the way, not even hamlets where you can get a night's respite."

"I know," Jo responded. "We have Fernlover and one other mule to carry our supplies, and spring has come to the land. We're strong enough. We'll find the box, hopefully before it arrives in Armstead."

Sir Graybow nodded. "That's unlikely, Jo, but not as far-fetched as we had at first thought. I sent messenger pigeons to a few knights on reconnaissance along the Duke's Road south of Kelvin, telling them to ride west to Riflian and north to Verge and Threshold. Perhaps they'll arrive in Threshold before the box does."

"Should we try to meet them in Threshold?" Jo asked steadily.

Sir Graybow shook his head. "No, continue on through the village, heading straight northwest until you reach Armstead, then backtrack along the trail to intercept the box."

"Right," Jo said lightly. "If that's all, then, we'll be on our way. We've a good hour or two before sunrise, and we can be well out of Penhaligon territory by then." She paused and then added, "Have you any last words of wisdom?"

The castellan smiled, his second chin wobbling slightly. "Yes, but only this: have faith in yourself. I do." He stepped away from Jo's horse. "That's all I can ask, and that's all I want." Sir Graybow held up his hand, and a guard opened the wide doors to let Jo's party out through one of the secondary exits.

Jo's throat constricted, and she could only nod one last time to the castellan. Then she touched her heels to Carsig's flanks. The big gelding leaped forward, his metal-shod hooves ringing on the cobblestone pavement. Behind Jo rode Karleah on a mare every bit as gray as the wizardess herself. Dayin followed after, again on one of Braddoc's long-legged ponies. Brisbois took up the next position. He'd protested upon seeing Jo's mount, for the gelding used to be his. Jo cut his complaint short. Brisbois was given the choice between several sturdy horses, but, to everyone's surprise, he'd picked a stocky, short-coupled, piebald mare. She was an ugly thing, but Brisbois insisted that she was what he wanted. He led a pack-laden mule, as did Braddoc. The dwarf rode his jet pony, Onyx, and led Fernlover, the mule.

The seven animals cantered down the narrow road leading to one of Penhaligon's lesser gates. There were few people around at that early hour, and Jo was sharply reminded of the last time she had made such an exit; Flinn had stopped her to show her the rising sun split by the Craven Sisters. Jo now looked eastward and saw the two pointed hills, but the sun was not yet ready to rise. Another time, she thought. Another time to see again the beautiful split sun that gives the castle its name.

Jo turned Carsig north along the Duke's Road and gave the gelding free rein. He broke into a long, loping canter, a pace that could eat the miles away while the terrain remained smooth.

There was no suitable ford for miles around, and Jo

wasn't about to travel southward to the nearest one at Kelvin. No, they'd try crossing a few miles north of Penhaligon where the River Hillfollow widened out. Sir Graybow suggested the route, though he cautioned Jo. The spring rains were likely to have swollen the river's banks, and the current might be too strong. But they had to cross the Hillfollow somehow.

The chill darkness of early dawn gave way to warmth as the sun rose. Thankfully, the sky revealed no clouds. A flock of birds, cackling noisily, rose from nearby trees as Carsig clattered by. Startled, Jo heard a similar cry from behind her. She turned in her saddle to look at Karleah. The old wizardess was intent on the departing birds, and every now and then she opened her mouth and cackled in an excellent imitation. Jo smiled and turned her attention back to the road ahead. She shook her head and thought, Karleah is a funny, strange woman, but I'm glad to count her as a friend.

Jo glanced behind her again, checking on her comrades. A few lengths separated each person, just as she had instructed. Once again Sir Graybow's warning about bandits attacking travelers echoed through Jo's mind. Not unlike the gangs infesting Specularum, Jo thought and shuddered. She'd had enough of gangs to last a lifetime.

The fair weather and easy road made for excellent progress. It was only midmorning when Jo turned off the road and headed due west, toward the river ford. It's a good thing Sir Graybow made me memorize so much of the map, Jo thought as she urged Carsig through the spring undergrowth. I would have passed right by the three dead elms otherwise.

Water glistened just ahead. The land that sloped down to the river was not as flat as it had been around the

Hillfollow when Jo and Braddoc had traveled south to Kelvin. Knotted roots and grassy hillocks stood in thick clumps along the ground.

Approaching the bank, Carsig slipped on the soft spring soil, the earth saturated with rain and wet leaves. Jo gripped the reins firmly, giving the gelding just enough leather to recover. When he regained his footing, Jo pulled him to a stop. She turned around and yelled back to Karleah, who was following at some distance, "Karleah! Dismount; the way's not safe. Pass it on!"

Jo lightly jumped off Carsig, her own booted feet slipping as she landed on the slick earth. She grabbed her saddle to keep from falling, while her feet shuffled underneath her. Carsig turned his head to look at the squire and nickered at her. "Yes, yes, I hear you," Jo responded aloud. She held out her hand and added, "I'm off, aren't I?" Carsig nibbled her fingers, and then wheezed in disgust when he found no treat. Jo fished a carrot from her pocket and said, "All right, all right!" The gelding turned his head back to Jo and then delicately took the proffered carrot.

"What's it like ahead, Jo?" Karleah asked as she led her gray mare down the narrow path Carsig had taken.

"Not so good," the squire responded. Jo grabbed the gelding's reins and started to walk. The water lay less than a hundred yards away, but getting there was going to take some doing. The trees here—mostly willow and cottonwood—grew thick and tangled along the riverbank. Roots twisted above the soil line, and Jo saw signs of high water having flooded the land in the past. She led the big gelding down the straightest and safest path between the trees. She took care to get out of Carsig's way whenever the horse slipped. Johauna had been stepped on by a horse once at the hostler's, and the experience was not one she would willingly repeat.

Jo panted with her exertions. The sun was hot and high in the sky, and the spring leaves on the willows didn't entirely filter it away. Occasionally Jo had to struggle to keep her own footing, and sometimes she had to force the gelding down the route she had chosen. They drew closer to the water.

In front of them lay a wide depression, and just beyond it a border of marshy river plants. Jo looked behind her and saw that the others were slowly winding their way down the embankment. She called back to Karleah and pointed to the depression, "Let's hold up there, Karleah, and wait for the others. There's enough room to meet up and plan our crossing." Jo stepped forward, guiding Carsig carefully over the tangled roots of a willow.

A layer of old leaves covered the ground beyond. Overhead arched tree boughs with dark, wet bark and long, probing branches. Sunlight streamed into the large open space and invited Jo forward. She and Carsig took a few steps into the depression.

They sank immediately to their knees.

Jo looked down in dismay. "Oh, well," she murmured. "Live and learn, Carsig. Come on, we'll turn around and get out of this mess." She clucked her tongue and pulled on Carsig's rein, then tried to lift her leg to turn around. She couldn't. The shiny black mud beneath the deceptive layers of leaves held her legs firmly. Jo locked her hands behind one knee and lifted. Slowly, her leg pulled free from the mud encasing it. With a final *schlupp!* her leg came loose and Jo had the good sense to not set it down. She leaned against Carsig for support, and the gelding responded with a snort.

Karleah stopped on the edge of the sinkhole and cackled.

"You're in a situation, if I may say so," she chortled.

"You may, and you did," Jo answered with pretended frost. "Now help me out of here before I sink any deeper!"

Karleah found some short pieces of old fallen wood she could dislodge and carry. She brought them to the sinkhole and threw them toward Jo. The squire caught the wet logs one by one and grimaced as a spray of mud and sowbugs hit her in the face. "Thanks, Karleah," she said wryly as she began arranging a platform to stand on.

Tentatively Jo put her loose, mud-caked leg on the platform. She shifted her weight and was pleased to see that, though the logs sank slightly, they looked as if they'd hold her up. "Okay," Jo muttered to herself while Karleah collected more wood for another step. "Brace yourself! You need to do this right the first time."

Jo pushed off Carsig, at the same time shifting her weight heavily forward onto the platform. With the same reluctant noises coming from the ground as before, Jo withdrew her leg. She stood on the platform and panted, caked with mud. A stray sowbug climbed onto her waist, and she flicked it away.

"I take it a city girl like you isn't aware of sinkholes," a voice rang out.

Jo look up, flustered. The words had come from Brisbois, still mounted on his piebald mare. The man's voice made Jo's teeth grate. Jo caught the wood Karleah threw to her and prepared for her next step before she spoke. "That's enough, Karleah," Jo said, then turned to Brisbois. She looked directly into his insolent eyes. "I'll thank you, Sir Brisbois, to kindly turn your attentions elsewhere."

"Such as to helping your horse escape your . . . miscalculation?" Brisbois quipped. He turned and smiled at Braddoc and Dayin as the two rode up.

Jo chose to ignore his comment. Gathering herself, she leaped to the next platform. She slipped and almost lost her balance as one log sank beneath her foot. She took the next jump immediately, landed at the edge of the sinkhole, and scrambled upward onto safer ground. She spun around and sat on the wet ground. Carsig turned his head, looked at her, and nickered in distress.

"I know, Carsig, I know," Jo told the gelding while she caught her breath. "We'll get you out somehow." With a nearby stick Jo began scraping the layer of mud off her legs. *The river will wash this off, thankfully,* Jo said to herself.

"How are we going to get Carsig loose?" Dayin asked. "I think he's sinking."

Jo stared at the gelding. Sure enough, the horse seemed to have sunk. "Carsig!" she called. The animal turned his head toward his mistress and whickered.

Braddoc pulled two ropes off Fernlover's pack and handed one to Brisbois. Quickly the two men began tying them into lariats. They slowly twirled the ropes overhead and threw them at Carsig's neck. Brisbois missed, but Braddoc's toss landed on target. Carsig groaned indignantly. At Jo's congratulatory smile, Braddoc smiled and said, "Comes from years of practice at rounding up ponies." Brisbois snorted and threw his rope again; this time it caught. Jo averted her eyes from the knight and said nothing.

The man and dwarf pulled in tandem while Jo called coaxingly to Carsig. The ropes tightened around the gelding's neck, and the horse whinnied fearfully. Carsig's roan haunches rippled with effort as he struggled to move in the quagmire. On the bank, Braddoc and Brisbois strained against the ropes, but not enough to hurt the horse's neck.

"Come on, Carsig! Come on, boy, you can do it!" Jo shouted. She held out the stubble of a carrot; beside her, Dayin waved some succulent grasses. Carsig heaved once more, his back arching as if trying to buck away from the clawing mud. For a moment it looked as if the gelding would pull free; his front hooves surfaced to the sounds of wet mud smacking. Jo cheered, and Braddoc and Brisbois strained harder against the ropes.

Carsig twisted and turned, his hooves coming down in the mud. He tried frantically to maintain his momentum, but his rear haunches would not move in the mire. The gelding thrashed about, his front hooves clawing at the mud as he tried desperately to free himself. Braddoc and Brisbois threw their weight farther back and the ropes tightened about the horse's neck, but even their combined strength couldn't budge the horse. Jo began to call out again, but the words faltered. Her eyes were locked on the struggling horse, her ears hearing only his throaty rattle as he tried to whinny. Carsig's throat had grown raw from rope burns as he threw his head forward and back.

Stomping over to the men, Jo threw her weight against the rope and cried, "Now!" It was their last chance, Jo was sure. She, Braddoc, and Brisbois strained against the rope, while the gelding screamed. He arched his back, churning the mud between his hind legs. With a fierce kick, Carsig toppled sideways, his legs pulling free. He thrashed his way through the mud and onto the firmer ground surrounding the sinkhole. With a last, shuddering pull, Jo and the others hauled the filthy, shaking horse out of the mud.

Carsig stood before Jo, his entire body quivering with fatigue and terror. After assuring that the horse would not suddenly bolt, Jo removed the two ropes from his neck and inspected the rope burns. The rope had dug deeply into the horse's neck, but Carsig would recover. Next Jo inspected the creature's legs to see if he had pulled any muscles or torn any joints. Jo breathed a sigh of relief. The Immortals must have been smiling on them: the horse's shivering legs were free of the knots of muscle that indicated a pull.

Brisbois rewound the ropes and sauntered over to Jo. He said without inflection, "It's good we were here to help you. I don't think you'd have gotten Falar out without us."

Jo's lips pursed. She said tightly, not bothering to look up at the tall knight as she checked the gelding's last leg, "His name now is Carsig." Carsig was the name of the hostler she had worked for in Specularum, a harsh and serious man, but one who knew horses—and had gained Jo's respect because of it. But, truth be told, she had named the horse after him not only to honor her former employer, but also so that she could order "Master" Carsig about. Johauna bit her lip and then added, "And I never would have gone into the sinkhole if I had been traveling alone."

Brisbois snorted and turned back to his own horse. Karleah and Dayin stood nearby, the boy supporting the old woman. Jo stood and looked at the wizardess. Karleah's face was pale and strained with fatigue, and she held one arm close to her side.

"Karleah . . . ?" Jo began.

The crone held up a hand and shook her head. "I'll be all right. I'm just not used to witnessing such trials of nature anymore," Karleah said wryly. She threw a quick glance at Dayin and added, "Though I don't mind a good rabbit hunt now and again." She and the boy broke into laughter, and Jo smiled in return, though she didn't know why they were laughing.

Jo grabbed Carsig's reins and said, "The river's just beyond those trees. I think Carsig can make it. We'll ford the river and see how much farther we can get tonight." Jo paused and added thoughtfully, meeting the eyes of everyone but Brisbois, "It's up to us to stop that box from reaching Armstead, my friends."

The squire turned and led Carsig the remaining distance to the river, and the others fell in behind her. They were approaching the marsh edge, where the ground sloped farther to the river. As they moved forward, wading into the water, cattails and saw grass snapped and bit at them, cutting their legs. Hillocks of grass rose up from the murky water, which grew progressively deeper. Jo grimaced. The water was up to her waist already, and still the river was a long stone's throw ahead. The expanse of marsh they were traversing had seemed such a short distance before they entered it. Jo looked ahead, trying to ignore the increasing grumbles of discontent behind her. Sunlight twinkled brightly off the water and almost blinded her. In the midst of the shimmering rays, though, Jo could see a sudden cloud of darkness rise up from the water.

Jo's eyes grew wide as she watched the cloud lift from the water and move with frightening speed toward her. "Mosquitoes!" she shouted, only moments before the horde descended on her and Carsig.

The air turned to night. Jo swatted left and right, splashing water on herself and the gelding; the insects stung and bit at Jo's exposed skin and even through her clothing. She flung about furiously, trying to shake the stinging beasts. Beside her, Carsig flung his head back and forth and swung his tail. His sharp teeth snapped at the insects biting his hide.

"Jo! Jo!" Someone reached through the curtain of insects.

"Jo!" It was Karleah, behind her in the marsh. Jo swatted her tormentors and looked toward the old wizardess. She was waving her hands forward. "Go, go! The river's slow enough! Keep moving!"

The squire grabbed Carsig's reins and threw an arm over her face, then stepped forward. All around her buzzed the mosquitoes, stinging her ears, crawling through her hair, and biting her lips and eyelids. Jo couldn't take it any more. She bolted forward and began a sort of swimming stroke by using the saw grass and cattails to pull herself along. Carsig, beside her, was floundering, but the gelding had the same intention as Jo.

Jo saw that only three more hillocks of saw grass stood between her and the open river, and the sky above her lightened as she reached the edge of the mosquito swarm. Jo floundered a few more steps, then caught the side of her saddle. With supreme effort, she hauled herself up out of the water and into the saddle. Carsig struck out in a slow paddle across the wide, smooth waters.

Jo called back to Karleah, who was just entering the river on her gray mare, "Keep going! The river's clear!" She looked ahead of her at the wide expanse of river. The waters here were sluggish, despite the spring rains, and by some miracle, the insects were not following.

Suddenly Jo's flesh crawled. The squire's eyes grew wide with horror and disgust. Her free hand crept beneath the hem of her chemise. She slid her hand along her skin toward the faint, tickling sensation at her side. Her fingers touched something soft and slimy, and she jerked them away reflexively. Steeling herself, Jo reached back into her clothing and pulled loose a six-inch-long leech before it could firmly latch onto her.

Shuddering deeply, Jo threw the thing as far down-stream as she could. She heard the leech land with a *plop*, and an instant later another *gulp* announced that a fish had found a meal. Jo smiled in vengeful disgust. Then her smile turned to a painful scowl. She felt a second leech, then a third, move inside her clothing. There was no way she could remove them now, not in midriver. Jo shud-dered again and lay close to Carsig, seeking solace in the gelding's strong back and trying desperately to ignore the crawling of her skin.

The Hillfollow was bright and wide and slow. The big gelding swam with sure strokes, heading always for the opposite bank. Jo looked down at Carsig's surging fore-hooves and saw a leech streaming away from the horse's side. She wanted to pull the thing away immediately, but held back. The head would likely detach and infest the horse. No, they'd have to wait until they reached the shore before Jo could rid her and Carsig of the bloodsuckers.

Jo looked behind her. She smiled. Her comrades were spread out behind her like a small flotilla. She waved encouragingly at Karleah, who didn't return the gesture. Jo didn't blame her. They must think I'm pretty stupid, Jo thought, to bring them across the river in such an awful place. Mud, stuck horse, saw grass, mosquitoes, and now leeches! What next? Jo shook her head and turned her attention back to the approaching shore.

The far side of the river sloped gently and was quite rocky. Past the band of rock, the ground sloped steeply upward. A stand of trees lined the bank, giving way to the rapidly rising Wulfholde hills.

Carsig struck bottom and gladly made for shore. When the creature reached shallow water, Jo slid off the gelding and let him continue on his own. She ran behind a tree and pulled off her clothes as quickly as possible, dropping them to the rocky shore. The others were approaching, but she didn't care. The leeches had to come off. Modesty didn't matter at a time like this.

Jo used her knife to flick off the leeches that hadn't yet attached themselves to her skin. She shuddered as she looked down at the six still remaining on her body. Little tendrils of blood trickled out of the leeches' mouths and spread across her still-wet skin.

Desperation welling in her eyes, Jo turned to the rest of the party. They had already landed, stripped, and begun plucking their own leeches. Jo picked up her knife from the pile of clothes at her feet. Shuddering one last time, she began digging the leeches off her body. If I die, I die, she thought fatalistically. Better that than feed these blood-suckers any more. Jo flicked the last one away, stabbed it with her knife, then turned to her clothing.

Beside the pile, a naked Brisbois stood looking at her. Jo felt herself flush with embarrassment, then anger. She picked up her tunic and bridled at the dishonored knight. Brisbois merely arched an eyebrow and then held out a small, wet pouch. He said, "At least rub the salt in your wounds." He turned on his heel and walked over to his own pile of clothing. Jo caught herself looking at the man's blood-and-salt–pasted body and turned away. She pulled out a handful of wet salt and rubbed her wounds, wincing. Jo inspected her clothing, found five more leeches, which she destroyed, and then dressed.

As the others finished tending their leech bites, Jo hurried to Carsig. The gelding's head hung low, and spasms rippled across his hide. Quickly Jo applied salt to the horse's bloodsuckers; she crushed them beneath the heels of her boots after they fell to the stony ground. She stroked Carsig's velvety nose and whispered, "Don't give out on me, boy. I need you. We can't stop now." The gelding pricked his ears, then began snuffling the ground for edible grasses. Jo began tending the other animals.

Nearly half an hour passed before the leeches were all removed and wounds attended. Jo squinted at the sun lowering in the west, then picked up Carsig's rein from the ground and turned to the others. "We've got a good three hours before nightfall. Let's head out."

Karleah wrung out the hem of one sleeve and snapped, "I'm wet, I'm tired, and I don't want to go on any more today!" Her swollen lips were turned down in disgruntlement. Jo looked at the others, wondering if she herself looked as bitten.

Brisbois shook his head and said, "I'm not budging, either." He eyed Jo slyly from the corner of his eyes. Be charitable, Jo thought. The man's next words dispelled her thoughts. "It's obvious you don't know what you're doing out here, particularly after you didn't travel a few miles north to the better crossing point." Brisbois shrugged nonchalantly and sat down on a rock.

Jo stared at the man, wondering if he was telling the truth. She couldn't let him get a rise out of her, however, so she said calmly, "Be that as it may, we are now across the Hillfollow. It's time to be on the move again."

"We're wet, cold, and tired," Brisbois snapped. His hazel eyes flashed at Jo. "And I say we set up camp just up there on that hill." The man gestured behind Jo.

The squire gritted her teeth. I can't lose face! she thought angrily. I can't let Brisbois take over! In a tense tone, Jo said, "And I say we move out—now."

She locked eyes with Brisbois, and the man raised a

sardonic eyebrow. Jo's eyes narrowed as she remembered that Flinn often used the same expression; on the dishonored knight, the expression seemed almost blasphemous. Brisbois broke gaze first. He turned to Braddoc and said with a smile, "Don't you think we should camp and rest, Braddoc? It doesn't make any sense to get in a few more hours of weary travel, does it?"

The dwarf looked at Jo for a moment, his expression inscrutable. Slowly he turned his gaze to Brisbois, who smiled, then to Karleah and Dayin. The wizardess was plainly out of sorts, and the boy was obviously upset by both Karleah's condition and the tension that had built in the group. Finally, Braddoc turned back to Jo and said solidly, "I agree with Brisbois that it's not the most sensible idea to continue traveling today." Braddoc paused, and Jo pursed her lips. She seemed unable to turn away from the dwarf's single-eyed gaze. "However," Braddoc continued, then nodded reassuringly, "you're in charge here, Jo. I stand by you." The dwarf folded his arms across his chest and splayed his stance.

Jo stared at her friend, and never had she felt more grateful for Braddoc's steadfast loyalty. She flicked her gray eyes toward the knight. All right, Brisbois, she thought contemptuously. Make your next move.

As if he had read her thoughts, Brisbois arched his brow again and smiled smugly. He turned to Karleah and Dayin and said, "And what do you two say?" His voice was warm with honeyed tones. "Surely you'd rather set up camp and warm up?"

Dayin put his hand on Karleah's arm, and the two looked at each other. Jo swore they could communicate without words. Karleah turned to Brisbois and scowled, "Every bone in my body, every muscle, agrees with you,

Brisbois." The old woman nodded at Jo and then continued, "But I'm with Jo. Dayin, too. You can stay here, for
all we care." As one, she and Dayin turned toward their
mounts.

Jo took a step toward Brisbois, who slowly rose. She
looked the tall man in the eye and said smoothly, "I'd
rather you stayed behind, Brisbois, but you are my bondsman, and Sir Graybow told you to accompany me." Her
face hardened, as did her voice. "So mount up."

Jo's eyes glittered. "We're going to Threshold and get
that box before it gets to Armstead."

***

They made camp that night on a rocky ridge that rose
above the desolate Wulfholde Hills. The stony crown of
the ridge was rimmed by scrubby brush that would mask a
fire from travelers on the barrens. Jo was pleased: she knew
she wouldn't be able to forestall a mutiny if she denied the
others a fire tonight. Her companions wearily tended their
mounts, changed out of their damp clothes, and lay down
beside the meager fire Jo had built. Only Dayin and Brisbois bothered with pulling any food from their ration
packs before falling soundly asleep.

By the stillness of her companions, Jo assumed she had
been chosen for first watch. That suited her fine: it would
give her a chance to contact Flinn through the stone she
had received. Making certain the animals were properly
hobbled and her companions fully asleep, Jo took a coal-
tipped branch from the fire and ascended to the top of the
rocky knoll. She scanned the black hills around the camp,
looking for signs of the bandits rumored to roam these
wastes. Nothing was moving through the Wulfholdes that

night, nothing but the wind in the rugged grasses.

The gem was already warm when Jo pulled it from her belt pouch. It rarely cooled, and Jo drew comfort from its heat, as though Flinn's spirit were beside her, his hand resting gently on her hip. Cradling the gem reverently in her palms Jo peered down into its deep, glistening depths.

"Flinn, it has been so long," she whispered, tears rising in her eyes. She dashed them away with one hand and steeled her nerve, then lowered the gem toward the red-hot embers. Waves of heat rose in the wan light of the coals, enfolding the gem and stinging her fingertips.

Then, in the dim glow of the embers, a face began to form. Shadowy and indistinct, the face might have been a trick of the light, a suggestion imposed on the facets by her aching heart. Whether true or illusory, one thing was certain; the face was Flinn's.

"Johauna," he seemed to say, his lips moving in the ghostly shades of the gem.

"Oh, Flinn," Jo whispered, her voice cracking, the resolve to be strong fading from her. "Oh, Flinn, I've missed you so."

"And I have missed you, my love, Johauna," the shade answered stiffly, his voice faraway and sibilant.

"I did as you would have done, my love," Johauna said. "I granted Brisbois mercy, though every part of me cried out to kill him. I—"

"You still have my sword," Flinn interrupted. "You still bear Wyrmblight in my honor, do you not?"

Jo nodded, wiping tears from her eyes. "Yes, Flinn, yes I do."

"The Great Green tried to destroy it once. Still he hungers to destroy it. I can feel his hatred in this place of shadows."

"Yes," Johauna said, a nervous laugh on her lips. "But he couldn't destroy it, Flinn. He can't. I knew he wouldn't be able to. Wyrmblight bears your glory."

Flinn's face darkened, and for a frantic moment, Jo thought it might disappear in the depths of the stone. She lowered the gem toward the embers, ignoring the searing heat on her fingertips. The face brightened, and Flinn whispered again, "Is the blade speaking to you, my dear?"

"It is," Jo replied with a tearful smile. "It speaks often to me. It tells me to have faith."

A steel-edged smile formed on Flinn's face, and he nodded. "Ah, I see. Yes, Johauna, have faith. Keep your faith in Wyrmblight."

"The bards are singing of your glory, my love," Johauna broke in, wanting to turn the conversation from the sword. "They say you are becoming an Immortal. They say you will be coming back to Penhaligon."

A light seemed to dawn on Flinn's face, and his smile deepened. "Yes, the bards sing the truth. I am coming back, Johauna. I am coming back to you, to fight by your side."

"When?" Jo asked, the word little more than a breathless gasp on her lips. But the crystal was dark, and the image was gone.

Chapter XII

fter camping for the night, the five riders reached Threshold midafternoon of the next day. Braddoc's pony, who had picked up a stone that had badly bruised his hoof, was on the verge of exhaustion, and Carsig still hadn't recovered from the strain of escaping the sinkhole. The two mules and Dayin's pony also seemed weary. Only Karleah's gray mare and Brisbois's piebald seemed still fresh. Jo realized she had misjudged Brisbois's choice in horseflesh; although the mare's conformation left much to be desired, the paint was a game creature.

Jo and the others approached Threshold from the east. They came down from the Wulfholdes into the valley that housed the tiny village. Peasant farmers stopped their tilling to stare at the strangers, and a blacksmith at the edge of the town set down a red-hot horseshoe long enough to study them. Jo nodded to a few people, only one of whom reluctantly nodded back. Friendly group, she thought ironically. Hope it's only because we're coming in from the wrong side of town. Jo recalled the maps she'd been shown, then looked eastward; they were coming in on the western branch of the Duke's Road, which passed through harsh, bandit-ridden territory before arriving in Threshold. She was thankful they hadn't encountered any of the wasteland's inhabitants.

Though it had its own garrison, the village was even smaller than Bywater. Six buildings composed the center of town, and perhaps a dozen rough cottages surrounded the wooden buildings. Jo saw two taverns—the Cock's Crow and the Maiden's Blush—and scowled. Two drinking establishments for one tiny village meant only one thing: a town divided. They'd have to be careful. Appear to side with one faction or the other, and they'd likely get no help from either. Johauna Menhir shook her head and turned Carsig toward the rundown stable. A sign, hanging by a single rusted hook, displayed the place's illegible title.

Jo dismounted, and the others behind her did the same. Brisbois tossed his reins to Dayin and said, "I'm getting a drink, boy. Take care of my horse." Jo scowled as the man turned on his heel and began walking away.

"Wait, Brisbois!" Jo called out sternly. The knight did not pause, and Jo clenched her fists. She raised her voice and said, "Bondsman! Attend me!" Jo's unblinking gaze apparently bored into the man's back, for Brisbois hesitated, then stopped. He raised his hands to his side and cocked his head. Jo wondered if she would have to say anything more, but then the man slowly turned around. He shook his head, a sour smile on his face.

"Whatever you say, *Mistress*," Brisbois said with a sneer. He lowered his hands and walked back to the group. Dayin held out the horse's rein, and Brisbois snatched it from the boy.

Jo's face hardened in response both to Brisbois's words and to his callous treatment of Dayin. She was about to rebuke the man, but the stable door behind her opened. Jo turned around to see a slight, aged man standing halfway behind the door. Only his balding head and his right arm were visible as he looked inquiringly at the people before him. His pale, colorless eyes were magnified by round lenses that balanced on his nose. Jo had seen glasses before, but never this close. She was intrigued.

Jo cleared her throat and said, "Ah, good sir—" she gestured up at the sign "—I'm sorry. I'm afraid I can't make out your name."

The man glanced up at the sign and spat tobacco juice from the corner of his mouth before replying. "Sign says 'Gelar,' but that was the previous owner. Name's Hruddel. What can I do for you?" He blinked at Jo, and she was fascinated by how his thin eyelids became wide when they fluttered behind the thick lenses of his glasses.

"We'd like to lodge our horses for the night, if we may," Jo began politely.

Hruddel looked at her yellow tunic suspiciously and then at the stained but still-recognizable blue of Sir Brisbois's. Hruddel turned back to Jo. "You wouldn't have anything to do with those four Penhaligon guards who were here the other day, would you?" The hostler opened the door reluctantly, and Jo smiled at him brightly as she murmured thanks.

"Why, no, good sir. We aren't connected with the people you mentioned." Jo looked suddenly concerned. "Did they do something wrong? Where are they now? I will be sure to report them to the castellan!" Jo looked about in pretended anger.

Hruddel shook his head and said quickly, "Oh, no, they've gone. Rest assured. They left day before yesterday." Hruddel continued speaking, voicing his displeasure over the guards' treatment of him and his stable girl, but Jo heard only "day before yesterday." *How are we going to catch them in time?* she thought desperately.

The hostler turned to the others and began tending to the animals. Karleah came up to Jo while the younger woman was lost in thought and said, "You couldn't have known the box was already gone, Jo. Besides, this is the path laid out for us by Sir Graybow."

Jo turned her frightened eyes to the wizardess. "But I *should* have known! You were right when you said I have no intuition!" Johauna whispered.

"I was angry, you mean." The old crone shook her head. "You did what you did; it cannot be undone."

Though Karleah and Jo had been talking quietly, the hostler's ears were sharp. He turned from the stall where he was putting Carsig and called out to Jo, "Did you say something about a box? Those guards had a box. Strange one, at that."

Jo and Karleah exchanged glances, then Jo turned to Hruddel and smiled. She moved closer to the short man. "These guards had a box, you say?"

Hruddel looked down at the straw on the dirt floor and shifted nervously. Jo glanced at Braddoc and Brisbois, who were both standing near the man, and jerked her head. They took the hint and busied themselves by putting the rest of the animals into their stalls. Jo walked closer to Hruddel, then leaned over the stall door. She smiled softly at the man, who stared at her from behind the thick lenses of his glasses.

"Hruddel," Jo asked frankly, "what do you know about the box?"

Hruddel responded by taking a step closer and leaning confidentially toward Jo. "There's something about that

box that ain't right," he said, shaking his head worriedly.
"It swallows magic, that's what."

"What's that?" Karleah snapped. The old woman flicked
a glance at Jo as if to apologize for the interruption. Jo
shook her head faintly.

Hruddel looked at the old woman, his lips pressing into
a line. "Karleah's all right," the squire said.

Hruddel blinked as he nodded, then said to Karleah,
"You know it swallows magic then, I s'pose? When the
guards held up that charm of the constable's and it disappeared, we were all amazed."

"Disappeared?" Karleah said sharply. Her black eyes had
drawn to thin slits.

"Aye, the guards waved the amulet over the box,"
Hruddel said. His eyes widened in remembered amaze-
ment. "And then the box opened up all on its own and
swallowed the charm."

"*Swallowed* it? The box opened? Did anything come
out?" Jo asked in alarm.

"Nothing—nothing I never saw, anyway," Hruddel
answered. "The lid opened, and this purplish light shone,
and then the constable's neck chain was gone. Just like
that."

Jo was about to ask the hostler more questions, but Karleah touched the squire's arm and said, "Thank you,
Hruddel. This seems a fine stable." The old woman
pressed a golden coin into the man's palm.

Hruddel pulled his forelock and nodded his thanks. He
looked from Karleah to Jo and then asked, "Will you be
staying long, miss?"

"No. We'll be off in the morning, Hruddel," Jo
responded. "Can you recommend a place to stay?"

"There's rooms to let over at the Maiden," Hruddel

answered. "Or old Keeper Grainger lets people stay in her barn, if you're short on gold. She's a might on the strange side, though." Hruddel looked down at the coin in his hand, then he tested it between his teeth. When his teeth sunk lightly into the soft metal, he pocketed the coin inside his waistband. Hruddel nodded, well pleased.

Jo, thinking about the two taverns and the obvious feud in the town, decided on the barn. They could handle an eccentric old biddy. Jo smothered a laugh. Isn't that what we do with Karleah? she thought. Besides, that'll save us some of Sir Graybow's money. Jo set her hand on Hruddel's and asked, "Why is she called 'Keeper'?"

Hruddel shrugged and said, "No one knows why, leastways no one I know. Her mother was called Keeper, and her mother before her. The Grainger women have always been called Keeper."

Jo nodded and then asked, "Can you point us the way to Keeper Grainger's then? And does this woman serve meals?"

"She will if you ask her to," Hruddel answered. "She's got the last place on the north end of town, even past the garrison."

Jo checked Wyrmblight's fastenings, then grabbed her belongings and said to the hostler, "Thank you, Hruddel. We'll be by in the morning for our mounts. Oh, and can you give a bran mash to the gelding and the one pony? They've had rough going the past two days."

Hruddel's eyes gleamed suddenly. "It'd be my pleasure, miss. I'll add a couple handfuls of coarse salt, too, to put the spring back in their steps. The pair—and the rest of the lot, too—will be fit as fiddles by tomorrow."

Jo gave the man a satisfied nod, pleased that Hruddel had suggested the addition of salt to the mash. The hostler knows his work, Jo thought. Carsig'll be ready to travel tomorrow. With the Black Peaks ahead of us, we *all* need a night to rest. Johauna and Karleah turned and left the stable. Braddoc, Brisbois, and Dayin were waiting for them outside the barn door. The dwarf was standing alert, watching the few townsfolk who walked by. Brisbois and Dayin were using their toes to flick stones in and out of a circle one of them had scribed in the packed dirt.

Glancing at everyone, Jo said, "We're going to stay at a place called old Keeper Grainger's. She'll let us sleep in her barn for a pittance and feed us a meal. Let's go." Jo started away from the stable.

Brisbois stood slowly, planted his feet, and crossed his arms. "I'm not going," he said. "I want a decent bed. A man just told us the Maiden's Blush has beds for let. I'm not going to sleep in a barn." There was a mulish pout around his lips, which were partly disguised by the moustache and goatee Brisbois was growing back. Jo was certain Brisbois had shaved them off so he couldn't be identified.

Jo dropped her belongings. She looked at Brisbois, then casually flicked loose one of the tabs holding Wyrmblight in its harness. "Over my dead body," she said insolently.

Brisbois drew his sword and shouted, "I can arrange that!" He advanced on Jo, rapidly closing the distance separating them. Jo yanked Wyrmblight from the harness in one quick pull and shifted to a crouching position.

From the corner of her eye, Jo saw Braddoc and Dayin racing between her and Brisbois. Angrily she waved them away and hissed, "Get back! This is between him and me!" The two did not stop, however. Braddoc stood before Jo, and Dayin put his hands on Brisbois's chest. The knight stopped and stared at Jo, his anger in check. Jo scowled.

Karleah stepped forward and said severely, "Stop it, you two! We've had enough. Now, just who's in charge here?" Karleah's black eyes flashed at Jo.

"I am!" Jo said quickly, jerking her thumb at her chest. She stared at Brisbois, but the knight only arched his brows in mockery.

"Then act like it!" Karleah snapped.

Jo stared at Karleah, suddenly chastised. I haven't acted properly, have I? she thought. Oh, what would Flinn do? Jo glanced at Brisbois, then at Braddoc and Dayin. She squared her shoulders and said firmly, "Pick up your things. We're going to Keeper Grainger's." Jo looked at Brisbois, forcing nonchalance into her manner. She picked up her things and set off, only just daring to listen to the footsteps falling into place behind her. Jo let out her held breath when she heard Brisbois's heavy tread join the others'.

The walk to Keeper Grainger's was a short one. The group met no one along the way, not even when they passed the little, walled garrison. A farmer from a distance did stop to look at them, and Jo wondered why the town was so suspicious.

She turned up the walkway toward the last cottage on the north end of town. A rough rock wall separated this property from the rest, and, on the well-tended lawn, scattered patches of flowers were beginning to bloom. The house itself, though small, was tidy and trim, as was the small barn Jo could see in the background. She knocked on the pine-green door and wondered how much help old Keeper Grainger employed. Keeper Grainger's home was the most well-kept place Jo had seen here in Threshold.

Braddoc, Karleah, Dayin, and Brisbois gathered behind Jo just as the door opened. A thin, long-limbed woman of indeterminate age stood there with a questioning expression in her green eyes. Jo guessed that the woman's age was closer to the cradle than the deathbed.

Her eyes are the color of those limes I saw at the market, Jo thought, recalling seeing the strange tropical fruit once at Specularum. It was a cool, clear color, like that of a depthless pool. Could this woman really be the one she was looking for? Jo shook her head and said tentatively, "Ah . . . Keeper Grainger?"

The woman smiled and nodded. "Yes. Is there something I can do for you?" Her pale eyes lingered on Jo, and her thin nostrils flared slightly. A shadow crossed the woman's face, then she quickly looked at the others.

Brisbois pushed forward, a dazzling smile on his face. Brisbois's eyes never left Keeper Grainger's as he took her hand and bowed low over it. "How do—"

Jo cut in. "We were told you rent out your barn?" She laid her hand warningly on Brisbois. Brisbois pulled back and said nothing.

Keeper Grainger cast a lingering, inquiring look at Sir Brisbois before turning back to Johauna. "Yes," she said simply, "but I do not use it to stable animals."

Jo shook her head. "We've already stabled our mounts over at Hruddel's," she said. "He recommended your place to us."

Keeper Grainger raised one brow. "Hruddel recommended my place?" she asked coolly. Her pale eyelids fluttered half closed.

Jo said, "It would only be for one night, please. We'd be willing to pay, too, for a meal tonight and something for the morning. We're leaving at first light."

Keeper Grainger looked at Jo, then nodded and said, "I'll let you stay the night, and I'll have a meal for you in an hour or so. But that'll be—" she looked over Jo's group quickly "—four goldens for all. I'll send you off in the morning with a full belly and something for your pockets, too. Fair?" Keeper Grainger's pale green eyes stared unblinkingly at Jo.

The squire nodded. "Aye, more than fair," Jo answered. Johauna took out the four goldens and pressed the coins into Keeper Grainger's palm.

"Thank you," Keeper Grainger said quietly, then hesitated. "May I know your names?" Her pale eyes flitted over the group and lingered on Brisbois again.

"I'm Squire—" Jo began, then stopped as Karleah's bony fingers clenched on the young woman's arm.

"I think it's best we remain anonymous travelers, Keeper," Karleah interjected. Jo looked at the old wizardess and saw that she wore a carefully blank expression. Am I missing something? Jo asked herself, though she found she suddenly felt Karleah was right.

Keeper Grainger nodded her head. Jo felt compelled to reach out and grasp the woman's hand, but Karleah's fingers tightened. Jo restrained herself.

"Of course. As you wish," Keeper Grainger said a moment later. "Please, let me show you the way to the barn. It's quite warm and comfortable, for I haven't used it to stable animals in many a year." She closed the door to her cottage and picked up two lanterns resting on a nearby stone. With slow, deliberate steps, Keeper Grainger led the way past her house and to the barn behind the cottage.

Jo glanced over at Brisbois, who seemed almost enchanted by their new host. Jo realized that she also felt an odd attraction to the alluring woman. Watching her carefully, Jo tried to analyze what made the Keeper so compelling. She was physically intriguing, her tall, solid frame giving the impression of inner strength. Her face, too, bespoke strength—and beauty. Jo continued to study their host as the woman led the way to the one-story barn. Every move she made was filled with such fluid grace that Jo felt instantly clumsy.

As though in confirmation of her feelings, Jo tripped over a root half-buried in the soil. She fell to the ground, her arms and legs sprawling. Keeper Grainger was immediately at Jo's side, inquiring after her. Brisbois, too, leaped to Jo's side and helped the squire stand. Jo murmured her thanks to Keeper Grainger and shot an acid look at Brisbois. The man never noticed, for his eyes were once again on their host.

Jo brushed off a few leaves and dirt, while the Keeper bent and picked something up from the ground. "I believe you dropped this," the woman said and handed Jo the pouch that held the giant gem she had received from the stranger in Kelvin. The pouch felt strangely chill as it dropped into Jo's hand. She blushed, her secret seeming suddenly conspicuous. But the woman knelt again, noticing something else on the ground. "And this."

Keeper Grainger stared at one of the small abelaat crystals she carried.

"Oh, thank you, Keeper Grainger," Jo said nervously. "My birthstone. I would have been crushed to have lost it." She held out her hand, but the woman only lifted the crystal to light. Her pale green eyes were wide with fear. Karleah moved forward suddenly and snatched the crystal from Keeper Grainger's hand. The old wizardess helped Jo stand.

Keeper Grainger looked at the people who surrounded her. Her eyes were calm and clear once more, her hands serenely tucked into her shift. She stood slowly and gestured toward the barn door, only a few steps behind her. "Please," the woman said, with only the faintest break in her voice, "make yourselves comfortable inside. I must prepare your meal." Keeper Grainger turned to go, then pulled up short. "And then we must talk," she whispered.

ﾞﾞ ﾞﾞ ﾞﾞ ﾞﾞ ﾞﾞ

Karleah huddled farther back into the gray horse blanket she had wrapped about herself. She was cold, it was true, but she also wrapped up to remain just beyond the light cast by the fire in the brazier. As Keeper Grainger tended the fire, Karleah and her comrades finished their meal and waited for her to speak. Setting aside their plates, Jo, Brisbois, and Dayin arranged themselves on their blankets between the old wizardess and Keeper Grainger.

Karleah breathed a tiny sigh of relief. Her companions provided yet another screen between her and the other witch. Despite her wariness around the Keeper, Karleah was glad they had found the woman. Discovering the secrets that the Keeper kept could well arm them for battling the box once they had intercepted it. Still in the shadows, Karleah nodded her approval when Jo gestured for Braddoc to stand guard with his battle-axe. Not that the dwarf could do much good against the Keeper, Karleah thought spitefully.

Keeper Grainger stood gracefully and began collecting the emptied plates. The woman's eyes met Karleah's, and for a moment Karleah let herself feel the strange, sad attraction the woman engendered in people. Then Karleah snorted "Harrumph!" and turned away. The wizardess would not be lost in those pale eyes of green, not her.

It was easy to see that the others had been lost—particularly Brisbois. The man acted as if he had never seen a woman before. Dayin, usually so intuitive, had also been completely taken in by the Keeper. The boy had spent the better part of the evening helping her with the meal and making sleeping arrangements in the barn. His bright blue eyes shone when he looked at the woman, and Karleah felt a twinge of jealousy.

The old woman shook herself. I'm much too old to feel that way, she thought, then turned her musings to the dwarf and the squire. Karleah couldn't read Braddoc. He seemed respectful of the woman, though not awed or infatuated, as Dayin and Brisbois were. Braddoc had been unusually silent since they had arrived, and Karleah wondered why. The old wizardess's eyes flickered over to the dwarf, standing nearby. Braddoc held his battle-axe crosswise in his arms, in his standard ready position. His good eye remained focused on Keeper Grainger as she walked about the barn, plumping pillows and smoothing blankets. At least the dwarf, if no one else, seems to have his senses about him, Karleah thought.

She turned to look at Jo, sitting cross-legged in front of her. The young woman had tidied her clothing and rebraided her hair. Jo's expression was intent upon the Keeper, but every now and then the squire's brows knit in anxiety. Karleah saw Jo stroke Wyrmblight, which, as usual, lay beside the girl. The crone smiled. Ah, so the blade is talking to you again! she thought. Good. If anything can help you keep your wits, it's Flinn's sword. In her other hand Jo clutched an odd pouch she had been wearing on her belt. When the squire lifted her hand from it to adjust one of the buckles on her boot, Karleah noticed that Jo's moist handprint remained on the pouch.

A moment later, she was clutching it again.

The old woman's tired eyes flicked to Keeper Grainger, who now sat cross-legged beside the brazier. Beneath the folds of her long dress, the Keeper's legs curved gracefully away. Karleah doubted she had ever seen a more physically perfect woman. And with a brain to match, too, the crone thought suddenly. Perhaps that is the secret of her allure.

Karleah pursed her thin lips. The crone rested her chin in her hands. "Tell the tale as you know it, Keeper," Karleah whispered softly, "Your time has come."

Keeper Grainger added one last piece of peat to the brazier and stoked the embers. Pungent smoke swirled up and away toward a hole in the barn's ceiling. Keeper Grainger's pale eyes flicked from one person to another, apparently trying to see past the shadows that enfolded Karleah. The woman turned back to the brazier and began speaking quietly.

"I do not know your names, it is true," Keeper Grainger said, "but I know your purpose—and your destination."

"What?" Jo cried out.

Karleah shook her head. You must learn more control, girl, she thought. You *must*. Your impetuousness will be the end of you someday.

Apparently the young squire had the same thought, for she calmed herself and said, stiffly, "What do you mean, Keeper? It's true we are on a journey, which of course means we must have a destination."

Keeper Grainger nodded at Jo and smiled. The light from the fire illuminated her radiant face. She said, "Perhaps it would be best if I first explain why I am called the Keeper. Then we can discuss your journey."

"We would be delighted to hear your tale, Keeper."

"Then listen, and listen well, child," Keeper Grainger

said softly, though the words rang clear to the rafters of the barn. She folded her legs together and leaned toward Jo, Brisbois, and Dayin. Braddoc took a step backward and hid in shadows, much as Karleah had done.

The old crone hunched down even farther into her horse blanket, as if seeking protection in the wool fibers. She wondered just how much the Keeper would reveal, and what she in turn would have to tell her comrades. Let it fall as it may, Karleah warned herself. She clutched her staff a little tighter. No spells had returned to the oak, but she felt more secure with it anyway.

"Why I am called Keeper, I will tell you now, as I was told, as my mother before me was told," Keeper Grainger began. Her pale eyes focused on the rafters above, and the shadows from the fire distorted her upturned face. "I am the last Keeper, for I did not believe the tale—until tonight, when I saw your stones of abelaat blood, Squire-Without-a-Name."

Karleah saw Jo's fingers clench on Wyrmblight, but she did not cry out. The old woman nodded approvingly.

"I did not believe the tale handed down from mother to daughter in my family," Keeper Grainger continued. "I did not wish to be Keeper, as my mother had before me. I did not wish to have a daughter to pass on the secrets I was taught, so I spurned all advances and offers of marriage. I wished the line of Keeper to end with me, that the secret burden of eons could end with me as well."

"What burden is that?" Brisbois asked gently. Karleah turned to watch the man. Could he really be looking at the Keeper with something other than his usual wanton lust? It seemed unlikely.

The Keeper surveyed the group before her. "Thousands upon thousands of years ago, so long ago that even the

elves and the dwarves—" she inclined her head toward
Braddoc, who responded in kind "—have but the slightest
memory, our world, Mystara, was closely tied to another,
whose name I dare not mention. It was a place of darkness
and shadow and powerful sorcery, though not an evil
place. Indeed, it had a beauty and nobility that Mystara has
never attained. For in that world, there lived a race of sur-
passing grace. In the old tongue they were called the
a'bay'otte, a name which has been corrupted by the
tongues of men to abelaat."

Jo reflexively touched her scarred left shoulder, and
Dayin crossed his arms, his fists guarding the marks on his
inner elbows. Interesting, Karleah thought, that memories
can be provoked from a single word.

"Abelaats . . . beautiful?" Jo asked, incredulously. "I
have never seen a fouler creature in all the world."

"Yes," the Keeper said simply. She added, "Those
abelaats that live now are horrible perversions of the creatures of old. The original abelaats roamed their own world
in grace and constructed magical gates into Mystara—for
they were a sorcerous race, and their world a sorcerous
world. But Mystara, in those days, was not magical at all.
Was it, dwarf?" Keeper Grainger turned to Braddoc, who
stood in the shadows.

Braddoc cleared his throat clumsily and said, "No . . .
not as it is today—or so legends say."

"Why didn't you tell us about the abelaats before, Braddoc?" Jo asked.

The dwarf shrugged. "It was an ancient, ancient tale, so
old no one believed it anymore. I've plenty of ancient
dwarven tales that I haven't bored you with."

"Believe the tale, dwarf," Keeper Grainger said huskily.
"Believe the tale, for it is true." She turned back to the

others and continued, "The abelaats multiplied across their twilight world, where they were the master race—beautiful and shining. They crossed their magical bridges to reach Mystara, and spread out here as well." Keeper Grainger paused for breath, and the fire crackled in the silence that fell.

"But, in the dawn-time of Mystara, new races crawled from their birthing beds. The elven race slowly gained a foothold on Mystara, as did the dwarves. The abelaats lived contentedly with these new folk, trading with the artisan dwarves, and teaching small magicks to the elves. They even traded their blood crystals to the young races of Mystara.

"But the abelaats had not realized the power of their crystals. They did not know the magic inherent in their blood and spittle. It was their essence, their magical essence, that they were gradually trading away to the dwarves and elves. And the land changed because of the abelaat crystals. Mystara began to crave magic, as a starving man craves food. It began to draw magic away from the abelaats' home world, through the sorcerous portals and gates the abelaats themselves had built.

"Then Mystara gave birth to a new race, the humans." The Keeper paused, looking at Johauna and Brisbois, a faint edge of accusation in her eyes. Karleah pursed her lips and wondered how the woman knew not to look at her or Dayin.

"Go on, Keeper," Dayin whispered. "Go on."

The woman nodded. "The birth of humans marked the doom of the abelaats, for humans hated abelaats and called them the creatures of the night. Humans multiplied quickly and took over the land. The abelaats were forced from their homes and hunted." Keeper Grainger lowered her head momentarily. "The butcheries they brought on the abelaats were great. They hunted them for fear and sport and cruelty, and they left their bodies to lie in waste.

"That's when the abelaats began their ceaseless war with the humans. They started to hunt them for food. But even that was no great crime—for millennia, the abelaats had fed off one another as well."

"The abelaats . . . *ate* each other?" Jo asked, horror lacing her words.

Keeper Grainger shook her head. "No. They drew sustenance from each other's blood. But as their numbers dwindled on Mystara, and as their gates to their home world collapsed, one by one, the abelaats began to seek sustenance from human blood."

The Keeper's voice hardened. "Humans destroyed all but a few of the abelaats. The survivors hid in the mountains and the valleys and the deepest gorges, seeking escape from the encroaching hordes. In the end, only one true abelaat remained: Aeltic was his name."

"Abelaats had names?" Jo asked hesitantly. Her hand rubbed her scarred shoulder nervously.

"*Have,* squire, not had," Keeper Grainger gently chided. "Even the pathetic creatures who attacked you and the boy had names."

Jo shot an amazed glance at Dayin, who returned her look. "How . . . how did you know we've been . . . we've *both* been attacked by abelaats?" Jo asked uncertainly. Karleah felt a pang in her heart for the two of them. Neither wanted to be reminded of those awful times.

The Keeper's pale green eyes flickered in the firelight as she gazed from Jo to Dayin. "The bile of the abelaats lingers in your bodies. It . . . gives off a distinct odor. Some of us are sensitive to it."

Karleah leaned forward intently. Will the Keeper reveal her secret? she wondered.

Keeper Grainer looked down at her white hands, then slowly added another piece of peat to the brazier. Her furrowed brow smoothed, and a certain calmness seemed to enter the woman. For a moment, it seemed as if the Keeper would not continue.

"Tell them, and be done," Karleah hissed.

The pain in Keeper Grainger's eyes deepened, and she closed them as she spoke. "What none of the legends say is that the abelaats' world was drained of so much magic that the abelaats who were still there grew weak and, eventually, turned slowly to stone. Magic was their life essence, and without it, they became crude, slumbering statues. As the magic energy ebbed, the last gates between their world and this one fell. The abelaats on Mystara could not return home, could not bring back magic to awaken their sleeping brothers from the stony ground."

"And Aeltic descended from those few survivors," Karleah supplied.

"Yes. Aeltic was the last true abelaat."

Karleah huffed and drew the blanket back from her features. "A pretty and tragic tale, the Keeper tells. But it is only half true."

Karleah stood and gestured for the others to remain seated. A wry smile formed on the crone's lips. "Your story has told us much that we needed to know. Now let me tell my companions the rest. The abelaats were a beautiful race indeed, as are vampires and other creatures of darkness. Their beauty is cold and lethal. Abelaats have no love for the children of the day, treating them like cattle, subsisting on their blood. Humans, elves, and dwarves alike."

"Abelaats are vampires?" Jo asked, confused.

Karleah shook her head. "No. They are like vampires, but are living creatures, not undead. Abelaats are born of sorcerous darkness and blood-lust."

Jo looked worriedly at the Keeper, expecting her to take offense. But the woman's drawn features stared emptily into the brazier.

Karleah approached Braddoc, jabbing a finger into his chest. "The dwarves feel a kinship with the abelaats because they were, like the dwarves, creatures of stone and darkness. According to dwarven legends, abelaats and dwarves were brothers. That is rubbish. It was only by trickery and illusion that the abelaats could even move among Braddoc's folk."

"You've said enough, old crone," Brisbois growled, rising to his feet and setting a protective hand on the Keeper's shoulder.

Jo interposed herself between the enraged man and Karleah, Wyrmblight raised and ready in her hands. Though her eyes sternly warned Brisbois back, she spoke to Karleah behind her, "Please, Karleah. Isn't it obvious Keeper Grainger is in pain—"

"Pain?" the old witch cried. "Pain? You yourself should know about pain, Johauna. You know what it feels like to be attacked by an abelaat. And you, idiot knight. Has this woman's spell so completely enraptured you that you cannot guess the source of her allure?"

Stunned, Brisbois stared at the Keeper.

"It's from the abelaat blood," Dayin murmured without peering up.

Karleah nodded, keeping her blazing eyes on the two fighters. Brisbois blinked as if he had been slapped in the face, and Jo's arms dropped heavily from their defensive posture.

"Yes, it's true," Karleah said. "The abelaats have many magical powers, and this 'attraction' is one that has allowed them to live among humans all these years," the old woman said. "All the abelaats that came to Mystara before the gates collapsed share in that beauty. Those who are gated in now are twisted by their journey, transformed into horrible monsters." Karleah pointed a crooked finger at the Keeper, who still sat on the floor beside the brazier. "The Keeper is from the old line."

Keeper Grainger nodded. A tear rolled down her cheek. "Aeltic—the last true abelaat on Mystara—was my father."

Chapter XIII

our father!" Jo exclaimed. Stunned, she stared in disbelief at Keeper Grainger. The others around her, even Karleah, in the shadows, leaned toward the woman beside the brazier.

The Keeper nodded. "Yes, my father, though so many times removed as to no longer hold the meaning you have for 'father.' He was the father of the Keepers—we who keep the memory of the abelaat alive. Aeltic was the last abelaat, and he took as his consort a human. Their offspring, a daughter who bore traits both abelaat and human, mated also with a human. And so it went for a thousand years, until at last I was born. I, the last Keeper, have only a bare trace of my father's blood left in me."

"This is all neither here nor there," Karleah spoke up in her raspy voice from the shadows. "You are the last Keeper—tell us what we need to know."

Keeper Grainger stared in the direction of Karleah's voice. "You are bold, Karleah Kunzay of the Red Ones," she said angrily. "Though I was but a babe when last we met, I thought it might be you."

"The ancient traditions demand that you answer our questions, Keeper," Karleah said sternly, drawing the blanket up to shade her features.

"I have denied my vows of tradition, witch," Keeper Grainger rejoined, "for I have taken no mate. The line of Keepers ends with me."

"Of course it does," Karleah snapped. "But the time has come for you to give us what the Keepers have passed down from generation to generation—and you know that."

Keeper Grainger's face clouded over. Her pale skin flushed as she bent her head, and Jo had to strain to hear the woman's voice. "You have come to find the abaton— what you call simply the puzzle box—which Auroch has unleashed on Mystara."

"Yes," Karleah said, her bony frame finally entering the circle of light.

The Keeper continued, "The abaton was created to save the abelaat race, to give them one final portal for entering and leaving Mystara."

"Wait a moment," Jo said, shaking her head in confusion. "What good is a portal if there aren't any abelaats to use it? In their home world, the abelaats are asleep—slumbering statues of stone, like you said. And those abelaats that are here are hideous monsters who wouldn't think to use a gate."

"The portal is not so much for the abelaats to cross," Keeper Grainger replied, "at least not initially. The portal's first function is as a drain, to draw magic out of Mystara and deposit it into the abelaats' world. Only when it has drawn enough magic to awaken the first abelaats, only then will the abaton begin to serve as a portal for the creatures themselves."

"But, why would they want to come to Mystara, where they are hated?" Dayin asked quietly.

The Keeper smiled wanly at the young apprentice. "The abelaats desire more than all else to draw their magic back to their own world. They want to revive their slumbering kin. After they are awakened, they will march upon Mystara, to reclaim it as their own."

Jo turned and looked at Brisbois. The man was obviously confused. But she had a sudden revelation, a horrible realization that no one had voiced. "That must mean Teryl Auroch is in league with them!"

"Yes."

"Because he, like Keeper Grainger, is part abelaat," Karleah conjectured.

The Keeper nodded leadenly and added, "Teryl Auroch's mother was a human sorceress who dared to travel to the land of the abelaat. She took enough magic with her to awaken one of the ancient creatures. She never returned, but gave birth to a son—"

"Who built the abaton to shift the balance of magic back," Jo concluded.

The Keeper simply nodded.

Dayin whimpered slightly, tears running down his face. Jo knelt beside him, sliding her arm gently about his shoulders. "It'll be all right, Dayin," she said stupidly. Censoring herself for the platitude, she elaborated, "You are your own person now, Dayin. That man, Auroch—he isn't your father any more than I am your mother. The evil that he's done can't touch you."

The boy's sky-blue eyes regarded Jo coldly. "You don't understand," he said, his voice uncommonly bitter. "I've got abelaat blood in me, too. You just heard about how they've been hunted and tortured. You've heard their tragic story. It has *everything* to do with me. Teryl Auroch *is* my father."

Karleah sat down next to Dayin and held him in her arms. She said, "The boy is right, Jo. Let him feel what he feels."

Brisbois had begun to pace nervously. "So, if we don't intercept this—this stupid box, we'll have an army of monsters marching down our throats. Is that what you are saying?"

"Yes."

"Why are you helping us?" Jo blurted, suddenly, rising from Dayin's side and clutching Wyrmblight nervously. "You've got abelaat blood in you, too—"

"Teryl Auroch is an abomination to the abelaats. He wants vengeance, he wants Mystara to suffer for stealing the abelaats' magic. I don't want that to happen. You must understand, Mystara is *my* world, the only one I've ever known. I don't want it to be destroyed any more than you," the woman said, finally standing from her place. "Besides, he will desire my death in his quest to purify Mystara of all its human traces. As his power grows, he will become more and more aware of me. He will come for me soon. I have seen it."

"Come, Dayin, we must find other accommodations tonight," Karleah whispered, slowly rising. She helped the boy to his feet, and he sadly clutched her side.

Jo shook her head in outrage and confusion. "There must be something we can do!"

"There is," the Keeper said despondently, moving toward the door, which Braddoc pulled open. "Find the abaton. Remove it from any source of magic. Find a way to destroy it." She paused and reached into a pocket in her dress. "Take this." She held out her hand, presenting a

beautiful amber crystal, eight sided and pointed on the
ends. "It is a crystal from my father—the most powerful
magic I can give you.

"Now I think you should go. You can find lodgings at
the Maiden's Blush," the Keeper said. As she stepped out
of the barn, she added, "Do not come this way again."

ła ła ła ła ła

Jo tossed fitfully in her bed, wishing they could set out
for Armstead. But earlier that evening she had lost the
argument about pushing on before morning. Even Braddoc had refused, saying that she obviously had never traveled through the Altan Tepes Mountains. Karleah, too,
noted wryly that in order to capture the abaton, they must
first reach Armstead alive. Despite all the good reasons for
staying in Threshold that night, Jo wanted to leave, if only
to pay Brisbois back for his sneering taunts. "I should have
killed him in the alley," she told herself, rolling angrily
over.

Brisbois wasn't the only surly malcontent. When they
had checked in, Jo asked the innkeeper about sending a
message back to Penhaligon and was answered with a stupid stare. The man was irritable enough, having been
awakened after midnight, and that request sent him over
the top. He'd even charged them for four separate rooms.
Brisbois, of course, took full advantage, demanding a
room for himself. Too tired to quibble, Karleah and
Dayin, Braddoc, and Johauna each took the other rooms.
The waste of gold irked Jo to no end, but, clearly, they
would acquire no other accommodations tonight.

There was a shattering of glass, a man's scream, and a
pounding thump from the room above Jo—Brisbois's

oom. As she leaped up from her bed, Jo heard Braddoc
ise in the room next door, heard the rattle of his axe
eing lifted from the doorknob, where he had hung it. Jo's
and reached for Wyrmblight but drew back: the sword's
great length would make it useless in the man's room. She
lipped a shift over her shoulders and, grabbing her belt,
lung it around her waist. She tore open the door and
olted up the stairs. As she checked to make sure her dagger was in its sheath, Jo heard Braddoc's solid footfalls on
he steps behind her.

Jo reached the head of the stairs, rushed for Brisbois's
loor, and threw it open. In the wan light of an oil lamp,
he saw Brisbois standing, stunned, beside a broken win-
low. Shattered glass lay in glittering triangles across the
loor, blood showing on a few of the edges. Then she
loticed that the dishonored knight's arm was bleeding.

"What happened in here?" Braddoc demanded, appear-
ng in the doorway behind Jo and hefting his axe.

Brisbois gave a dismissing gesture and winced from the
ain in his arm. "Nothing," he slurred. "An owl or some-
hing was looking in the window at me."

"Looking in the window?" Jo asked, glaring at the man.
"You're drunk, aren't you?"

"No," spat Brisbois. He suddenly straightened and,
linking, tried to look Jo straight in the eyes. "It *was* look-
ng at me," he insisted, his voice still thick with liquor. "I
hink it was Verdilith, the Great Green."

With an expression of disgust, Braddoc turned to leave.
"Yeah, Verdilith, the Great Green Owl. You'd better do
omething about that arm." He disappeared from the
loorway.

"So you thought you'd punch the window out to let
his owl come in?" Jo asked sarcastically. She walked over

to the window and peered outside, her heart pounding with excitement.

"No, my mistress," Brisbois said with a mocking bow. "I tried to stab it with my sword." He gestured toward the bloody blade, leaning in the corner of the room.

He's a fool, a drunken fool, and nothing more, whispered a voice inside Johauna's head. She felt the warmth of the abelaat stone in her belt pouch. Yes, Flinn, she thought, I know he's a fool. She looked out the window toward the ground below. "Where's this owl's body?"

"I thought it fell," Brisbois said, leaning over her shoulder to see out the window.

By the odd smell of Brisbois's breath, Jo was sure he was drunk. She pulled away from him and snarled, "There wasn't any owl, Brisbois, except in your drunken imagination. You didn't stab Verdilith. You stabbed yourself. And you'll pay for that window out of your own pocket, come morning."

Brisbois whirled on her, some stinging retort on his lips, but when his eyes met hers, he averted his gaze and fell silent. Shuffling to a hook on the wall, he gingerly opened his pack and removed a small box. He flipped the lip back, revealing a bolt of gauze, a few sharp-edged knives and needles, and a small bottle. Uncorking the bottle, he took a swig, then spattered his wounded arm with the rest. Tearing away a piece of the gauzy bolt with his teeth, the man began to wrap the wound. Jo watched from across the gloom as he attended himself.

Brisbois paused long enough to glare at the young squire. "If you're not going to help, get out."

Jo felt an involuntary sneer cross her face. "I wish I could say the same to you," she muttered under her breath. She stalked out of the room, leaving the door ajar.

The dishonored knight kicked the door shut with his boot and continued to bandage the wound. He smiled.

A poisonous tendril of gas rose from his nose.

🐾 🐾 🐾 🐾 🐾

Spring had only newly come to the Black Peak Mountains as Jo and her companions rode through the range. Jo set a north-by-northwesterly route, seeking the tiny village of Armstead, somewhere in the wilderness ahead. Although the path she chose wound through the mountains, her sense of direction was true. Unfortunately, the mountain paths were too treacherous to chance fast travel.

Lost in thoughts of the abaton, Jo didn't notice when the mountains' heights changed the climate from one of spring to one of winter. Patches of ice and unexpectedly deep snow lined the ravines and passages between the Black Peaks. Much of the rock was obsidian, which lent the range its name, as did the sheets of ice, black from the underlying obsidian, lingering along some sides of the mountains.

The trail was rugged, little better than forging across country. In fact, when the path turned east, the group abandoned it, preferring instead to continue to head north by northwest. At one point, Brisbois said he saw hoof prints whose horseshoes bore the emblem of the castle, but none of the others could spot them in the trampled ground.

At midday Jo held up her hand and halted the group. She patted Carsig's neck and watched the horse's white breath curl lazily away. The big gelding was holding his own. Jo blew on her hands and rubbed them to warm them; she pulled her woolen cape closer. She hadn't really

believed Sir Graybow when he had said she would need
such a warm garment for the mountains, but she was glad
now that the man had insisted.

Johauna looked up at the sheer rock and ice surfaces of
the mountains surrounding her. "And I thought the
Wulfholdes were rugged," she murmured to herself. She
had never seen mountains before. She let Carsig have his
head so that he could snuffle the ground for something
edible, and Jo jumped off to stretch her legs.

The few harsh grasses that could survive this arid land
had not yet turned green with spring growth. Carsig and
the other animals contented themselves with the dried
blades, snorting puffs of frosty air as they nibbled the
mountain grass. Every now and then a horse or mule
would find a tasty, succulent snow crocus or other early
blooming flower.

Jo joined her comrades. Braddoc was smiling to himself,
and Jo realized the dwarf felt at home in these mountains.
Karleah snorted and sat on a nearby, flat rock. She drank
from her waterskin, oblivious to the walls of ice and rock
surrounding her. Only Dayin's expression remained one of
wonder and disbelief as he stared at the cliff faces.

"Have you seen any more sign of the guards' passage?"
Karleah asked testily. The crone clutched the tattered remnant of a gray silk shawl around her bony shoulders. Dayin
came and stood next to her.

Both Jo and Braddoc shook their heads. Braddoc said,
"Not since this morning, Karleah. Johauna stopped us at a
good point. There're two ravines ahead that could be the
paths the guards took. I'll scout ahead and see if I can find
any more tracks."

"It's hard with all the rock and ice," Jo said. "But maybe
they'll have gone through a snowdrift or two, and we'll get

ıcky." Johauna went to Fernlover and pulled out a loaf of
►read and a chunk of dried venison. She returned to her
riends and, using her knife, began slicing and handing out
he food.

Karleah grunted her thanks, bit a huge bite from her
ood with her strong white teeth, and said, "Give me a
ninute to—heh, heh—'wolf' my food, and then I'll
heck out the passages. Maybe I can scent something."
Karleah smiled, her canines gleaming in the bright light of
he midday sun that shone overhead. An eagle, attracted
erhaps by the travelers, circled above. Its piercing cry
choed off the mountainsides.

"Can I go with you, Karleah?" Dayin asked. He began
ɔ eat his food quickly, too. "Maybe I can scent something
ou might miss," he said through a mouthful of bread.

The wizardess shook her head. "No, son. You'd only
ow me down and be a cause for worry," Karleah said.
he pointed a thin finger up at the circling eagle. "She'd
ave you in her talons before I'd even hear her dive to the
round. Out here I can't protect you like I could in my
voods. *There* everyone knows not to touch my young rab-
it." The old woman took another bite. She chewed her
nouthful and said at the same time, "Why you chose to
e a cottontail is beyond me."

"Karleah shapechanges into a wolf and you into a rab-
it?" Johauna asked. She sliced another strip of venison
nd handed it to Karleah. At Braddoc's nod, the squire
iced him a strip as well.

"Why a rabbit?" Braddoc asked. "And why can you
hange into only one animal? That doesn't seem very use-
ıl." He gestured at the bird flying above. "If you could
ırn into an eagle, I'll bet you could spot the guards carry-
ıg the abaton. Then we'd know for sure which way to

go—and could even cut them off, if possible." The dwar[f] chewed his food slowly.

Dayin shrugged, his shoulders lost beneath the thick fu[r] vest that Flinn had given him. "I like rabbits, and I wante[d] to be one," the boy said. "They're lots smarter than peopl[e] give them credit for. Besides, they're small and can wiggl[e] into places most other creatures couldn't. They're fas[t], too." Dayin smiled widely at the old wizardess. "I've give[n] Karleah quite a run in the woods."

The crone snorted, then turned to Braddoc. "To answe[r] your question, dwarf, there are mages who can learn t[o] shapechange into more than one creature, but they tak[e] on merely the animal *form* and not the animal *spirit*. Whe[n] I am the wolf, I *am* that animal. I wanted Dayin to experi[?]ence that same sensation, and he does." She nodded he[r] head toward the boy. "Gather up the animals, will you? [It] wouldn't do to have them panic and desert us in thes[e] mountains." Dayin agreed and left the others to thei[r] meal.

"But as a *rabbit?*" Braddoc asked again. Dayin frowne[d] at the dwarf, ending the conversation.

Karleah reached for Jo. The younger woman held ou[t] her hand, thinking the older one needed support. Th[e] wizardess's dry, bony fingers touched Jo's palm, and the[n] Karleah withdrew her hand. Jo looked down at her palm[.]

"This . . . this is a crystal from a *real* abelaat?" Jo aske[d.] She held up the eight-sided crystal. It was fully twice a[s] large as Jo's other crystals. The sunlight flickering throug[h] it shed prisms of color into the young woman's eyes, an[d] she was dazzled by its beauty. She heard Brisbois gasp an[d] move closer to her.

Karleah nodded. She said, "Yes, that's what Keepe[r] Grainger gave me. Her people have been the keepers n[?]

only of the history of the abelaats but also of their crystals. This is the last true abelaat crystal—a crystal made from Aeltic's own spittle." Brushing her hands and sniffing the wind, Karleah said. "It's time for me to change."

Braddoc and Jo stared at Karleah as the old woman began her transformation. Her lanky gray hair shortened and then spread over her body while her face lengthened and ears grew. Karleah pulled off the last of her clothing as the rest of the shapechange occurred.

"How long will you be gone?" Jo asked the wolf-woman.

"Not long," Karleah said in painful half-growl. "Take . . care of . . . the crystal," she continued. "It is my . . . only protection . . . from the abaton." Her black eyes turned golden, and her pink tongue lengthened and fell out of her not-quite-changed jaw. The woman flexed her fingers as the digits shortened and claws grew. Karleah's arms and legs grew leaner, the muscles rippling beneath her black fur. Finally, her torso changed shape and a tail grew. The old she-wolf yelped once and leaped away from Johauna and Braddoc.

Jo enviously watched Karleah's sure pace carry her into the mountain passes. She said to Braddoc, "I wish I could shapechange. I think it would be wonderful to transform into a wolf like Karleah and roam the land, at one with it in a way humans never are."

Braddoc shrugged noncommittally. "She'll be back soon. I want to check the pack on the mule. I think it needs rearranging." The dwarf stood.

"I'll come with you," Jo said. "I packed Fernlover a little quickly myself." Dayin accompanied them to the animals. Brisbois, who had said nothing since discovering the original sign of the passing guards, moved solicitously out

of the way. With a confused glance at the man, Jo began
checking the bundles on her mule. Silent moments passed,
then Jo said, "What are you looking at?"

Brisbois smiled slightly and shrugged. "What would
you do if Verdilith attacked you right now, in these mountains?" he asked.

Braddoc stared up at Brisbois. Jo once again stood in
silence for a moment. "What kind of question is that?"

"A legitimate one, I should think," the man replied.
"You're so vulnerable out here, on an open mountain
range, with no way to fight, nowhere to run."

"You're as vulnerable as we," Braddoc interjected.

Brisbois shrugged, "More so, I bet you think. After all, I
don't carry Wyrmblight, scourge of the Great Green, do
I?" The man moved with reptilian grace toward Jo, his
hand reaching out to the blade harnessed to her back.

Jo backed away, watching the yellowish steam rise from
Brisbois's nose. "What's gotten into you?"

Brisbois withdrew to a nonthreatening distance and
said, "You have a lot of faith in that sword. Too much
faith, if you ask me."

"I didn't ask you," Jo shot, checking the straps on
Fernlover.

"You think that sword will save you," Brisbois pressed, a
gleaming grin on his mouth, "but it didn't save Flinn."

Jo whirled, wrenching Wyrmblight from its harness and
leveling it before Brisbois's heart. "You mention Flinn one
more time, and I'll cut your heart out with this."

"Jo," Braddoc said, with a warning glare.

Brisbois smiled and waved the dwarf off with a ban-
daged hand, "She doesn't mean it. That sword is everything to her. She holds on to it and thinks she's holding on
to Flinn. But Flinn failed her, and so will the sword."

Jo lunged forward, a snarl of rage on her lips. The tip of
Wyrmblight sliced through the dishonored knight's tabard,
punctured his breastplate, and slammed the chain mail into
his sternum. With a slight gasp, Brisbois slipped and fell to
the ground.

Jo stepped up, setting the blade back on the gash and
towering over him. Braddoc clutched her arm, trying to
pull her back, but Jo gritted her teeth and began to lean
into the blade.

"Mercy," Brisbois cried out with mock fear. "I beg you
mercy on this battlefield, squire of the mighty Flinn. Will
you kill me, though I beg mercy of you?"

A confused frown crossed Jo's face and she colored. Her
pressure on the sword relented as Braddoc pulled her away
from the knight. As Brisbois painfully rose to his feet, the
dwarf led Jo back to the mules and locked the gaze of his
good eye with hers.

"You lost that one, Jo. Don't let him manipulate you
like that," the dwarf said evenly. "Everybody already
knows he's an idiot. Don't let him make an idiot out of
you."

Something half-human and half-wolf suddenly streaked
toward them. Karleah had returned from her search. Braddoc turned his head away politely as the wolf-thing transformed back into a naked old woman. The wizardess
pulled on her clothing. She said with some asperity, "I'm
sure a woman's body is nothing new to you, Braddoc.
Seen one, you've seen them all."

"Not one as withered as yours, old hag," Braddoc
quipped, apparently to lighten the tension. He threw the
crone a smile to soften the words.

Karleah responded with only a "Harrumph!" then said,
"I found their trail. They've taken the western pass." The

old woman shook her head. "They've got a good day, da
and a half, on us. They aren't in any hurry, but I doubt w
can gain much ground on them."

"You know it's cracked, don't you?" Brisbois murmure
to Jo as he wandered stiffly to his horse.

"What?" Jo cried, rounding on him with fiery eyes.

Brisbois busied himself with the straps and buckles (
his mount. "A hairline crack. I saw it in the sunlight whe
I was on the ground."

Jo held Wyrmblight up in front of her, studying th
blade with anxiety. Looking up, her blush deepened i
hue and she snorted. "I don't see anything."

The defamed knight shrugged casually and swung u
into the saddle in one motion. "Let's be off," he sai
"We're burning daylight!"

Braddoc's hand gripped Jo's trembling arm and he sai
"Let it go, Johauna. Let it go." He took Wyrmblight fron
her hands and began to snap it into the harness on he
back. As he did so, his eyes scanned worriedly along th
blade's white steel.

Chapter XIV

Karleah held up her hand, and the three riders behind her halted their mounts immediately. They were near Armstead, the wizardess knew, and they did not dare come upon the village unprepared. Through the leather of the pouch around her neck, Karleah could feel the heat radiating from the abelaat crystal as it grew closer to the abaton. She only hoped she was right in supposing that the crystal would prevent the abaton from draining her powers a second time. Karleah took heart in the fact that she had begun to regain her powers faster once the crystal had come into her possession.

The wizardess gingerly dismounted from her gray mare. "I'm too old for this," she mumbled. "Far too old. I want to go back to my valley."

"What's that, Karleah?" Jo asked curiously.

Karleah turned to face the squire. She thought that the trip had done the young woman good; the despair and anger that had consumed Jo at Flinn's death were still there, but were under slightly better control. Karleah hoped it wouldn't be too much longer before Jo was able

to put those emotions behind her. The old woman shook
her head.

"Nothing, Jo," Karleah said. She cocked her head
northward. "I think Armstead's just beyond that bend. At
least I think the abaton's there, according to this crystal."
Karleah touched the crystal's pouch. "I suggest you and
Braddoc lead the way, in case we run into the guards.
Dayin and I'll bring up the rear—and hopefully not be
engulfed by the abaton."

"That box wouldn't open up and 'swallow' you like it
did the charm in Threshold, would it, Karleah?" Braddoc
asked.

"Why, is that *concern* I detect?" Karleah cackled suddenly to hide how touched she was at the dwarf's words.
She tapped Braddoc with her oaken staff. "Seriously,
friend dwarf, I think being swallowed by the box might be
one of the nicer things the abaton could do to me."

Riding, Jo led the way north, with Braddoc right
behind her. Each led one of the two pack mules. Karleah
gestured for Brisbois and Dayin to go before her, then she
joined the group as they filed forward through the last of
the Black Peaks.

The mountains had brought two days of misery to Karleah's ancient frame. The cold, biting wind of late winter
whistled through the Black Peaks. Despite a fire, nothing
could warm their stony beds at night. To make matters
worse, the moon had turned full, and Karleah had felt the
call more than once to turn to wolf form. Someday soon,
she mused now, I will stay that way forever. I shall roam
the hills and live and die as an old she-wolf. Some days, I
am so weary of my human form. But the old wizardess
hadn't dared to give in to her desires so near the abaton.

The group wound steadily through the last of the Black

aks, the icy obsidian trail gnawing through even Kar-
h's thick boots. The ground was treacherous afoot, and
 crone wished she were back on her mare. The obsid-
 chips blended so well with the patches of ice that it
s often difficult to distinguish which was which. The
dafternoon sun did not light the land either, for it was
structed by all the towering mountains, which added to
 difficulty of the journey.

Or is something happening to me? Karleah thought
ldenly. Surely I shouldn't be having this much trouble?
e others are doing fine. Or am I really, truly growing
d at last? A part of her was troubled by the idea, while
other part—a most ancient part—savored the idea of
aring the end of her existence. Karleah eyed Jo's young,
e form with a twinge of jealousy.

The old woman quelled those thoughts ruthlessly. "I am
t yet ready for the next life," she muttered to the wind.

An hour passed before Karleah and her comrades
nded the last bend. By this time, the heat from the
laat crystal was nearly scorching, and Karleah won-
ed if she would be able to withstand it any closer to the
ton. "At least it seems to be protecting me," Karleah
rmured to no one. She held out her oaken staff, which
d recently served as nothing more than a walking stick.
'ith this stone, I can sense my powers returning."

Up ahead, Jo exclaimed in surprise. The squire stopped
lking, her horse and mule halting behind her. Braddoc
ned Jo, and Dayin and Brisbois hurried after him. Kar-
h heard their startled murmurs and prayers and tried to
h forward. She cursed the rocky ground and fought for
h unstable step, wishing her staff could clear a path for
r, as it had done in her own valley. The wizardess
mbed her way to the top of the small crest where Jo,

Brisbois, Braddoc, and Dayin stood. Shouldering her wa
between the dwarf and the boy, she looked into the valle
beyond. The old woman gasped.

Armstead lay in ruins.

Not a single tower had been spared. The area looked
if it had been the center of a great bonfire that had sprea
in sudden waves out into even the forest beyond. Th
ground was blackened and striped with coal and ash. Th
buildings lay in smoldering ruin, walls toppled as thoug
pushed over by a giant's foot. Even the outer wall, mo
decorative than anything else, had been flattened •
rubble. The stream that had flowed into Armstead was
scorched bed of rock and ash, and piles of uprooted tre
and shattered bridges and buildings formed a natural da
that let only a timid finger of water through. A fine ha:
of charcoal dust filled the air, creating dull and ironic rai•
bows. Karleah accidentally took too deep a breath and w
caught in a fit of choking.

She stumbled forward, her step uncertain as she hurri•
down the slope leading to the village. "No, no," she whi
pered. "Not Armstead . . ." Her mind was filled with
red-hot pounding sensation, so much so that she forg
the hot pain radiating from the abelaat crystal.

The group slowly headed through the broken archw
in the outer wall. Karleah stared at the scorched rock. H
eyes fell on the smooth pavement of the road leading in•
the village, then shifted to the destroyed buildings nearby

The tiny village had housed no more than fifty or
mages at any one time. Its one-time buildings—grea
soaring structures of incredible creation—were considere
some of the finest pieces of architecture ever created. •
spires formed the famous Mages' Circle, at the center
which was the amphitheater where all public meetin•

were held.

"Karleah!" Jo asked. "Is this the work of the abaton?"

"Yes," Karleah muttered. "We didn't arrive in time. Look at that spire!" The wizardess pointed to the remains of a tower. "Wazel lived there—an old friend of mine. When the time was right, I was going to send Dayin to him for polishing."

Braddoc asked, "Karleah, just what was Armstead?"

The old woman sighed heavily as she started down the main avenue that led to the center of the village. Karleah remembered wonderful, exotic trees lining the way. They had all been snapped in two. "Armstead," Karleah said heavily, leaning against her staff as she shuffled along, "is—er, was—a place of wizardry. How old the village is—was—is unknown." She stopped to flip over a large, flat piece of debris.

Karleah leaped back as the withered husk of a human body, swaddled in charred robes, fell over.

The wizardess carefully turned over another pile of charred cloth, finding the same desiccated cloth and flesh. She stared down the avenue at other piles of what she had thought were debris. She shook her head sadly.

"What, Karleah?" Dayin asked, the boy's keen ears picking up his mistress's words. "The dead people?" The boy's eyes were wide with morbid curiosity. Karleah touched his hair sadly.

"The abaton was brought to this village. The energies here must have been immense." Karleah pointed at scorch marks and some blasted buildings that had to have been hit by lightning bolts or similar spells.

"My guess is, the wizards of Armstead let the abaton in, believing the guards when they said it was a simple puzzle box," Karleah continued. "Then the abaton opened up and began drawing in all the magic present here in Armstead—which was considerable, needless to say."

"But what about the wizards?" Johauna asked as they continued to walk toward the center of the town. "Why are they dead? Why weren't they just drained like you and Dayin were? Why?"

"More importantly, that box has to be around here still, Karleah," Braddoc added. "Are you and the boy all right?" He pointed to a trio of dried husks. "You're not going to turn into that, are you?"

Karleah touched the crystal's pouch, suddenly thankful for the burning pain. "No." The old woman shook her head. "Leastways, I don't think so. Dayin, are you in any pain?"

The boy shook his head, staring.

"We should be fine as long as I carry the abelaat crystal," Karleah answered. "It seems to be working very hard to block the abaton's draining powers." The ancient wizardess leaned heavily on her staff, driving herself forward as the others passed her. They had already slowed their pace for her, and she was determined they should not a second time. "Yes," Karleah said huskily, "the abaton drained these wizards of all their powers—to the point of death. I'm thankful the abaton was very weak when last I was in contact with it."

Karleah pointed to the left. "That used to be an inn," she informed the group. "I had hoped we could stay there tonight, for they made the best onion soup I've ever tasted—thick, rich, and savory."

They had reached an amphitheater, where the mages of Armstead once had held magnificent celebrations and rituals. Karleah took the first step down the chipped stairs. Her gait was necessarily slow, for arthritis had set in her old bones some years ago. The long, cold days in the saddle had aggravated it severely.

"Look!" Jo cried out.

It took a moment for Karleah's eyes to focus on the playing stage a hundred feet down. The early evening light seemed to play tricks on her eyes.

The abaton stood in the middle of the stage, somber and black. Its lid was closed, but Karleah could still feel its power.

Jo raced forward, her feet pounding out a frantic rhythm on the stone steps. Braddoc following at a more sedate pace. Brisbois remained at the top of the stairs, offering no comment. Dayin put his arm around Karleah's waist to help her down the steps, but the old woman shooed him away. "I'm not that old," she said testily. Karleah touched the pouch to reassure herself; yes, the abelaat crystal will protect me from the abaton. The old wizardess sighed once and then stepped forward hurriedly.

Only then did she see Jo pull Wyrmblight from its sheath, moving calmly toward the abaton. She walked with a confidence that said she thought she knew how to destroy it.

"Jo!" Braddoc shouted, hurrying down the steps now. "What are you doing?"

Jo didn't answer, for she was almost at the stage now. The dwarf's short legs carried him forward with surprising speed. He reached the stage just after she did and threw himself at Jo as she swung Wyrmblight in an overhead arc. He slammed into her, his arms wrapping around her midsection and dragging her to the ground. Together, they collapsed onto the hard granite floor of the amphitheater. To the squire's credit, she didn't lose her hold on the sword, though one hand flew off and most of her breath was knocked out of her.

"Johauna Menhir," Karleah said evenly, only now reaching the stage. "If you ever try anything that foolish again, I'll make sure you never live to make a third attempt. What were you thinking, girl?"

Jo hesitated a moment, then hung her head in shame. "It suddenly seemed like I could destroy it with the sword." She paused, apparently realizing how idiotic she sounded. "I heard this voice in my head that said, '*Wyrmblight can destroy the abaton. Wyrmblight can destroy it.*' " She murmured an apology, but the old witch was not interested in excuses.

"Look," Brisbois said, still standing at the top of the amphitheater, "we've got to destroy this thing somehow. Let her use Wyrmblight."

"Close your mouth and open your eyes," Johauna said to Brisbois. "We need a lookout up there."

"That's what I'm doing," came the snide reply.

Karleah tapped the granite between Braddoc's feet and said, "See if you can pick up the box. See if you can carry it out of here."

The dwarf nodded grimly and sidled over to the box. It was one of the first times he had ever responded immediately to Karleah, without some disparaging comment about the "old crone." Stooping over the abaton, Braddoc grappled it sides and pulled. It didn't move. He tried again, taking a lower purchase on it. Still the box would not budge. Placing his foot against one edge, he thrust, seeing if it would even slide on the stage.

"Won't move," Braddoc said, looking up red-faced.

Karleah's expression was solemn. "It is as I thought. The thing is rooted. When it absorbed enough magic to become a true portal, it must have affixed itself to this spot on Mystara."

"If its swallowed that much magic," Jo interrupted, "and has become a portal, shouldn't we be expecting some abelaat visitors?"

Karleah seemed to consider. "That's why we need to camp right here, to guard the box until we can learn how to move it or destroy it."

"Camp here?" Jo asked, gazing about at the blackened seats and ash-strewn foot wells. "With this kind of blast, Auroch would have to know exactly where his little box ended up."

"Precisely," said the old crone.

Chapter XV

Karleah leaned back against the charred steps of the amphitheater and frowned. The nighttime sky above was black and starless due to the drifting ash in the air. Even with Jo and Braddoc on guard duty, Auroch could easily slip through that seamless night and trigger the abaton. But he hadn't. In the faint glow of the abelaat crystal in her hand, Karleah could see that the abaton was still there, and still closed. The box that destroyed Armstead now sat silent and cold.

"Concentrate," the wizardess told herself. Turning her attention from the box, she peered into the flawless golden depths of the stone. Surely the crystal could tell her the weakness of the abaton. She lowered the stone atop a smoking brazier, letting the heat embrace its edged form. Again Karleah concentrated on the box, on Auroch, or her hope to destroy the abaton. With avid interest, she watched the dim facets of the crystal glow and fade. Smoky forms swirled about the outside of the stone. But the inside remained empty.

It was no use. The crystal lay silent, lifeless in Karleah'

palm. The old woman's gnarled, scarred fingers closed about the stone, and her eyes lifted to the black sky overhead. She sighed and let her mind rest for a moment. You're trying too hard, deary, she told herself. That's why you aren't seeing it. The abaton was too dangerous, too powerful for Auroch to have lost track of it. Surely Verdilith's possession of it was part of the mage's plan. Surely Braddoc's theft of it, the castle's examination of it—even their removal of it to Armstead must have been set up by Auroch from the beginning. And now, the fact that he hadn't attacked them to regain his precious prize showed that they also were playing right into his hands.

Perhaps I should have let Johauna use Wyrmblight on the box, Karleah thought. Or, perhaps that's exactly what Auroch wanted me to do.

"No," Karleah said aloud. That's just running myself in useless circles. It can't be that everything I think of is part of Auroch's plan.

Karleah shut her eyes to the darkness around her and whispered, "You haven't forgotten what Armstead was like. You remember how lovely Armstead was in the spring. You remember the blossoming crabs lining the cobblestone pavement, the crocuses and tulips peeking beneath the trees."

The old woman sighed, trying to hold back the flow of tears. She couldn't allow herself the luxury of giving in to her pain.

Karleah opened her eyes and gazed down at the five smaller crystals Jo had given her. They lay arrayed dimly before her, as inert as the true abelaat stone. Karleah had hoped these other crystals might be key to unlocking the master crystal. But she had searched each of them, looking for some answering response, some glimmer of motion or color within the stones. Every time, she had failed.

The wizardess again contemplated the box. A clear seam outlined its lid, and a simple clasp connected the lid with the bottom of the box. Free from all ornamentation, the abaton was a marvel of simplicity.

Karleah knit her brows in concentration, clasped the master crystal in her hands, and stared at the box, suddenly wishing it would open for her. She wanted to see this marvelous place where the legendary abelaats lived, wanted to see them before they became twisted and evil creatures. She wanted to step across the bridge between worlds.

The crystal in her hand dug into her flesh, adding its heat with that of her blood.

♨ ♨ ♨ ♨ ♨

As Jo stood watch, she distractedly ran her finger along the edge of Wyrmblight. Its hard, sharp edge nearly cut her skin. The sensation surprised her, for she had once believed it would never cut her. But much about the blade surprised her lately.

She should have given it to the baroness. That much was clear. The blade was fully an inch taller than she, and it had been stupid for Jo to think she could wield it.

Worse yet, she now knew she was ruining the blade. It was a sensitive, intelligent blade, drawing strength from its wielder. When Flinn fell from honor, the sword was blackened by his bitter soul, and when his honor was regained, the sword again glowed bright. Only four days after Flinn's death, the blade was so strong that Verdilith couldn't break it. But, in Jo's meager hands, the fabled Wyrmblight had slowly diminished to being even weaker than a normal blade. It was so brittle now that jabbing

Brisbois had cracked it. She hadn't found the fracture, but she knew it was there. She could sense it.

And the sword hadn't spoken to her since Kelvin. A kind of gnawing desperation had begun inside of her. She was afraid to even pull the blade from its harness, lest she might break it. If only she could bear it back whole to the Castle of the Three Suns so that they could encase it, a relic, in glass. That's what it had become: a glass sword.

Even Flinn had sensed her discomfort when last they had spoken through the crystal. He had asked repeatedly about the blade, kept saying he could feel that something was amiss with it.

Weary of her ruminations, Jo looked across the fire to check on Dayin. He slept soundly, as though unaffected by their bleary surroundings. Brisbois lay nearby, still but not asleep, his eyes open and staring toward Wyrmblight. There was something akin to lust on his dark features. Apparently aware of her attention, he stroked his short beard and twirled the ends of his moustache.

Jo turned Wyrmblight away from the dishonored knight, and he gave a slight whimper of disappointment.

"What are you looking at?" the young squire demanded.

Brisbois shook his head and smiled. "Nothing. I was just trying to think of how Verdilith is going to smash that thing."

"He will not."

"Well," the man said, rising and shuffling over to where Jo stood. He stared her straight in the eye. "I hope, for your sake, you've got some other plan for the Great Green's demise. Something gruesome you've been thinking of. Cutting his throat and letting him choke on his own blood; disemboweling him and letting him slip on his entrails; you know, that sort of thing."

"What about cutting his arm off and beating him with the bloody stump?" Braddoc asked wryly from his nearby guardpost. He shook his head in disgust.

"Say, that's a good one. Well, what are you going to do Jo? Are you going to beat him to death with his own limbs?"

"What business is it of yours what I plan?" she spat.

"I think it's everyone's business," Brisbois replied, indicating the rest of the group with a sweep of his arm. "Obviously, Verdilith is searching for us. It's only a matter of time—"

"How do you know he's searching for us?" Braddoc interrupted.

Brisbois directed his response to Jo. "He hates that blade, Johauna. And he hates the person who wields it. He hates the blade so much I'll bet he'd betray anyone to see it destroyed, even an old ally like Teryl Auroch."

"How do you know that?" Jo asked, pulling Wyrmblight closer to her for comfort.

"How could I not?" Brisbois replied incredulously. He brushed the ash from his side and added, "Wyrm—that sword was created with a single purpose: to destroy Verdilith. It's very existence is an abomination, as far as the dragon is concerned."

"But, the Great Green would have to be a great fool if he hasn't found us yet," Braddoc shot back.

"Just so, just so."

"You two are a couple of gasbags," Jo said, a chill running down her spine.

"If I were Verdilith and I knew that sword was forged to be my bane, I would destroy it this instant, and you just after. Especially since it is the fallen sword of Flinn the Fallen."

"Flinn the Mighty, damn you!" Jo hissed, jumping to her feet. "Don't think I've forgotten what you and your plans did to him, bondsman. And don't think your debt will be easily paid!"

Brisbois appeared shocked and backed away a step. He held up his hands in a gesture of peace and said, "I'm sorry, Mistress Menhir. I meant no disrespect."

"What was the point of all this, again?" Braddoc asked, tersely motioning for Jo to lower the blade. She resented Braddoc's continual interruptions of the feud between her and Brisbois, but did as she was told.

Brisbois pulled on his goatee a moment, a dubious expression crossing his features, then he sat down again by the fire. He said, "All I was saying was that Verdilith is sure to find us eventually, drawn to that sword like a moth to a flame. Here, in this blasted town, we have no defense. There's nowhere to run, and nowhere to hide. He could kill us all with a single breath."

"We've got to guard the abaton," Jo said, glaring askance at the man.

"One of us does," he replied. "The rest should wait in reserve to attack if needed."

"And what do you suggest?"

"I have no suggestion," he replied. "That's why I asked if you have any other plans for your defense."

"Why don't we ask Karleah? She knows this place better than we do. She could probably find a place for us to stay that isn't quite so . . . exposed," Braddoc suggested.

Brisbois shook his head. "I don't think that's a good idea just yet. The old woman seems engrossed in whatever she's doing."

"For once I agree with you," Jo said. "And I hate to say it, but you are right about us getting out of the open."

The squire looked over her shoulder to the unmoving form of the old woman. "We might be here a little while."

"Then let's start now," Brisbois said, rising and dusting himself off again. "You keep guard over Karleah and Dayin while Braddoc and I go off to find someplace to hole up."

Jo was about ready to agree with the proposal when a voice in her head said, *Don't let him have the upper hand. If he chooses the place where you'll camp, he'll know it better than you.* But neither did she trust him to guard Dayin and Karleah. Jo made an angry cutting motion with her hand. "You're staying near me, bondsman! Braddoc will post guard and you and *I* will find better cover."

Brisbois turned to Braddoc and shrugged. The dwarf made no reply as he leaned on his axe. "Fine by me."

Jo turned to Brisbois, who stood waiting, sword hand on the pommel of his weapon. The young squire made a commanding gesture, and the two headed off into darksome Armstead.

&. &. &. &. &.

As Karleah forced her will upon the amber crystal, she felt it press into her palms, cutting through the flesh. And there was blood. For the first time since she had taken the true abelaat stone from its pouch, she broke contact, letting it drop to the ground beside the other crystals.

"It's this damn box, sapping the stone's power," she said to herself as she stared at her hands. The blood was running faster than she had expected. Karleah blinked and wiped away what she could. She stared at her new cuts with annoyance, not wanting to cease her efforts to divine the abaton's weakness. But the lines of blood slowly spreading down her arms convinced her to bandage the wounds. She shook her head, grasped the hem of her robe, and began to rip off strips of it.

As she applied the crude bandages to her hands, Karleah glanced up toward the campfire at the top of the amphitheater. Her eyes widened when she saw that there was nobody by the still-burning blaze except the sleeping boy and the dwarf.

"How goes the magical folderol?" Braddoc shouted down to her.

"Fine," she lied, tying off one of the bandages. "Where are the others?"

"Went to . . . explore," Braddoc replied.

That seemed a bad idea to the old witch, and Braddoc apparently sensed her uneasiness.

"Do you want me to try to stop them?"

A smile formed on the crone's lips. Despite their bickering, she and Braddoc were growing psychically sensitive to one another. "Yes."

Nodding, the dwarf tromped off into the darkness. Karleah peered nervously after him, noting once again the still form of Dayin. In the flickering light of the campfire, he seemed as dead as the buildings of Armstead. He had been despondent since Threshold. The news of his father's heritage, of his own abelaat bloodline, must have crushed the boy, Karleah reflected.

"And no wonder," she whispered to herself, continuing to stare at the boy's dark form. "He now knows more about himself than he ever needed to know."

She turned back toward the box, and only then realized with horror what she had done. The true abelaat stone had left her grasp, had left contact with her flesh. Its protection of her had ended.

She groped about on the ground, but the stone was gone. Looking up, she saw with fear that the abaton's lid was slowly cracking open.

And the blackness within it was enormous.

She couldn't scream, feeling the life force already draining from her body. She couldn't move, her body seeming hollow, like a stone statue, imprisoning her soul. And, though she knew the box's lid was only open a fraction of an inch, she felt as though she were staring into eternity.

She saw everything, and nothing. She saw fireballs as big as Mystara itself, as big as a thousand worlds, hurling in reckless courses at speeds unimaginable. She saw nations spread like lichen across a barren rock, breaking it down into sand and soil. She saw worms boring through the bodies of the dead. She saw the color of pain and the shape of screaming. But, worst of all, in the roaring rush she saw the purpose of the evil abaton—she saw what Auroch would do.

"He's coming back for Dayin!" she hissed through lips no longer her own. She struggled to rise, but the box dragged her stony body forward. Her head struck its coal-black side and bone shattered like glass in her mind. Then Karleah saw another vision, a vision of Teryl Auroch coming down from the skies and taking Dayin into the abaton, back to the world of the abelaat.

Dayin—run! she struggled to say, but her body slid off her, like a robe of silk slides from the shoulders of a young woman. And then, solid and black and heavy as the sun, oblivion embraced her.

ta ta ta ta ta

Jo and Brisbois cautiously picked their way through the catacombs beneath Armstead. They formed a vast network of naturally and magically carved caves that honeycombed the bedrock of the village. If Jo's guess was right, the catacombs connected every site in Armstead, including the amphitheater. Finding the trunk that led to the amphitheater would allow them an excellent hiding place, and a post from which to guard the abaton.

As the two carefully made their way through the passages, Jo held up a small lamp she had found among the wreckage. The flickering glow of the lamp seemed to make the caves jitter and sway, and it cast evil shadows over Brisbois's grinning face.

"I told you we could turn up something worthwhile, if we only looked," Brisbois said, stepping carefully over a fallen column of stone.

"All we've found yet is ruin and corpses," replied Jo. Although she knew Brisbois was right, she couldn't bring herself to admit it to him. Peering ahead, Jo mentally retraced their steps, hoping they were still heading toward the amphitheater. The passage ahead narrowed, and cracks in the stone walls showed that the ground had shifted in the blast. "I think the connecting passage will be just after this section."

"Lead on," Brisbois replied with a leering, self-satisfied smile.

Jo pursed her lips, declining comment. She stepped cautiously into the tight corridor, leaning to avoid the dark jags of rough stone that protruded from one wall. Brisbois followed close after, too close, in Jo's opinion. She could feel his hot breath on her back, and his hand occasionally brushed her side.

She turned in the tight space and scowled at Brisbois. "Back off, bondsman," she said, intentionally lifting the lantern close to his face.

The man didn't wince, a lascivious light in his eyes. He nodded, his gaze tracing out the ash-smudged contours of her chest and hips.

Jo's eyes narrowed. She set a hand on his shoulder and pushed him backward. "Keep your mind on your duty, soldier." Pivoting, she continued into the passage. She raised the lantern and turned sideways to squeeze between two boulders. As she worked one leg past the encroaching stone, she could feel his eyes still on her.

"I know now why Flinn fell in love with you, Jo," Brisbois said luridly, "why he wanted you."

A sharp retort died on Jo's tongue as the caves shifted violently around her. The lantern dropped from her hand, and, with a shattering of glass, the flame guttered and almost went out. Jo frantically tried to pull her foot free from the boulders. But, in the shuddering darkness, she couldn't find a handhold. Dirt fell from the ceiling in a choking cloud and billowed out through the passage.

"Brisbois?" Jo shouted, anger and fear and alarm mixing in her voice.

For one awful moment, she felt him, his body pressed next to hers, his hands groping along her sides, his lips rubbing hungrily against hers. She broke away, drawing a breath to scream, but a burning, biting vapor filled her lungs, and she spasmed with coughing.

"You'll be an excellent prize, Johauna Menhir," he seethed eagerly.

Jo lashed out with her fists, but struck only the stone of the passage. Although she flailed in both directions, her knuckles struck nothing.

Thunder rumbled in the distance, and the caves shook again. In desperation, Jo wrenched her foot free of the rock, drew her knife, and searched the cave floor for the lantern. After dragging across the shattered glass, her hands at last settled on the lantern's handle. She adjusted the wick and the flame grew bright again. Lifting the lantern into the dusty air, she drew her knife, but the defamed knight was nowhere to be seen.

"Brisbois! You bastard!"

᛫᛫ ᛫᛫ ᛫᛫ ᛫᛫ ᛫᛫

The amphitheater was lighted by an unholy glow as luminous vapors swirled thickly through it. The magical storm rose from the abaton and spiraled up into the black night above Armstead. Its twining mists reached like spectral claws up to the clouds high above and tore a hole in them, revealing the starry heavens. White-hot jags of lightning erupted through the center of the storm and danced in spinning circles across the devastated village. The ash that had settled on the charred ground lifted on the winds and filled the air like snow.

And, suddenly, Teryl Auroch stood in the midst of the storm, as calm as if he were standing on land. His face bore no expression, and, as he was lifted on the rushing winds, his piercing blue eyes settled on the campfire atop the amphitheater.

With a motion of his hand, Auroch awakened his son. Dayin rubbed his eyes and looked upward, shielding his face from the radiant mage. Then, lip trembling, he stood. Resignation hung plainly in his features, as though he knew in that moment what his father had planned, always had planned, since the moment of his birth.

The storm heightened, a moaning roar rising from the abaton itself. The charred remains of a blasted home collapsed in the gale, and rubble from the rock walls jiggled uneasily. Abruptly, fire erupted in the core of the vapors, flames that leaped to the very clouds. The sudden blast of heat sent winds howling and thrumming through the surrounding forests, bearing with them flocks of leaves, torn from their boughs.

The boy seemed mesmerized, unaware. He didn't flinch as the crackling thunder shook the ground. He didn't wince as the flames roared in huge, spiraling sheets from the box. Without expression, Dayin calmly stepped up from the earth, as though on an invisible stair, and walked to his father. The mage put his arm around the boy and held him close, as if to protect him from the ravages of the still-growing storm. Dayin glanced up at his father, the gazes of their brilliant blue eyes locking.

🐾 🐾 🐾 🐾 🐾

Jo burst out from the catacombs entrance just before the building above her toppled into the caves. She dropped the lantern and gripped Wyrmblight in a firm, two-handed grasp as she rushed toward the storm-swathed amphitheater.

"Karleah!" she shouted in fear, though the wind ripped the word from her throat. Leaning into the gale, she ran, stones sliding beneath her feet. Her legs slipped out from under her and she fell. Crying out in surprise and pain, Johauna gripped a charred root to keep from being blown backward.

Blinking, she stared into the raging storm. A blue-white column of mist rose from the amphitheater, its core blazing with fire. A shower of sparks and embers emanated from the storm's heart, raining down on the land around her. And there, at the heart of the storm, she saw Teryl

Auroch holding Dayin.

"Dayin!" she cried, but the wind blew too hard for her to hear her own voice.

A tremendous pillar of light pierced the sky, stabbing at an angle through the heart of the storm and entering the abaton. The pillar had a beautiful, pearlescent glow. Teryl Auroch gently gestured his son to walk into the slanting light. Jo watched helplessly as the boy floated on the air, entering the glowing shaft without a backward glance. The mage shot Jo a last enigmatic look, then stepped in behind his son.

"No! Dayin!" she screamed. "Dayin, come back!"

Struggling to her knees, Jo lifted Wyrmblight, wanting to feel the four runes of the Quadrivial pulse and glow with heat. But the sword was dark and cold.

All was lost—Armstead, Dayin, Flinn, Wyrmblight . . . Jo didn't even want to guess what had happened to Karleah and Braddoc. Auroch had defeated them. Brisbois had escaped. Honor, Courage, Faith, and Glory were dead, and Jo's heart was dead with them. Her pledge to Sir Graybow and herself—her pledge of mercy—rang hollowly in her ears.

Rising unsteadily to her feet, Jo grasped the blade of Wyrmblight and set the hilt firmly on the ground. Leaning the sword toward her, she placed the tip against her left breast and closed her tearful eyes.

"No, Jo, there is another way," a voice said from behind her, a voice she actually heard, one she recognized.

Johauna Menhir whirled around, Wyrmblight clattering loudly to the ground. Her heart leaped. It was impossible. It was true. For a moment, the fury of the storm was nothing.

Standing in the blasted city, framed by the flames of the

burning buildings, stood Flinn the Mighty. He was clothed in scintillating light, his armor blinding. His smiling face glowed with strength and health.

And life.

Chapter XVI

nvoluntarily, Jo crumpled to her knees and buried her face in her hands. She felt suddenly unworthy, suddenly ashamed of her despair. Reflexively, she reached out for comfort to Wyrmblight, lying beside her. It was cold to her touch, *cold with the taint of your unworthiness,* the voice in her head told her. Only the stone in her belt pouch was warm and comforting.

"Rise, Johauna," came Flinn's voice from the brilliant light. "Your fear can wait. Now we must act."

Jo's eyes remained averted, and she trembled upon the ground.

"I said rise!" the voice commanded, its tone tinged with anger.

Slowly, Johauna stood, lifting Wyrmblight with her. "Oh, Flinn," she breathed, her voice just audible over the storm. Still her eyes would not meet his. "I have missed you, so."

"And I, you, my dear," the radiant figure said. He reached out gently toward her, cupping the side of her head in his hand. "Give me the sword, my love."

"Yes," she said, her heart pounding painfully. She turned Wyrmblight toward him, pommel-first. "You are an Immortal now, aren't you? You have the power to set things right, don't you?"

Flinn smiled a polite smile and reached out for the blade.

Only now looking him full in the face, Jo saw the way the wind blew his hair, and remembered riding with him in the days when they first had met. She remembered her joy when fighting side by side with Flinn the Mighty, hero of legend and song. She remembered the thrill that had traveled up and down her spine, and she wondered why she didn't feel that same thrill now. The young squire suddenly withdrew the blade. "Promise me."

Flinn's brow furrowed, but he maintained his smile and still held out his hands. "Promise you what?" he asked, his voice resonant above the howling wind.

"Promise me you'll save Dayin and kill Auroch and Verdilith and Brisbois." Jo took a single step closer, fixing her gaze on the eyes of the man she loved. "And promise me you'll never leave me again."

Flinn let his arms fall to his side, the smile on his face quickly fading to an expression of deep pity. For a moment, it seemed to Jo that the man—the Immortal—might fall to his knees and beg forgiveness for leaving her to die all alone. But she understood in her heart and soul that whatever Flinn had become, through whatever fiery lands he had walked, he didn't need her forgiveness for any act, past or still to come. He was beyond guilt and innocence now. Though he stood resplendent before her, Flinn would never truly be the same man she had once loved.

"Johauna Menhir," Flinn said gravely, "I promise to do

these things. And I promise that even death cannot separate us now." He raised his hands again to accept Wyrmblight.

Jo lifted the heavy blade without hesitation, pushing it forward into Flinn's arms. The runes of the Quadrivial blazed brightly, almost angrily, in the hands of the glowing creature. Johauna gazed at it with awe, guessing that whatever holy essence was used to create the sword, the blade knew when it was in the hands of its wielder.

Flinn gripped Wyrmblight with both hands, the perfection of his body reflecting the brilliant white radiance of the pillar of light, which seemed now to be drawing the mists and winds into it. Jo watched with fascination as every muscle contracted with power—more power than any mortal man could wield. She felt hypnotized, staring at his graceful, muscular body, and all other thoughts fled her mind: she forgot the destruction of Armstead, the disappearance of Karleah and Braddoc, the abduction of Dayin. None of these things were important any longer. Flinn was back from the dead, and she knew he would set things right.

"What would you have me do, Johauna Menhir?" Flinn asked, his arms slowly lifting Wyrmblight above his head, as if to strike Jo down. She did not move, but stood entranced. "What would you have me do? Shall I travel to this other world to retrieve Dayin, kill his father, and ensure the abelaats never return?"

Jo nodded slowly. "Yes," she said above the winds.

"Shall I smash this pillar of light and destroy the abacon?"

Jo nodded again. "Yes."

"Shall I find Karleah and make her your equal in youth so you may share your lives as closest friends?"

Jo's head dropped to her chest. "Yes."

Flinn placed the tip of Wyrmblight under Jo's chin and lifted her head to face him. She felt the metal on her flesh as the storm winds buffeted her, as the crackling lightning split the sky.

Her love had returned from the land of the dead.

He would set things right.

"Shall I take you as my one true love, above whom I will place no other?"

Jo said nothing. She moved forward, letting the edge of Wyrmblight caress her skin, drawing a thin line of blood across her check. She felt no pain, only the joy of being closer to Flinn. She raised her arms and clung to him, daring to hold him close, embrace him, feel the power beneath his once-dead flesh. His heart beat loudly in his chest and his breath was hot.

Jo gently parted her lips and looked up toward Flinn's face. With a trembling hand on the back of his neck, she pulled his lips down onto her own, tasting what she had longed to these many months. The kiss was a gift of forgetfulness, purging her mind of all that had past. As long as he held her close, as long as she clung to him, she would never feel pain again.

"Jo, dear," he whispered, huskily, pulling back from her. "To stop the wizard, I must regain *all* of my life force."

Jo staggered backward a step, staring doe-eyed into her lover's face. She wanted to continue the kiss, so safe a haven from the maddening storm.

"Wyrmblight," Flinn continued, "holds a small part of my soul. I must release it if I am to stop Teryl Auroch."

Jo gave a vague nod, her eyes blank. "I remember. You spoke to me."

"Yes. It is as I said to you. To release it, I must break the blade. But to break the blade, I need you to will that it be broken," Flinn replied. He knelt, digging the tip of Wyrmblight into the ground and laying the great length of the blade across his bent knee.

Jo nodded again. She blinked as if to clear her thoughts and looked to see what Flinn was about to do.

"Desire it to be broken, Jo. You must abandon your faith in Wyrmblight, or my soul will never be freed," Flinn explained. "I must destroy Wyrmblight."

Jo's limbs felt as heavy as stone. Her mind, whirling in a haze, believed Flinn when he said he must break the blade. But her heart screamed at the thought; if Wyrmblight was the soul of Flinn, it must not be destroyed. It had been her source of guidance, her source of hope in the dark times since Flinn's death. She had wielded the blade against Verdilith and nearly slain the beast. She had listened to its wise counsel to *have* faith, not abandon it.

Flinn's fist came down on the blade. A shower of sparks arched from his knuckles and were drawn into the insatiable winds. The four runes of the Quadrivial flared brightly at the man's touch. Flinn's fist came down a second time, and his expression twisted with pain as his hand rebounded from the hard metal. The runes flamed again, sending shafts of light into the air and into Jo's dazzled eyes. The blade cracked across its width at the third blow, and the Quadrivial blazed once more before it went black.

Jo staggered back another step, feeling the pulse of the abaton's pillar of light. In the pearlescent glow, Flinn seemed huge and monstrous as he raised his fist for the final blow. Anger twisted his face, and, in his eyes, Jo saw something she had never witnessed before in the man she loved.

Madness.

Flinn would never have destroyed Wyrmblight. He would never have made the runes of the Quadrivial go black. *You will be an excellent prize, Johauna Menhir.* The words of Brisbois echoed in her mind.

"Not Brisbois," she murmured, incredulous. Jo screamed her rage and lunged forward. She grabbed the hilt of Wyrmblight, yanking it from the glowing creature's grasp. "For Flinn!" she cried, running the blade through the man's heart. Coruscating bands of white light streamed from the wound.

Flinn's eyes opened in sudden horror, revealing vertically slitted pupils: the eyes of Verdilith. With a roar, he reached out to grapple her, his arm suddenly maimed and bleeding. Jo pushed the great sword farther into Flinn's body. He shrieked in agony. His eyes rolled back into his head and his hands clawed at the air, mouth now opening without a sound.

Jo twisted the blade, and Wyrmblight snapped in two, lodged in the ribs of the statuesque figure. Flinn's body fell back to the ground, but Jo leaped atop him and battered him with the jagged edge of the broken sword. The blows fell on that muscled form with equal measures of hatred and love, and the runes of the Quadrivial blazed brightly on the shattered blade.

"Mer—Mercy," the dragon whispered through the lips of Flinn the Fallen.

Jo paused for a moment, staring down blankly at the ruined form. Setting the razor edge of the broken blade on the creature's throat, Johauna Menhir said, "No. Not mercy. Justice."

Epilogue

he black gateway of the Realm of the Dead opened.

Flinn arose in flames. Stepping from a burning building at the center of Armstead, Flinn breathed the air of Mystara into his lungs again. His memory of what had just happened was vague, shrouded by a haze of forgetfulness, like the drifting ash that shrouded the village. He didn't even know his own name.

But he *did* remember the abaton, the evil box of Auroch and the abelaats. He remembered, too, the instruction he had received from Diulanna: Destroy the abaton or remove it from Mystara.

There it was before him, its white-hot pillar drawing the magic from Mystara. Flinn could feel the life of his world gradually drain away into the pearlescent column, feel the balance of magic slowly shift and sway to favor the abelaats' world. He must destroy the box, or every creature on Mystara would be dead within the year. Diulanna had shown this to him. Thor, the Thunderer, and Odin, the All Father, had confirmed it.

Flinn flexed his muscles and felt his immortal form
writhe with power. His mortal body had been strong, but
now he wielded an otherworldly power. Even so, his powers were new to him, and he did not know them all. But
he would learn them, and learn them quickly if he was to
destroy the abaton.

The knight took another step, feeling the ground
beneath his feet—a sensation he thought he would never
feel again. He remembered that his pyre had been much
like the ruined building that burned now behind him. Yet,
something was missing, something that danced just
beyond the edge of memory.

Flinn shook his head in confusion. "Not something," he
said to himself. "Someone." But he couldn't remember
who. Soon he would remember—as he learned his powers, he would remember. "I must build my strength," he
stated.

"Since when do dead men have to build their strength?"
a voice asked from behind him.

Flinn slowly turned. His eyes narrowed with remem-
brance.

"You don't remember me," said the stranger flatly.
"That's no surprise. You've been dead quite some time."

"And who are you?" Flinn asked.

"Do you remember anything? About who you are, who
you knew. Who you loved?"

Flinn shook his head. "No. Very little."

"Then let me help you remember. Your name is great
in these lands—of course, partly due to me. Your name is
Flinn . . . Flinn the Mighty."

Flinn nodded, trying the name out on his lips. He felt
no threat from this stranger and guessed it was somebody
he had known in his mortal life. Blinking, Flinn pointed

down to the remains of a body on the ground, "Who was that?" he asked.

The stranger paused introspectively before replying. After a moment, he said, "That was your greatest enemy, a dragon named Verdilith. He took your form in perfection, as there is a perfect copy of everything on the Plane of the Dead. It was one of the many events that allowed you to return to this world." The stranger eyed the column of light. "Let's go. It'll drain both of us of our souls unless we get away from it. Besides, you've much to learn before you can destroy that thing."

"Very well."

Flinn let himself be led away from the pillar of light, the pillar that was the gateway to his enemy. As he walked, he asked, "What is your name?"

"Braddoc, of Rockhome, of course."

The Penhaligon Trilogy

If you enjoyed *The Dragon's Tomb*, you'll want to read —

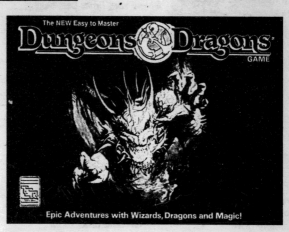